Amanda McCabe lives in Oklahoma with two very spoiled cats. When not reading or writing romances, she loves doing needlework, taking dancing lessons, and digging through antique stores. A RITA and *Romantic Times* award finalist and a Booksellers Best award winner, she loves to hear from her readers via e-mail at Amccabe7551@yahoo.com.

Allison Lane's lifelong love affair with reading perfectly complements the writing career she began in 1994, a career that allows her to use her interest in English history to create vivid plots and characters. In addition to being named as finalists for the RITA, her books have won numerous awards and been nominated for many others. For more information, check her Web site at www.eclectics.com/allisonlane.

Edith Layton, critically acclaimed for her short stories, also writes historical romances, and has won numerous awards. She loves to hear from readers and can be reached at www.edithlayton.com.

Barbara Metzger, one of the stars of the genre, has written more than two dozen Regencies and won numerous awards. Her newest Regency-set historical is *A Perfect Gentleman*. Her Web site is www.barbarametzger.com.

Sandra Heath is the ever-popular author of numerous Regencies, historicals, novellas, and short stories. She has won Readers' Choice awards for Best Regency Author and Best Regency Romance, among others. She can be reached at sandraheath@blueyonder.co.uk.

Regency Christmas Magic

Five Stories by

Amanda McCabe
Allison Lane
Edith Layton
Barbara Metzger
Sandra Heath

A SIGNET BOOK

SIGNET
Published by New American Library, a division of
Penguin Group (USA) Inc., 375 Hudson Street,
New York, New York 10014, USA
Penguin Group (Canada), 10 Alcorn Avenue, Toronto,
Ontario, M4V 3B2, Canada (a division of Pearson Penguin Canada Inc.)
Penguin Books Ltd., 80 Strand, London WC2R 0RL, England
Penguin Ireland, 25 St. Stephen's Green, Dublin 2,
Ireland (a division of Penguin Books Ltd.)
Penguin Group (Australia), 250 Camberwell Road, Camberwell, Victoria 3124,
Australia (a division of Pearson Australia Group Pty. Ltd.)
Penguin Books India Pvt. Ltd., 11 Community Centre, Panchsheel Park,
New Delhi - 110 017, India
Penguin Group (NZ), Cnr Airborne and Rosedale Roads, Albany,
Auckland 1310, New Zealand (a division of Pearson New Zealand Ltd.)
Penguin Books (South Africa) (Pty.) Ltd., 24 Sturdee Avenue,
Rosebank, Johannesburg 2196, South Africa

Penguin Books Ltd, Registered Offices:
80 Strand, London WC2R 0RL, England

First published by Signet, an imprint of New American Library,
a division of Penguin Group (USA) Inc.

First Printing, October 2004
10 9 8 7 6 5 4 3 2 1

Printed in the United States of America

Contents

Upon a Midnight Clear

Amanda McCabe

Chapter One

December 21, 1816

"Oh, Aunt Antoinette, *please* won't you come to Bath with us? Christmas won't be *Christmas* without you!"

Lady Penelope Leighton's childish voice piped into the fire-warmed air of the sitting room. Her large, green eyes were wide and beseeching as she leaned against Antoinette's knees.

"Grandmama's house in Bath is always jolly, but it won't be if you're not there," added Penelope's brother, Edward, hanging off the back of Antoinette's chair with his sturdy, chubby little hands. "We're going to see a pantomime."

"*And* a lecture on Greek theater," said Penelope, her eyes growing even larger, if that was at all possible. She reached out to clasp a handful of Antoinette's red silk robe. "Or, if you don't care for Greek theater, there is sure to be something on philosophy or theology at Aunt Chat's Philosophical Society."

"Or herbs!" cried Edward. "You always like to hear about herbs."

Baby Louisa, still scarcely able to toddle, glanced up from her building blocks and gurgled an agreement.

"Oh, *mes petites*," Antoinette said softly, putting an arm about Penelope and Edward and drawing them close to her. "You know I would love nothing better than to spend Christmas with my favorite children in all the world. But, as I have said, I must finish this new book on winter herbs very soon, or my publisher will be most unhappy with me. And in Bath there would be far too many 'jolly' things to distract me."

"We would not distract you, Aunt Antoinette!" Penelope declared, going up on tiptoe to loop her small, slender arms about Antoinette's neck. "We would be so good and so quiet when you were working."

Antoinette laughed, for she knew all too well that the Leighton children's idea of "quiet" consisted of tiptoeing while they shouted out about their newest discovery in Greek history (Penelope), horses (Edward), and solid food (Louisa). She pressed a quick kiss to Penelope's tousled dark curls. "I know you would, dearest, but the lectures and dances would not be resisted. We will have a grand party when you return home next month."

As Antoinette hugged them close, she caught a glimpse of their little group reflected in the gilt-framed mirror hung above the fireplace. Anyone looking at them would realize immediately that she was not the children's *true* aunt. Not their blood aunt. Their milky-white complexions, Edward's silvery blond cap of hair, were in sharp contrast to Antoinette's own coffee-colored duskiness, her midnight eyes, and the thick, wavy fall of her matte-black hair. They were as far opposite as people could possibly be.

Except in their hearts. In Antoinette's deepest soul, they *were* her nieces and nephew, and she loved them beyond all else. They never watched her with doubt or curiosity or hostility, as so many others did. In their clear eyes there was only love and respect.

Or beggary—as there was now. It hurt her heart to see them, to know that they would go away in only a very few moments and leave her alone at the one time of year when *all* families should be together. She almost jumped up, grabbed a valise, and shouted, "Of course I will go to Bath with you!"

But she could not. Some urges were too strong, some hurts too deep for even Christmas to heal.

"We will find you the most wondrous Christmas present, Aunt Antoinette," Penelope said. "I promise. And I will write you every day."

"So will I!" Edward said stoutly.

"You do not know your letters yet," Penelope said, disdain heavy in her young voice. "And that is because you don't apply yourself to your lessons. You only think about horses."

"I do not!" Edward shouted, and the two siblings were off on their oft-repeated quarrels.

Little Louisa used her tiny sticky hands to pull herself up by Antoinette's skirt, adding her babble to the fray.

Thus was the room full of chaos when the cottage door was pushed open and Cassandra Leighton, Countess of Royce, the children's mother and Antoinette's best friend, appeared. A heavy, fur-lined white wool cloak swathed about her so that she appeared a ghostly apparition. Everyone at Royce Castle knew a great deal about ghosts. One could not avoid them in one of the most haunted houses in Cornwall.

The illusion faded, though, when Cassie pushed back her hood and stomped dew from her stout half boots. She took in the fray with one sweeping glance, and laughed. "Ah! I see I have come just in time. My children are obviously being carried away by naughtiness."

"Mama!" Penelope cried imperiously, propping her tiny fists on her hips. "We were not doing anything *naughty*. We simply asked Antoinette to come to Bath with us for Christmas."

"Did I not tell you, before I let you come here, that you were not to bother your auntie?" Cassie scooped up Louisa into her arms, and leveled her steady, motherly gaze on her eldest daughter.

Penelope's pugnacious stare faltered. "Yes, Mama. But . . ."

"No buts. You were quite clearly disturbing her. There is no time to discuss it now, though. The carriage is waiting, and if we do not hurry your papa will vanish back into his library for another hour. So, kiss your auntie, and be on your way. Papa will settle you in the carriage with warm bricks and blankets."

Penelope turned back to Antoinette and dropped her a perfect little curtsy. "Good-bye, Aunt Antoinette. I will write to you every day and tell you what we are doing." The image of impeccable young ladyhood was ruined, though, when Penelope threw her arms around

Antoinette's neck and kissed her once, twice, three times. "We'll miss you! But we *will* have a party when we return home, right?"

Antoinette kissed her back. "Of course, my dear. Be a good girl for your grandmama, and enjoy yourself."

"I love you, Aunt Antoinette."

"And so do I!" Edward piped up, kissing Antoinette's other cheek.

Louisa just gurgled, and thrust a silk tassel from her mother's cloak into her little mouth.

Antoinette's throat tightened, and she blinked hard against the sudden rush of hot tears behind her eyes. "I love you too, *mes petites*."

With one last kiss, the children dashed past their mother and out the cottage door. Their shouts and laughter could be heard clearly on the crisp, cold air until they turned the corner on the pathway to the castle and were gone.

Cassie leaned against the doorway, Louisa still propped on her hip. Her dark eyes were shrewd and all-seeing as she watched Antoinette. They had known each other for far too long for Antoinette to hide much from Cassie, or Cassie from her. It had been ever thus, since they were little girls running on the beach in Jamaica, neither caring that one was the daughter of an English landowner and one the child of a freed slave.

Antoinette tried to give her friend a light smile. She pulled her Kashmir shawl closely about her shoulders, yet could not entirely rid herself of her chill.

The chill that was always with her. It could not be banished by the crackling fire, and did not melt with the English snows in the spring. It was a chill in her very soul.

"The children are not the only ones who would beseech you to come to Bath with us," Cassie said. "There is still time, you know. Phillip would not mind waiting one jot while you packed a trunk. Christmas in Bath is so jolly!"

"I know. Edward told me." Antoinette stood from her chair, and took up the cast-iron poker to stir at the fire. Tiny orange-red embers crackled and fell out onto her stone hearth, almost catching the hem of her robe. "And

I have been there with you every Christmas for the last five years."

"But not this year?"

Antoinette smiled back over her shoulder at Cassie. "Not this year."

"Because you must work."

"Indeed. Because I must work. My last book on herbal soaps and lotions did so very well that my publisher is eager for a volume on growing herbs in winter. He is willing to pay me twice as much if I can send it to him next month. I would be too distracted to write in Bath."

Cassie shifted Louisa to her other hip, still frowning. "If it is a question of money . . ."

"It is not!" Antoinette cried, a sharp pain pricking behind her eyes. She whirled back to face the fire, pressing her fingers to her temples. She loved Cassie as her own sister, she truly did. But she was seized with such a need to be alone, a desperation for silence. She could not bear to talk about money, or Christmas, any longer, to try to explain yet again.

And, really, how could she explain something to her friend that she did not understand herself? If she tried to voice these strange, unvoiceable feelings she had been having of late, it would only worry Cassie, and to no good end. Her friend could not help Antoinette; no one really could. And Cassie deserved a joyous holiday with her husband and children, enjoying all the delights Bath could offer.

And Antoinette needed this time alone.

She felt a soft touch on her sleeve, and turned to see that Cassie had drawn nearer, reaching out to Antoinette with her gloved hand. Her pale, heart-shaped face was creased in worry—which was the last thing Antoinette wanted to cause.

She forced herself to give another merry smile and a light laugh, and reached up to press Cassie's hand with her own. "Don't look so melancholy, my friend. I will be fine here, truly. I will work, and rest, and finish a new batch of lotions for Mrs. Greeley's store in the village."

Cassie still did not appear happy, but something shifted behind her eyes. Some sort of surrender, some giving-in, which was quite amazing. Though Cassie was a full foot shorter than Antoinette's own towering six feet—and a full year younger, to boot—she still tried to be the arranger, the overseer.

"If you are certain this is what you want . . ."

"It *is*," Antoinette answered firmly.

"Then we will honor your wishes." As if she had any choice.

"Thank you, Cassie. I will write to you often and assure you that all is well here."

"If you get too lonely, at least go up to the castle. Cook will be delighted to ply you with her cinnamon cakes, and your guest suite is always prepared."

"I shall probably avail myself of the cakes, but I cannot stay there. The eternal quarrels of Lady Lettice and Jean-Pierre would be too great a distraction."

Cassie had to laugh at the reminder of the noisy antics of Royce Castle's resident ghosts—an Elizabethan lady and her faithless French swain. "Indeed they *are* a distraction. I sometimes wonder when they will move on, but Lady Lettice is so good with the children."

"Yes. And I know someone else who must 'move on' now," Antoinette said. "Your journey is a long one, and if you do not leave soon you will never make it to your first stop by nightfall."

Antoinette reached for one of the small willow baskets arrayed on her sitting room shelves, and took out a small black muslin bag stuffed with fragrant herbs and tied with a pink ribbon.

She pressed it into Cassie's hand. "Take this. The black is for protection, and it is filled with rose for friendship, lavender for even more protection, and marjoram for happiness. I know this will be the happiest of holidays for you."

Cassie stood on tiptoe, much as her daughter had, and kissed Antoinette's cheek, holding the precious bag out of Louisa's grasping reach. "I will keep it close by me. Happy Christmas, Antoinette."

"Happy Christmas, Cassie." Antoinette kissed Cassie's cheek in return, and urged her out the door and back into the wet morning.

She leaned against the wooden frame, tucking her

hands into the sleeves of her silk robe for warmth as she watched her friend hurry along the narrow path leading from Antoinette's cottage to the castle. Cassie turned just before disappearing at the bend and waved, along with little Louisa. For just an instant, the baby's chortles could be heard, then they turned away and were gone.

The only sound was the wind in the bare trees around the cottage, the winter's whispers on the faintly salty Cornwall air.

Antoinette was alone.

She hugged her arms closer about her waist and moved to the edge of her small front garden. The herbs and flowers were mostly sleeping for the winter, but a few things flourished still, including a tough clump of rosemary beside the low stone wall. Antoinette picked a stem, toying with it between her fingers as she leaned against the cold wall. The wind caught at her loosely tied-back hair, tossing the dark, coarse strands about.

Antoinette pushed them back impatiently and studied the scene spread out before her. She could not see the cliffs or the sea from her cottage; they were hidden by thick stands of trees, precious trees that gave her solitude and camouflage. But she could hear the song of the waves, chill gray and pale blue water crashing against the rocky shore.

A shore so very different from that of her birthplace, Jamaica. As different as if they were on another planet. The sea in Jamaica was turquoise and emerald green, always shifting, sparkling under a warm golden sun. She and Cassie had often run across the sand, white sand as soft as a baby's breath under their feet. The thick breezes had borne the scents of jasmine and plumeria to them, as well as the rich spices from the kitchens. From the open doors there, they could hear the cook and her assistants singing the old Trinidadian song "The Virgin Mary Had a Baby Boy."

Antoinette thought she heard an echo of their song on the cold breeze now. It was a song her mother used to sing at this time of year, as her nimble needle created her exquisite gowns and shawls. "Ah, Antoinette, *ma belle*, one day you will find your own destiny," she would say, when Antoinette expressed a desire to sew like her. "Greater things await you than stitchery. One day, you will see. One day they will find you. . . ."

Well, it had not found her yet. Nothing she would call *destiny*, anyway. Yet a part of her mother's prophecy had come true. She did not make her way by the needle. She made it by her pen, by the herbs she grew in this garden and in the small conservatory behind her cottage. Her books about the uses of herbs sold well in London bookshops. Many women swore by her lotions and tinctures, vowed they made their skins younger and softer. She was glad of that—glad that her knowledge made her the money to buy this cottage, to be independent.

She did not share *all* of her knowledge of herbs, of course. That would be foolish in a place where her acceptance was so very precarious anyway. She could not share it with the white English who, in their ignorance, would call her a witch. Only Cassie and her family knew the true power to be found in an ancient, secret book hidden beneath Antoinette's bed.

It was the greatest gift of Marie-Claire Duvall to her daughter. The secrets of the Yaumumi priestesses were safe in Antoinette's hands. And they had served her well in many ways.

Antoinette tipped her head back to stare into the empty, slate-gray sky.

"Oh, Maman," she whispered. "Why could you not have taught me to cure an unsure heart, as well? How to fill an emptiness, when I do not even know where the wound lies?"

There was no answer, of course. Antoinette had not expected any, yet there was always a half-hidden hope. A hope for a reply, a *sign* that she was doing the right thing in her life.

She did not regret leaving Jamaica to accompany Cassie to England when Cassie's father died and his plantation was sold. Antoinette's mother had died many years ago, and she had no other family. Only Cassie, who was like her sister. And Cassie's family was likely the only one Antoinette would ever know—there were not very many suitors in southern England for women such as her!

Antoinette could have stayed in Jamaica, of course, could have purveyed her herbs and spells to people of her own sort. But she knew she would have been just as alone there, in a hut on the beautiful beach, as she was here. Just less cold.

Antoinette shook her head hard and laughed, trying to push away her sudden rush of self-pity. She was usually far too busy to wallow in maudlin thoughts. Indeed, she ought to be busy now, tending her conservatory, writing, brewing a new batch of lavender-rose lotion. She had no time to loll about, moaning like some hapless heroine in one of the horrid novels Cassie loved so much.

She pushed back from the wall and strode back down the pathway to her cottage door, brushing off her dew-dusted sleeves. It was only Christmas making her feel so sad, she thought. Christmas was a time for families, for children, for evergreen boughs and holly wreaths and red-ribbon bows. Not for strangers in strange lands.

It was chilly in the sitting room again, the fire died down to mere embers in the grate. Antoinette grabbed the poker and stirred them to life again, while she shivered under her robe.

Why was this blasted country always so *cold*?

Chapter Two

Cold. Freezing cold, like ice or snow. Or death.

The nightmare was the same as it always was, the full horror of those moments rushing back onto him as if eleven years had not passed. As if it were happening again—and again. He always knew it was a nightmare, yet he could never pull himself out of it, pull himself back into the reality of his life now. He just had to watch it once more, until the bitter ending.

The explosion that tore half his ship away hurled him into the churning waves. At first, he welcomed the chill of the water, the freezing bite of its depths. The entire left side of his body burned with a frigid, heavy flame, his uniform torn away, the gold braid cutting into his raw flesh. But then the full force of the cold salt water slapped against him, bringing new agony.

He began to sink, dragged to Davy Jones' locker by an inexorable force. He welcomed it, welcomed the dark, sweet oblivion that he knew waited for him there, promising to soothe away the unbearable pain. He was a sailor; had been since he was a boy of fifteen. It was a fate he was familiar with and had always half-expected.

Then, as the waves closed over his head and he shut his eyes against the waning of the light, he saw her face. *Elizabeth.* His fiancée, his love. Her golden curls glowed with all the brilliance of the sun. Her violet-blue eyes beckoned to him, begging him to stay with her, to not leave her, not lose their love. She reached out to him, as if to pull him back to the land of the living.

Her eyes were stronger than the force of the sea. He

reached out for her beckoning fingers—and his hand brushed the hard, splintering wood of a piece of flotsam. A plank from his ship. He grasped it and, with every bit of strength left in him, every ounce of willpower, pulled himself up into the air.

Into a new hell.

His ship was dying, sinking fast, but all around him the battle still raged. Cannon fire turned the air thick and rancid, the black clouds mingling with flames and blood. Shouts and cries swirled above him, while all about him was the detritus of the ship he had been entrusted with. Burning wood, guns, bits of steel—the bodies of his men.

He recognized Lieutenant Bridgers, as the young man's body floated past him, eyes wide open yet unseeing. He stared down at his own arm that wouldn't seem to move, and blinked in disbelief at the sight of raw, red flesh where his blue wool sleeve was torn away.

Bits of burning sail landed on that arm even as he watched, bringing fresh waves of agony. He gasped, and fell back onto his lifesaving plank. The battle around him, the cacophonous noise, the light fading left him with only one thought.

Elizabeth.

Mark Payne sat straight up in his bed, a shout strangled in his throat. *Of course.* A nightmare. That was all it was, all it ever was. It was not real.

But once it had been. It had been a real hell, fresh and hot around him, burning his nose with its stink. Eleven years. Eleven years he had been haunted by that day. Would the memory of it, of his failing, never leave him?

Mark longed for it to be gone, yet he knew it never would be. Not until he could lose the ache of guilt that gnawed at his belly.

At least here, in his isolated little house in Cornwall, there was no one to be disturbed by his nighttime shouts. Or the endless pacing on the nights when he could not sleep at all. Here, he could hurt no one.

He knew that the villagers speculated about him, made up tales, as they had ever since he came here seven years ago. He knew they asked endless questions of the old woman who came in to cook and clean for him, questions she could not answer, though she certainly tried to with fantastical speculation. Perhaps he was a werewolf? A devil, cursed and cast out of hell? An exiled prince from a faraway land?

Mark laughed now to think of those stories—and they were only the ones that had come to his own ears. He could not even begin to imagine the ones he had not heard. The Cornish were ever fond of wild tales. Perhaps that was why he had come here, and not to one of his family's estates in Kent or Devon. Here, he was only one more haunt among many.

Even his nearest neighbor, the grand and ancient Royce Castle, was said to be haunted. Full of ghosts and spirits and devils of all sorts—even an island witch. Though Royce Castle was above two miles away from Mark's small abode, on clear days he could glimpse the turrets and speculate about those creatures, speculate about what an island witch could possibly want with such a cold and desolate land.

Such speculations were one of his life's few amusements.

Mark threw back the heavy bedclothes. He knew he would find no more sleep this night. The fire in the grate had died away, leaving the small bedchamber chill and dark. He lit the candle on the bedside table, casting a small circle of light in the gloom, and reached for his dressing gown. The fur-lined velvet slid over his nakedness, caressing his damaged flesh with its softness. As he tied the corded sash, he turned to the window, pushing back the draperies to let the night in.

And such a night it was, as different from the landscape in his nightmare as it could possibly be. He might have suddenly landed on the moon. The same moon that peeked from behind thick clouds to cast a brief, silvery glow over the night.

Rare snow from early in the evening lay in a thin white layer, light as an eiderdown, over the ground, shimmering in the new light. Frost hung from the bare branches of the trees in his sadly overgrown and tangled garden, and a new snowfall drifted like magic from the skies. It was not yet thick; every flake could be seen in its own individual perfection.

It was a breathlessly beautiful scene. Mark was reminded of a story his mother used to tell him and his brother and sister when they were small children. A tale of an ice princess, who was incredibly lovely but very, very lonely. She lived all alone in her palace made of winter, because no one understood her or her magic. They all shunned her. So she spent all her time creating snowflakes, no two alike, each a picture of cold perfection.

Thoughts of his family—his mother, and Charles and Edwina—far away in London, reminded him that it was very nearly Christmas.

Christmas. The holiday the ice princess and her snow minions—and his own mother—loved above all others. When had he last thought of it? Not for a very, very long time.

His mother always wrote to him at this time of year, of course, urging him to come home, to share the holiday with them. Yet how could he? How could he ruin this time of year for his family, the people he loved the most, by showing his face in their elegant drawing room? He did not belong around their pianoforte, singing Christmas ditties, or around their table with roasted goose and berry tarts.

Every time he was tempted to go back, he remembered the revulsion that swept over Elizabeth's beautiful face when she first beheld him after the battle. He heard again her scream of despair, remembered how she had turned away.

No. He would not put his family through that. They deserved the perfect Christmas.

Mark pushed back his brocade sleeve and stared down at his left arm. By some miracle, it had been saved from the surgeons' knives, but the skin was puckered, crisscrossed with scars and welts. In the sunlight, it was a strange, shell-pink color; in the moonlight, it was pale, disguised. The left side of his face was the same, scarred, marked forever by what had happened that day. He could usually hide from it, by being alone, by having no mirrors in his house except the tiny one above his shaving stool.

At night he was exposed for what he was: A living haunt.

Mark laughed roughly at the fanciful thought. He was so very rarely *fanciful.* "You are moon-mad, Captain Payne," he muttered to himself. "Or perhaps bewitched? There are many curses floating about in Cornwall. One must have landed on you."

He started to turn away, to reach for the bottle of brandy sitting on the bedside table, when some noise startled him. He swung back toward the window.

"What the devil was that?" he said out loud, peering into the night. It had sounded like some low cry or moan. Not a scream or shout; something beckoning, enticing. Like the ice princess's lonely song.

There was nothing else. Only the silence of the snow-blanketed night. But Mark's nerves still rang. Something was out there. He could sense it, just as he had once sensed enemy ships lurking in the sea fogs. He suddenly felt alert, alive, as he had not in months and months. He had to find whatever was in the night.

He shrugged off his dressing gown and reached for the clothes he had carelessly piled on the chair before retiring. As he tied back his overlong dark hair and searched for his greatcoat, one thought reverberated in his mind.

He was moon-mad, indeed.

Chapter Three

Antoinette sat straight up in bed, gasping for air. She felt the edges of some tantalizing dream floating away from her, snatched away before she could grab onto it. What *had* she been dreaming? It dissipated like so much smoke, leaving her with only the remnant impressions of something unbearably sweet.

The blankets fell away from her shoulders, and she shivered despite her long-sleeved muslin night rail. The cottage was chilly and dark, the scents of her dried herbs and flowered soaps heavy in the crisp air. Antoinette shrugged her thick braid back over her shoulder and collapsed against the piles of feather pillows. She closed her eyes and breathed in slowly until she felt her fevered blood slow in her veins.

The dream was completely gone, and she was all alone in her familiar cottage. The moonlight spilling from the mullioned windows cast a glow over her brightly colored silk quilts, the bottles and pots on her dressing table, the bundles of dried herbs suspended from the ceiling beams. She could see the snow falling out there—the first snow she had seen in a very long time.

Antoinette had always felt safe in the cottage. The whitewashed walls seemed to embrace her from the first day she saw them. But right now, in this quiet midnight, it seemed as if those very walls were closing about her. She needed air. She needed to talk to someone. She needed . . .

She needed her mother. Her mother would be able to help her decipher all the strange feelings that were swirling inside her of late. Antoinette had tried before to contact her mother, but it had always been in vain. Maybe now, on this strange night, the winter solstice, it would work. Antoinette felt the magic in the snow-dusted moonlight on her very fingertips.

She climbed down from the high bed, and without even lighting the lamp, pulled open the doors of the carved wardrobe. The moonlight fell on the array of gowns, cloaks, and robes hanging there, the bonnets and slippers and shawls arranged on the shelf. One silvery beam glistened on the sleeve of one of her robes.

Green. Emotional healing and growth, the Great Mother in her nurturing form. *Perfect.*

Antoinette drew the soft silk of the robe over her night rail and fastened the gold frogs up the front. As she slipped on her sturdiest half boots, she reached into a small box under the bed and pulled out her most cherished possession. The red leather binding of the book was worn to a satin smoothness by all the women's hands that had touched it over the years. Her mother. Her grandmother. Her great-grandmother, who had inscribed much of the ancient knowledge on its parchment pages.

Antoinette smoothed her palm over the book's precious cover before placing it carefully in an oilskin pouch. She added candles, a flint, an array of herbs.

She was ready.

The night was colder than Antoinette expected. Cornwall was usually quite mild, at least compared to the rest of the freezing island of England, but not this night of rare snow. Her breath escaped into the air in tiny smoke-like puffs, and her boots crunched on the thin layer of moisture underfoot. New flakes, delicate as the lace many of the local villagers made, landed on the hood of her cloak and caught in her eyelashes and the braid of her hair. The sky had become strangely clear, though, stars blinking down at her like diamonds from between a wide break in the clouds.

She had no idea where she was going. She simply turned out of her garden gate and walked, letting her feet lead her where they would. She would not be surprised to discover she was still in her bed, dreaming. It was not like her to leave the safety of her house to go wandering alone in the night, especially since some villager on his way home might see her and carry the tale of her midnight ramblings back to his neighbors. People there were suspicious enough of her, despite the friendship of Cassie and her family, and of the vicar and his wife.

"Do not be silly, Antoinette," she told herself, turning down a different pathway. "No one is fool enough to be out on such a night. No one but you."

Indeed, it *was* silent. So silent she could almost hear the new snow falling on the ground. She heard no supernatural whispers, no one calling to her. Even the ghosts of Royce Castle were asleep, as all sensible people—human or spirit—should be.

Antoinette laughed softly. It felt a bit like when she was a child, and she and Cassie would slip out to go swimming in the ocean at night—exciting, a strange fluttering deep in her stomach. Only back then their environs had been considerably warmer.

Her laughter faded when she saw where her steps had led her. She was atop one of the steep, rocky cliffs that fell straight down into the roiling winter sea. She stared out over the water, mesmerized for an instant by the waves and the sky.

She came to the shore often, of course. The rocky sand was a favorite picnic spot of the Leighton children, and the old smugglers' caves there contained very strong ghostly vibrations. But she seldom came here at night, and never like this—all alone, in the snow and cold, atop the sharp cliffs.

She shivered, yet somehow this felt *right*. This was where she was meant to be, for this moment.

Tucking her woolen cloak beneath her knees, she knelt down on the ground and took her treasures out of the pouch. Candles—white, silver, purple, blue, gold—were neatly arrayed, protected by their glass globes. Antoinette lit them, and sprinkled thyme, lavender, meadowsweet, and dried rose petals in the snow around them. As she did this, she closed her eyes and focused all her thoughts toward the love of her mother, toward all her mother's teachings. She rose and, at her feet, the ancient book fluttered open, the pages shuffling in the cold breeze.

"Mother of all days," Antoinette called, "come to us this night, touch us with your presence. Bring me your wisdom, your peace, your power. Help me to find the right path."

Help me to find my way out of this loneliness, she added silently, with every ounce of her being.

She held out her arms, and the hood of her cloak fell back. A new wind arose around her, sweeping at her skirts, skittering the candles' flames, though they did not go out. Indeed, they seemed to glow even brighter.

The cord binding her braid fell and her hair blew free, the waist-length strands whipping across her face and throat. A warmth kindled deep inside her, growing hot and brighter.

Antoinette raised her arms higher, palms up to catch the moonlight. "Come to me," she chanted. "*Help* me!"

She lurched a step forward, and another. She felt light, so very light, as if she could fly free of all her confusion . . .

"*No!*" she heard a man shout. At first disoriented, she thought it was part of the spell. A strange part, one she had not conjured herself, but many times things happened she had not counted on when she was in a meditative state. She did not have the powers of her mother. She closed her eyes tighter, trying to will the strange voice away.

Yet it came again, closer this time, more insistent. "No, miss! Please!"

Antoinette opened her eyes and spun around, seeking the source of that shout. The magic of the night dissipated, the wind faded to a mere cold embrace.

She turned too quickly, though. The soles of her boots slid on the coating of snow, and she felt them slipping beneath her. Almost as if time had slowed down, allowing her to see herself falling, she coasted backward. Her arms flailed, trying to grasp onto something, *anything*.

There was nothing behind her but empty air.

She fell toward the earth. The sky arched overhead,

black and cold and void. Something hard struck at the back of her head—and then she saw nothing at all.

Oh, *blast*! He had killed her!

Mark ran from the ring of trees toward the edge of the sea cliff, his boots slipping on the new layer of snowfall. The woman lay there, so very still, a crumpled heap of silk and wool.

He dropped to his knees beside her just as the moon disappeared behind a veil of clouds, leaving them in deepest midnight shadows. The only light was from the flickering ring of candles, sheltered from the cold by glass globes. The scent of lavender and dried rose was sweet and rich—and strange, in the middle of winter.

Mark had no time to ponder such oddities as candles and flowers, though. His only thought, his entire being, was concentrated on the woman lying still on the ground.

"I'm sorry I startled you," he muttered. "Please don't be dead."

Very carefully, he bent down toward her, watching her for any sign of breath and life. He took her hand in his, and pressed his fingertips to her slender wrist. "Thank you," he whispered, when he detected the thready hum of her pulse. Her chest rose in a steady, though shallow, rhythm.

So she was not dead, but not yet out of danger. Mark recalled how, on the second ship he sailed on, a cabin boy had been struck on the head by a falling bucket. The lad had remained unconscious for many days before dying, never once awakening. Head injuries were quite perilous and unpredictable.

He quickly stripped off his greatcoat and made a cushion of it on the ground. Slowly, gingerly, he moved her head onto its softness, probing gently for an injury. There was a small knot near the base of her neck, but none of the stickiness of blood.

He had been quite right all these years to resist his mother's letters urging him to come home. Look what happened when he ventured outside his door! He was a menace to other people. A curse. Here he had merely meant to prevent the girl from throwing herself over the cliff, and instead he had nearly killed her.

He should go for help, he thought, as he reached for one of the woman's candles and brought it closer. But where could he go? The nearest house after his own cottage was Royce Castle, and the woman who came in to keep house for him had said that the Leighton family had gone to Bath until after the New Year, and most of the servants were home in the village with their families. The physician was in the village, too, more than thirty minutes' ride from here. Mark would just have to take care of her himself.

He lifted up the candle so he could see her better—and gave a strangled gasp. It wasn't merely that she was beautiful, though she certainly was, extremely so. It was that she was so completely unlike anyone he had ever seen before, and not at all what he would expect to find here in this remote corner of England.

She was more like something he would find in a dream, a fantasy of warm seas, waterfalls, and jasmine flowers. Maybe she *was* a dream, truly. This whole bizarre night was a dream.

His fingers tightened on her wrist. No, she was too warm, too solid to be a dream. Or a ghost.

The woman's skin, though ashen at the moment, was a dark, burnished color, like cream in coffee, undulating like smooth silk over high cheekbones and an aquiline nose. Her hair, spread around her on the snow, was a wild riot of thick, black waves. She was dressed unlike anyone else, too. Her dark cloak had fallen back to reveal a strange robe of green silk, embroidered in gold with exotic flowers and symbols, fastened up the front with gold braid frogs. She was very tall. If she was standing, she would probably be about as tall as Mark's own six foot three, yet she was slender as a reed.

"You must be an illusion," he whispered to her. "What else would you be doing on this godforsaken shore?"

Then he remembered—the island witch. Of course. This must be she.

When Mark first joined the Navy at age fifteen, he

was sent to the West Indies station, where he stayed for over five years. Jamaica, Barbados, Bermuda. There he had seen many women like this one, dusky, willowy, impossibly exotic. He had never seen one to approach her aura of elegance, though. Even unconscious, she exuded a certain power surely unknown to any English lady.

"Who are you?" he asked her. "How did you come to be here?"

And *was* she a witch? Mark was certainly not a man to put stock in village gossip. He had been the subject of it far too often himself. But something odd had been happening here this night. Look at her robe, the candles.

The necklace she wore. It was a heavy silver pendant, suspended on a long chain, etched in its center with a crescent moon image, surrounded by a circle of rough-cut gemstones. They glowed in the candlelight, seeming to entice him, to beckon him. . . .

The tips of his fingers were grazing the cold silver, when she let out a soft moan. Her long fingers stirred and reached up toward her temple.

"You're awake!" Mark shouted in jubilation, a relief unlike any he had ever known rising up in his heart. She was *not* dead, nor in an endless stupor. He had not killed her.

"Am I?" she whispered roughly. Her eyes opened, focusing up on him. They were wide, as black as the night around them, and as clear as if she was simply waking from the most refreshing of slumbers.

Her brows, as silken and arched as a raven's wings, drew down slightly when she saw him, as if puzzled. Too late, Mark realized he held the candle near to his face—his ruined face. It was sure to send this goddess back into her unreachable sleep to see *that*! And he had not put his gloves on, either. He hastily blew out the candle and cast it away into the snow.

She did not scream or gasp or turn away, as other ladies often did. Nor did her expression dissolve into pity. She simply watched him, that tiny puzzled frown on her brow.

Perhaps her wits were still addled from the fall.

"Who are you?" she asked, her voice low and soft,

touched with a French island lilt. She stared up at him warily, her slender body stiffening. "What happened to me? Are you a ghost?"

He swallowed hard past the sudden dryness in his throat. "No, I am not a ghost. Not yet. My name is Captain Mark Payne, madam," he answered her, the words escaping before he could even catch them. Captain? He had not called himself by that title in many years. But there it was, the sound of it hanging in the air between them. "I fear you took a fall and hit your head. I thought you were about to jump off the cliff, and I called out to you. I fear I startled you—I'm sorry."

"A fall?" Carefully, wincing a bit, she turned her head to see the sputtering candles, the scattering of herbs now being covered by the new snowfall. "I remember coming here now. Do you live nearby?"

"Yes. In Thornbush Cottage. I could not sleep, so I came out for a walk. I thought no one would be about."

She studied him very carefully, her dark eyes narrowed. He did not know what she saw there, but whatever it was obviously somewhat reassured her. She finally nodded, and said, "You saved me? Thank you very much."

Mark could only nod brusquely, unable to take his gaze from her. She appeared to be waiting for him to say something. Her perfect stillness, her very aura of some unfathomable serenity, seemed to invite confidences of all sorts. Even from a man who had confided in no one, relied on no one, for seven long years.

But she was far too fragile to listen to any of his nonsense, and he would be even more of a boor than he already was to burden her with his apologies. *She* was the one he must take care of.

"You're welcome," he said simply.

"Well, Captain Mark Payne," she said, her voice a bit stronger though still shaky. "I am Miss Antoinette Duvall, and pleased to meet you, despite the less than auspicious circumstances. Do you always walk in the snow in your shirtsleeves?"

Mark gave a bark of laughter, suddenly realizing that he was indeed in his shirtsleeves, and it was demmed cold. "No, madam. I am not quite as foolish as all that. My coat at present resides beneath your head."

"Oh!" Her trembling hand darted up to feel the soft, crumpled wool of his greatcoat. "Here, sir, you must take it back. I would not have you catch a chill for your good deed. You must be freezing. Unless you really *are* a ghost? Then you would not be cold at all."

He *was* cold, but she was probably much more so, lying on the ground. The snow was drifting thicker and faster around them. And he worried about her rambling talk of ghosts. "Do you feel well enough to rise, Miss Duvall?"

"I feel as if my bones have turned to jelly."

"Put your arms around my neck," he told her. As she wound her silk-clad arms weakly about him, he slid his own beneath her legs and lifted her carefully as he rose to his feet. He was glad to find all of that wood-chopping he had done, all the new thatching on his roof, the evening rides along the cliffs, had not been for naught. Antoinette Duvall was not a small woman, but she fit easily into his arms.

With a low, pained sigh, she rested her head on his shoulder. Her hair smelled of jasmine and candle smoke. "Thank you, Captain Payne," she whispered. "You are truly a knight in shining armor."

"Rather tarnished armor, I fear."

"Not at all." She still clutched his coat in her shaking hand, and awkwardly shook it out to spread it over one of his shoulders.

He carried her away from the cliff, toward the meager shelter of the trees. Once on the pathway, though, he was struck by a sudden doubt—where to take her, where she would be safe and cared for? The Leightons at the castle were gone; he had no idea where Miss Duvall lived. The closest residence was his own cottage.

His thoughts were interrupted by her sudden panicked cry. "My book!"

"Your what?"

"My book. I left it back in the snow. Oh, it cannot be ruined! It's all I have."

Mark glanced around them, and saw a fallen log that was as yet only lightly dusted with snow. "If I put you down here, can you sit for a moment while I go to fetch it?"

"Yes, of course."

He was not sure he completely believed her; her head bobbed against him weakly. But he could not argue against the urgency in her voice. She obviously *needed* that book, whatever it was, and she would not be easy until she had it. He placed her carefully on the log, making certain she would stay upright and that her cloak was tucked warmly beneath her.

Mark turned and ran back toward the cliff, thrusting his arms into the sleeves of his greatcoat. The book was indeed there, beside the dying candles. A few flakes melted on the antique parchment pages, but it appeared to be undamaged. As he brushed off the moisture, he saw printed there words in some strange language, the dark brown ink faded with age.

He had no time to ponder the volume's mysteries, though. He closed it with a snap and pushed it inside his coat. There was Miss Duvall he had to return to with all haste, or she would surely faint away again.

Indeed, she was listing quite alarmingly when he returned to the fallen tree; her head wobbled on her slim neck. She smiled radiantly, though, when he handed her the book. She cradled it against her as if it was made of the rarest rubies.

"Thank you," she said. "That is twice you have saved me this night, Captain Payne."

"Ah, but my rescue will have been in vain if we do not get you home this minute. You will surely catch a chill," Mark said, scooping her up into his arms again. "Do you have a maid or companion waiting at your house? You should not be alone with a head injury. You need someone to keep you awake until a physician can be summoned."

"No, I live alone," she answered, her voice soft, almost drowsy. Her head drooped back against his shoulder. "There is a girl who comes to clean for me, but only in the afternoons."

Mark cursed beneath his breath. That was what he was afraid of, that she was as solitary as he.

"What is it?" Antoinette asked complacently, not at all fazed by any use of impolite language. He wondered nonsensically if she had perhaps grown up around sailors and become used to their ways. "Is something amiss? Beyond the obvious, of course."

"If there is no one where you live, then there is only one place for you to go, Miss Duvall. At least for this night."

"Oh? And where is that?" Her tone held only casual curiosity, as if her immediate future held only marginal interest for her. He sensed her deep weariness.

"My house. Thornbush Cottage, it's called. Someone must look after you for the next few hours. They are the most vital after someone sustains a head injury."

If he had expected missish protests, cries, or tears, he was to be pleasantly disappointed. She merely gave a quiet laugh, and said, "That is *three* times now you have rescued me, Captain Payne. I am so very sorry to inconvenience you, but I fear you are correct. I have some knowledge of healing myself, as you obviously do, and I know I should *not* be alone right now. I feel so very—odd."

Her arm tightened about his neck, and she cuddled closer with a gentle sigh. Her breath was cool against his bare throat.

He had indeed been correct, Mark thought, as he turned down the hidden lane toward his cottage. Miss Antoinette Duvall was unlike any other woman he had ever met.

Chapter Four

Antoinette's head throbbed with a low, dull ache, giving a fresh twinge every time her rescuer took a step. The cold wind blew her cloak and robe about her, and her senses hummed with the force of her interrupted spell. Yet none of those discomforts were stronger than the one thought reverberating in her mind . . .

How very intriguing her rescuer was.

She rested her head against his hard shoulder and studied him carefully in the moonlight. She was certain she had never seen him before, or she certainly would have remembered him. He was quite unforgettable, and not only because of the scars tracing a delicate white pattern over the left side of his sun-bronzed face. Her heart ached at the knowledge of the pain he must have suffered, the agony that etched those marks on his flesh.

Even with those scars, he was a handsome man, with a strong jaw shadowed by a day's growth of beard, a slightly crooked nose, and eyes that glowed a strange pale silver even in the night. His hair was dark and overlong, falling over his collar in rich waves that escaped from their loose tie and tickled softly at Antoinette's fingers. He was very tall, and strongly built—strong enough to carry her over the uneven ground, and she knew she was no featherlight female. The muscles that moved and bunched across his shoulders and arms were as powerful as those of any farm laborer.

He was no laborer, though; she knew that for certain. She had never met a farmer with such an air of command, of aristocratic self-possession.

It was not just his good looks, but his innate strength that drew her to him, that made her quite unable to look away from him. It was the deep, cutting sadness she saw hidden deep in his eyes, a despair deeper than any she had seen before.

Antoinette longed to know who he was, where he came from. What sorrows he carried in his heart. Whatever they were, she would vow they made her own loneliness, her own sense of displacement, seem insignificant indeed.

But her powers of discernment were muted by the pain in her head, and by a sweeping wave of exhaustion threatening to drown her beneath it. She closed her eyes, and felt the heavy weight of her limbs.

She must have sighed out loud, for she sensed his gaze upon her. "We are very nearly there," he said gently. "I'm sorry for jostling you."

"I am fine," Antoinette assured him. "Just very, very tired."

He lifted her higher in his arms, and beneath her skirts she felt him reach out and push open a squeaking gate. "You must be exhausted after everything you have been through this night, Miss Duvall, but you must not go to sleep yet. Not until we can ascertain the true extent of your injuries."

"I know," she answered, her words breaking off on a wide yawn. She grimaced when she realized she had not even covered her mouth. "Forgive me. You must think I was raised in a barn somewhere."

Captain Payne gave a low chuckle, which vibrated warmly through her body. "I will confess to a curiosity about where you were raised, Miss Duvall, but I think you are in no condition to answer at the moment. You should be quiet, and rest as well as you can."

Antoinette opened her eyes at the sound of a soft click and a thud. He had opened the door of what appeared to be a cottage. It was smaller than her own abode, and darker, covered with a thick climbing ivy that concealed even the windows. The captain ducked his head down as he took them through the narrow doorway into a room even darker than the night they left behind.

Antoinette could see nothing in the gloom, but it was obvious that he knew his way easily. With a gracefully balanced movement, he bent down and gently deposited her on a soft settee.

"Wait here, Miss Duvall, and I will light a fire. We'll have you warm in no time," he said.

"I'm warmer already," she answered. The room still held the memory of an earlier fire, and already the chill was receding from her fingertips and earlobes. The pain in her head was also muted, yet the fatigue only grew greater now that she was warm and still. Antoinette untied the ribbons of her cloak and pushed it back from her shoulders, settling against the cushions of her new seat.

She listened to the sounds of the captain's movements, her senses heightened by the rich darkness. He was near, she could feel that. She heard the hollow thunk of wood being piled in the grate, the rustle of paper, and the click of a flint—once, twice. A flare of light broke the gloom, and soon a merry blaze glowed in the fireplace.

Still kneeling before the grate, he turned to look at her, his expression solemn. In the orange firelight, his scars were more pronounced, a puckered pale pink, and she saw that his left hand and wrist were also damaged. They were injuries that were healed, though, and nothing at all to some of the wounds she saw in Jamaica.

And they could not compare to the glory of his hair, autumn-brown, waving to his shoulders, or to the wary intelligence shining from his eyes.

"So this is your home?" she asked, slowly shifting her gaze from his to examine the room around her. The whitewashed walls and gray stone hearth were the same as those in her own home, but there the comparison ended. Where hers was full of pictures, books, and the scent of herbs, his was just—bare. The few pieces of furniture were old and shabby; there were no rugs, no draperies at the windows. The only painting was a print of a frigate cutting through the churning gray waters.

It gave her no clues whatsoever as to the personality of her rescuer, yet its clean starkness did confirm one thing she had suspected, even before he gave her his rank—he was a military man. Judging from the print, a navy man.

"It is very cozy," she added, when he was silent.

He gave her a half smile, sitting back on his heels to watch the flames he had kindled grow brighter. "Tiny, you mean."

"Hm, yes, that is one way to put it. But, as I reside in a rather small cottage myself, I am keenly aware of the advantages of a less than grand space. Not so much dusting, for one. And, even better, it is easier to keep the dreadful English chill away."

His smile widened just a fraction, slowly, as if his mouth had grown rusty from a long lack of mirth. He seemed to fear his face might crack if he dared smile further, or, God forbid, laugh aloud. Antoinette decided that when she was not so tired, she would wrack her brain for the most ridiculous jests she knew, just to see if he could indeed laugh.

"Compared to the cramped conditions aboard a ship, Miss Duvall, this cottage is a veritable palace," he said. "And everything stays where you put it, with no pitching or rolling about."

"Ah, so you *are* a navy man. I suspected as much."

His faint smile faded away altogether, and he glanced away from her into the fire. "*Was* a navy man. A very long time ago." He pushed himself to his feet and sat down in the only other chair in the room, a twig rocker by the side of the mantel. He closed his hands on the chair's wooden arms, curling his long fingers tightly. The only sound in the room was the crackling of the flames, the rasp of their breathing, and the rhythmic ticking of a strange, oval-shaped gold-and-ivory clock on the mantel.

Antoinette gazed up at its pale face. It was after one o'clock, still hours until the dawn. It was obvious that Captain Payne was not a man for light chatter, but Antoinette was itching to talk, to make *some* sort of noise. Otherwise, the warmth and the ticktocking of the clock would send her straight to sleep.

"Have you lived very long in the neighborhood, Captain Payne?" she asked him, rubbing at her temples. The pain was already muted, receding away. "I myself have been here for five years, yet I am sure we have never met."

He turned to her, very careful, Antoinette noticed, to keep the left side of his face in shadow. "I have lived here for seven years now, but I do not mix very much in society."

"Nor do I. Not that there is very much of what most people would call 'society' hereabouts. Not very many balls or routs. Though there are some agreeable people."

The corners of his mouth turned down a bit in obvious doubt. "Indeed, Miss Duvall? You do not find them to be a rather—gossiping lot?"

Antoinette thought of the individuals who had tried so very hard to make her feel at home here, such as the vicar and his wife, Lady Paige, Mrs. Greeley. Then she thought of the others, too many to count, who stared at her wide-eyed as she walked through the village, whispered behind her back as she passed.

She hated that so much, hated always having to hold her head high and pretend she did not hear them.

Were they really so very different, though, from the people in Jamaica, people of her own sort, who whispered and speculated about her friendship with the white Richards family?

"They are no more gossiping than any other set of people, I suspect," she said.

"That is too true. London, a ship, Cornwall—there is truly no escaping the curiosity of others. Not even, I imagine, in an Indian jungle. At least I have found what I was looking for in Cornwall."

"What were you looking for, Captain Payne?"

"As you say, Miss Duvall, a lack of society."

"And where did you come from before?" Antoinette suddenly noticed how very uncomfortable her damp boots had become. She bent to unhook them—and winced at the fresh wave of pain in her head.

"Here, let me do that. You should remain still." He left his chair and knelt down at her feet, his elegant fingers deftly unhooking the pearl buttons from the stiffening leather. "I fear I am out of practice at playing host. You ought to have something warm to drink. I think there may be some tea about."

"Tea would be most welcome, Captain Payne. Yet I fear you are evading my question."

He looked up at her, that tiny, rusty half smile on his lips again. In the firelight, his hair glowed with the burnish of October leaves, waving damp and silky to his shoulders. Antoinette longed with a sudden, tingling passion to touch that hair, to sink her fingers through its softness and trail them down his damaged cheek to his jaw, his lips. . . .

She tightened her hands into fists before they could go wandering of their own accord, and sat back in her chair.

"If you are so perceptive with a head injury, Miss Duvall, I should hate to see you with all your wits about you," he said. "You must be formidable indeed."

Antoinette's throat was suddenly so dry, she wasn't sure if she could speak clearly. Sitting here, with this strange, glorious man at her feet, the night and the fire wrapped around them, she did not feel like her usual sensible self at all. "I am not sure about formidable," she managed to say hoarsely. "But I am incurably curious. Some might even say a busybody."

Captain Payne gave a low chuckle that was really no more than a rumbling deep inside his chest. He slid her boots from her feet and lined them up neatly next to the fire, then stood up to stroll away through a narrow, half-hidden doorway. Antoinette surmised, from the rattling of china and metal, that that must be the kitchen.

"You cannot possibly be half the busybody my housekeeper is, Miss Duvall," he called back to her. "But in answer to your question, my family lives mostly in London. They have country estates, also, which I am sure they still travel to now and then."

"You do have family, then?" Antoinette asked, her breath held with the apprehension that she had gone too far, asked too much. His silence stretched on too long.

Distance, though, seemed to lessen Captain Payne's obvious reticence. Perhaps it was the fact that he could not see her face while he spoke from the kitchen. Or perhaps he sensed, as she did, the odd intimacy of this midnight, this feeling that they were the only two people in the whole world.

Probably not, though. That was surely all a product of her head injury, her disordered brain.

"I do have family," he said finally. "I am the younger son of the Earl of Havelock. My brother, Charles, is the earl now, and my mother and sister live with him at

Havelock House in Portman Square. Edwina, my sister, is much younger than Charles and myself—she is to make her bow in the spring. I am sure she will be quite the toast of the Season if she is as beautiful as I remember."

There was obvious affection in his tone as he spoke of this family, yet Antoinette saw nothing of them in his house. No portraits, no mementos. Nothing arranged on the mantel except the clock. "They do not care to visit you here?"

"No. They do not." There was cold finality in the words, his previous, ever so brief words gone like so much candle smoke.

Captain Payne came back into the sitting room with a tray arrayed with mismatched china cups and saucers and a plate of biscuits, as well as a kettle which he placed on the hob to warm.

"There is no sugar or milk," he said, with that stiff formality he had only barely begun to throw off.

"That is quite all right," Antoinette answered, not sure what else she could say to continue to draw the captain out.

Much to her surprise, *he* was the one who continued the conversation. "And where is your family, Miss Duvall? You are obviously not a native of Cornwall."

Antoinette gave a little laugh. "Ah, so you noticed that, did you? No, I am not English. I was born in Jamaica. My mother was a freed slave from Saint-Domingue. She and my father came to Kingston before I was born, and he died shortly thereafter. He was a blacksmith, I believe, the son of a French merchant and his placée, though I have no memory of him at all. My mother was a seamstress, a very fine one."

Antoinette had *never* told anyone of her family. Not even Cassie knew the truth about Antoinette's father. Most English people would be shocked to their core by this litany of slavery and illegitimacy. Captain Payne, though, was not like other Englishmen; she had sensed that the moment she first saw him. He merely nodded at her words, and reached for the kettle to pour hot water into their cups.

"Your mother, too, is deceased?" he asked, carefully steeping the tea.

"Yes."

"And how ever did you come to find yourself here?"

"That is a long story, Captain Payne."

"We have all night, Miss Duvall." He passed her the cup, and gave her a wry grin. It seemed less stiff now, as if he was remembering at last how a smile went.

"It is a dull story, as well."

"Ah, but I am seldom bored."

"Very well, then." Antoinette stretched her stockinged feet out toward the fire, and sipped at the strong, bracing tea. She told him of how her mother was employed as seamstress to Cassie's mother, of how their families became close and Cassie became like her sister.

"So, when her father died and she came here to live with her aunt, she asked me to come with her," Antoinette finished. "I could not say no."

He nodded thoughtfully. "You were very brave to come to a new land."

Antoinette gave a disbelieving snort. "Brave? Nay, Captain, I was a coward, unable to make my own way in life without my friend to cling to."

Captain Payne shook his head. "I lived in the West Indies for five years, Miss Duvall. I know what you left behind; I know how very different it is from this place. It is warm, full of flowers and sun and strange, compelling music. To have that, and come to this cold, narrow-minded, inhospitable place—that is courage indeed."

There was a sudden passion in his voice, a pain, a longing, that seemed to echo that in her own heart. "I have not always found England to be so terrible."

His head swung toward her, his gaze, like quicksilver, piercing her to her very core. "Do you not?"

"I—no. It is not all one could wish for, of course, but what is? I often miss the sun, and the way the sea looks there, so very different from the cold waves here. But there are compensations. Such as tonight."

His dark brows drew down. "Tonight? You enjoy being knocked unconscious and falling in the snow, then? You *are* a strange female."

Antoinette laughed, feeling an odd rush of sudden lightness. "Of course not! Snow is *horrible*. So cold. But if all that had not happened, I would not have met a new friend."

Those brows arched up in surprise, as if the word "friend" was one he had not heard in a very long time. Then he chuckled, a sound more warming than the fire and the tea. "Indeed, Miss Duvall. I would have been most unhappy to be deprived of making your acquaintance."

"And, considering everything we have been through this evening, could you perhaps call me Antoinette? Just for tonight?"

"If you will call me Mark."

"It is a bargain—Mark." Antoinette took a biscuit from the plate and settled back happily in her chair. Despite everything—her injuries, the cold, her spell gone awry—she felt more content here in this tiny, bare cottage than she had in a very long time.

"I think that captaining a navy vessel is far braver than anything *I* could have ever done," she said. "And far more exciting besides."

"It was mostly deadly dull," he answered.

"I do not believe that. You must have a great many tales to tell."

Mark shrugged, and reached for a biscuit of his own. "A few. But they are hardly suitable for a lady's ears."

"Ah, yet as we have established, I am not your typical English lady. Come now, Mark. We have many hours until dawn. Tell me some of your sea tales."

He gazed into the fire, perhaps trying to recall a story that was not too gruesome, or too personal. Antoinette doubted he would tell her how he came to get his scars—not yet, anyway. Their friendship was too new, too delicate.

Antoinette was a patient woman, though. One day, he would tell her. And it was the Christmas season, after all—a season when anything was possible. She had not believed that before, but now she was beginning to.

"When I was a mere ensign," he began, "I was sent to the West Indies, to Jamaica in fact, and there an old sea captain told me a most fanciful story indeed. . . ."

Chapter Five

Dawn was just beginning to break over the landscape with the palest pinks, lavenders, and oranges when Antoinette made her slow, careful way out of Mark's cottage door. She leaned on his arm, steadying herself against residual waves of dizziness. Mark had wanted to carry her out, tried to scoop her up out of her chair into his arms. She laughingly resisted, insisting that she was not an invalid. She *had* been sorely tempted to give in, though. To feel his arms about her one more time, holding her safe above the earth and all its mundane cares.

It was a most extraordinary night that had just passed, she thought, as she moved slowly down the uneven stone walkway to where Mark's saddled horse waited. They had talked for hours, of nothing in particular. She told him stories of the Leighton children's antics, the beauties of her island home, the books on herbals she wrote, and the lotions and soaps she made for stores in the village and in London. He related tales of his years at sea and all of the exotic lands he had seen. But only light tales he thought might amuse her, make her laugh; nothing of what had caused his scars, what had driven him from a life of seafaring adventure he obviously loved to one of isolation in Cornwall. Nothing more about his family.

She wanted so much to know all those things, to know *everything* about this intriguing man. But she did not want to press, and ruin this lovely night they shared. For it had been a lovely night indeed, filled with talk and tea and firelight. She had not felt so—so *light* in a very long time.

Strange, considering that it was all thanks to a man whose heart was the heaviest she had ever sensed.

Antoinette paused to lean against Mark's rusting garden gate, watching as he untethered the horse. "The snow has ceased," she said.

He gave her a small smile. "So it has. Judging by that sunrise, we should have a clear day. Warmer."

"I thought the saying was 'red sky at morning, sailors take warning,'" she answered, remembering a little rhyme her mother had sometimes recited. "Can we look for new storms?"

"Ah, but that is not quite red, is it? More like—pinkish." His strong hands came around her waist, lifting her carefully and easily into the saddle. All too briefly, his warm touch, soothing and incredibly exciting at the same moment, landed on her leg, smoothing the silk of her robe. "If it is clear tonight, will you go back out to the cliffs to finish what you began last night, Miss Duvall?"

Antoinette turned her face up to the glories of the sunrise. Last night, when she ran out to the cliffs in a dark fit of loneliness, seemed so very far away now in this new dawn. She went there wanting to find *something*—what, she knew not. She relied on her book and her herbs to send her an answer.

She began to think now that they had done just that, though in a manner she could not have predicted. She felt so strange, so uncertain—so tired.

"I thought I asked you to call me Antoinette. And I do not know," she answered him. "I rarely go walking along those cliffs at midnight, though I often do so in the early evenings. There is no one about then, and the sounds of the sea and the birds are very peaceful."

He smiled up at her. "I am quite fond of a good evening walk, myself."

"Are you indeed, Captain? Well. Perhaps one evening we shall meet there."

"Perhaps we shall." Mark swung himself up into the saddle behind Antoinette, his arms coming around her to take the reins. She leaned back against him, savoring that sensation of warm safety. His breath was cool, scented of the spice from their tea, as it brushed against her temple and stirred her hair. "Now, Miss Duvall—Antoinette. Would you be so kind as to give me the direction to your home?"

Mark stood outside the garden gate of Antoinette Duvall's cottage long after she disappeared through the door, turning to give him a wave and a smile before the red painted wood closed behind her. The draperies at the old-fashioned mullioned windows never opened, but in good time a plume of silver-gray smoke rose up from the chimney.

He knew he should rush back to his hideaway before the countryside stirred to life and someone saw him lurking there. Her maid would be coming in soon, or a woodsman might pass by on the way to his morning's task. Even worse, Antoinette herself might glance out of the window and see him still there, and wonder with growing horror just what sort of shambling beast she had let into her life.

But he found he could not leave. Not yet. He felt like a beggar child, gazing longingly into the window of a warm bakery. There were delights of all sorts there—comfort, beauty, good humor, intrigue. But not for the likes of him.

Antoinette's cottage looked much like his own—small, square, built of rough gray stone. There the resemblance ended. Where his garden was wild and overgrown, hers was trim and perfectly ordered, with beds outlined in red brick. It was cut back for the winter, but in the summer it would be a riotous glory of color and scent. Her walls were free of choking ivy, her gate neatly painted and oiled.

He wondered what she would do if he walked up to her door, knocked on it, and begged admittance as he longed to do. He even took one step forward, his hand reaching for the latch on her gate, before he remembered himself and fell back. She was exhausted. She needed to sleep and recover from her fall—a fall *he* had caused—not to be pestered by a retired sailor begging for just another moment in her company.

In the firelight he could pretend she could not see him clearly, that he was as he had been eleven years ago. In the daylight, his flaws were all too obvious.

Mark swung back up into the saddle and turned the horse toward home. Yes, indeed—firelight and shadows could conceal much, could even allow a foolish man to pretend he was not as he was. Those long hours of night had been a precious time out of time, where he could enjoy the company and the laughter of a beautiful woman. He told her half-forgotten tales of the sea and basked in the musical cadence of her voice as she told him stories of her own.

Stories that were funny, and interesting, and even a bit eerie, as when she related ghost stories from her homeland. But nothing that told him what she had been doing on the cliffs last night, what she thought of her life in England. It could not be easy for her. Her skin marked her as an outsider, just as his scars marked him. There was only the merest trace of that in her wide smile, in the dark pools of her eyes.

He had the sense, though, that she would understand about his own life, his own pain. She would listen, and *know*. If he could just tell her, which of course he could not. He didn't even have the words to explain it to himself. Long years in the navy had frozen off that part of himself, and not even Antoinette Duvall's Jamaican sun could thaw it.

He liked conversing with her, though. He liked looking at her, at her exotic beauty and the elegance of her long hands. She never glanced away from him uneasily, as everyone else did, as Elizabeth did. Antoinette watched his face as they conversed, touched his damaged left hand as he lifted her from the horse. It was as if she noticed not a thing amiss. They were merely two neighbors, sharing an amiable chat and a pot of tea by the fire.

Perhaps he *would* go strolling along the cliffs one evening soon, where they could meet and talk and walk together in the fading daylight.

And perhaps he would not. For Mark Payne, who had faced the French navy and fierce squalls at sea without flinching, found he was an abject coward before a beautiful woman.

Chapter Six

"Oh, Miss Duvall, I vow your lotions smell more luscious every time!" Mrs. Greeley gazed down at the array of bottles and pots on her store counter, and inhaled deeply of a dab of chamomile cream. "I cannot tell you how happy I am for a new batch. These fly off the shelves as quickly as I can put them there."

Antoinette smiled, deeply gratified by the compliment. She had worked long and hard over these preparations, concocting exactly the right recipes and mix of herbs. "There are soaps too, Mrs. Greeley," she said, reaching into the large hamper and bringing out small, muslin-wrapped squares. "Rose, lavender, sandalwood. I am working on some toilette water; it should be ready to bottle after the New Year."

"Lovely, Miss Duvall! These soaps will be just the thing for customers looking for Christmas gifts."

Antoinette thought of the little fragrant bars she had carefully wrapped up at home, waiting for Cassie and Penelope. "Indeed you are right, Mrs. Greeley. The sachet bags would be very nice too. Perhaps you could make a pretty display of them here on the counter? Then people coming up to pay for their purchases would see them, and you could persuade them that their mother or daughter needs just one more sweet little gift."

Mrs. Greeley laughed. "How clever of you, Miss Duvall! I shall do just that." She turned the small, colored glass bottles so that their facets caught the sunlight from the windows. Her store was quiet at this time of day, and she was obviously primed for a bit of chatter. "Now, Miss Duvall, speaking of the festive season, I hope you are not working so very hard that you cannot enjoy it. It *is* Christmas, after all, and it only comes about once a year."

Christmas. Of course. How could Antoinette forget it, when every shop in the village was bedecked with greenery over the doors, every window festooned with ribbons, every horse's bridle merry with bells? She had even given into it herself, bringing holly and evergreen in to decorate her fireplace mantel and staircase balustrade.

Much to her blushing shame, she went so far as to make a kissing bough to hang in her sitting room, just on the slight chance that Captain Mark Payne might come calling. She thought better of it as soon as it was made, though, and tossed it in the fire.

A very good thing too, for Captain Payne had *not* called. She had not seen even a glimpse of him in the past two days, not since he left her at her garden gate. She went walking in the evenings along the cliff, just as they had talked of, and he was not there either. Now tomorrow was Christmas Eve, and it seemed the holiday would pass without another meeting with the intriguing captain.

Not that she cared, of course, for she did not. Not one jot. Truly.

"Of course I am enjoying the season, Mrs. Greeley," she said, with a smile that even she could sense seemed overly bright and false. "Who could not?"

The shopkeeper gave her a shrewd glance. "We heard that the family up at the castle has gone to Bath to visit the dowager countess."

"Yes, that is true. They go every Christmas."

"Since they are your nearest neighbors, and your cottage lies such a distance from the village, it must get very quiet there. Very lonesome."

Antoinette peered closely at Mrs. Greeley, wondering what the lady was insinuating. Had she seen Mark leaving Antoinette's cottage at daybreak? Was there gossip?

That would be the very last thing Antoinette needed. It was difficult enough to overcome the villagers' suspicions as it was. But Mrs. Greeley merely looked complacent and innocent, her faded blue eyes wide as she peered up at Antoinette.

"I do well enough in my home, Mrs. Greeley," Antoinette said cautiously. "I am very cozy."

"Yes, but one shouldn't be alone at Christmas, Miss Duvall. You should come to the assembly tomorrow evening at the Hare and Hound. Mr. Greeley and I would so enjoy it if you came with us."

"An assembly?"

"Yes, for Christmas Eve. Lady Paige is sponsoring, and the whole village is ever so excited—the assembly rooms haven't been used in an age, and they are so much more spacious than the old rooms we used for the Christmas Eve assembly last year! There will be supper and dancing and cards."

Quite against her will, Antoinette was tempted. She generally disliked social events, where everyone watched her and whispered, and only a few people actually conversed with her. She usually only attended parties at Royce Castle or supper at the vicarage. She never went anywhere without the Leightons.

But she did love to dance, and was not averse to cards either. And she had not really been looking forward to a solitary holiday. She had hoped, oh so briefly, that perhaps she could invite Mark for a Christmas supper and a hand of piquet. Since that appeared to be a distant possibility, she should go to the assembly with the Greeleys and try to enjoy herself.

Be brave for once, Antoinette, she told herself.

"Thank you, Mrs. Greeley," she said. "I happily accept your kind invitation."

Mrs. Greeley's smile lit up her round, lined face. "Excellent, Miss Duvall! We will see you tomorrow evening, then."

Antoinette tucked the payment for the soaps and lotions into her reticule, and stepped out onto the walkway, the bells on the Greeleys' door jingling merrily behind her. It was a quiet time of day for the village, and not very many people were out and about on the street, going in and out of the half-timbered shops. Only the vicar drove by in his gig, raising his hat in greeting to Antoinette, and Mrs. Brown, the dressmaker, was arranging a new display of fabrics and ribbons in her bow window.

Antoinette turned her steps toward home, but then paused, considered, and glanced back at Mrs. Brown's window. The mantua-maker sometimes had gowns ready to purchase, or at least some shawls and dancing slippers or headdresses. Something new, and dashingly attractive, might be in order for the assembly. After all, Mark Payne might, just *might*, attend.

Antoinette laughed at herself, and forced her feet to turn once more toward the outskirts of the village without going back to the shop. She was acting like a silly schoolgirl, mooning about for a man who cared nothing for her. She had thought, after their evening together, that they were forming a new friendship. But his silence these past two days gave the lie to that.

Ah, well, she thought, as she walked briskly along the clifftop pathway. So she had been wrong about the captain. She was certainly no worse off than she had been before.

And, with the winter wind whipping at her hems, the cold, pale sun shining down on her, she could almost believe that. She hummed a bright tune under her breath, a Christmas carol in honor of the season.

"*It came upon a midnight clear, that glorious song of old, from angels bending near the earth to touch their harps of gold. Peace on the earth, goodwill to men . . .*"

The tune quite died away in her throat as she turned the corner that led to her cottage and she saw the tall figure waiting by her garden gate.

Captain Payne. *Mark*. He had come after all. Her heart gave a flutter in her breast, and she felt a very foolish grin catch at the corner of her lips. For an instant, she feared he might be an illusion, a phantom with his back toward her, tall and broad in a dark blue greatcoat.

Then he turned, and she could clearly see his strong, scarred face, half-shadowed by his hat brim. He gave her a slow, tentative smile.

"Miss Duvall—Antoinette," he said, his rich, rough voice carried to her on the wind. "I have called to see how you fare."

"Mark," she answered, through her own silly smile. "I fare very well indeed."

He should not be here. Mark knew that very well. Antoinette Duvall had enough to contend with in her life without him adding to her troubles by tagging along at her skirt hems. She was far from home, making her life among strangers who whispered of "island witches."

He had resolved to leave her alone. She was a beautiful lady, obviously busy with her work, and this would be for the best.

That lasted only two days. Two days of chopping firewood and shoveling snow, of scything back the undergrowth from his garden. He worked himself hard during the day, worked until his muscles burned and the sweat trickled in itchy rivulets down his back and shoulders.

But at night—at night there was nothing to occupy his mind. He tried to read, yet he just ended up staring into the fireplace, remembering the dark mystery of Antoinette's eyes, the way her face lit with a smile as she recounted some antic of the wild Leighton children. He wanted to know more about her, more of what lay beneath her smiles and her amusing stories.

Sometimes, when she thought he was not looking, her smiles faded a bit and some shadow of loneliness lowered over her fine eyes. A loneliness he knew all too well, and one he would banish from her eyes for all time if he only could.

He had not thought so much about a woman since the heady early days of his courtship of Elizabeth. *Elizabeth.* He grimaced now to think of her, to remember how he had been foolish enough to fall for her golden loveliness, her air of light charm. How he had never seen the shallowness behind her pretty, flirtatious manners.

Antoinette was nothing like Elizabeth. Mark would stake his ship—if he still had one—on that. She had charm, but there was no heartlessness in it. She was marked by life, as he was, and that left no room for a shallow heart. Her dark eyes spoke of miseries and joys that a girl like Elizabeth, now safe in London as Lady Penworthy, could know nothing of.

It was that gleam in Antoinette's gaze that drew him here today, when he could stay away no longer. It was why he found himself standing outside her garden gate, wearing his best coat, a dark blue superfine the height of fashion twelve years ago, his boots shined and his hair neatly tied back.

Yes, he had done his best to make himself appear presentable (a hopeless endeavor on the best days). But now it appeared his efforts were in vain, as Antoinette was not at home. There was no smoke from her chimney, no stirring at the window draperies.

"Well, now," he said to his waiting horse. "It appears I *am* a foolish old sailor after all."

He gathered the reins up, and turned to mount the horse when he heard a lightly lilting voice call, "Good afternoon, Captain Payne—Mark! I trust you have not been waiting too long?"

His heart gave a jolt to hear that voice, crisp and sweet in the cold air. Grinning like an idiot, he stepped back to see Antoinette hurrying down the pathway toward him. She was not dressed in her green silk robe today, but instead wore an ordinary walking gown and pelisse of burgundy- and cream-striped muslin. Her glorious hair was tucked beneath a burgundy turban, and the dark fur collar of her pelisse lay sleekly against her throat.

In the pale winter sunlight, dressed as a respectable English lady, she did not have the wild, untamed beauty of her midnight self. Yet her eyes still glowed, her tall figure radiated energy and vibrant good health. He felt his own spirits rise just watching her, and his reticence of the past two days seemed foolish indeed.

His life held little enough cheer. Why should he not enjoy the company of a lovely lady, if she was willing to bestow it?

He resolutely pushed back the niggling doubts, the revulsion of Elizabeth and her ilk, and returned Antoinette's smile with one of his own.

"I have only just arrived," he answered her. "But I saw you were not at home, so I was about to take my leave."

"I am glad I returned in time, then," she said. As she

reached his side, she held her hand out to him, and he bowed over it. She smelled of jasmine and the fine kid of her glove, and he wanted so much to hold onto her hand, to absorb her warmth into his own flesh.

She withdrew it even before his clasp could tighten, though, still smiling, her cheeks painted with a pink flush over the coffee and cream.

"Won't you come inside, Mark?" she said, pushing open the garden gate and leading the way to her door. "I gave Sally the afternoon off, but I'm sure I can find some tea to offer you."

"Thank you, Antoinette," he answered, following in her jasmine-scented wake. He was afraid his tone and demeanor were ridiculously stiff, but he was not accustomed to paying polite calls. Even before his injuries, he had been poorly equipped to perform social niceties. Life aboard a ship held little in common with a drawing room.

Antoinette did not appear to notice, though, and he relaxed as soon as he stepped through her door. Her home was not grand, as his mother's was; there was no delicate gilt furniture for him to worry about smashing, no porcelain gewgaws. Antoinette's abode was filled with fine Jacobean antiques and glowing garnet and blue rugs, fine paintings of seascapes and portraits of small children, and rich draperies at the windows. But it was all very welcoming and cozy. The air was scented with the bundles of herbs hanging from the ceiling rafters and the leather bindings of books.

Not the book she had with her on the cliff, though. That volume was nowhere to be seen.

Antoinette took his coat and hung it on a peg beside her pelisse. "Please, sit down, Mark," she said, gesturing toward the chairs drawn up by the banked fire. She went to open up the draperies, letting light spill into the sitting room, before joining him there.

Mark instinctively drew back away from the light, into the shadows where she could not see his face so clearly.

"I wanted to see how you were faring after your—adventure," he said.

Antoinette laughed. "Oh, I am quite well! I had a terrible headache the day before yesterday, but it is gone now. I walked into the village, to deliver some of my special lotions to Mrs. Greeley's store. She wanted them before Christmas in case any of her customers needed last-minute gifts." She reached for the fireplace poker and stirred the embers, coaxing them to flame anew.

Mark leaned back against the velvet cushions of his chair. He felt his qualms of the past two days fading away at the sense of *rightness* in this moment. It felt so pleasurable and strangely comfortable to sit here with her, feeling the soft magic of her presence around him. Her ease in his presence, her informality, gave him a sense of comfort he had not known in a long while.

"Actually, Mark," she said, "I am very glad you came to call. I was going to send a note around to you this afternoon."

He smiled at her, ridiculously pleased that she thought to write to him. "Were you?"

"Indeed. You see, Mrs. Greeley invited me to an assembly at the Hare and Hound Inn tomorrow evening. It is in honor of Christmas Eve. I believe they have it every year in different locations, yet I have always spent the holiday in Bath until now. I would like to attend, and I need an escort. Would you care to come? I know it is not at all the thing for a lady to invite a gentleman, but perhaps I could be excused by my island upbringing."

Mark stared at her, aghast. An *assembly*? At the village inn, where there would be dozens of people in attendance? People who would stare and whisper.

He liked *this*, just sitting with her by a quiet fire, listening to her speak, enjoying her smiles. It was comfortable. It was—safe. He could not imagine walking into a dance, where everyone would wonder how such a damaged cripple had found such a rare and exotic beauty.

Besides, his dancing skills were beyond rusty.

"An assembly, Antoinette?" he asked her, still wondering if perhaps he had misheard her. "Where there will be—dancing and such?"

She just nodded serenely. "Of course. And cards too, for those who do not care for dancing. I confess I myself quite enjoy a lively country dance."

"I thought you did not care much for mixing in society."

"Generally, I do not. In such a small place, someone as—different as I can have a difficult time finding a niche. I am sure you have found the same. But Mrs. Greeley said, and I concur, that it *is* Christmas. A time for new beginnings, new friends. It would be too sad to spend it all alone when one could spend it with music and dancing."

Mark felt himself being swayed, even against his very instincts. The thought of dancing with Antoinette was too much for a red-blooded male to resist.

She gave him a cajoling smile. "Come, Mark, for me? I have a ballgown I am aching to show off, and if you are not there I shall sorely lack for partners."

Mark was sure *that* was not true. Yet he found he was nodding, and saying, "Of course, Antoinette. I would be honored to escort you to the assembly."

Chapter Seven

In the daylight, the Hare and Hound was a perfectly ordinary village inn. Cleaner than most, perhaps, with a fine ale and a friendly landlord, but still like dozens of other half-timbered, stone-chimneyed relics of the Tudor era.

On this Christmas Eve evening, though, it was quite transformed. Golden light spilled from every window and doorway onto the innyard, covering everything with a fairy-tale sparkle. Laughter and chatter rose and fell like music from the revelers making their way up to the third-floor assembly rooms. Strains of actual music also floated down from a village orchestra demonstrating little finesse but a rich abundance of enthusiasm. The entire tableau was one of great frivolity and holiday good cheer.

Antoinette began to think that this had not been such a good idea after all. The crowd was large, loud with merriment. What would happen when they saw *her* here?

She stood on the front steps of the inn behind the Greeleys, who had paused to greet some acquaintances of theirs, staying back in the night shadows for as long as she could. Her hand, encased in her most elegant silk evening glove, was tucked into Mark's elbow, and, much to her embarrassment, she felt that hand tremble.

He peered down at her, his lips tilted down in a slight frown. He looked very distinguished and quite elegant in his black and white evening clothes, a fur-lined cloak tossed back from his shoulders, and a bicorne hat tucked beneath his arm. His hair was brushed back and tied with a black velvet ribbon, shining chestnut-brown in the candlelight. Yet, despite all his handsome looks, he, too, seemed distinctly ill at ease. His face was taut, expressionless as a stone statue.

As her own was, she was sure. Her skin felt like it would crack if she stretched it even further.

She saw his free hand reach yet again toward his scarred cheek, and she pulled at his elbow.

He gave her a startled glance, as if he had quite forgotten she was watching him. Then he smiled at her ruefully.

"Are you certain you want to attend this assembly?" he whispered. "We could go back to my cottage and share some brandy. You could tell me more tales of Jamaica."

Of course she didn't want to attend this assembly! How could she have once thought she did? A nice fire, a snifter of brandy, and some convivial conversation seemed far preferable to staring crowds. Especially now that she was actually faced with that crowd—the farmers and shopkeepers and local gentry who whispered about her. Why had she thought this was a fine idea in the first place? She must have been addled by her head injury.

Antoinette glanced back over her shoulder. They were apparently the last to arrive, for no one waited behind them in the innyard. It would be easy to make their excuses to the Greeleys and depart. . . .

Except that Antoinette's mother had not raised her to be a coward. She would not become one now. She had wanted a Christmas party, and here it was. She would hold her head up, and laugh and dance and chat. And she would make Mark Payne do it with her.

She gave him a mischievous smile, and tugged again at his arm. "Certainly not, Captain. You promised me a dance, and I intend to hold you to it. Besides, I have not yet had a chance to show off my ballgown."

He laughed, and laid his free hand over hers, briefly squeezing her fingers. "Quite right, Miss Duvall. I will happily dance with you, if you do not mind ruined slippers. I am not as light on my feet as I used to be."

The Greeleys moved forward then, and Antoinette

and Mark followed them into the inn's common room. After surrendering their cloaks to a waiting attendant, they made their way up the stairs to the assembly rooms.

Antoinette paused just outside the door to glance into a mirror. She had only this one ballgown, but she loved it, loved the inky-blue color of the silk, the shimmering gold embroidery on the low-cut bodice, the Elizabethan slashing of the tiny puffed sleeves. Now she only wondered—what did *Mark* think of the way she looked in it?

Her gaze met his in the glass, and she had her answer. His quicksilver eyes warmed like a summer sky, and his polite smile turned slow, sensual.

"You look most elegant tonight, Miss Duvall," he said deeply.

Antoinette gave him an answering smile. "As do you, Captain Payne." She reached up to untangle her long earring from her blue silk turban, and then turned back to clasp his arm again.

Somehow, with his warm, muscled strength beneath her hand, she no longer feared the crowd. She no longer feared *anything*.

"I believe I hear a Scottish reel starting," she said.

The long, wide assembly room was filled with gaily dressed revelers; young couples joining the dance, matrons watching them, chattering together; old men speculating on sport and the weather. On a table along one wall was arrayed a variety of delicacies, salmon patties, roast goose, mushroom tarts, a large plum pudding, and three punch bowls.

Yet the room did not feel crowded or overly warm. It sent out an atmosphere of holiday cheer and welcome. Even Antoinette felt it, deep inside of herself, and for the first time since their arrival at the Hare and Hound she felt some small flame of—was it *excitement*?

She gazed around, and noticed that while some people did give Mark and her startled glances, most did not even notice them.

Yet.

"Miss Duvall!" she heard someone call out, and she turned to see Mr. Lewisham, the vicar, hurrying toward them. His plump, cheerful wife followed, artificial holly woven into her pale blond hair in honor of the holiday. "Miss Duvall, how very charming to see you here. We thought perhaps you had gone off to Bath with the Leightons, until I saw you in the village this morning."

"It is good to see you as well, Mr. Lewisham, Mrs. Lewisham," Antoinette answered. "I stayed behind this year to finish some writing."

"Work? At Christmas? I thought only the vicar had to do *that*!" declared Mrs. Lewisham. "We are glad you had time to join this evening's revels."

"As am I," Antoinette said, and found, rather to her surprise, that it was true. The music, the holly, Mark's arm beneath her touch, all conspired to give her a rather breathless Christmas warmth she had not felt since childhood. "I do not believe you have met Captain Payne. Mr. and Mrs. Lewisham, this is a neighbor of mine, Captain Mark Payne, late of His Majesty's Navy. He came here with the Greeleys and myself this evening. Mr. Lewisham is incumbent of St. Anne's." She pulled Mark from the shadows into the flickering candlelight, fully to her side.

Mr. Lewisham only gave a welcoming smile, and reached out to shake Mark's hand, but Mrs. Lewisham's eyes grew wide at the sight of his face. Her glance darted from Mark to Antoinette and back again.

"It is always a pleasure to meet a newcomer to the neighborhood, Captain Payne," said Mr. Lewisham.

"Thank you, Mr. Lewisham," Mark answered, not bothering to correct the vicar and say he had actually been in the neighborhood for seven years.

"And, of course, any friend of Miss Duvall's . . ." added Mrs. Lewisham, a sly undercurrent of speculation in her voice. The vicar's wife fancied herself the village matchmaker, and she had not had a "victim" in quite a long while.

"Perhaps we will have the honor of seeing you at St. Anne's tomorrow, for Christmas services," said the vicar.

"Thank you," Mark answered slowly. The music changed from a reel to a schottische. "Ah—a dance I believe I can manage. Miss Duvall, may I have the honor?"

"Of course, Captain Payne. Please do excuse us, Mr. Lewisham, Mrs. Lewisham." Antoinette gave them a smile, and followed Mark to take their places in the set. She could feel the interested gaze of the vicar and his good wife all the way across the room. As she and Mark took their places in the dance, conversation hushed around them. Ladies whispered behind their fans.

She ignored them as she smiled across at Mark. No gossip could bother her at all this evening—not with the lively tune making her toes tap and Mark's silver-blue gaze on hers.

"The Lewishams seem quite—congenial," he said, as their hands met and they made a turn and a leap.

"Indeed they are. They have been quite kind to me ever since my arrival in Cornwall."

"Unlike certain others?"

"Perhaps."

They were separated by the patterns of the dance. When they came back together, to promenade the length of the set, Mark leaned closer to her and whispered, "They were surely only jealous."

Startled, Antoinette stared up at him, almost missing the step. "Jealous? Of *what*?"

"Of your beauty, of course. Of how very—special you are." His voice was deep, touched with a sweetly surprised ardor.

Antoinette wanted to kiss him more than she had ever wanted anything in her life. She wanted to lean over and place her lips on his, to hold on to him and never, ever let him go.

If he meant what he said—what could it mean for her? For them?

She felt the very foundations of her life shift and reform beneath her feet.

Mark did not know where his words came from. He meant them. By Jove, but he *did* mean them! She was beautiful, beyond beautiful, and so special. He had realized that the moment he saw her on the cliff. And now, seeing how radiant and glorious she was, laughing in the dance, her deep blue gown flowing around her like the night, he knew she was a veritable goddess. A goddess of the sea and the wind. She made him see the beauty of life again.

No other woman could help but be jealous of her. She was more magnificent than any mortal woman could hope to be. But he hated it—hated it with a rage—that she had been hurt by any ignorance or lack of understanding. And she *had* been hurt; he could see it in the hidden depths of her eyes.

He wanted her only to have joy in her life from now on. Yet he was the last man to bring joy to any lady.

He did not regret his words, though, even as he was not a man given to poetic sentiment. He meant them—and more. So much more.

The dance ended, and Mark led Antoinette to the edge of the room, his arms already aching to hold her again. "Would you care for another dance, Miss Duvall?"

"Later, perhaps," she answered, with a gentle smile. "Right now, I'm in need of some refreshment. The claret cup looks inviting."

"Of course. Allow me to fetch you a glass."

They found two chairs in a quiet corner where they sipped in silence at the watery punch. Mark listened to the laughter, the movement around them, and urged himself to speak to her. Speak *now*.

"Miss Duvall—Antoinette," he began. "There are things I must tell you . . ."

She turned to him, her eyes wide with expectation, her body leaning slightly toward him. But anything he might have said was drowned out by a burst of music, a rush of voices raised in familiar song.

"*The holly and the ivy, when they are both full grown, of all the trees that are in the wood, the holly bears the crown.*"

Several of the villagers had joined the musicians on their dais, and sang out the old carol with great enthusiasm and holiday cheer. Antoinette looked to them, her eyes shining with enjoyment of the song.

And Mark knew that whatever he wanted to say could wait, *should* wait until a quiet moment. A moment when he could clearly decipher his own emotions toward this most unique lady. He sat back in his chair, carefully situated in the shadows, to watch her as she listened. Just—watch. And greedily drink in her beauty.

More voices joined in as the song came to its close. "*The rising of the sun, and the running of the deer, the playing of the merry organ, sweet singing in the choir.*" A half smile touched Antoinette's rose-pink lips, and she swayed slightly in her chair, whispering the lyrics. She obviously loved music; it seemed to infuse her entire body, lifting her from the dim surroundings into a realm no one else could invade.

As the carol ended, Mrs. Greeley leaned toward Antoinette and said, "Miss Duvall, why do you not favor us with a song? Lady Royce has told us you have a beautiful voice indeed."

The smile faded from Antoinette's lips, and her shoulders stiffened. "Oh, no, Mrs. Greeley," she protested. "I have a mediocre talent at best. And I am sure no one would be interested . . ."

"Nonsense!" Mrs. Greeley interrupted. "Mr. Greeley and I would so enjoy hearing you, as, I am sure, would Captain Payne. Is that not so, Captain?"

Mark would more than "enjoy" hearing Antoinette sing—he would pay his last farthing to do so. To hear her voice moving around him, showing him what music, what *Christmas*, could truly mean. He was only just becoming aware of the truth of so many things.

"Yes, please, Miss Duvall," he said. "Do favor us with a song. Something from your homeland, perhaps?"

She stared into his eyes long and hard, her own dark pools unreadable. Finally, she nodded. "Very well, Captain Payne. To please you. But please do not ask me to go up on the dais!"

"You may sing right here, Miss Duvall," Mrs. Greeley answered her. "We will be near."

Antoinette slowly rose from her chair, her head held high, hands folded at her waist. The candlelight glittered on the gold embroidery of her gown, and her gaze swept over the swiftly quieting crowd. She looked like a princess, Mark thought. No—a queen. A grand, magnificent queen. Only the slight trembling of her gloved fingers betrayed any nervousness.

She closed her eyes and parted her lips, and the most astonishing sounds, lively and bright, emerged.

"*The Virgin Mary had a baby boy . . . and they say that his name was Jesus. He come from the glory, He come from the glorious kingdom, oh, yes, believer! The angels sang when the baby born . . . and proclaim him the Savior Jesus.*"

As she sang words and melodies that were strange, exotic, yet achingly familiar, Mark could not turn his stare away from her face. She sang of love, redemption, transcendence, her eyes closed, a rosy glow on her cheeks. Her hands fluttered, raised in the joy of the song, the season. Her body swayed. She did not look at him, yet the words seemed only for him. They called to him—they told him that he was not alone, that someone else understood the agony of having one's world torn to bits with nothing to replace it, nothing beautiful to cling to.

Before him stood something beautiful beyond anything he could have imagined.

And he knew then, without a shadow of a doubt, that he was falling in love with Antoinette Duvall. She was an angel, a goddess, a woman of infinite understanding. She was beyond him—perfection did not mate with a monster, he knew that. But he also knew that he was compelled to tell her what she had brought him. What she meant. He had to try to bring her some surcease from her own loneliness, no matter how meager.

"*He come from the glory, He come from the glorious kingdom!*"

The last jubilant notes died away, echoing into the profound silence of the room. The revelers stared at Antoinette, dumbstruck. Many jaws gaped most inelegantly, and more than a few ladies wiped at damp cheeks. Something had shifted in the crowd, just as something had shifted in Mark's own soul.

Yet Antoinette clearly did not see that. Her shoulders were stiff, and slowly, painfully, her eyes fluttered open. Her hands twisted together. She appeared ready to flee, like a wounded gazelle.

Then a clapping began, slow at first, growing as it swept across the room, a tidal wave of emotional sound.

A tentative smile again touched her lips, and she made a small, elegant curtsy.

Mark stepped up to her and took her gloved hand in his, bowing over it. "Miss Duvall—Antoinette," he murmured, so no one else could hear. "I must talk to you—I must tell you something. May I come to your cottage tomorrow? To speak to you privately?"

She stared at him for a moment, silent. Then something shifted behind her eyes, something that told him she understood his sudden desperation. She nodded, and her fingers tightened on his for a fleeting instant. "Come to my cottage later tonight," she answered. The last word barely escaped before she was swept away by people demanding another song.

Yes. Later tonight.

Chapter Eight

Antoinette moved one porcelain ornament from the left side of one of her pier tables to the right then back again. It was the fourth time she had done so since she returned to her cottage from the assembly more than an hour ago. Mark had left before she departed with the Greeleys, saying he preferred to walk home, and she began to think she imagined his words to her.

Imagined the entire strange evening. The dancing, the music—the tentative conversation of people she always imagined disliked and suspected her. Above all, she must have imagined the way Mark looked at her as he bowed over her hand.

He looked as if he—admired her. Yet how could that be? He was the son of an earl, a naval captain who had bravely served his king and country, even though he seemed determined to forget all that, to bury himself forever here in Cornwall. She was a nobody. Less than a nobody.

Yet that could not erase the indisputable fact that she also—admired him. *Admire* was an inadequate word for what she felt. There could be no words. She felt she knew him in a way she could never have imagined. The lonely ache of her soul filled up when she met him, and every encounter added to that warmth.

For the first time, she felt at home in England, felt there could be no place else for her.

Soon, Mark would surely go back to his family, his true place, and she would stay here with her work and her friends. But it would not be the same as before. Her memories of this brief time with this very special man would sustain her, and she intended to seize every moment she could with him.

If he would just appear, as he had promised he would!

Even as she thought this, a low knock sounded at the door. She spun away from the table and dashed to open it, her heart rising in a wild flutter of giddiness.

Mark stood on her doorstep, wrapped in his greatcoat, hat in hand. He smiled at her, yet he seemed rather unsure, as if now that he was here he was not certain what to say to her. Antoinette would have none of that. If their time was to be short, she would, by heaven, make the most of it!

She reached out, took his hand, and pulled him into her sitting room. As the door clicked shut behind him, he took her into his arms and held her close, so close they could not possibly be parted. Not yet. Antoinette looped her arms about his neck and closed her eyes, inhaling his scent of sandalwood soap, leather, and night air. They were much of a height, and she could turn her head to kiss his rough, scarred cheek, his strong jaw. Her lips trailed over the faded burns, healing them with all the love she had in her heart.

"I missed you," she whispered.

Mark gave a hoarse moan, and his lips claimed hers. Their kiss was not gentle—it was full of desperation, of passion, of all the love and need they possessed.

"Antoinette," Mark muttered, his kisses trailing along her throat. "Antoinette, I must . . ."

"Shh," she whispered. "You do not need to talk. I know."

"I *do* need to talk," he protested. He stepped back from her a fraction, his strong hands sliding up to hold her face between them. "I have been a coward for far too long, but you—you extraordinary, perfect woman—make me brave again."

"You? A coward? No!" Antoinette protested. She grabbed at his hands, holding them tightly in hers. "Never, Mark. You fought in battle, you were horribly injured!"

"I did fight, for many years, and I thought nothing of it. But I vow to you I *am* a coward. I have hidden from life—from myself—for all these years because I could not face myself, could not face that my life had changed so irrevocably."

"Yes," she answered quietly. "Yes, I know how that feels."

"I know you do. And that is why I feel I can tell you about what happened to me. About how I came to be—as I am."

Mark took her arm and led her to the settee. She went without a protest, though she was not certain she truly wanted to hear what he would say. She could not bear to think of the terrible pain he must have endured, both of the body and the heart, the soul. But she sensed his need to tell her this, and she would listen.

They sat at opposite ends of the settee, only their hands touching in the middle. "I was the captain of the *Royal Augusta* at Trafalgar, a forty-four-gun frigate with almost three hundred crewmen. Things were going well, or well enough for the heat of battle, anyway. We had lost very few men, and we had already destroyed two French ships. Victory was in our grasp, and then . . ." His voice faded.

Antoinette folded her hand about his. His clasp tightened, but he did not look at her.

"One of our guns exploded, and I don't know how it could have happened. But there was a fire, an explosion, and many—most of my men were killed."

"It was not your fault," Antoinette said softly, hearing the bitter tone in his voice, the self-recrimination he carried after all these years. "Terrible things happen in war, but you are a good man. I know you were a good officer."

"I did my best," he answered. "And that day—it was simply not enough. I know I did not cause that explosion. But I will carry the knowledge of that failure with me always. As well as the knowledge that I am not fit for proper society."

"What happened when you returned home? Was your family not—welcoming?" Antoinette could not imagine how a family could not welcome back such a son. Yet she knew—knew all too well—the immense capacity for cruelty some human beings could possess.

"Oh, no. They were quite welcoming, quite solicitous. Quite—pitying." He gave a wry little smile. "It was my fiancée, Lady Elizabeth Morton-Haddon, who found that her feelings for me had changed quite utterly. She took one glance at my new face and cried off. One could hardly blame her."

Hardly blame her? Antoinette jolly well could. A fire of anger at the unknown Lady Elizabeth burned in her throat. "She was a fool." Antoinette leaned forward to kiss Mark, the softest, gentlest touch of her lips on his. "A great fool to lose a wonderful man such as you."

His arms came about her waist, holding her close. "Most would have called her a fool if she stayed."

"Not I."

"No. Not you, Antoinette. You are quite unlike anyone I have ever met. But I have not told you this story to gain your pity, or even to get another kiss from you."

Antoinette grinned up at him, twining a long strand of his hair about her finger. "Oh, no?"

He laughed, his head thrown back against cushions of the settee. "Well, perhaps just a bit. I do enjoy your kisses. But I told this to you because I wanted you to know I understand what it is like to be lonely. I saw how people treated you when we first arrived at the assembly, whispering behind their fans and staring. Did their parents never teach them proper manners?"

Her grin faded. She did not want to be reminded of the cold winter world outside her door. She only wanted this moment, this perfect time. "It is of no matter," she said, striving for a light, careless tone. "I have my own friends, my own life. The gossip of people so wholly unconnected to me means little."

His arms tightened. "Your life here cannot have been an easy one."

"Who does truly have an *easy* life? Everyone has trials and tribulations, and mine have not been so great." She cuddled closer to him, resting her cheek on his strong shoulder. "No one has thrown rotten vegetables at me as I walk along the street or anything of the sort. They respect the family at the castle far too much. But most of them do keep their distance, I admit. They do not understand me—they don't know where I came from, my customs. I cannot blame them. I do not understand myself most of the time."

"What do you mean?"

Rather than answering, she disentangled herself from his arms and stood up from the settee. She went to the small, locked cabinet in the corner and carefully withdrew her precious book, clutching the silk-wrapped bundle protectively in her arms. Slowly, she turned back to face him.

"I have told you about my family," she said. "Yet there is one thing about my mother I never speak about, something very precious and secret."

He slid to the edge of the settee, his folded hands clasped before him and dangling between his knees. His expression was still and solemn, as if he sensed the true seriousness of her words. "Of course, Antoinette. You may tell me anything you wish. All your secrets are safe with me."

"You'll remember this book, I think," she said, "since I sent you back to rescue it from the snow on the night we met." She placed the bundle carefully on a low table and folded back the silk.

He watched her closely, his expression unreadable in the firelight. "Yes. I remember it."

"This book belonged to my mother, and to my grandmother before her. I do not know where it came from originally. Africa, my mother said, but I don't know if that is true." She opened the book to the pages in the middle, and caressed her hand over the soft, smooth vellum. She could feel the slight indentations of the ancient words written there, the stiffness of the painted images. The pages seemed to warm under her touch, leaping to life.

"What is this volume about, Antoinette?" Mark asked quietly.

Antoinette lifted her gaze from the pages and met his across the table. He looked serious, but not alarmed, merely curious. But she had never shared the book with anyone before, had only ever shown it to Cassie, and her stomach lurched with anxiety.

"It is about many things," she answered. "My mother was a great woman, a powerful woman. She knew many things, things ordinary people cannot conceive of, and she learned them from this book. She could heal people, could see beyond this world to others we know nothing of."

"Witchcraft?" he whispered.

"No!" Antoinette cried, recoiling from the word. "My mother was not a *witch*. She was a devout Christian; she brought me up in the church to be one as well. These were just—gifts she had, abilities that not every person possesses. She said they were gifts from God, given to her so she might help His people on earth. And that is what she did. She healed people; she never harmed anyone!"

Antoinette could feel a frenzy rising up in her as she defended her mother, tried to explain her powers. It was always thus when she spoke of or remembered Marie-Claire Duvall. But now it was more vital than ever that she should make Mark understand. It was the only way she could help him. Help *them*.

He reached over and caught her hand in both of his, cradling it against the warmth of his skin. She calmed at his touch, and felt her breath slow in her lungs.

"I see," he said. "Your mother was a—a priestess of sorts."

"A Yaumumi priestess," Antoinette explained. "It is an ancient tradition, from Africa."

"And she cured people of their illnesses?"

"Yes. Of both the body and the heart, the spirit."

Mark nodded slowly. "I met women of that sort when I was in the West Indies. What they could achieve was remarkable."

Perhaps he *did* understand, then, at least a little. And soon he would see more. Antoinette stepped around the table to stand before him, framing his face in her long fingers. She traced the pattern of his scars gently with her thumb, feeling the silky tightness of the damaged skin. He flinched, but did not pull away.

Antoinette caught and held his stare with her own, not letting him go. She felt a strength, a power growing in the center of her being. She could do this. She *must* do this. The future of the man she loved depended on it.

It would be a future away from her, back with his

family, his old world. But she had to do this. She had to try to set him free.

"I do not have the powers of my mother," she said. "I am weak compared to her. But she can help us now, if you will let her."

Mark stared up at her, and covered her hands with his, clutching at her tightly. "What do you mean?"

"Do you trust me, Mark?" she whispered.

"Yes," he answered, not even hesitating for a heartbeat.

"Then all will be well." Antoinette was far from believing that herself. For, truly, how could all be well if she had found true love only to cast it from her? But she *did* love Mark—she saw that so clearly now, as she looked down upon him in the firelight. He was brave and caring. He deserved better than this solitary life he had been living, a life whose pain and loneliness Antoinette understood all too well.

She had to try to set him free.

She stepped back away from him. He reached out for her, trying to catch her back. "Antoinette . . ."

"No," she said. "Trust me. It is Christmas. The most magical time of year."

She quickly gathered candles from the cupboard, red, pink, white. She arrayed them about the book and lit them. Then she gathered herbs—cinnamon, clove, lilac—and sprinkled them along with salt between the candles, whispering all the while, calling on her mother for help. Mark watched her, a small frown tight on his brow, but he said nothing and never moved.

Finally, all was in readiness. Antoinette released her hair from its pins, letting the thick mass float about her shoulders. She lifted her hands above the book and closed her eyes, keeping the image of Mark in her mind. The familiar tingling sensation grew, spreading from her toes to her fingertips. Her thoughts turned misty, and she turned her hands toward Mark, palms upward.

"Be renewed from this day," she chanted. "All pain, all fear, all loneliness washed away. Carry my love to where he'll be best, let his heart be open and free. Cleanse and consecrate our hearts, and lead us forward from the pain into the light."

A brilliant warmth such as Antoinette had never known suffused her, shooting energy and joy and even pain from her heart until she cried out with the force of it. A bright golden light flooded her mind—and then it was gone. The burst of magic ebbed away from her, and her legs were as weak as a new kitten's. She felt herself falling, yet before she could collapse to the floor, she felt powerful arms catch her, lifting her and holding her close, safe.

Mark had rescued her, just as he had on the night they met. He held her safe in his warm strength.

Antoinette's head sank against his chest. She was so very weak she could not even hold it up. She felt his lips press to her temple, her cheek, her mouth. And there, as his kiss met hers, she tasted the salty wetness of tears.

She opened her eyes to see that he was indeed crying, silent, crystal tears that fell onto her own cheeks in a sort of baptism of released pain and new freedom.

"No, no," she murmured. Her own voice seemed to echo from a very long way away. Exhaustion flowed through her veins like a heavy syrup, and she gave in to it, allowing the darkness of healing sleep to overcome her, right there in Mark's arms.

Chapter Nine

Mark sat by the window in Antoinette's cottage, watching the sun come up on a new day—Christmas Day. He had seen many a dawn, over the waves of the sea, over rooftops of London and cliffs of Cornwall. Yet never had he seen a dawn so exquisitely lovely. Pink and orange and soft lavender swirled in the morning sky, pierced by arrow-pricks of purest gold light, like a halo crowning the heavens.

As exquisite as the sunrise was, though, it could in no way compare to the lady he held cradled in his arms.

Antoinette slept, her head resting on his shoulder, her breath soft against his throat where he had loosened his neckcloth. Her beautiful silk gown was rumpled now, covered by the paisley shawl Mark had drawn warmly around her. Her hair fell in a loose, wild cascade over his arm. Earlier, at the assembly, she was the perfect lady, fashionable, poised, elegant; now she seemed the wild island girl she was born.

And Mark loved both aspects of her. He loved *her*, Antoinette, in a way he had long surrendered hope for. As he sat there in her house, the scent of her jasmine perfume all around him, he felt more at peace than he ever had. Even before the fateful battle that ended his life as he knew it, he had always been seeking, striving, moving. Never still, not even for an instant. His heart could never be serene, never trust that things were right just as they were.

Now he knew that all was right. A quiet contentment settled over his mind, his very soul. The pain of the past was gone. It was behind him, and there was only the future to be faced, full of—of whatever he wanted it to be! And what he wanted, now and always, was Antoinette. By his side, for the rest of his days.

He did not know if this new peace was due to the spell she performed. But he *did* know that when he saw her face as she chanted those words, so intent, so focused, he realized he loved her truly. And she had feelings for him too. Feelings of love? He was not certain. It had been many years since he had even thought about romance; his facilities in that direction were rather rusty.

He had to sharpen them now, though. He had to persuade Antoinette to marry him and go with him to face his family again. It would not be easy. She was as settled in her solitary ways as he had been for so many years. It would be frightening for her to go to London with him and meet his grand family, though they would surely accept her as his wife. But she *had* to do it. She must!

For he could never do it without her.

Antoinette stirred in his arms, her eyes blinking open as the morning sun washed over her. Her hands drew the shawl closer about her shoulders, and she gave him a small smile. "Good morning," she murmured.

"Merry Christmas," he answered. "My love."

His love? Had Antoinette heard aright, or was she still dreaming?

She sat up straight, pushing slightly away from his warmth so she could study him closer. He seemed—different this morning. Younger, somehow. More open. His silvery eyes were clear as he looked back at her, his smile wide and brighter than the morning sunshine.

Had her spell worked, then? Was he free? Were they *both* free?

It was what she had wanted, more than anything. But now that he was free of the past, would he fly away from her?

She reached out to touch his face, her fingers light against his scars. He did not flinch or draw away, ducking into the shadows as she had often seen him do. He turned his head to kiss her fingertips, raising his own hand to hold her there.

"Merry Christmas," she whispered, echoing his own words. *My love.*

"I vow it must be the finest Christmas ever," he answered. "With sunlight, and the sea, and the most beautiful lady by my side."

Antoinette's head spun, making her giddy. This change, this new brightness, was all too much for so very early in the morning. "I fear I have no roast goose, no plum pudding, and no gifts. It is a very shabby Christmas indeed."

"You have the most valuable gift of all, right here." He cradled her hand in his, her palm up.

"What do you mean?"

He bent his head to plant a kiss right there, in the center of her palm. It lingered, warm in the cool morning air. "Antoinette Duvall, will you do me the great honor of giving me your hand in marriage?"

Marriage! Antoinette pulled away from him, startled—no, *shocked.* She jumped to her feet, holding the shawl protectively around herself.

She was not sure what she had been expecting or hoping for. But this was beyond anything she might have dreamed! To be Mark's *wife* . . .

For one moment, she let herself believe that it could be, that they could love each other, make a home together, a *family*, just as she had dreamed.

But then reality came in, like the cold waves of the English sea. He might be a recluse like her, but he came from a titled family, a family who would welcome him back into their fold. She was a nobody, an "island witch." It would be selfish of her to grab at her own happiness at the expense of his.

"Mark, I . . ." she began.

But he sensed her wavering, and jumped up to catch her in his arms before she could go on. "No! No, Antoinette, I won't let you do this. I won't let you refuse me."

"I can do nothing else," she said, feeling her own heart wavering. It felt so good to be in his arms, so safe. So *right.* "Your brother is an earl. Your family would never want to see you wed someone like me."

"My family would want to see me wed any woman who makes me whole again—as you do." He drew her even closer, his hands buried in the mass of her hair, cradling her against him. "Even if they do not, I am my own man; I have been making my own way in the world since I was fifteen. My choice of wife is my own. Please, Antoinette. I was in darkness before you—you are my light. Do not take that away from me. Say you will be my wife, that you will never leave me."

Antoinette shook her head, confused. How could she ever think straight, with his arms around her and his words pouring over her like gold from heaven? She felt tears spilling down her cheeks onto the loosened folds of his neckcloth, and she could not stop them. "I only want your happiness," she choked out.

"*You* are my happiness!" He framed her face in his hands, forcing her to look up at him. "And if you marry me, I will spend the rest of my days making you happy too. We do not have to stay here in Cornwall, or even in London. We can go back to Jamaica together, anything you want."

Antoinette's heart surrendered then, completely. Yes, there *would* be hardships in their future, obstacles aplenty. But she knew now that she—*they*—could face anything at each other's side. They would not be alone anymore, not ever again. Whether here, or on a beach in Jamaica or a town house in London, it did not matter. Only their love mattered. Now and forever after.

The magic had worked. She felt its sparkle in her own heart, and she knew it would never fade away.

"I do not care where we make our home," she told him, "as long as we are together. Yes, I will marry you, Mark. I love you, with all my heart."

Mark gave a loud, whooping laugh of joy, and swept her up into his arms, swinging her about. "As I love you! I told you this was the finest Christmas ever, Antoinette."

Antoinette laughed too, her soul overflowing with exultation. "And so it is! The finest, most *magical* Christmas ever."

And, as they kissed beneath the swags of holly and red ribbon, the pages of her mother's book flickered gently and closed with a soft, satisfied sigh.

The Ultimate Magic

Allison Lane

Chapter One

December 22, 1818

"How dare you call me foolish?" snarled Diana Russell. "Wedding Giles is a mistake, I tell you. There's no magic when we're together. He won't even talk to me! I *won't* tie myself to a man who ignores me. I won't! So leave me alone!" She slammed out of the room.

Cursing, Edith Knolton followed. If Diana made it to the altar without scandal, it would be a miracle.

"Only four more days," she reminded herself as she strode down the hall. Once the wedding was over, she could return home, celebrate a belated Christmas with her family, then relax while she studied the employment offers she was already receiving—but only if Diana avoided scandal. Who would hire a finishing governess who couldn't control her charge?

The fear of scandal loomed larger every day. Diana was arrogant, selfish, and willful at the best of times. Now that doubts about her betrothal to Giles Merrimont had set in . . .

Nothing Edith said helped. Diana expected him to mimic the fawning cubs who formed her court—her blue-eyed, blonde loveliness had turned heads all her life. But Giles was a man in his prime, his temperament perfectly suited to the sober negotiations he conducted for the Foreign Office. Girlish whims annoyed him, especially Diana's insistence on daily proof that she was the center of his world.

She wasn't.

Edith shook her head. There was no ignoring that Giles was often called to his office with little advance notice. If Diana fell into hysterics every time the Crown disrupted her plans, no one would blame Giles for shutting her away. Such antics could jeopardize his position.

No footsteps clattered up the staircase, so Edith hurried toward the side door.

She should have followed her custom and taken a new post the moment Diana accepted Giles's offer. Her job was to prepare girls for their Season, then chaperon them until they made a match. This was the first time she'd agreed to remain through the wedding—and the last. Between Lady Russell's fragile nerves and Diana's megrims, what should have been another feather in Edith's cap threatened to become her first failure.

As Edith rounded the last corner, she saw Diana slip outside. Since fleeing Edith, the girl had donned her smartest cloak. What did she intend this time?

Edith hoped it would be a brisk ride to settle her nerves, but that wasn't likely. Diana wasn't wearing a habit. The girl would never climb on a horse without proper attire and an admiring audience.

Edith feared that Diana was headed for an assignation. This latest outburst seemed contrived, the petulance false, the tears feigned. That she'd stashed a cloak nearby before staging her little drama made it a certainty. She was probably meeting Mr. Jessup. Their flirtation last night had raised more than a few brows.

Even last week Edith would have trusted Jessup—he was Giles's cousin, best friend, and official witness for the wedding. But he'd been behaving oddly since arriving at Russell House four days earlier, as if determined to prevent this marriage. Giles's diplomatic mask revealed none of his feelings, but something was clearly wrong between the men.

Icy wind slammed into Edith's face when she reached the terrace, but she had no time to fetch her own cloak. Diana was already out of sight, probably in the wilderness walk that skirted the drive. Shivering, Edith ran after her.

The breeding that gave Edith access to society let her command a high salary. But the nature of her work meant that few posts lasted more than a year. Even a small smudge on her record could affect future employment. If Diana jilted Giles, many would blame Edith for the resulting scandal.

She'd known that accepting this post had been risky, of course, but Sir Waldo Russell had offered a huge premium for her services. One meeting had convinced Edith that Diana was as spoiled a beauty as walked the earth, but she'd felt up to the challenge. Hadn't she got the impish Bedford twins safely settled?

And she *had* managed until now, softening Diana's arrogance enough that the girl had caught Giles's eye. He was the son of a viscount and had excellent prospects—many believed he would be Foreign Secretary one day—so it was an outstanding match for the daughter of a minor baronet. Edith should have left Sir Waldo's employ the next day. But she'd known that Diana needed further training in protocol and world affairs if she hoped to succeed as a diplomatic hostess, so she'd agreed to stay. Now . . .

"Four more days," she repeated as the path twisted through shrubbery so thick she could rarely see more than a dozen feet ahead.

She shivered in the icy cold, cursing her own stupidity. She should have spoken to Sir Waldo last night. Yes, he would have lectured Diana about responsibility and duty, putting the girl's back up and likely making her worse. And yes, his opinion of Edith's competency would have fallen, jeopardizing her bonus. But he would have designated a couple of footmen to watch his daughter. Edith couldn't do it alone, as this latest start demonstrated.

"Well, well. A delectable morsel rushing to join me."

Not now! Edith nearly snapped as she skidded to a halt. Diana's dissolute brother stood squarely in the path, drunk, though it was barely three. A mad dog could pose no more danger.

Peter grinned maliciously. "You've been avoiding me, my sweet."

"My duties keep me busy with Diana." She warily backed a step, then another. At twenty-two, Peter was a vicious bully who took what he wanted—which just now was her. Not that he liked her, but she had stupidly made her disdain clear when he'd tried to steal a kiss last week. He hated rejection.

"Your duties are whatever I say they are," he snarled, springing.

Even as she turned to flee, he slammed her into a tree.

A scream escaped. She clamped her mouth shut, horrified. If anyone discovered her with Peter, her reputation would shatter.

"Shout all you want," he panted, rubbing against her. "No one can hear."

It was all too true. Few would brave today's harsh wind, so she was on her own. "Leave me alone!" she spat, stretching until she could sink her teeth into his neck above his cravat. As he recoiled, she jerked a hand free and gouged his face, drawing blood.

But there was no escape. His backhand snapped her head sideways. Fingers closed around her throat even as he hissed, "Claw me again and you'll die, bitch. But if you satisfy me well enough, I'll let you live."

Live? she wanted to shout. *How?* Without her reputation, she had nothing.

Closing her eyes, she again scratched at his face. Death was preferable to ruination. Even if she somehow escaped this encounter, she would be ruined. All he had to do was brag that she'd begged to be taken. No one ever believed a servant over a gentleman. Her life was over. Her mother—

She was suddenly free.

Peter roared in pain.

Her eyes flew open, but it took a moment to believe the sight. Peter stood six feet away, half bent over, one hand clutching his privates, the other twisted upward behind him. As someone inched the arm higher, Peter whimpered.

Edith shakily straightened. Only then did she recognize her savior—Lord Charles Beaumont.

She closed her eyes in horror.

She'd often glimpsed him in London, for he stood out in any crowd. The best looking of the Three Beaux—society's favorite rakehells, whose closeness made them nearly brothers—Lord Charles was six feet of glorious manhood. Broad shoulders. Trim waist. Muscular legs that were the envy of every dandy in town. His auburn curls framed an arresting face dominated by a full, sensuous mouth and the seductive emerald eyes that had lured half of society's matrons into his bed.

Today those eyes flashed with fury, she realized when she looked again. And his lips drew back in a snarl she suspected few had seen.

Mortification chased away her terror. Of all possible rescuers, why did it have to be him? He already thought her a clumsy fool. His droll account of their first meeting had amused society for days. His account of their second had raised suspicions of her competence. Now he would think her wanton as well. One word would destroy her, and she had no reason to think he would stifle that word. He entertained all of London with his exploits, so turning this encounter into another hilarious anecdote was exactly like him.

Not that he seemed amused at the moment, she admitted as he murmured something that drained the last color from Peter's face.

"The Beaux will be watching," he continued, stepping back. "Make one false move in town, and I'll know. Set one foot wrong here, and I'll hear about it. Hawthorne lives across that hill, and Hughes just beyond him," he added, naming his fellow Beaux. "You haven't a prayer of avoiding them."

Peter fled.

Edith cringed as Lord Charles turned his sardonic gaze on her.

"You again." He shook his head. "Did he hurt you?"

The question was so unexpected, her jaw dropped. "N-no."

"Liar. He was choking you when I arrived." Before she realized his intent, he'd tilted her head back to expose her throat. "That will bruise. You'd best pin a ribbon around it until the marks fade. Adding a sprig of holly will forestall questions and let you wear it all day. 'Tis the season, and all that."

"Th-thank you." His touch burned clear to her toes.

"He won't bother you again," he continued, turning her so he could brush bark and moss from her skirts.

"There. Nothing to raise eyebrows. Are you sure you're all right?"

She nodded, though if he didn't stop touching her, she would likely faint.

"Excellent." He backed away. "You'd best return to the house before you freeze. I'd lend you my coat, but someone would wonder how you came by it." He grinned. "At least it survived this encounter intact. Let's keep it that way. My valet will be most upset at another disaster. We brought only one trunk on this jaunt." He headed for the drive, adding, "Good job on Russell's face, but a hard knee to the groin is more effective. You might want to remember that."

And he was gone.

Edith collapsed against a tree, cursing steadily under her breath—at Peter for his attack, at Lord Charles for the reminder of her most embarrassing moments, at herself for her damnable infatuation. . . . Thank heaven he didn't know about that, or he would roast her worse than ever—if he could stop laughing long enough to speak.

Why had he rescued her?

She frowned.

Gentlemen never interfered with one another's pleasures, especially when the sport involved servants. Yet he had been furious at Peter. Only Peter. His threats had terrified the younger man—itself a shock, for even Sir Waldo couldn't control his heir. And not once, by word or deed, had he suggested that she had enticed him. Everyone made that assumption when a servant was discovered with a gentleman.

Damn Charles anyway! How was she to be sensible now that he'd revealed the honor and compassion she'd sworn he didn't have?

Shoving the thought aside, she headed for the house. It was too late to follow Diana. All she could do was pray that no scandal erupted. In the meantime, she must hide evidence of Peter's attack. There was a chance it would remain secret after all.

Charles remounted his horse, castigating himself for interfering. Yet what else could he have done? He hated men who forced unwilling women.

Russell would pay, he vowed as he trotted up the drive. For the attack. For abandoning honor. But especially for reminding Charles of the day he'd found his sister's governess broken and bleeding after a brutal rape. She'd died that night. He'd been barely ten.

At least this time he'd arrived before anyone was hurt. But why the devil did the victim have to be the annoying Miss Knolton, bane of his existence?

Oh, he'd known that she worked at Russell House. That was why he'd originally declined the invitation to this house party. But Castlereagh had ordered him to attend. Baron Schechler was another guest. Since Merrimont had failed to wrap up a trade agreement with the Prussian, the Foreign Secretary had sent Charles to deal with the matter.

He would have welcomed the assignment if it had taken him anywhere else, for it gave him an excuse to skip his family's Christmas gathering. They would present him with a bevy of suitable young ladies, but he wasn't ready to reconsider marriage. Six months ago Emily had jilted him practically at the altar. Not until he figured out how he'd misjudged her so badly would he try again—though he could hardly explain his reluctance to others; no one must suspect that Lord Charles Beaumont's judgment was faulty.

But it was.

His spirits plummeted, for the problem could so easily destroy his career. He'd battled Schechler for years. The man was an uncompromising ass at the best of times, but Charles had previously held his own in their discussions. Or so he'd thought. Now he had to wonder. No one who missed fundamental truths could negotiate even a simple contract. Had Schechler taken advantage of his incompetence all this time? Would the wool fall from Castlereagh's eyes, revealing how incapable Charles really was?

Drawing a deep breath to settle his nerves, he passed between the columns of Russell House's massive portico and plied the knocker on the front door.

Chapter Two

That evening Edith retreated to a corner of the ballroom, hoping to escape further notice. Three men had already complimented the ribbon around her neck. Had Charles meant to draw attention to her?

Yet his suggestion had been sound. Bruises decorated her throat. Even the high-necked evening gown that marked her as an employee didn't cover them completely. But she wondered at the experience that could both recognize her problem and devise a remedy suited to her means and position.

Her eyes sought him out before she could stop them. He was murmuring into Lady Cavendish's ear, his words bringing a blush to the lady's aging cheeks. Edith could only pray she did not figure in his conversation.

She'd avoided him since coming down to dinner, an easy task since she always knew where he was. The air in his vicinity pulsed with energy, and people seemed more vibrant when he was nearby.

Pulling her eyes from the emerald winking in his cravat, she concentrated on her job. It had been Diana who had suggested informal dancing this evening—several neighbors had joined the party for dinner, so there was a sizable crowd. But the last-minute change of plans raised Edith's suspicions, for it had been Diana who had originally planned an evening of cards and the games at which she excelled.

The girl was clearly up to something. She was avoiding Edith, deliberately separating from each dance partner on the opposite side of the room—which kept her close to Charles. People were beginning to notice. Not that Diana was flirting with him, but—

A footman dropped a tray in a crash of glassware, drawing all eyes. As Miss Parkes fled the scene, Edith whipped her gaze back to Diana in time to see the girl slip outside with Jessup.

Damnation! Miss Parkes was Diana's closest friend, so this was no accident. Diana must have asked her to create a diversion so she could leave unnoticed.

Edith glanced wildly around, wondering how to follow without drawing attention to Diana's misbehavior.

"What's wrong?" murmured a voice in her ear.

Edith sighed in relief. The Earl of Hawthorne might be one of the Beaux, but he claimed to owe her a favor. "Miss Russell slipped outside. Can you fetch her back?" He had recently made a love match, so Diana's reputation would be safe. No one would suspect him of trifling with her.

He smiled. "Miss Russell's betrothal removes many restrictions on her behavior. A turn on the terrace does no harm."

"If that was all . . ."

"What do you fear?"

She couldn't explain while they might be overheard, so she led him to the hall. "Miss Russell has become almost fey, flirting and carrying on until people are whispering about it. Mr. Jessup is encouraging her. He followed her outside."

"Does she disapprove this match, then?" He frowned.

"I don't believe so. She was in alt about her betrothal, and I honestly think she cares for Mr. Merrimont. But she is young and foolish—and accustomed to constant adoration."

"Ah." Hawthorne smiled. "My ward had the same problem. But Merrimont is not a man to fawn."

"No. Nor should he. I believe he cares for Miss Russell, but he won't spout nonsense or turn his back on duty when she demands attention."

"So she's trying to bring him to heel?"

"I fear so, and the excitement she derives from clandestine meetings doesn't help. Her determination and Merrimont's stubborn pride are a dangerous combination—

especially now. I can no longer trust Mr. Jessup. His eyes hold a desperation I neither understand nor like. I doubt he will stop with flirtation this time."

Hawthorne nodded as her analysis increased his already high regard for her. He could rescue Miss Russell easily enough. Jessup would never dare counter the Beaux, who were known to punish those who crossed them. Men knew that one word from a Beau was the only warning they would get.

Normally, he wouldn't care a fig about Miss Russell's conceits—or about Merrimont, who was a stiff-necked prig with more pride than sense. But he owed Miss Knolton a favor for preventing his ward from causing a scandal last Season.

Yet rescuing Miss Russell from folly would not solve Miss Knolton's problems for long. Her next charge might be worse than Miss Russell. Or the one after that. What she really needed was a husband.

Charles would be perfect.

Hawthorne had vowed to find wives for both of his friends—payback for an incident last spring. He'd succeeded with Richard Hughes, but Charles was proving to be a challenge. Miss Knolton could meet that challenge, for there was something about her . . . something beyond the beauty she tried so hard to hide.

"You are right to be concerned," he said. "I will see that no harm comes to her tonight, but I am not staying at Russell House."

"I can manage."

"Not alone." He flashed the smile that had brought countless women to his bed before his marriage. "Charles will lend a hand until the wedding."

She paled. "That won't be necessary, my lord. And he will be too busy, in any case."

"I hardly—"

"I appreciate the thought"—she actually interrupted him—"but he will never agree. He despises me."

Charles despise a female? Impossible. Yet now that he thought on it, there was some truth to her claim. He couldn't recall a single moment when the pair had kept less than the entire width of a room between them. Such extreme separation could not be coincidence, for both mingled freely with the crowd.

Something must have happened after he'd left town last Season. Something Charles had not shared with his friends. And if it was still affecting him . . .

"You wrong him, Miss Knolton. He is perfect for the job. Your problem goes beyond tonight's escapade. I can see that you fear this betrothal might collapse. Charles works with Merrimont and can discover his thoughts. And if Miss Russell threatens scandal, Charles's diplomatic skills and family ties will be useful. His father is the very powerful Marquess of Inslip, you might recall."

Giving her no chance for further protest, he slipped away.

Charles relaxed the moment Miss Knolton left the ballroom. Perhaps he would survive the evening without another embarrassing confrontation after all. How so clumsy a lack-wit held a responsible position was a mystery.

He made sure that Russell didn't follow her, then put her out of his mind. It was time for another try at the baron.

Their afternoon meeting had been less than auspicious. Schechler was as intransigent as ever, and Charles had been loath to push too hard lest he reveal his shortcomings by demonstrating an insufficient grasp of the situation. But perhaps these agreeable surroundings would make Schechler more amenable—or the quantity of wine the man had consumed at dinner. Charles had limited his own intake so he would be sharp if he managed to corner the Prussian.

Braying laughter drew his gaze to the punch bowl where Schechler was entertaining several ladies. As Charles watched, Schechler threw himself into his tale, broadening the gestures meant to clarify his heavily accented words—or so it might appear to innocent eyes.

But Charles was no greenling. He could have written the script himself, so it was no surprise when the contents of Schechler's glass spilled across Lady Frobisher's bosom.

Horrified, the baron burst into apologies, producing a wholly inadequate handkerchief to daub the drips from her flesh before rushing her away, ostensibly in search of her maid. Charles would wager anything the search would end in the baron's bedchamber.

He shook his head, wondering if he could use the incident to pry a few concessions from the man. Lord Frobisher was hot-tempered and very protective of his property. If Charles could confirm the baron's liaison—

"Don't frown in public."

Charles flinched, then cursed himself for betraying surprise. "Jacob! Why the devil are you sneaking about?"

"Sneaking? In a room packed with a hundred people?" Hawthorne grinned.

"Yes. Well . . ." Charles shrugged.

"If I didn't know better, I'd suspect you were planning a tryst. What is it this time? Negotiations going badly?"

"Schechler's an ass."

"That's hardly news. You've known that for five years."

"Handling him doesn't grow easier. But if I can verify that he and Lady Frobisher—"

"He isn't that stupid."

"I would have agreed if I hadn't watched him pour wine down her bodice."

"Really?" Hawthorne's eyes suddenly gleamed. "That does bear checking—but not by you," he added as Charles turned to leave.

"You?"

"Hardly. We need to talk, and you can't be caught prying." A gesture brought his wife to his side.

"Charles!" she exclaimed, offering her hand. "We've had no chance to speak this evening. You look well."

"As do you. Quite ravishing, in fact." He wondered if it was marriage that made her glow, or her advanced pregnancy. Probably both. And he was happy for her. She hadn't looked nearly this content when she'd accepted *his* proposal—which should have warned him that offering for her was a huge mistake. Jilting him to wed Hawthorne had been right for all of them—the two were wildly in love—but it had tossed them into a storm of gossip.

She laughed. "Don't look so appalled, Charles. You needn't fret. I shan't deliver for weeks yet, and I'm not carrying twins. The midwife insists that all Hawthorne heirs are large." She exchanged a glance with her husband that nearly set the room ablaze.

Charles thanked Providence that they'd discovered the truth before he'd married her, then raised a brow at Jacob. "Where is Richard? I'd expected him tonight."

"We were to drive over together, but one of their tenant cottages caught fire. He tried to send Georgiana anyway, but she insisted on helping."

No surprise there. Richard's wife was never content to play while others worked. Charles wasn't used to having his fellow Beaux married, though. Or to their staying in the country. London wasn't the same without them.

"We'll get together before you return to town." Jacob murmured something to his wife, who immediately left. "She'll discover the present occupation of your baron. Which means you are free to do me a favor."

"Anything."

Jacob smiled as he stepped into an empty alcove. "Since I knew I could count on you, I already promised the lady you would help."

Alarms jangled in his mind. "Lady?"

"Miss Knolton. She—"

"No."

"You haven't heard me out."

"No. The woman is a menace. I want nothing to do with her."

Jacob's eyes gleamed. "I wasn't aware that you were acquainted."

"We're not."

"Then do me the courtesy of listening instead of jumping down my throat." He rarely used that tone on his friends.

Charles snapped his mouth shut, cursing himself for losing control. He would still refuse, of course, but first, manners demanded that he endure the tale of the poor exploited Miss Knolton, who was being unjustly persecuted by the villainous Peter Russell. That it was true fanned his fury. But he had to stay away from her. She'd already made him the butt of gossip twice. He would be hard-pressed to maintain his dignity at the Foreign Office if it happened again.

"Miss Russell's flirting is out of control," said Jacob bluntly. "If something isn't done, her antics could jeopardize the wedding."

"Which is no more than she deserves," growled Charles to cover his surprise.

"Probably. She is demanding attention, and Merrimont is ignoring her. They are both being ridiculous. If they don't suit, they should say so. I don't care what happens to their betrothal, but a scandal will hurt Miss Knolton. We can't let their idiocy destroy innocents."

"Are you sure Miss Knolton is innocent?" Inciting the girl to riot sounded more like her.

"Of course. Miss Knolton is the most levelheaded female I know, my wife excepted."

"Levelheaded? She causes trouble wherever she goes."

"You must have her confused with someone else."

"Hardly."

"What do you know about her?"

Charles shrugged. "Her baronet father died in debt. Her mother and sister now live in a cottage. Her brother perished in Spain—volunteered for the Forlorn Hope since he lacked the blunt to buy a commission." He kept his voice light, as if everyone knew the story, though it had taken him several days to discover that much. And once he had, he'd wanted to kill Sir Richard for the trouble he'd caused his family. "A sad tale, but hardly unique."

"Also incomplete. Her mother tries to support herself as a village dressmaker, but it is Miss Knolton who keeps a roof over the family's head."

"Which explains why people tolerate her incompetence. They feel sorry for her."

"Are you blind?" demanded Jacob. "She's worth every shilling she makes—and more."

"A clumsy fool?"

"You are absurd."

"Absurd! Who destroyed my best coat by smearing it with cream cakes in the middle of Lady Beatrice's drawing room? Who gave me a concussion that kept me in bed for a week?" He snapped his mouth shut as laughter sparkled in Jacob's eyes.

"O-ho . . . Sits the wind in that quarter, eh? Since I've never known you to hold a grudge, you must have a yen for the girl."

"Absolutely not! She's a menace, I tell you."

"The gentleman doth protest too much, methinks. You're in love with her."

"Impossible. I don't know her—and I don't want to. I can't risk another concussion when I'm involved in negotiations."

"Keep repeating that, and perhaps you will come to believe it. In the meantime, you promised your help. Word of a Beau. I owe Miss Knolton a favor. Since I'm returning home tonight, I'm counting on you to help her. You know Merrimont well enough to do the job."

Charles cursed. Refusing after he'd agreed would strain a friendship that dated back twenty years. And he had to admit that his animosity was entirely personal and possibly overdone. He'd never heard a word against her, and so few people knew about her family woes that she would hardly win so many positions through pity.

"Very well. What does she want?"

"Nothing. She thinks she can handle Miss Russell herself. But the girl is too determined for a single guardian to keep her in line, no matter how competent. Then there's Jessup."

"Jessup?"

"He's behaving quite oddly. It isn't done to toy with a friend's betrothed."

Which was why Charles had resorted to subterfuge to make Jacob and Emily admit their love. He raised his brows.

"They slipped away a quarter hour ago. I found them in a heated embrace on the terrace. Since I don't believe Jessup cares a fig for the girl, I put the fear of God into him—or at least fear of the Beaux—and vowed you would watch him closely. But I don't know why he's taking such risks. It takes a powerful motive to ignore both friendship and kinship. My ignorance bothers me."

"And me. I'll look into it. And speaking of the Beaux, I told Russell that you would watch him. I caught him attacking an unwilling female this afternoon."

"Who?"

Charles shook his head. If he was wrong about Miss Knolton's character, he could not risk harming her. Jacob would never mention the incident, but the ballroom was too near. One whisper could doom her.

Jacob scowled. "I'll deal with him. He's young enough to settle."

"I doubt he has the brains. It seems to be a family failing. How Merrimont can believe Miss Russell will suit, I don't know."

"Find out. If he's decided she won't and is trying to make her end it, you can help them avoid scandal."

Jacob slipped away before Charles could respond, but this explained why he hadn't just spoken with Sir Waldo, which would have settled the matter. If Jacob thought the betrothal should end, he would expect Charles to manage it cleanly. After all, he'd survived his own jilting virtually unscathed. He knew how it was done.

But he'd not done it alone. The Beaux had rallied around, shielding him from the most vicious gossip, showing their support, deflecting criticism. . . . And Emily's immediate marriage to Jacob had blunted much of the talk. They were so obviously in love.

He doubted that he could arrange a similar disposition for Merrimont.

Shaking free of the memories, he returned to the ballroom to seek out Miss Knolton.

Chapter Three

Edith relaxed when Diana returned barely a minute after Hawthorne had headed for the terrace. There was no sign of Jessup.

Hawthorne's warning should keep Jessup in line, but eliminating that threat didn't solve Edith's problems. Even the width of a candlelit ballroom couldn't hide the fury simmering in Diana's eyes. It was clear Hawthorne had put her back up. Pride would make the girl prove that she could do as she pleased.

It didn't take long. Within a quarter hour Diana was laughing with Mr. Tomling, her hand on his arm as she leaned far too close and whispered in his ear. Tomling flushed.

Edith started to join them, but she'd covered barely half the distance when someone whirled her into a waltz without warning.

"My dance, I believe." Charles's green eyes laughed down at her.

She ignored the sudden warmth. "My lord! This is most improper. I'm a chaperon."

"This is an informal evening at a country house party. You can do anything you like, Miss Knolton. Is Russell behaving himself?"

"I— Of course, he is. You threatened him with the Beaux."

He raised his brows. "You mean he actually understood the threat?"

"Everyone understands *that* threat." She erased her scowl lest people notice.

"How unfortunate. I'd hoped for another encounter. You aren't his only victim. He is no gentleman."

"I know, but—"

"He will benefit from an extended trip abroad. I'll see to it."

"But—" She stopped, confused and more than a little dizzy as he spun her into a complicated turn. The dizziness had to come from the unaccustomed motion. Or maybe from surprise—his actions belied his reputation. It had nothing to do with laughing green eyes or the way his hand burned into her waist. Or so she insisted.

He grinned, twirling her faster. "I hear your charge is causing trouble."

"No. I mean, I never—" She stopped, not sure what she was trying to say. Why did she always sound like a ninny around him?

But Diana *was* giving her trouble, and it was getting worse. Gathering her wits, she peered around Charles's shoulder to see Diana dancing far too close to Tomling. If something wasn't done—and soon—they would all be in trouble.

For the moment, people smiled indulgently, attributing Diana's behavior to high spirits as she approached her wedding. But that wouldn't last. Already Giles was glaring. Since gentlemen could not honorably terminate betrothals, he must see his future going up in flames.

Swallowing her pride, Edith sighed. "Miss Russell is an arrogant, spoiled peagoose. I fear she will never make it to the altar if she keeps this up."

"Is that what she wants?" He twirled her onto the terrace.

Edith knew she should object, but they could hardly discuss Diana in a crowd. Hawthorne had insisted that Charles could help. The alternative was admitting her failure to Sir Waldo.

The moment they were out of sight, she stepped out of his arms so she could think. The darkness helped, for it kept her from seeing the green, green eyes that haunted her dreams far too often. "I suspect she wants Mr. Merrimont's attention—according to Miss Russell, he has all but ignored her since their betrothal."

"He has a job."

"I know that. I've explained that. I've made sure that she knows her duties as his wife—duties beyond paying calls and hosting at-homes for society ladies. He will have to entertain often, especially if he stands for Commons."

His face twisted into surprise. "Did he actually share that ambition with her? Few gentlemen know of it."

"Of course not, but I was hired to prepare her for the future. That means finding out what skills she will need."

He shook his head slowly, as if in shock. "Then why is she balking?"

Edith turned toward the yew tree overhanging the balustrade and brushed its delicate foliage. "Lord Hawthorne said I could trust you." She glanced over her shoulder, waiting until he nodded. "Miss Russell has been the local diamond since the age of fifteen, so she is accustomed to men who fawn over her, accede to her every wish, and praise her at every turn. Her previous governess encouraged her."

"Why?"

"I don't know the woman, so I don't care to speculate. I've tried to explain that contrived adulation is the fashion and thus means little. Mr. Merrimont lacks the temperament to indulge in excessive flattery. Nor does he waste his time in idle flirtation."

Again she glanced back until he nodded.

"Miss Russell equates flattery with love. She thinks his reticence means he doesn't love her, which raises fears that her beauty is fading. That causes panic, which increases her determination to prove his love by forcing him to flatter her. I suspect tonight's goal is to make him jealous."

Charles choked.

"I agree, but she no longer listens to me. She is a devotee of romantic novels and expects love to transform the world into a magical place. So far, it hasn't. We spent last month in town. When Giles refused to forego a Four-in-Hand Club outing so he could take her shopping, she snapped."

"She expected him to escort her around the shops instead of driving out to Salt Hill?" He sounded appalled. "Merrimont's prowess as a whip is legendary.

I've never seen such light hands on the ribbons—or such absolute control. He can trot through a gate with less than an inch of clearance. Hell, he could turn through a gate that tight—at speed. Driving is how he relaxes after tense negotiations."

"I am aware of that. I've explained it very clearly. But Miss Russell is spoiled—still very much a child in some ways. She needs constant reassurance."

"No wonder Merrimont is making no progress with Schechler."

It was her turn to raise her brows.

"I was sent out here because he can't keep his mind on his job," he explained bluntly. "I expected to find him caught up in wedding preparations. Instead, he is so distracted that I'd barely greeted him before he treated me to an outburst on the insanity of females." His glare made it clear that he shared that view, at least when it came to her.

Edith ignored it. Diana's future was more important than Charles's opinion. She faced him. "I fear he is close to walking away. On the other hand, if he truly doesn't care . . ."

Charles paused, then shook his head. "I suspect he cares too much. There was something in his voice. . . . Hawthorne and Hughes use that same tone when speaking of their wives."

"Then why doesn't he tell her?"

"Do you honestly suggest that he lay his heart on the floor for Miss Russell to trample?"

"She wou—" Edith bit off the denial, for Diana undoubtedly would, if for no other reason than to prove she could. "You have a point," she said instead, sighing deeply.

"I have several points." He ducked into the library to hold his hands over the fire. "This is not the weather for tête-à-têtes in the garden," he explained when she joined him.

"No. But you were saying—" She shivered now that the air was warmer. Or maybe it was the dismal room, which qualified as a library only because one shelf contained a dozen volumes of old sermons. None of the Russells were scholars.

"Merrimont's reticence is more than protection against pain. He is a diplomat. We are trained never to reveal our thoughts."

"That hasn't stopped *you.*" She glared, recalling the names he'd called her after she'd slipped and knocked him into a suit of armor back in July. The clatter as he and the armor crashed to the marble floor had drawn a dozen spectators.

"That's different."

"Really?"

"We are discussing Merrimont," he snapped. "Most gentlemen are taught from birth that emotions are vulgar; thus indulging in them reveals inferior breeding. And love is the most vulgar of all, suited only to the lowest classes. Merrimont won't acknowledge such a feeling and won't admit he can't handle Miss Russell. Pride won't allow it."

"So it's all right to be emotional around inferiors, but not your equals?" she asked, suddenly angry.

"That's not what I said."

"Really? Mr. Merrimont, younger son of a viscount, can't tell Miss Russell, daughter of a baronet and his affianced bride, that he loves her. But you, who are a great deal higher, think it's permissible to attack, revile, and otherwise disdain a lowly governess."

"That's not true!" he snarled, slamming his fist on the mantel in a vivid show of temper. "I said *most* families eschew emotion. Mine doesn't. We're not quite respectable, if you need the truth, though we've enough power that all but the highest sticklers overlook our oddities. We don't deride emotion. We even champion fidelity after marriage. But that is not the point." He sucked in a calming breath. "Does Miss Russell want this marriage?"

"Yes, but on her terms. I think she's terrified that he doesn't care and that she might face living with a man who ignores her. Somehow I must convince her that compromise is necessary—and trust. That will be easier if Mr. Merrimont makes even a small show of approval. Can you convince him to abandon pride long enough to admit he wants this match?"

"I doubt it. If this has been building for some time,

he will see any concession as a defeat. And while he is trained in the art of compromise, he never makes the first move."

"Damnation," she muttered under her breath. "Fools, both of them, standing on pride when they ought to trust each other enough to be honest. Why did he offer for her anyway? Surely he could see what she is."

"Which supports my contention that he loves her. It's the only reason he might abandon sense. But he won't admit it even in his mind, and he won't risk being hurt. Pain is never pleasant. A smart man learns to avoid it."

The pain in his voice halted her reply, for he'd been trampled rather badly himself not long ago. London had talked of little else for weeks after his fiancée jilted him. "Then we need another approach. What if he finds her in danger? The shock might break down his pride."

"No." His tone was final.

She stared. "Why?"

"I once arranged that scenario to force two other proud fools to admit the truth. Despite precautions, one of them nearly died. I won't risk it again."

"I see."

"I doubt it, but it doesn't matter. I swore then that I would never again meddle in other people's affairs. I'm already uneasy about involving myself in this. I won't tempt fate."

"Very well. What do you suggest?"

He paced to the window, stared over the grounds, then returned to the fire. "You said Miss Russell expects love to produce a magical transformation. How?"

"She is fond of romantic poetry, and her favorite novels always end with the characters transformed by love. So the idea that marriage will saddle her with a host of responsibilities and surround her with serious-minded diplomats instead of fawning suitors does not sit well."

"She is mad."

"You asked what she expects."

"Didn't she foresee this when she accepted him?"

"I doubt it. She was too caught up in the Season. Reveling in her success left little time to think about how marriage would change her life."

"Hmm." He clasped his hands behind him and resumed pacing. "Magical transformations . . . Does she believe in magic, then?"

"How should I know? I don't include magic in my lessons." But her irritation faded when she met his eyes. "What do you have in mind?"

"A magic amulet. Wearing it would force those around her to speak only the truth."

She snorted. "She won't believe anyone but Mr. Merrimont, and she won't accept anything short of capitulation to her demands."

"I wonder how true that is. Using an amulet might force her to see herself in a different light."

"How?"

"Suppose I encourage Merrimont to repeat today's outburst. Suppose Miss Russell overhears him." His gaze sharpened. "If she's as selfishly arrogant as you imply, I doubt his words will contain much flattery. It will be up to you to control her."

"I'll manage."

"Good girl."

His smile pooled heat in her womb. Ignoring it, she concentrated on business. "When?"

"It will take a day or so to arrange," he admitted. "Not the amulet. I can cobble something together easily enough. But I need time to prime Merrimont so he'll talk, and you'll need time to convince her that the amulet is truly magic. Start tonight. Mention that I know Granny Gibbs."

"The witch?"

"She has that reputation, though I've seen nothing to warrant it. I know her as an excellent healer. She patched me up more than once when I was a boy."

"While you were visiting Hawthorne and Hughes?" He hadn't lived in the area himself.

"Exactly. Tomorrow morning I'll give Miss Russell an opportunity to ask me about it. I can produce the amulet the next day."

"All right. But don't speak with her alone. If I'm wrong and she's given up on this match, she may attach a replacement before jilting him—that's one lesson she would have learned from your imbroglio last Season. Only your betrothed's immediate marriage to Hawthorne mitigated the scandal. You are the greatest catch in residence just now. More eligible than Merrimont, if truth be told, and far more eligible than Jessup. If she's looking, she'll know that."

Shock flared in his eyes.

Leaving him to brood, she returned to the ballroom. Diana was waltzing with Jessup, much too closely. So much for Hawthorne's warning. Glaring in the earl's direction, Edith settled in for a long evening.

Following her habit, Edith entered Diana's room as the girl was preparing for bed. She liked to discuss the day while its events were still fresh.

"Did you enjoy the dancing?" she asked once the maid left.

"Mostly." Diana frowned. "But Giles is making me look a fool."

"How?"

"He ignores me! People notice. He's hateful!"

"I saw nothing to criticize. He led you out for the first set and again for the fourth, then spent the rest of the evening entertaining your relatives. It would be ill-bred of him to hang on your arm."

"Ill-bred! We are betrothed! He didn't even notice my new gown."

Edith sighed. "Men rarely notice appearance unless your attire is inappropriate. We've discussed this before."

"Mr. Jessup noticed. Mr. Tomling noticed."

"Because they have little to do beyond flirting with the ladies, so they need things they can praise. Giles has business to conclude before your wedding—business that is not going well from all accounts. He spent the afternoon in meetings with Baron Schechler and Lord Charles."

"At *my* house party? How dare they!"

"The Regent expects an agreement this week," she snapped crossly, then stifled her temper. "You know Giles has responsibilities. We speak of it every day. As long as he works for the Foreign Office, he will have little control over where or when he conducts business. And if you wish to leave on a wedding trip, you will cease disturbing him. Let him finish his negotiations so he is free to go." She wondered if the baron was taking advantage of Diana's antics to wring concessions from a distracted Giles. Not that Charles would let him get away with it, but—

"What business was Lord Hawthorne conducting when he decided to follow me about?" demanded Diana.

"I wasn't aware that he was," lied Edith.

"Though I suppose someone as beautiful as I must expect every man to watch her," Diana continued with complete illogic.

"Having seen the way the earl looks at his wife, I can guarantee that he has no interest in you, no matter how beautiful."

"Nonsense. Everyone loves me—except Giles. If you'd heard Mr. Tomling praise my eyes, you would understand."

"Diana!" Edith shook her head. "A man may enjoy looking at beauty. A young man may play at worshipping beauty. But a husband needs more than an ornament." She sighed. "If you are dissatisfied with Giles, perhaps you should reconsider wedding him."

"He's mine!" She flung herself across the bed. "He offered prettily enough, so why won't he even compliment my new gown?"

"Because you treat any notice as a skirmish won in a war only you are fighting. Yes, a war," she repeated when Diana tried to object. "You have criticized him so relentlessly that he must conclude you are a shrew."

"I'm not!"

"Think, Diana. What did Giles see tonight? It wasn't your gown, lovely though it is. It wasn't your face, either. What he saw were flirtations that went well beyond propriety, vulgar laughter, abominable manners. . . . In short, he saw a girl whose behavior will embarrass him at best and possibly harm his position with the Foreign Office. Slipping outside to kiss Mr. Jessup was not well done."

"How did you—" The words were out before Diana remembered that a denial might serve her better.

"I heard about it, which means that others might also hear about it. Especially Giles. Do you really believe that Jessup will remain quiet? He is working hard to discommode Giles, so he will certainly trumpet his triumph. And if Lord Hawthorne caught you together, Giles can hardly doubt Jessup's word. Jessup may have arranged for Hawthorne's presence himself."

"What are you talking about? Mr. Jessup loves me."

"Jessup loves only himself. Haven't you noticed that he is most attentive when Giles is watching?" It wasn't strictly true, but she needed to penetrate Diana's arrogance. "His goal is to harm the man you vowed to marry, and you are helping him."

Diana was off the bed in a trice, palm extended to slap. "You wrong him. He loves me more than Giles ever will."

Edith caught her wrists. "No, Diana. Calculation fills his eyes. Determination stiffens his jaw. You are too young to recognize it and too determined to see only what you want to see. But in truth, he is using you to further his own goals." That much was real.

"Why should I accept your so-called truth?"

"Because I am older than you, with more experience of the world." She shook her head to cut off another protest. "But if you don't believe me, then seek the truth for yourself. There are foolproof ways to discern it."

"Then use them and prove yourself wrong."

Edith nearly smiled, for the words played into her hands. "Only you can use such methods, Diana. The best way to divine truth is through magic, but magic only reveals truth about its user. It cannot uncover secrets about others."

"Magic?" Surprise threaded her voice.

"Exactly. I am not skilled in its use, but I overheard Lord Charles discussing Granny Gibbs this evening—he is well acquainted with the woman. She concocts amulets that reveal truth. Perhaps he can obtain one for you. But beware. Truth can be uncomfortable."

Diana surprised her by nodding. "I will think on it."

Chapter Four

When Edith arrived at breakfast the next morning, Diana and Jessup occupied opposite ends of the table. It made her wonder if Charles had reinforced Hawthorne's warning to Jessup.

That hope died five minutes later when she intercepted an exchange of sly glances that left Diana nearly bursting with suppressed excitement. They were up to something.

Her fears increased when Peter slid into the seat on Jessup's right and murmured something into his ear. Jessup nodded briskly, then murmured a reply that brought a smile to Peter's lips.

Edith hid a frown. Jessup had ignored Peter since arriving at Russell House, so why did they suddenly act like the best of friends?

Peter rose to address the company. "The ice is finally thick enough to be safe. Anyone wishing to skate should meet in the hall at ten. We'll walk to the lake together."

Diana squealed in delight. Jessup started to smile, but a word from Peter pulled his face into a scowl.

Edith chewed thoughtfully. Was Peter warning Jessup away from his sister—even the worse cads could be protective of family—or was he pressing Jessup to do something distasteful? She suspected the latter. Peter cared only for himself.

"More trouble?" murmured Charles, sliding into the vacant seat on her left.

She nearly jumped out of her skin, and not just from surprise. Heat sizzled along her nerves until she had to inhale twice to keep her voice steady. "Puzzles rather than problems, my lord. Jessup's odd behavior extends beyond Miss Russell and Mr. Merrimont."

"To whom?"

"Mr. Russell." She nodded toward the pair.

"Did they arrive together?"

"No. Russell chose to sit there. Jessup doesn't like him, yet he seems to be listening, almost as if Russell had some hold over him."

"That sounds ominous." His gaze remained on Peter.

"Very. Jessup is full of surprises today. Did you speak to him last night?"

"There was no need. Hawthorne had already done so."

"With minimal effect. He was waltzing with Miss Russell when I returned, and holding her far too close. They've been exchanging secret glances this morning."

"I'll see that he—"

"No." She grasped his wrist when he began to rise, keeping him in his seat. Electricity sparked. Her lungs tightened until she had to fight to draw her next breath. "Something powerful is driving him—why else would he ignore Hawthorne's warning? *Nobody* defies the Beaux. I doubt he cares a fig for Miss Russell, and I don't like that Mr. Russell can seemingly influence him."

"Nor do I." He paused to chew bacon. "Have you mentioned your fears to Miss Russell?"

"No. I only just noted the connection. And she swears that Jessup loves her." She sipped her coffee. "But she may have doubts she won't admit aloud. My mention of magic last night intrigued her. On the other hand, the news that we can skate this morning produced excessive excitement. Jessup may have sent her a note. I hope she's not planning something drastic—like eloping. She has become almost frantic for attention, and Jessup is supplying it. His ministrations could easily scramble her wits. Will you be skating?"

"I'm supposed to meet with Schechler."

"I hear he is stiff-necked and refuses any compromise."

"Too true." He sighed.

"Then bring him along. The other guests are already

caught up in the Christmas spirit, though the festivities won't begin until tomorrow. Perhaps their excitement will work some magic on him. It can't hurt. And be sure that Merrimont joins us."

"Is that wise? Watching Miss Russell flirt with Jessup is bound to irritate him."

"Good. They need to confront this problem, not ignore it."

"Do you want them to call off the wedding?" he asked softly.

"Personally, no. The scandal would make it difficult to find a new position. But neither do I want them to live fifty years in misery." She frowned as Jessup and Peter left together, heads bent in earnest conversation.

"Yes, that does seem odd," he agreed. "And eliminates my own suspicions."

"Which were?" She finished her coffee.

"That Jessup is obeying Merrimont's orders. If Miss Russell creates a large enough scandal, Merrimont could jilt her with impunity."

"Is that what happened to you?" The question was out before she could stop it.

"No." He scowled her into silence. "Russell's involvement cannot be good. I will postpone my morning meeting and join you at the lake."

She nodded, then followed the pair from the room, hoping to learn something useful.

Charles watched her leave, grateful that she was gone. He was angrier with her today than he'd been after she'd cracked his skull. He knew it was unfair, but he couldn't help it. She was walking proof that his judgment was hopelessly impaired.

He'd assumed that Miss Knolton was incompetent, ignorant, and lacking common sense.

He'd been wrong.

Yet more than his faulty assumptions irritated him. Everything about her triggered his temper. He'd wanted to destroy last night's monstrous gown and replace it with a fashionable creation that would show off her intriguing bosom. He'd wanted to slide his hands into her lustrous hair, loosening pins until that severe knot softened to dark waves framing her heart-shaped face. Silky waves that would draw attention to her silver eyes. Those eyes had haunted him since the day she'd fallen into his lap, smearing a plate of cream cakes all over his coat. They were mesmerizing, drawing him into depths he'd not expected. And her mouth! Sinfully red lips begged to be explored. . . . Once he dressed her properly, he would drape rubies around her neck, bringing roses to her creamy cheeks and tempting—

He broke off the thought, appalled. Damn Jacob for planting ideas in his head! It was bad enough that she stirred lust. He didn't need—

"Good morning, my lord." The sultry voice shattered his thoughts.

"Miss Russell." He rose to execute the expected bow, then spotted the gleam in her eyes and sighed. Miss Knolton was right to fear Miss Russell's intentions. The girl was exploring her options and would jilt Merrimont in a trice if a better offer appeared. At least the breakfast room contained a dozen people.

His cold tone dimmed her gaze, but she quickly rallied, batting her lashes outrageously. "We were delighted that you could accept our invitation, my lord."

"My presence is purely a business matter, Miss Russell. If I didn't have to speak with Baron Schechler, I would be with my family."

"Oh." She'd obviously expected a compliment.

Laughter rippled from the corner where Riley was entertaining the crowd with the latest *on-dits*. A Home Office investigator, Riley was another of Merrimont's friends.

Miss Russell tugged on Charles's arm. "I need to speak with you, my lord. Privately."

"So speak. No one is paying attention. It is unseemly to slip away from the others."

She flashed a smile she must have practiced before a mirror. "But a gentleman of your high breeding can hardly care what others think, my lord."

"On the contrary, Miss Russell. A diplomat must always consider appearances. Merrimont certainly does."

"Hardly. Ignoring me cannot do his credit any good."

Charles laughed. "You really are a peagoose, aren't you?" He dismissed her indignation. "Don't you know anything about society? Living in your pocket would reduce his credit—and yours, too, for doing so implies that he cannot trust you to behave."

"How dare—"

"Surely your companion has explained the ways of the world. I pitied Merrimont last night. How he maintained his dignity is a mystery, for your antics would horrify the most broad-minded gentleman. I cannot imagine having a wife who makes such a vulgar cake of herself. If you don't learn proper manners, he will never advance at the Foreign Office. Nor will he find supporters if he chooses to stand for Commons."

Her mouth hung open in her first genuine show of emotion. "If that is how he feels, then he should let me find someone who appreciates me," she snapped.

Charles suppressed a sigh at the arrogance that could twist criticism so far around. "I don't know how he feels, Miss Russell. All I know is that your behavior affects both of you—not that you seem to care. But I don't want to see Merrimont's life ruined by an arrogant little witch. He's a good man."

"How dare you, sir!"

"I dare because accepting his offer made you part of him, so your misbehavior harms him—I know what Hawthorne found on the terrace last evening. I dare because I despise selfish girls who don't care how their actions affect others. You are calling censure down on your family. You are branding Jessup a cad. Staying on this course will force Sir Waldo to turn Miss Knolton off without a reference, which will prevent her from finding a new position. All that damage just so one spoiled miss can soothe her sensibilities and flex her claws. I won't allow it."

She stepped back, all thought of flirtation gone. "*You* won't allow it?" Her voice could have frozen a raging river.

"Exactly. Rather than let you destroy innocents, I will have your father lock you in your room until the wedding."

"He would never do such a thing! Papa loves me."

"Of course he loves you, but that won't stop him from dealing with this tantrum. What do you hope to accomplish?"

"This is Giles's last chance to prove he loves me. If he doesn't, I won't wed him."

"Childish." But when tears glinted on her lashes, he relented. "This is not the way to prove anything, Miss Russell. No man worth his salt will give in to blackmail."

"Blackmail!"

"What else can one call your threats?"

"I'm not threatening anyone. Since most men adore me, why should I tie myself to someone who doesn't?"

"The so-called adoration of cubs unready for marriage is but a game, Miss Russell. They pretend admiration and profess undying devotion, but anyone of intelligence knows it's all pretense. A pleasant way to pass the time. No more—as is obvious from the frequency with which they change idols. Those of an age to wed look beyond the color of your hair or the tilt of your chin. Gentlemen need a lady, a hostess, an heir."

"But I need someone who cares."

"Don't confuse caring with poetry. Are you a good person?"

"Of course." She glared.

"Are you beautiful?"

"Naturally."

"Then why do you need to be told twenty times an hour that it is true? Are you afraid it is false?" He held up a hand to prevent an explosion of temper. "Think about it, Miss Russell. If you don't believe it, then being told so will change nothing. If you do believe it, then it matters not what others might think. Compliments are nice—and they can make you feel better when things are going badly, as they always do from time to time. But they can't change truth, so demanding them with every breath makes you seem childish. And any compliment that you coerce is worthless."

"You are hateful." She twisted her mouth into a pout.

"I don't believe it, so your opinion doesn't matter." He drew a breath. "But if you are seriously questioning your betrothal, perhaps you should consult Granny

Gibbs. She is quite skilled at helping people choose the right course."

"So I've heard. Does she really make amulets that reveal truth?"

"Yes." He paused, but though her eyes begged, she couldn't bring herself to ask. Perhaps she found the request too embarrassing. Or maybe his harsh words made it impossible to beg a favor. He finally took pity on her. "If you want one, I can call on her for you. But be wary of magic," he cautioned softly. "It can reveal things you don't wish to know."

"I'll chance it." She dimpled prettily, satisfied to have achieved her main goal. "Thank you, my lord."

The skating party convened on a shallow cove half a mile from the house. Footmen carried benches and baskets of skates to the shore, then built a fire to warm frozen fingers and let an undercook prepare chocolate. Children shouted, weaving among their elders in games of tag and crack the whip. Laughter followed in their wake, as did gasps of feigned terror as young ladies sought steadying arms from favorite gentlemen.

By half past eleven, Edith had moved beyond the cove itself, gliding in random zigzags that let her keep one eye on Diana and the other on the rest of the company. Too many dramas were disturbing the carefree pleasure of the crowd.

Peter was clearly stirring up trouble. He wouldn't attack Edith with others nearby, but he'd spoken with Jessup, leaving the man white-faced. Then he'd paused by Schechler, who had speared Charles and Giles with glares the moment Peter skated away. A quarter hour later, he'd cornered Giles.

Perhaps he was seeking revenge for Edith's escape yesterday. Disrupting Diana's marriage would hurt Edith, and turning the baron against Charles would repay him for interfering. But that didn't explain why he could influence Jessup.

A short time later Schechler had surprised her by inviting her to skate. As a chaperon, she should have refused, but she'd taken his arm, hoping to discover what

Peter was saying. Diana was skating with Tomling, a picture of propriety this morning.

"The Russells you know well, *nein*?" Schechler asked once they were moving.

"I've been with them for eighteen months."

He nodded, then maneuvered around several slow-moving couples before continuing. "I know it is not done in your country to speak of certain matters, *fraulein*, but I have heard a disturbing tale. If true, it could affect my business."

"Who told you this tale?"

He seemed surprised by her question. "Herr Russell. The son."

"I see." She spared a moment to thank Fate that Schechler was less credulous than Peter thought. Schechler might be an incorrigible, stiff-necked ass, as Giles had once described him when he'd thought himself alone, but at least he checked claims before accepting them. "When I hear gossip—and what can one call tales about others if not gossip?—I first consider the source, asking myself if that source has reason to lie. Who was this tale about?"

"Lord Charles Beaumont. Herr Russell brought it to me because we engage now in delicate negotiations. The charges are quite grave."

She smiled. "I'm sure they are, but I am equally sure they are false. As you say, I know the Russells quite well. I know that Mr. Peter is a dishonorable cad and that he hates Lord Charles. I also know that Lord Charles is an honorable gentleman with a gift for finding equitable solutions to any problem."

"But his reputation!"

"You speak of the Three Beaux, I presume?"

He nodded.

"The Beaux make exciting drawing room chatter, but they have never drawn true censure. And since society scrutinizes their every move, we would all know instantly if they behaved badly."

"I do not understand your country."

"I doubt that it is much different from your own," she dared. "People abhor dishonor, cruelty, and vulgarity. But they love scandal, as long as it does not touch them personally, and discussing rogues makes them feel dashing. One reason the Beaux are so beloved is that they are larger-than-life men who often flirt with scandal yet never cross that final line. The gossips can exaggerate their exploits, fan themselves furiously over their reputed prowess, and recall every hint of impropriety, but everyone knows the Beaux never abandon honor, so it is a harmless pastime. If you want my advice, share Mr. Russell's claims with Lord Charles and ask for the truth. He will give it. Then put it behind you and finish your business so you can enjoy the remainder of your holiday."

Giving him no chance to argue, she'd turned the conversation to the differences between English Christmas customs and those he knew, particularly those that dealt with peace, goodwill, and the burial of old quarrels.

Diana had still been with Tomling when Edith left the baron, but Edith had intercepted another glance between the girl and Jessup. So when Jessup headed for the thicket covering a spit that protruded into the lake just beyond the cove, Edith had positioned herself where she could keep an eye on him. She didn't think Jessup had noticed her. Nor had Diana, who had begun picking a fight with Tomling.

Diana shoved Tomling away and left, ostensibly to be alone.

Jessup practiced a lazy spin behind the spit, pointedly ignoring Diana's tantrum.

Edith knew better. They had planned this interlude well. Miss Parkes, undoubtedly following Diana's orders, chose this moment to fall in a flurry of skirts. While everyone else rushed to her aid, Diana headed straight for Jessup.

Edith caught Charles's eye, nodded toward the spit, then picked up speed, flailing her arms as if fighting for balance. As she neared Jessup, she screamed.

Jessup whipped around so fast he tripped.

Edith flattened him.

"Oh, my. Oh, my," she squeaked, scrabbling along the ice to his side. "Oh, dear. Are you all right, sir? Oh, I'm so terribly sorry. I don't know what happened. I must have caught the blade— Are you hurt?"

He cursed, tried to sit, then fell a second time when her attempt to help him knocked him over, slamming his head against the ice.

She ignored the thud, keeping to her role. "How awful. You're bleeding, sir! Let me look. We need help. Yoo-hoo! Over here," she called, noting that several skaters were following Charles around the end of the spit.

"What happened?" demanded Jessup shakily.

"I'm not sure. I was skating—slowly, so I wouldn't fall. I am not very accomplished, you understand. Then my toe caught on something. I think it was my toe, or maybe it was the heel. But I lost my balance. Falling is so embarrassing that I tried to catch myself, but that just made my feet move faster, and I couldn't control anything, and then there you were, so I tried to turn, but you turned, too, and I couldn't help it, but I ran into you, and you fell so hard, and that awful thunk when your head hit the ice, and now you're bleeding. Did I kill you?" She finished this artful mishmash by tugging on him until she managed to fall across his chest.

His breath whooshed out.

Charles arrived, closely followed by Diana, Giles, and Miss Richland.

"Mr. Jessup!" squeaked Diana, shoving Edith aside.

Charles caught Diana's arm so she couldn't throw herself atop Jessup. "Control yourself, Miss Russell. I know he's a guest, but you could cause more damage if you aren't careful. Are you all right, Miss Knolton?"

Edith let Charles pull her to her feet. "Just a tumble. But Mr. Jessup cut his head."

"I can see that. Have you other injuries, Jessup?" His censorious look struck Jessup square in the eye, raising the hair on Edith's arms and blanching all color from Jessup's face. For the first time she understood the Beaux' power.

"Dizzy," murmured Jessup as Giles squatted beside him.

"I'm not surprised. Head injuries have that effect." Charles winked at Edith, then shifted his gaze to Giles. "Take Miss Russell to the fire, then send a pair of footmen to help Jessup to his room."

"Right." Giles grabbed Diana's elbow. "Time for chocolate," he announced to the growing crowd.

Miss Richland turned to Charles. "Miss Knolton also fell. Escort her to the house. I will see that Mr. Jessup avoids doing anything silly—like trying to rise before the footmen arrive." Miss Richland was a formidable spinster who could keep the devil himself in line. She'd been supervising the children who had joined the skating expedition.

"An excellent suggestion," he agreed, offering Edith his arm. "Are you hurt, Miss Knolton?"

"Merely clumsy," she said as they moved away.

"Hardly." He chuckled. "I've seen you when you were clumsy. This performance was a work of art."

She didn't know whether her blush arose from mortification or gratitude. Probably both. "They'd planned an assignation behind the thicket—or so it seemed. I fear Mr. Russell might be involved in some way." She shared her observations, including her conversation with Schechler.

"Your fears are well founded," he agreed when she finished. "Russell is clearly stirring up trouble. I will have to deal with him sooner than I'd planned."

She raised her brows.

"I'd hoped to put it off until after the wedding, but now . . ." He shook his head. "I don't believe he would ruin his sister merely to spite you, though. There is something we don't yet know. Once you are settled, I will speak to Riley. He hears news that escapes even the gossips. In the meantime, Jessup's head will keep him in bed for the day and give you a chance to divert Miss Russell. I doubt she planned to elope."

"Elope?" While she had suggested the possibility that morning, she hadn't thought Diana was ready to abandon Giles just yet.

"After our conversation, I asked my groom to keep an eye on Jessup's horse so I would have notice of any unusual plans—he has no carriage. My groom sent word an hour ago that Jessup had ordered two horses to wait for him beyond the lake, one with a sidesaddle. He also ordered a carriage from the village. I made sure the horses remained in the stable." His satisfied smile warmed the air. "Since Miss Russell still seemed undecided when she asked me to procure an amulet, I doubt she had plans to leave with Jessup. And I'm certain that someone of her character would never forego the spectacle of a lavish wedding in front of an admiring crowd."

"Abduction, then. He must be desperate. But why?"

"I'm hoping Riley will know." He seated her on a bench and removed her skates, his fingers warm as they unaccountably wandered above her ankles.

Edith tried to ignore the heat blazing up her leg, but she couldn't control her tremors.

"Are you sure you didn't hurt yourself?"

"Quite sure. I landed on top of him."

He grinned. "Deliberately, I suspect. Miss Knol— What is your name anyway?"

"Edith."

"Good. If we are to work together, I prefer less formality. You can call me Charles." When she nodded, he led her toward the house. "As for diverting Miss Russell's attention, I heard a rumor that Jessup lost at cards last week. Perhaps you should mention it—or even exaggerate it. She must know that gamesters make bad husbands."

The blood drained from Edith's face as his words revived old horrors. Before she could slam the door against them, memories engulfed her, encasing her in fog. She barely felt Charles pull her into the walled garden beyond curious eyes.

"Forgive me," he begged. "That was an abominable suggestion. I'd forgotten—"

"—that Papa killed himself after losing everything at cards?"

"That you found his body. I should not have reminded you."

She turned away to hide the face she could no longer control.

He pulled her back. "Since I've already walked into this bumble broth, why don't you tell me about that day? I suspect you've never discussed it."

"I c-can't," she admitted, fighting tremors, though his touch soothed some of the horror.

"Talk to me, Edith. If you hoard the images, they will never fade."

"You sound as if you know."

"I do know. I was first on the scene of a rather bloody horror myself. I was ten."

"So young." She sighed. And maybe he was right. She hoped so, for she couldn't refuse him. Besides, nothing she said would lower his opinion of her. . . . "Finding Papa was only the first shock. We'd had no idea that he was a gamester—he'd apparently flirted with ruination before. And the timing hurt as badly as the loss itself. I was supposed to come out in London only a week later."

He murmured something soothing, though she couldn't make out the words. His hands warmed her back.

"When I entered the library that m-morning—" She gritted her teeth until they no longer chattered, then shook her head, hoping to dislodge the images. When that didn't work, she forced her tongue into motion. "There was so much blood. And then his note . . . He'd lost everything. We had two days to vacate the house. Mama collapsed. Jaimie was nearly as upset. My brother," she added, shaking her head. "In the end, I had to take charge. I'd salvaged my pearls, but even frugality couldn't make them support four of us for long. Jaimie tried to help, but he was barely sixteen, and without patronage he had no hope of obtaining any sort of post. He finally accepted the king's shilling, hoping to make a name for himself in the army. He died in Spain."

"I understand you've been supporting your mother and sister ever since."

"Who else will do it?" she demanded. "Mama tries, but her clients use her mostly from charity, for she never was much good with a needle. Nor is my sister. She is a dreamer every bit as bad as Papa and still thinks wishing will somehow restore our former life." Her control snapped. Before she could stop herself, she was weeping on his shoulder.

His arms pulled her close. She should have protested, should have backed away, but she couldn't. For once in her life, she let down her guard long enough to accept the comfort he offered. That it was Charles himself who held her . . .

The tears flowed faster.

Charles let her cry even as he cursed Sir Richard for leaving her with so many responsibilities at so tender an age. If only the fool were alive so Charles could call him out.

He eased her closer, stroking his hand down her back. She fit perfectly against him, triggering a ripple of desire, though he felt no need to act on it. Most unusual.

Her sobs finally slowed.

"Forgive me, my lord," she murmured, trying to push free.

"Charles." He let her pull back just far enough that he could see her eyes—silver disks now rimmed with red. "We agreed you would call me Charles."

"Charles." She sighed. "My apologies for subjecting you to that."

"I expect you needed it. Have you ever let yourself grieve?"

She shook her head. "There was never time, but that's no excuse for discommoding you."

"You haven't."

He cradled her head between his palms, his thumbs wiping the last tears from her cheeks. Then he dropped a comforting kiss on her mouth. Sparks kindled, burning clear to his toes. Her eyes widened in more than shock. . . .

His own closed as he kissed her again, dragging her close enough to plunder, to savor, to revel in discovery.

Not dragged, insisted the corner of his mind that still functioned. *She isn't fighting.*

It was true. Her arms closed around his waist. Her mouth opened to his darting tongue. Heat burned him to a crisp, igniting the familiar lust. But unfamiliar sensations also raged. Trying to identify them awakened him to reality.

He was assaulting a well-born innocent without invitation. Just like Russell.

"Forgive me," he begged, praying her eyes would not

hold condemnation when they opened. "That was not well done. You should have used that knee I mentioned yesterday."

She inhaled twice before finding her voice. "There is nothing to forgive, Charles. It's an unusual approach to dissipating tears, but quite effective." She pulled against his grip, reminding him that he still held her.

He thrust his hands into his greatcoat pockets, speechless from her interpretation—and thoroughly irritated. No one ever dismissed his kisses.

Edith blew out a long breath, then turned the subject. "We were discussing Jessup's gaming. You suggested I inform Miss Russell of it, but that is not a good idea. She would either ignore the news or assume that her devotion would cure him of the habit."

"Is she mad?"

"She is young. And she dotes on romantic novels in which love resolves all problems, if you recall. If she thinks her dowry would remedy a financial crisis—serious losses might explain his current course—then she would expect a lifetime of gratitude in exchange."

Charles choked. "Throwing that in his face every day would likely earn her a beating."

"I know, but she believes herself irresistible and refuses to hear anything to the contrary." She headed for the house.

"Merrimont might be better off without her," he mused, catching up so she would not appear to be fleeing him. "I wonder if they settled anything just now."

"I will ask."

"Do that." He clasped her wrist so she had to look at him. "And I'll talk to Riley. Meet me in the library after lunch." Schechler was again murmuring into Lady Frobisher's ear, so there would be no negotiations today.

Edith held his gaze for a long moment, then nodded and slipped away.

He headed for the billiard room, still shaken by that kiss. It was unlike anything he might have expected had he ever considered kissing her—and nothing like Emily's kisses. Edith's were far more seductive, and thus very dangerous. Her sensuality frankly astounded him. How had he missed it? Was he too blind to see beyond the surface trimmings of a governess's garb? It did not say much about his wits.

She was intriguing in character as well as in looks. Quick-witted. Logical. Competent. It was something else he'd missed. She'd been in London with one charge or another for several years, yet he'd not even noticed her until the cream cake incident. Now he couldn't get her out of his head.

Chapter Five

The library was empty when Edith slipped inside. At least she needn't fret over Diana for the moment. The girl was shepherding the ladies to tea at the vicarage. Sir Waldo had taken most of the men out shooting. Jessup remained in bed.

But Edith found it impossible to relax. Charles's kiss had left her so shaky that she'd barely managed to speak lightly afterward then walk away as if nothing had happened. He was amazingly skilled, raising sensations she'd not known existed.

Stupid! she castigated herself. She should have followed her instincts and stayed far away from him. Harboring a *tendre* for a notorious rakehell was bad enough. Now that she'd discovered a host of virtues beneath his public façade, he was even more desirable. And his touch was more incendiary than she'd thought possible. If his auburn curls had burst into flames, he couldn't have scorched her more. And the way he'd comforted . . .

She was more than stupid. She very much feared she'd fallen in love with him.

Nothing could be worse. She'd locked away dreams of love and marriage eleven years ago, then built a satisfactory career, first as a companion and then as a finishing governess. Pride in her accomplishments helped overcome any lingering regret for her family's fall.

Now Charles had revived those dreams. Worse, he'd pushed them beyond girlish fantasies by evoking adult passion. How could she ever be satisfied squiring silly young girls now that she knew how much she'd really lost? She should never have stayed with Diana this long. Christmas with her family would have kept her world intact.

As footsteps approached, she unclenched her fists.

"Did Riley know anything useful about Jessup?" she managed with credible calm when Charles appeared in the doorway.

"More than useful. Nothing of a financial nature slips past him." He closed the door and joined her by the fire, raising the temperature in the room. "Jessup's recent losses landed in Russell's pocket."

"What?" The information dissipated her nervousness. "Why doesn't Merrimont know that?"

"Keep your voice down. Even the walls have ears." He dropped his own to a seductive murmur. "Merrimont probably never asked. And the Foreign Office doesn't hear about Home Office investigations. They've been watching Russell since autumn."

"Why?"

"That isn't relevant, but they know a great deal about him."

"Such as?"

"Because Sir Waldo keeps him on a tight financial leash, Russell turned to gaming to increase his income. Stupid," he agreed, overriding her protest. "But he's made it work, for though he loses as often as he wins, he has never lost a large wager, whether at cards or dice."

"That doesn't sound honest."

Charles smiled. "You go straight to the point. No one wins all their large wagers while losing most of their small ones. He has to be cheating."

That smile melted her knees, so she toyed with a vase of spills to avoid meeting his eyes. "If Mr. Russell holds Jessup's markers, it would explain why he can command him."

"Exactly."

When he stepped closer, she circled the terrestrial globe, placing it between them.

He leaned against the mantel. "According to Riley, Jessup lost everything he owns and more. Russell gave him until Twelfth Night to redeem his vowels. The total exactly matches Miss Russell's dowry. Ten thousand pounds."

Edith bit back a curse. "So that's it. I couldn't explain why Jessup might wish to harm Giles, but Peter resents Diana's extravagant dowry and hates that her husband will wind up with money Peter considers his own."

"I wish you had mentioned that earlier."

"That argument began before Diana even met Giles, so it did not seem relevant until now. Did Peter suffer any setbacks last week?"

"Why?"

"Something must have pushed him to cheat Jessup. It's been six months since Diana accepted Giles. Why wait until the last minute?"

"Good question." He frowned. "I'll ask Riley."

"Do that. Something prompted him to act."

"Maybe he only recently discovered his sister's ambivalence."

"Maybe he's responsible for her ambivalence. But there has to be more. If his goal was to wrest a fortune from his clutch-fisted father, he could have cheated someone months ago—an elopement before the Season would not have jeopardized the family name."

"Sir Waldo might have canceled the dowry for an elopement. That is still true, for he has no contract with Jessup and thus no obligation to pay anything."

Edith was surprised she hadn't considered that possibility. Perhaps she should remind Diana that Sir Waldo could keep her dowry if she jilted Giles. Without a dowry, she would never find another suitor. Beauty might draw second looks, but there were plenty of well-endowed beauties on the Marriage Mart. "I doubt Peter would think of that. He's rather stupid."

"But Jessup should know." He frowned. "I wonder how he can assure that the dowry is paid."

"It doesn't matter, because we'll stop him. The only question is how."

"Let Sir Waldo do it. Once I tell him about the card game and the Home Office investigation, he will send Russell abroad. And he can forgive Jessup's debts on the grounds of fraud, which will prevent Jessup from plotting further, though I doubt his friendship with Merrimont will survive."

"And just as well. No one needs that sort of friend. In the meantime, this doesn't address Miss Russell's arrogance. Sir Waldo can force her to the altar, but I can't in good conscience subject Merrimont to a life of misery. She has to grow up and start thinking of more than herself. Are you still making her an amulet?"

He nodded. "I will give it to her in the morning, then try to arrange a frank discussion with Merrimont. I'll signal you when I succeed, so you can see that Miss Russell overhears."

The timing couldn't be worse, Edith admitted. Christmas festivities began tomorrow. Everyone would be caught up in decorating the manor. It could take Charles all day to corner Giles. In her present mood, Diana would not welcome Edith as a constant companion. But they could not postpone it for even a day. The wedding was too near.

Footsteps jolted her from her thoughts. She slid into the shadows lest she be discovered alone with a gentleman, but they passed the door without pausing.

Charles stared at the door, then moved to Edith's side so they would not be overheard—or so he told himself. But the words no longer rang true. Something about her drew him, as if she could supply the answers to all of life's riddles. Her scent enveloped him, weakening his knees. When he leaned down to whisper in her ear, she jumped. He nearly smiled.

"Use Miss Russell's desire for truth to convince her to listen when I'm speaking to Merrimont," he murmured, stroking her arm, his bare hand against the warmth of her bare skin. "I doubt she'll admit she has a magic amulet, but after all her complaints, she can't be surprised that you know what she seeks."

"That will work. And perhaps I can weave some Christmas magic into our discussions—peace on earth and the like. 'Tis the season to dismiss old grudges and start anew in the spirit of goodwill. You might try that with Giles, too. He and Diana must either accept their differences or part before it is too late." Silver eyes stared up at him, limpid pools sparkling in the sunlight streaming—

He pulled himself together. "You make parting sound easy. It isn't."

"You would know."

He waited for the inevitable questions, but she said nothing, merely staring into his eyes. Perhaps that's why he found himself sharing thoughts he'd not even told the Beaux. "Ending a betrothal is never easy, even when everyone agrees. And it leaves lingering questions. I still can't understand my stupidity. How could I have thought us suited?"

"Everyone makes mistakes."

"I know that!" he snapped, then strode to the window so he could tighten the reins on his temper. "Mistakes happen every day—walking into Tattersall's when the one man you need to avoid is standing just inside the door, or misplacing your favorite hat, or not suspecting that an unusually spicy sauce is hiding bad fish. But that betrothal was more than a mistake. It was a case of atrocious judgment. Why didn't I see it? How many other ways am I blind? How the devil can I stay in a job where faulty judgment can cost the Crown so dearly?" Not until she grabbed his wrist did he realize he was tearing at his hair.

"Sit down, Charles. No one expects you to be perfect."

"My father does."

"Then he is stupid."

He was so surprised, he let her push him into a chair. "Stupid?"

"Exactly. He must know that no one is perfect. If he holds you to a higher standard than is humanly possible, then he's an idiot. I don't care what his motive is. Comparing people to impossible ideals never works."

"But he doesn't consider his standards impossible," he snapped back. "He adheres to them himself, so why shouldn't others?"

"That has nothing to do with perfection," she countered. "That is demanding that you make the same choices he does, which is absurd. There are many acceptable choices in life. One is no more right than another."

"It is when it creates scandal. That damnable betrothal—"

"Surely a man of his background cannot expect you to wed someone who would make you miserable."

"No, but he had plenty to say about my judgment. I should never have jumped into that betrothal to begin with. And I certainly should not have done so without discussing it with him first. To prevent a recurrence, he is taking matters into his own hands by choosing a wife for me. Thank God duty keeps me here instead of at home this Christmas."

"Which proves he is stupid. A man who teaches that marriage should encompass love and fidelity cannot expect an arranged match to work. And denigrating your judgment proves that his own is flawed."

"What—"

She swept on. "I've heard no tales that suggest your judgment is faulty, Charles. If there was any evidence, you can be sure Lady Beatrice would notice," she added, naming London's most prominent gossip, who prided herself on knowing everything. "Everyone takes a wrong step at times. Competent men recognize those wrong steps. If their characters are strong, they immediately retreat—as you did last Season. If they are weak, they freeze, bemoaning Fate or blaming others until everything collapses onto their heads. Stupid men never recognize that they are wrong. They forge ahead even after it is obvious to everyone else that they will fail. You are intelligent enough to recognize that a misstep you rectified months ago cannot mar your otherwise excellent judgment."

"You've a unique perspective." His head was whirling.

"And a forward tongue. Lecturing you is impertinent, so I must beg forgiveness. I have been instructing people too long, I fear." She shook her head.

"That wasn't a criticism. You are making me reconsider ideas. No friend could do more."

"You claim your betrothal was a case of bad judgment. Since I'm already guilty of hopeless impertinence, I'll ask what you mean."

He shrugged. "I let lust blind me."

She waited silently until he again felt compelled to continue.

"Emily was my best friend's sister, making lust inappropriate. So I convinced myself I loved her."

"A reasonable assumption, given your family's history."

"A stupid assumption. Just because she'd turned into a lovely lady since I'd last seen her didn't change that I'd treated her as a sister most of her life. When push came to shove, she remained more Richard's little sister than anything else."

"You blame yourself for twisting attraction into love." It wasn't a question.

"Of course. I should have recognized the truth far sooner—I didn't offer for her until a month after she reached town."

"But you did recognize the truth, and in time to rectify your mistake. I see nothing odd about you tumbling into such an imbroglio. A rake of your renown must be attracted to many women. Only friendship pushed you to twist the attraction in that case. Now that you recognize the trap, it won't happen again."

"My friends have no more sisters."

"See? The problem is gone."

His head whirled faster, for she'd somehow twisted his stupidity into a minor irritation rather than the earth-shattering dilemma that had plagued him for months. He opened his mouth to question her further, but she again surprised him by turning away.

"If you'll excuse me, I have several tasks to see to before Diana returns. Lady Russell will be unhappy if they are not done."

He wasn't sure if he wanted her to leave or stay, so he merely nodded. "Very well, Edith. And I'll take care of Russell."

The moment she left, he paced to the fireplace and back, pondering the past half hour. He felt as though she'd torn him apart then pasted him back together in a totally new way.

All his life his father had loomed just over his shoulder, watching every move he made. Though he loved his father with a devotion he accorded no other man, that constant watchfulness had never been comfortable—probably because Inslip had never been satisfied with his son's behavior. No matter what Charles did, Inslip found fault. Knowing that his best was never good enough stripped most of the enjoyment from his achievements and kept him in constant fear that others would note the same faults Inslip saw so clearly. He had never considered that Inslip himself might be wrong. . . .

Until now.

He cautiously reviewed their most recent clashes in light of Edith's interpretation, fearful that he would discover a flaw in her reasoning. But she was right. Inslip wasn't all-knowing or all-seeing. He was merely a man who, believing his own ways were best, expected his sons to follow precisely in his footsteps. But striking out on his own did not mean Charles was wrong.

Relief flooded him. And the return of confidence. He *was* competent. He *was* intelligent. He *could* negotiate with Schechler to a mutually satisfying end.

And he had Edith to thank for it. She had a knack for seeing past the surface to the core of a problem. And she had a knack for convincing people to reveal more than they considered reasonable. He'd actually shared his fears with her. If she told others . . .

But she wouldn't. He didn't know why, since she was nothing like he'd expected, but he trusted her.

He shook his head over the impressions he'd formed last Season. He should have recognized that her stammering had arisen from embarrassment rather than stupidity. Thrusting her into the public eye with his droll recounting of the cream cake affair would have revived memory of every cut she'd received after her father's death. She'd made one small mistake by tripping on the carpet and landing against him. If she hadn't been carrying a plate of pastries, the incident wouldn't have rated more than passing notice. But her squirming as she tried to rise had literally plastered him with cream cake. To divert attention from his embarrassment, he'd figuratively rubbed her face in the incident instead of letting her recover her poise.

His guilt increased when he realized that his ridicule

might have directed Russell's attention to her. Had that attack been his fault?

Recalling how shaken she'd been when he'd pulled Russell away revived his fury. Russell deserved more punishment than mere exile. Perhaps he should personally escort the cad to the docks. . . .

He went in search of his host.

But Sir Waldo was nowhere to be found. An emergency had demanded personal attention. No one knew when he would return.

Chapter Six

Christmas Eve dawned colder than ever, though that didn't stop everyone from gathering to collect greenery. Excitement mounted as people filled the hall and spilled into adjacent rooms. For the moment, the magic of Christmas pushed all other concerns aside. Wedding plans, negotiations, even grudges didn't matter today.

Or so Charles hoped as he pushed through the crowd. He wasn't up to facing trouble. Though he'd gone to bed full of hope for the morrow, dreams had plagued his sleep, leaving him groggy. The lascivious ones of Edith hadn't surprised him—he often dreamed of women who stirred his passions. What disturbed him was the jumble of Inslip's worst lectures overlaid with crashing thunder and ominous fog. Threats seemed to hover just out of sight. He'd no idea of their form, but they promised a disaster he couldn't escape.

Enough! He shoved the images aside. He faced too many real problems to waste time fighting imaginary ones, especially when the imaginary ones did nothing but rehash old pains.

He finally spotted Edith and drew her into a corner. "I gave Miss Russell the amulet after breakfast," he murmured. "She must wear it next to her heart if she wants it to work. The magic disappears at midnight."

"I hope you can maneuver Giles into talking today, then." She sighed. "Diana was so sullen this morning, I fear it is too late."

"We will see. Sir Waldo was gone yesterday, so I

couldn't talk to him about Russell, but I'll see him as soon as possible. Until I do, take care that Russell doesn't find you alone. I don't trust him."

"Nor do I, but he would never stoop to notice underlings when he is surrounded by his equals, so I'm safe enough."

"Humor me. He is not behaving normally at the moment. Stay in sight. If I can speak with Merrimont, I'll tug on my ear so you can lead Miss Russell close enough to hear."

Edith stayed with Diana as the group headed for the woods, wondering at the girl's odd humor. Not only was Diana content with Edith's company, but she avoided every man in the party. Edith hoped the amulet was responsible, but she couldn't trust the change.

Jessup remained in his room, turning away all visitors. She'd meant to ask Charles about the man's condition, but his sudden appearance at her side—and the heat of his fingers on her arm—had made her dizzy. She'd been too busy hiding her reaction to remember her questions. And too dull-witted, she admitted. Sleep had eluded her much of the night.

Now she feared that Jessup might have caused Diana's malaise. Had he sent her another note? If he'd heard about last evening's high spirits, he might fear losing his chance to redeem his vowels.

Edith gripped her basket harder and stayed with Diana when the guests scattered. Charles had already followed Giles in another direction, so it was too late to warn him that Giles was reaching the end of his rope.

Diana had thrown herself into charades last night, laughing immoderately, flirting with every man in the room, and executing her pantomimes with so much sensuality that Giles had drawn Edith aside.

"Do something about her unseemly exuberance," he'd hissed.

"Do you want her in hysterics?" She'd been too irritated to temper her words.

"This frivolity has to stop. She'll ruin herself—and me."

Edith had sighed. "I agree, but controlling her will be

difficult. It was a mistake to combine your wedding with Christmas. The excitement has gone to her head."

He'd blinked. "Is that what it is?"

"What else? She is only seventeen, too young to completely control the most turbulent emotions. By next week, she should again be levelheaded. Another year will see her firmly settled."

"If you say so." He clearly didn't believe her.

"I do," she'd insisted, praying it was true. "In the meantime, she needs support from both of us. For all her seeming poise, she lacks confidence—a common problem with long-standing beauties. They've been taught that their appearance defines their worth, yet they can't truly trust that the accolades are sincere." She'd wanted to add that Giles's silence increased Diana's fears, but Riley had drawn him away. And perhaps that had been good. She had given him something to think about without triggering his defensive pride.

"Ah, Miss Russell!" Mr. Tomling bowed theatrically before Diana, pulling Edith from her thoughts. "Beautiful, as always. A golden rose blooming in a sea of gray."

Not quite accurate, decided Edith as Diana simpered. While some of the trees were gray, more were evergreen, and the guests wore cloaks in every color of the rainbow. But the compliment restored Diana's spirits—probably because of the amulet, which would give it more weight than it deserved.

She was still wondering how to deal with this new problem when Diana sent Tomling off to cut mistletoe from a distant oak, then continued into the woods, making no protest when Edith followed.

"There!" the girl said five minutes later. "My favorite holly tree. It always has the best berries."

"It's lovely." The ancient tree grew against the rear of an empty woodcutter's cottage. Had Diana arranged to meet Jessup inside? Yet she invented no errand for Edith. Instead, she set down her basket and began cutting.

Their baskets were brimming by the time the cottage door creaked, alerting Edith to danger. To avoid overhearing a tryst, she reached out to draw Diana away, but Sir Waldo's voice arrested her hand.

"Is this private enough for you?" he demanded.

"Quite." It was Charles. "This subject is too delicate to risk being overheard." He paused as if gathering his courage. "I dislike meddling in your affairs, but if I remain silent, your family's name will be dragged through the mud."

"Impertinence, sir!" snapped Sir Waldo. "How dare you malign my daughter's high spirits? Is this how you repay my hospitality?"

"Miss Russell's high spirits are another matter entirely and not my business. Hear me out, then judge for yourself. When I am done, I will depart Gloucestershire if you so desire." He waited until Sir Waldo grunted agreement. "Last week your son Peter fleeced Jessup of a great deal more than he owns. Peter is pressing Jessup to abduct Miss Russell—her dowry matches the debt, which is at least a thousand more than he can raise."

"Never!" The denial was automatic. "You cannot mean it."

"Quiet," whispered Edith when Diana opened her mouth. "They will be furious to find you here. Come away."

Diana shook her head, then clamped her lips firmly shut and put an ear to the wall.

"I do mean it," continued Charles. "Fortunately, the abduction failed, thanks to Miss Knolton's vigilance. But the setback will not make Peter abandon his scheme. This is not the first time he has cheated, as Riley can attest—the Home Office has received complaints. But this time Peter is determined to hurt all of you. He hates Merrimont, who refused him a loan the day before that fateful card game. He despises Miss Russell for being your favorite. And he is still smarting over your latest refusal to increase his allowance. So he means to steal some of his inheritance."

"Does Diana—"

"No. She knows nothing of his plot—even the most reckless high spirits would not push her to dishonor. Yes, she's a hoyden," he added as if speaking over a protest. "But she would never seriously consider wedding Jessup—he's a well known here-and-therian."

"I'll wring his neck!"

"People would ask why. So far, few know of the plot, and Jessup is not your greatest danger in any event. Riley also revealed that the Crown is poised to arrest Peter on other charges. A trial will blacken your family name. The best way to avoid scandal is to send him abroad. Have you property he could manage?"

"A small plantation in Jamaica." He paused. "I knew he was wild, but I hadn't wanted to believe— I will speak to Riley immediately. Thank you for bringing the problem to my attention, Lord Charles."

The door creaked, then slammed shut. Footsteps moved away, shuffling leaves and snapping twigs.

Diana turned as if to follow.

"No," whispered Edith. "Sir Waldo will be furious if he finds out you overheard."

"How—" Her chin quivered.

"No tears. You know they leave your eyes red."

Diana nodded, inhaling deeply several times. She was opening her mouth to continue, when a voice rang out.

"Sir Waldo! Are you out here?" Jessup.

Again the door creaked. Someone had remained behind. "What do *you* want?" growled Sir Waldo.

"We have business to discuss," said Jessup pleasantly, though the desperation underlying his voice made Edith fear he might ignore yesterday's clear warning from Charles. Surely he wouldn't demand Diana's hand in marriage. She tensed, wondering if she should draw Diana aside. But Diana again had her ear pressed to the wall.

"I've no business with a cur," snapped Sir Waldo.

"Yes, you do." Jessup must have shouldered Sir Waldo inside, for the door slammed shut, bringing the men closer to the rear wall and making it easier to hear. "I need a thousand pounds to meet a pressing debt. Unless you supply it, I will tell Lady Beatrice about my assignations with your daughter."

"Scoundrel!" Flesh thudded against flesh.

"I may be a scoundrel, but I have no choice," Jessup growled painfully. "Without the money, I'm ruined."

"Then marry the chit. Merrimont has eyes like a hawk and will know of any assignations. He won't wed soiled goods, so she'll be free to entertain an offer."

"It is true that Giles would be appalled, but he's been too busy with Schechler to notice. I don't want a wife, especially this one. Her petty demands would drive me to distraction. So you have a choice. Pay me, and she'll live respectably as Giles's wife. Refuse, and she'll become an outcast. Can you tolerate having her under your roof for the rest of your life?"

Tears flooded Diana's face, but she remained silent. Edith pulled her close.

"You won't say a word," said Sir Waldo ominously. "No, stay in that chair. It's your turn to listen. You are alive only because I know Diana has done nothing wrong. She might flirt more than is seemly, but she would never ruin herself."

"Truth matters not," countered Jessup. "Society believes the worst of anyone, and I can supply that worst."

"I told you to listen!" Another thud reverberated through the cottage. Jessup must have tried to rise and been forced back. "You're a weak fool, Jessup, but I will overlook it this once because I've been just as weak. For years I denied that Peter is a villain, blinding myself to all evidence. That is no longer possible. Peter cheated in that card game, so you owe him nothing. I will incarcerate him when we return to the house, and he will leave on the first ship I can find. You have no debts, sir. But neither are you welcome under my roof. Use this reprieve to embrace honor. And never forget that I'll be watching. If you bend honor again, I will destroy you."

Edith pulled Diana away, tiptoeing so they would not be heard. The girl was too distraught to remain quiet much longer.

"H-he lied to me," Diana wailed when they were alone.

"Yes, he did."

"And he lied to Papa." This time anger threaded her voice.

"True."

"What can I do?"

"Nothing." She forced Diana to look at her. "You will do nothing. Sir Waldo has settled the matter, and Peter cannot hurt you again. Rejoin your guests and behave like the innocent lady you are."

"Truth." Bitterness dripped from the word. "I wish I had never sought the truth."

"Truth is often painful," Edith agreed. "But it is better than lies, for lies invariably come to light in the worst possible way. And if you think about it, you will admit that you never cared for Jessup. You were using him to make Giles jealous, just as he used you to seek his fortune." She lightened her tone, hoping her explanation was close enough to the truth that it would not cast doubt on the amulet. "Wedding preparations often drive people a little mad. It is unfortunate that you let excitement push you into hysteria, but people will forgive your exuberance if you henceforth present an image of perfect propriety—something that should not be difficult now that you know how an unscrupulous man can twist the slightest slip into scandal."

"I'm confused," admitted Diana. "I thought Jessup was a gentleman. He wooed me constantly, yet he doesn't even like me. All he wanted was money. How can I trust that Giles isn't the same? He's made no effort to please me since our betrothal."

"Giles is nothing like Jessup. Nor does he need to wed money. He has enough of his own. If you've learned anything, it should be that truth is more important than pride. Why don't you swallow yours long enough to ask *him* these questions, calmly and without recriminations? Tell him your fears, then judge by his response."

The last of Diana's color fled, leaving her white and shaking.

Chapter Seven

Charles hid his irritation as he tromped through the woods in search of a suitable Yule log. So far his newborn confidence had achieved nothing. He'd expected to make progress with Merrimont that morning, but it hadn't happened.

Unlike Inslip Manor, where the groundskeeper maintained a special grove to provide holiday decorations, Russell House boasted only a half-wild wood spread over an entire hillside. When the party had scattered in search of greens, he'd quickly lost sight of Merrimont. Miss Russell had led Edith in another direction entirely, so he'd abandoned his plans and dealt with Sir Waldo.

At least that had gone well. Sir Waldo had lured Russell away while everyone was busy in the woods. No one yet realized that Russell hadn't returned.

But Charles was still kicking himself over losing sight of Edith. Miss Russell had seemed strained when the group had gathered around the fire for chocolate and carols. Edith had looked worse. Something had clearly happened, but he'd been unable to get her alone to ask about it.

Now he faced another delay. Schechler had refused to resume negotiations. Charles couldn't get near Edith, who was with the ladies, plaiting garlands and making kissing boughs. So he'd had no choice but to join the gentlemen fetching the Yule log—and if Sir Waldo kept everyone too busy to note Russell's absence, hours could pass before they actually *found* the log that had been drying since midsummer for just this occasion.

Perhaps he should talk to Merrimont and convince him to confront Miss Russell directly. Not that he wanted to, of course. If he failed to break down the man's rigid pride, it would be impossible to resurrect the original plan. But they could at least talk about the negotiations. Schechler's latest ploy was probably meant to bring pressure on Merrimont. They all knew the man was under orders to sign an agreement before the wedding.

"Here's a log we can use," shouted Sir Waldo with false jollity.

"It's too small," complained his cousin. "That won't burn more than three hours."

Insults flew from all sides, denouncing the log with such fervor that Sir Waldo held up his hands in mock surrender. "All right. All right. We need something bigger," he conceded. "Let's keep looking." And they were off.

Charles worked his way through the crowd, which straggled badly. Half an hour passed before he admitted Merrimont wasn't there. Had he bolted?

"Damnation," he muttered. He'd not checked to see who was going before they'd left the house. Hunting the Yule log traditionally required every able-bodied gentleman in residence.

This had to be Jessup's fault.

Edith had paused before lunch long enough to report that Jessup was gone after trying to blackmail Sir Waldo. They'd been interrupted before she could supply details, but maybe Merrimont was following his erstwhile friend to find out what had happened.

He hoped not. Merrimont might blame Miss Russell.

"Here's a log that's big enough," called Sir Waldo as they reached a clearing. A massive trunk fifty feet long and nearly four in diameter lay along one edge. Years of exposure to the elements had stripped off all the bark.

"It's *too* big," someone shouted. "It won't fit in the fireplace."

"We'd need a hundred men to carry it," cried another.

"I do not understand this custom," complained Schechler as the crowd happily insulted the behemoth.

"The Yule log?" asked Charles.

Schechler nodded.

"It is a symbol of warmth and good cheer, bringing luck for the new year. Choosing the right log is important, for it will be lighted tonight and must burn through the end of Christmas if the luck is to hold. The last brand is used to light the next year's log, carrying the luck forward."

"The good cheer I can understand," he said, gesturing toward their companions, most of whom had partaken liberally of wine at luncheon and many of whom were staving off cold with nips of brandy. "But how does the burning of this log bring luck?"

"Why do people in your country drag whole trees into the house at Christmas?"

"Tradition." Schechler shrugged.

"So is this."

Schechler sank into contemplation, so Charles let his mind drift to the jolts Edith had given him yesterday—and to the kiss he couldn't forget. She was far more than a clear-minded friend. . . .

Sir Waldo led them on another lengthy circuit of the woods, finally arriving at the real Yule log. Cheers rose from all sides.

"Perfect!" shouted the cousin.

"Excellent size."

"Easy to lift."

"We will have a prosperous new year after all."

"What luck to find it so near the house!" As if the groundskeepers hadn't dragged it that far so the gentlemen wouldn't have to exert too much effort carrying it inside.

Schechler unexpectedly laid a hand on Charles's arm. "What do you know of Herr Russell the younger?"

"You mean Mr. Peter?" asked Charles.

Schechler nodded.

"He is on his way to the Caribbean to avoid arrest for fraud. Why?"

"His word is not to be trusted, then?"

"No. He speaks only the words that will serve his own dishonorable purposes. This past week he has been pressing at least three separate feuds, spreading maximum ill will about each of them."

"Ah. She was right, then." Smiling, he stepped up to grasp one of the stubby branches left to make carrying the log easy. "We will carry this lucky log indoors, then perhaps we can complete our business."

Charles helped hoist the log. "I'm sure we can." He blessed Edith for her advice to Schechler yesterday. She'd made the man think—just as she'd made *him* think. It was a talent he wished he'd recognized sooner. . . .

Edith kept a close eye on Diana as they left the church that evening. She wasn't sure the girl would make it home without bursting into tears.

Christmas Eve was usually a day filled with excitement as the company decorated the house, shared fond recollections of previous holidays, tested the kissing boughs, sampled wassail and a host of special treats.

But Charles's amulet had turned it into the worst day of Diana's life.

She believed in its magic. Believed that everything she saw or heard today would be true. So for the first time in her life, she had focused her attention beyond herself, noticing much that she would usually have ignored—Giles riding down the drive with Jessup, deep in conversation, then retiring to his room without a word on his return; a cousin's parody portraying Diana as an arrogant queen who demeaned her suitors with frivolous demands; a gossip's speculation that Giles's mistress would offer him a refuge from his shrewish wife so, of course, he would keep her on. . . .

Diana had been close to tears twice, but she'd kept a smile on her face and remained cordial. Not until Giles arrived late for Christmas services and remained in the back of the church had she cracked. So public a cut was impossible to ignore.

Edith caught Charles's eye, silently pleading with him to do something. He tugged his ear, then pulled Giles aside when the others headed for the path that twisted through the woods to the manor. It skirted the dense thickets that crowned the low cliff formed when the stream had cut into the hillside.

"Let everyone get ahead of us," murmured Edith as

Diana's fists clenched. "This is your chance. You and Giles must talk honestly. Tonight. Share your truths, then listen to his. Only then can you decide what to do."

Diana nodded. Her hand clutched at her bosom as if drawing strength from the amulet.

"Good. Stay in control. Hysterics will make it impossible to learn anything useful." She nodded toward the vicar, who remained outside the church. "Since you don't want an audience, we will wait just beyond the first bend. When the men catch up, I will accompany Lord Charles to the house. Just make sure you and Giles return before we light the Yule log."

"Thank you." Diana relaxed, giving Edith hope that she would approach the coming scene calmly. Now all she could do was pray that Charles could draw some concession from Giles that would give this discussion a starting point.

"You seem oddly subdued for a man approaching the altar," said Charles as he and Merrimont left the church behind. With Edith waiting barely a hundred feet away, he didn't have time for subtlety. "Problems?"

"Schechler is an ass. Jessup has betrayed me. Diana—"

"Schechler is no longer a problem. We reached an agreement this afternoon. You can look it over tomorrow." Charles had gained more concessions than he'd expected. He owed Edith for puncturing Schechler's stubbornness, but in retrospect it was her effect on himself that had made the real difference. Now that he no longer feared that he was a fake, the wariness that had protected him from exposure was gone—which had turned their session into an exchange of ideas instead of a battle.

"Good work. Are you off, then?"

"I'll stay for your wedding."

"If there is a wedding."

"Why wouldn't there be? Jessup is no loss—the man is weak, making him a useful tool for those who would harm you. You have better friends."

Merrimont hesitated as the woods closed around them, blocking the moonlight. But perhaps the dark removed the barrier that had been holding his frustration in check, for he suddenly burst into speech. "But that's the point. I trusted him! I didn't see his weakness or understand how it might affect me until he told me about Russell's plot. Diana has been so odd lately that I fear she's another I can't trust."

"Odd?"

"She's a demanding shrew one minute and a spoiled brat the next. Hoyden. Flirt. Harpy. Wanton—" He fisted his hands. "How am I supposed to live with her? If I take her to London, she could destroy my reputation without a second thought. What did I do to deserve this?"

"She is young yet," Charles reminded him.

"Young! She is the veriest infant. I can't believe I overlooked such faults. I need a wife, not a daughter. It is not my place to teach her how to go on in the world."

"Her training is all that you could want," said Charles firmly. "Miss Knolton is an exceptional teacher."

"Which means nothing if the student refuses to learn." Merrimont slashed a shrub with his cane. "Can you imagine Diana at a diplomatic dinner? Her pouting will make me a laughingstock. And demanding that all eyes remain on her insults every other lady in the room."

"I can't believe she will be that bad. Granted, this house party is making her frantic, but she should settle quite well once you are wed. She has too much pride to embarrass herself."

"But what if she doesn't settle? What if she turns into another Lady Seaton?"

Charles had no response to that, for he could too easily imagine it. Lady Seaton was notorious for her liaisons—her husband had finally shut her in the country under guard until she produced an undeniably legitimate heir, then washed his hands of her, refusing even to share the same roof. But Merrimont was too sensitive to gossip to survive such a scandal.

"I was a fool to offer for her," Merrimont continued sadly. "All she cares about is herself."

Miss Russell let out a muffled shriek. Footsteps rushed away. Moments later her terrified scream slashed the night.

"Diana!" shouted Edith as the crack of breaking branches ended in a loud thud.

Merrimont shoved Charles aside and sped toward the ominous silence.

Charles followed to find Edith clinging to a tree. No one else was in sight. "What happened?" He grabbed her shoulders to make her look at him.

"She fled his truth. By the time I remembered the cliff . . ." She pointed to the edge, only ten feet away.

Merrimont's voice slashed the forest. "Diana! Wake up. Oh, God! Wake up! I need you, love."

Edith held Charles back when he would have followed. "Giles is with her. He'll call if he needs help, but I doubt she's dead. It can't be more than six feet down, and the shrubbery broke her fall."

Words tumbled from Merrimont's lips. Promises. Pleas. Vows of everlasting love. Eventually Miss Russell's voice responded.

"Did she fake this?" demanded Charles.

"No. Call it fate. Or perhaps your amulet is more powerful than you thought. Fleeing one truth has led her to another. We can let them settle this themselves. Finally." She turned toward the path and stumbled.

"Are you all right?" He pulled her against his side.

"Of course. Why?"

"You also screamed."

"What did you expect? When she disappeared over the edge . . . That cliff is a dozen feet high in places, with jagged rocks along the base. It took me a moment to recognize where we were."

"I see. Stay," he added when she picked up speed.

"Why?"

"My heart hasn't quite settled. Nor has yours," he added, feeling her tremors.

"I will be fine, my lord. And I should be there to cover Diana's absence."

"They will think you are with her. Are you afraid to stand in the dark with me?"

"Should I be?"

He wished he could see her expression, but no light penetrated the shadows beneath the trees. If that tremor meant what he hoped it did . . .

He wanted to wait until he was sure, but perhaps he should trust his judgment one more time, as he'd done with Schechler and Merrimont. It had been sound then. . . .

He kissed her.

It was better than the first time. Much better.

"Charles?" she murmured as he nibbled her ear.

"Hmm?"

"Why are you doing this?"

"Because I need to."

"Oh." Her hands moved under his coat, stroking his back as he pulled her closer. "Since you've been away from town for several days, I suppose you do."

He scowled. "That's not what I meant."

"It isn't?"

"I'm leading up to a marriage proposal. You deserve more out of life than parading chits through the Marriage Mart every year. Your family deserves more than struggling in a cottage."

"I'm not a charity case, my lord." She tried to pull away. "Nor am I a convenient way to thwart your father's matchmaking."

He refused to let go. "That isn't what I meant."

"You are saying a lot you don't mean tonight."

"Damnation!" He released her to drag his hands through his hair. "I'm making a thorough muck of this."

"That you are." Her voice sounded suspiciously light.

"Are you laughing at me?"

"A bit. I've not seen you this flustered since Lady Beatrice's drawing room."

He kissed her again—thoroughly—then led her out of the woods so he could see her face. It didn't improve his composure, for it was as impassive as the most accomplished diplomat's. "Let me start over, Edith," he said, laying his heart out for her to trample if she chose. "This has nothing to do with Inslip. I love you."

"You're serious!" She stared.

"Very. I don't believe in magic amulets, but I do believe in you. I need you, Edith."

"But you could have anyone."

"I want *you*. Is there any chance you want me, too?"

"Of course, but—"

He stopped her protest in the best way possible—with another long kiss that nearly set the grounds on fire. "Satisfied?"

"Not entirely." When he raised his brows, she sighed. "Are you sure, Charles? We've spent the day wrapped in the Christmas spirit and surrounded by good cheer, then finished with a scare. It is bound to affect your thinking."

"No. You forced me to trust my judgment, and I've discovered that it's as sound as you claim. It's love I feel for you, Edith. Not lust. Not infatuation. Not Christmas spirit. Love is more powerful than any of those. And far more lasting. I've lived around people in love all my life. They've always described love as the ultimate magic, and now I know what they mean. This is right, as nothing was before. You are right—right for me. Do you understand?"

She nodded, her hand lifting to stroke his cheek in wonder.

He pulled her into another heady embrace, his desperation easing when she joined him wholeheartedly. He nearly wept when he had to end it.

"More," she murmured huskily. "You stopped too soon."

"The rest will have to wait. One month, love. Long enough to gather my family and yours. Then we will wed."

Edith stared at him, speechless, still barely believing her ears. He loved her. He wanted to marry her. Her, a dissipated gamester's penniless daughter who had worked as a companion and governess for eleven years.

"You haven't said yes." His tongue flicked her nose.

"Yes." When he pulled her hard against him, she repeated it. "Yes, Charles. Yes."

"You're sure?"

"I've had a disgusting *tendre* for you since the first time I saw you. That tumbled hopelessly into love yesterday. Stupid of me, or so I thought."

He smiled. "Jacob was right. I think I've been in love with you since the day you ruined my favorite coat."

"I thought I would die of embarrassment, though it was your own fault."

"Mine?" He turned toward the house, keeping one arm firmly around her.

"Yours. I'd no idea you would be making morning calls that day—it isn't your habit. If you hadn't been suddenly in front of me in all your blinding elegance, I would never have tripped. Then I was so flustered, I couldn't get up again."

He laughed. "That's a story you can tell our grandchildren, love." Merrimont was embracing Diana under the kissing bough hanging from the portico, so he stopped, pulling Edith closer as he gazed up at the heavens. A falling star blazed a trail toward the Christmas star, its radiance adding to the joy bursting through his heart. "There's the Christmas star, Edith. Can you feel its promise? We belong together. Until the end of time."

She laid her head on his shoulder, raising a hand to cup the star's light. The night was so clear that it seemed to hover just beyond her fingertips. "It's beautiful, Charles. And you're right. Love *is* the ultimate magic. I'm yours. Forever."

"As I'm yours." Merrimont still blocked the door, so he pulled her closer. "Let's indulge in that magic one more time before we go inside."

His lips found hers and lingered. . . .

The Two Dancing Daughters

Edith Layton

His laughter was hollow, but so was his stomach. "I like sympathy as much as any man, but I don't want pity," the old soldier said.

"I'm not offering you pity, old man," his friend said, lowering his voice. "I'm offering a job of work. Christmas is coming. I thought you could use a few extra shekels. You'll have to work to get them, though. Ain't charity. Not that most men wouldn't be squeamish about charity, but few are as touchy as you! Offered to loan you a few quid and you almost bit my head off. So here's an offer of honest work. What's wrong with that?"

The other man smiled. "Henry, you offered me more money than a few quid. That isn't it. I *am* sensitive about being without funds. But I worked for my bread for the last fifteen years, and damned if I can get used to being without employment." He put up a hand. "It's not my fault, I know. No one wants a grizzled old gimp in their service."

"You ain't grizzled!" Henry protested. "A few gray hairs here and there, and you crop your hair so short no one could see them without a quizzing glass anyway. Been around, that's true. But there ain't a smarter, better man I'd want as a friend than you!"

"But I won't work at that. Friendship is pleasure. I need a job of work, Henry. A real one."

They sat in opposite chairs in one of London's most exclusive gentleman's clubs. The weak winter sunshine that struggled through the long-paned windows showed them both clearly. Sir Henry was a plump fellow, his portliness making him look older than his five and thirty years.

His guest, Major Gabriel Blanchard, ret., was a year younger and looked ten years older, at least at first glance. A second glance showed that the close-cropped hair had more brown than silver, the lines around his mouth were from pain, not age, and the hard planes of his face that made him look so flinty could be warmed to boyishness by one of his infrequent smiles. That smile was so winning it made a viewer forget the deep weariness in his gray gaze. He was lean, with wide shoulders topping a sinewy frame. He looked like a man used to work, and that work done with his body and not just his mind and hands.

His fitness wasn't the only thing that set him apart from his friend and the other gentlemen in the exclusive club. Major Blanchard's clothes were well-made and clean but years out of date, and the leather of his half boots, though shined to a high polish, was scarred, though not as deeply as the thin line that clove his left cheek.

"I'm a wreck," he said now, with one of those infrequent smiles. "They wouldn't take me back even if the war were still on. So I'm looking for work, my friend. Not a gift. The thing is, although I'm educated, I'm not trained to anything but cavalry and command. Know anyone hiring a private army?" he joked.

"Matter of fact," Henry said slowly, "I do."

Gabriel sat very still, but tilted his head to the side.

"There's this fellow I know . . ." Henry said, and then scowled. "Damn, but I don't like this, but it is work, and you did say . . ."

"That I wanted work. Yes. Not all of us are lucky in our forebears. You know my father went through the estate and what he left, he left to the eldest, my brother Francis. As second son, I got my colors bought and went to the army. If there'd been a third son, it would have been the church for him, poor devil, even if he'd had less religion than a stone. That's the way of it. Ours is an old family with old ideas. Puritan stock, to boot, only escaping the revenge of the Reformation because of family ties. The reason we never won a title was our stubbornness. We refused the favors of kings as well as the advice of friends down through the ages.

"The Puritan strain ran out fairly fast," he added with a sad smile, "though the stubbornness clung. My father went through our money in spite of what people told him. My brother did too, in his turn. There's nothing left but a house in Devon I inherited from an uncle, which I cannot afford to reclaim, and the manor where I spent my childhood, and it's moldering. Not that it matters to me—I can't even get an invitation to it."

"You and Francis on the outs now?"

Gabriel shrugged. "Who knows? He took what he could wring from the estate and went to Paris for the celebrations of the Peace. He was in Brussels before that. So was I. But I was on the battlefield and he was in the ballroom. He came to see me in hospital, after, and wished me well. He didn't stay long. I'd lent him money to repair his fortunes. He didn't repay it. I make no doubt my money's seen more fun than I have. At least it went to the gaming tables at the best spas in Europe. I came home."

Gabriel sighed. "I loaned money to more men than Francis. An officer has obligations and responsibilities. Someday, perhaps, I'll see those funds again. Even if I don't, I'd have done it anyway. We were taught responsibility as well as pride."

"Aye, and your brother has that?" Henry said angrily.

Gabriel's smile was crooked. "He's not dead yet. Who can say? But as for me, as of now, I'm little more than a bankrupt. I've enough for my rent here in town and can pay for my dinners, so don't put your hand in your pocket! But that's the extent of it. Now. Have you employment for me? I have Christmas gifts to buy."

Henry raised an eyebrow.

"For my men and their families, especially the families of those who weren't fortunate enough to come back to England to complain as I'm doing," Gabriel said. "So. Out with it. If it's honest work, I'll do it. Anything—except for being a dancing master, of course," he added, tapping the head of the walking stick by his side. "But be assured," he said quickly, "I can get around, and quickly if I must. Just not gracefully."

"Don't need a ballet master! I heard of a position where they need a guard, actually."

Gabriel raised an eyebrow.

His friend fidgeted. "Not a watchman, per se, or I wouldn't even have told you about it. Nothing so menial. More in the line of an investigator as well as a guard is what it is. And the pay would be fitting. That is, they'd come down heavy for whomever took the job."

"Then why don't they hire someone from Bow Street?"

Henry sniffed. "They did. Both times the Runners failed. And this job also needs someone who won't be out of place in the social world. I know some Runners have manners, but those who do are famous, and this friend wants someone who may be able to ask questions in high places as well as low without anyone knowing what he's about. The job would have some snooping to it."

"You interest me," Gabriel said.

"And they may need a man of action," Henry said worriedly.

"I'm even more interested. I can still use my fists, you know. As well as my stick, and my sword, and pistol. Tell me more."

Henry sighed. "This chap I know—a baron actually—has two daughters. Young and beautiful, both of them, and the family rich as they can hold together. The chits ain't girls, but they ain't on the shelf neither, just cosseted by their papa and in no hurry to marry—until now. One of them is in the toils of a foreigner, some prince is what he says he is, but he's a fortune hunter, for certain. Thing is, she's forbidden to see him. Other thing is, she is. Seeing him, I mean. Or so her father thinks, at least. There's evidence she sneaks out at night, her sister beside her, but no one has ever caught them at it."

"Why not?" Gabriel asked with interest.

Henry's honest face creased in a frown. "Smoky business. Footmen fall asleep, maids go to their beds early, the butler wakes up bleary-eyed and claims he never saw nor heard a thing in the night. But in the morning, the girls look exhausted, their finest gowns are rumpled, and their dancing slippers show clear signs of use."

His friend's shout of laughter woke some of the gentlemen drowsing in their deep chairs.

Gabriel bowed his apologies to the newly woken gentlemen. "Sorry about that," he said in a softer voice. "But it's your own fault. That was one of my favorite fairy stories when I was in nursery. Come now, what is the job, really?"

Henry looked affronted. "No fairy story. That's the *real* story."

Now Gabriel frowned. "Then someone's pulling your leg. Don't you remember? You must have heard it. 'The Twelve Dancing Princesses,' I think it was. About twelve sisters who stole out at night to dance with a demon king and his brothers."

"Ain't twelve," Henry said with awful dignity. "Just two, and if you don't want to pursue the matter, I'll let it drop."

"Don't get on your high horse with me," Gabriel said. "We've known each other too long for that. So, it's true? Well, then, it sounds almost too easy. I'll reread the story and take the job." He leaned over and swatted his friend on the shoulder. "Don't look at me like that either. I'm joking. And I'm sorry I doubted you. Actually, it sounds too good to be true, in that it seems like the perfect employment for me. In fact, if I do well at it, that could be a novel way to make my bread in the future—as an investigator. I'd like that. Enough intrigue to keep me interested, and I can use my skills, impaired as they are. Tell me where to go and I'll do it, and thank you for it too."

"You sure you can handle it alone?" Henry asked worriedly. "You've only been home a few months and out of bed for a matter of weeks."

"I can, and I will, and I should," Gabriel said, rising to his feet. "Now, though I'd love to join you for dinner, I have a previous engagement." Gabriel didn't mention the apparent fact that he couldn't afford a dinner in this club. He trusted Henry knew it, as well as the fact that he'd be insulted if a free meal was offered.

"I have to tell the baron I've found someone. I'll give him your name and put in a few words, then send you in his direction."

"Thanks, old friend," Gabriel said.

Henry brushed off the thanks, and then stood unhappily watching his friend make his halting way to the door. Fit as Gabriel looked, he walked with a stick, and it was clear from the way he had to work to move his stiff left leg that he needed it.

"I think I've found a job of work," Gabriel said when he came into his flat that evening.

"That so?" his valet and old battle companion, Hart, said with interest.

"Aye, my old friend Henry put me on to it," Gabriel said as he shrugged his greatcoat off into Hart's waiting hands.

Sergeant John Hart, recently retired from His Majesty's service, was a neat, sandy-haired man who had seen even more battles than his master.

"A well-paying job," Gabriel went on as he eased himself down in a chair at the table in the room that served as their kitchen and dining room. "And the first thing I'll do is give you your back salary."

"The first thing you'll do is see a proper physician," Hart said as he placed a bowl of soup and half a loaf of fresh bread in front of his master.

"Second thing," Gabriel said. "Your pay comes first. The physician would only take my money to say the same things the others did. You have to be paid because you keeping doing the same things, without pay." He took a spoonful of the thick soup, sipped it, and sighed. "Delicious. How you manage to cook this way from scraps I'll never know. And why you stay on with me to do it is a bigger mystery."

"November the third in the year 1811," Hart said promptly.

Gabriel broke off a piece of bread and dipped it in the soup. "It's an officer's job to protect his men. No thanks are necessary."

"None offered. I only gave you some soup, sir. So the job is . . . ?"

"Some rich gent's beautiful young daughters are sneaking out at night and carrying on with unsuitable company. They've either bribed, drugged, or outwitted the servants set to watch them, so no one knows where they're off to. I'd be expected to find out where the girls go, and with whom. It's thought that one of them goes to meet a lover, and that both girls go dancing with him. Speaking of which, it should be a waltz in the park for me, if I get the assignment."

Hart's silence was enormous.

Gabriel put down his spoon. "You don't think I can do it?"

"I know you can ride like the devil and fire and hit any target while you're at it. I know you can charge a pack of bloodthirsty villains without blinking. I've seen you best a man with your fives, and your sword. You can inspire men to walk up to death's door and knock on it with you. But outwit a female? No, *two* of them? Young ones, with all their wiles and graces? That I'd not make book on."

Gabriel blinked. "You think I'm too easily beguiled, do you?" he asked as he addressed his soup again.

"Nay," his servant said in a softer voice, "but you're too softhearted, sir, and I worry that they'll cozen you, and fill your heart with sympathy with their lies."

"It won't happen. These are ladies of Fashion. You don't know the breed. I do. They'll think of me as furniture. Trust me, they'll have absolutely no respect for the intelligence of any servant, especially an old broken-down soldier, nor any interest in him in any other way, either. And this old soldier has more interest in their papa's pocketbook than in all their wiles and graces. I intend for us to have a fine cooked goose for Christmas and," he added, with a flash of a smile, "I don't mean for it to be me!"

"Papa is hiring on a new guard," the young lady announced as she came into her sister's bedchamber.

"No!" her sister said, turning her head from her looking glass to stare. "A *third* one?"

Rosamund nodded. "And this time he's not even bothering to pretend the fellow will be a footman."

"And with Christmas coming! What are we to do?" her sister Sylvia moaned. She looked into the glass again and saw the reflection of their maid hovering nearby. "It's a great tribulation for one's father not to trust one," she said theatrically. "My hair is perfect, Iris. Thank you. You may go now. And if, perchance, you hear anything in the servant's hall about this new man, there'll be a new silver comb in it for you, if it's true."

The maid curtsied and left the room, leaving the two sisters alone.

"I'm not happy about this," Rosamund said as she wandered over to the window and looked down at the street. It was a bitterly cold day, and an exclusive district, so there was little to see but the bare branches of the trees that lined the entrance to the park.

"Oh, fiddle," Sylvia said. "Three's a charm."

"Exactly," Rosamund said gravely.

"A charm for me! For us, I mean. You know Alberon says the need for secrecy will be over soon. You know that silly rhyme he says, but it comforts me. He always says: 'I mean to make you mine by Christmas Day, when there's no more reason for delay.' "

She spun around in her chair and looked at her sister imploringly. "Oh, Rosie, dearest, please don't put on that face again! I know deception goes against the grain, but Alberon says he can't say anything to me before Christmas. He has an exalted title, so that must have something to do with it; I'm a foreigner to him too, you know. But then he says he'll have something to ask me. I know what I'll answer. Then we'll be engaged, and you can go your own way. . . . Though I do hope that way will be with Robin or Tom, or any of the gentlemen in Alberon's court. They all adore you. And why not? You're beautiful and wise, and so good and . . ."

". . . and not at all comfortable," Rosamund finished for her. "I can't be. I don't like secrecy."

"There'll be no need of it soon, I tell you. Papa won't let me keep seeing a man who hasn't declared his intentions, but Alberon has, to me. So, please, why can't we go on as we do for just a little longer? Where's the harm in a little dancing and a lot of laughter?"

Rosamund sighed. Sylvia was persuasive when she became emotional; it was devastating to see those haunting eyes fill with tears. She was so lovely and looked so fragile, with her golden hair and deep blue eyes. Sylvia's hair was truly her crowning glory, long, shining and fair, so like that of the princess locked in a tower that they'd heard about in fairy stories when they were girls. Rosamund could almost envision a prince climbing up a rope of it, except that Sylvia had a slender, graceful form, and surely the weight of a hero would have pulled her right out the window. When she'd told Sylvia that, the two had giggled like mad things every time anyone mentioned the story. They had that sort of easy communion with each other—until recently.

Rosamund, the older by a year, had a more buxom figure, inky-black hair and dark, upwardly tilted eyes. People scarcely believed she and Sylvia were sisters. Their mama had passed away while they were still in the nursery, and the two had become close and stayed that way, in spite of the fact that their temperaments were as different as their looks.

Sylvia was lighthearted and emotional. Rosamund was more thoughtful and kept her emotions to herself. Which was good, their father had joked, otherwise the house would be unlivable with two little minxes underfoot ready to set up a howl if their whimsical demands for odd fancies weren't instantly satisfied. What he didn't know was that Rosamund filled Sylvia's head with the fancies she would wail about.

"Snow White and Rose Red, Papa used to call us," Rosamund said sadly. "And so we were."

Sylvia smiled in remembrance. Their father was indulgent of his two motherless chicks. They'd gotten the name of Snow White and Rose Red when they were little, after they'd begged him for a dog that wasn't needed for the hunt or the chase. Inspired by their favorite fairy story, they picked a great brown shaggy beast and named him "Bear." Sylvia wept and Rosamund sighed when all their kisses failed to turn Bear into a "Prince" instead. Now that they were older, they had only to ask for clothes, or jewels, or treats and they were given them. But their fond papa wasn't as indulgent with their suitors.

"And so we shall always be as close as those two sisters were," Sylvia said promptly. "Alberon says he'd be happy for you to come to live with us."

"Where?" Rosamund asked quickly, seizing the opportunity.

"Why, in his country, silly."

"Which is . . . ?"

"East of the sun and west of the moon," Sylvia said with exasperation. "You know where. He's told you a dozen times."

"And each time a different name."

"Well, of course. That's only natural. The land's changed hands and names so many times in the wars even he forgets sometimes. That's why he hasn't been able to go back. But now, with the Peace declared, he waits for word so he can return home with all his honors intact. He's only a duke, but there he is a prince among men, he said."

"So he said, yes," Rosamund said. He said quite a lot, often speaking in teasing tones and rhymes, which ought to have sounded jolly, but sounded more sinister to her with every passing day. She saw what her sister admired in her foreign lord. What breathing female would not? The Duc d'Alberon was imperially slender, with a fiercely handsome face, dark and curling hair, and something even darker in his curling white smile and amused black eyes. She shivered at the remembrance of the look in those bold eyes.

Sylvia's lover ought not to look at her sister the way he did, Rosamund thought. Or was she only imagining it, because of her dislike for the fellow? Because no matter how charming he was, or how good his intentions, when he took Sylvia away, he would ruin Rosamund's life. He'd take his bride to that far-off foreign land, from which, he vowed, she'd never want to return. And Rosamund would regret the loss of her sister, even if it were true that Sylvia would go to a land where each day faded into a night filled with endless delight. That too, he always said.

Sylvia had met him in the park one day when Rosamund had been home with a headache. Now he courted Sylvia in the shadows. Rosamund didn't think Sylvia should continue to see him in secret, or that her beau should arrange for her to do it. But when she said so to Sylvia, her sister wept piteously and begged her to understand. She also said that Rosamund didn't understand because she had never experienced love or the pain of it. And that, of course, was true.

But Rosamund was the elder, if only by a year, and was always aware of it. So she couldn't let Sylvia go alone. And although all the couple ever did was dance through the night, Rosamund wouldn't stop going along with them, watching to be sure that was all they ever did before her sister's love made his formal declaration to her.

Until then she'd keep her sister's secrets, and that way, keep her counsel too. It pained Rosamund to deceive their father, but she did it because she and Sylvia were that close and loved each other that much, and she could no more betray her sister than she could trust her sister's suitor.

"And what shall you tell poor Arthur then?" Rosamund said softly.

Sylvia paused in her efforts to turn a silky lock of her golden hair so it would curl over one ear. She shrugged her white shoulders. "Why, I'll ask him to wish me happy, of course. And so he should. We've known each other forever, after all, and he would wish the best for me."

"He thought he was that," Rosamund said softly, remembering the young viscount's lifelong admiration for her sister.

"Well, so he was, until I met Alberon. Arthur will understand."

"Would you, if he'd been the one to find someone else?"

Sylvia spun around to look at her sister, her big blue eyes filling with tears. "I knew it! You hate Alberon! You don't want me to marry him!"

Rosamund wasn't sure what she wanted, except not to see her sister cry. It had always been that way. "I don't hate him," she said at once. "I just don't know him."

Sylvia smiled, her tears forgotten. "Well, so you will.

It's just that you haven't had the chance to speak to him very much. I've only known him since October. That's not a very long time, I know. But you don't know him as well as I do, because, I admit, I take up every minute of his time when I'm with him. I'll change that!"

"No, don't!" Rosamund said uneasily. "I'll get to know him in my own time. You know how awkward forced conversations are."

"Very well," Sylvia said brightly, forgetting her woes quickly, as she always preferred to do. "And so when do we get a look at this new guard?"

"As soon as Papa hires him on, I suppose."

"And what do you think we should do with him?" Sylvia said, with a curling smile that looked very much like her suitor's.

"The usual," Rosamund said, repressing a shiver at seeing the unfamiliar smile on that beloved familiar face. "That is, of course, unless we have to do the unusual."

Gabriel gave his coat to the butler and followed him to Baron Latimer's study, where his prospective employer awaited.

"Ah, Major Blanchard," the thickset, pleasant-faced older gentleman said as he rose from behind his desk. "Do come in. Have a seat. Can I offer you something to take the chill off the day?"

"Thank you, but no," Gabriel said. "It has never been my habit to drink on the job, and for all I know you may have one for me."

"Well said!" the baron laughed. "Very well, then, sir, let's get straight to it." He came out from behind the desk and took a deep chair opposite the one he indicated Gabriel should have. "You come highly recommended," he told Gabriel as he seated himself, his eyes assessing his visitor. "This job of work I have requires discretion, wisdom and stealth. As a former officer, I don't doubt you have the first two, but you seem a straightforward sort of fellow. Can you manage the last?"

Gabriel sat, and placed his walking stick at his right hand. He liked the fact that the baron was himself discreet enough not to stay behind a desk like a superior, but rather met him as a guest.

"Stealth?" Gabriel asked. "Let me be straightforward as you say I am. I heard that you have a problem with your daughters' meeting an unsuitable suitor on the sly. I also heard you've hired others to follow them who have failed to see what they've been up to. Therefore it follows that your daughters are alive and awake on every suit, on the lookout for pursuers. So I'll try to use stealth where I can. Obviously you see I can't creep. But there are other kinds of stealth. I wouldn't have survived the wars if I didn't know them. Observation, careful planning and surprise are as important to a campaign as stealth. So, if you mean can I track them without their knowledge? That, yes, I can, and I will."

"Ho!" the baron said with delight. "I like the cut of you, sir! To the point, and riding over rough ground as light as you can." He peered at Gabriel thoughtfully. "You have what I need, I think. Experience at command, bravery and good breeding."

Gabriel looked up at that.

"I'll be as straightforward as you are," the baron explained. "I had you investigated too. Your record of bravery and valor is commendable, unimpeachable. But your name is an old one and Briarwood is a grand estate, so I was shocked to see you seeking employment. Then I discovered the extent of debt and your brother's whereabouts, and all came clear."

He sat back, his pleasant face creasing in a scowl. "Right, then, to the crux of it. My daughters, who heretofore have always been honest as the livelong day, now no longer confide in me and I believe actively deceive me. They are good girls. The man—I will not call him a gentleman—responsible is a foreigner, though those who overheard him speaking to my daughters say he speaks English like a native. He styles himself the 'Duc d'Alberon,' though I've no notion what country he's a duke in, if any. Whatever he is, his intentions seem clear to me. I've money, Major. More than I inherited, because unlike many men in our world, I don't believe there's any shame in making more. Our title is not so very old, you see," he said with a rueful smile. "My father earned his title and paid too much for it too, in my opinion.

"So I admire a man who works for his bread," he

continued, looking at Gabriel with approval. Then he frowned again. "This fellow my daughters are involved with wants money he doesn't have to earn. I'd make book on it! He wants my daughters, and he doesn't want me to interfere with his courtship, so he's got them sneaking out to meet him every night!" He pounded his fist on the arm of his chair with each of these last words, and then sat back, the picture of frustration.

"I understand," Gabriel said. "But 'daughters'? Surely, he's only courting one."

"Aye. But though they're different as day from night, they're close as peas in a pod, and neither will tattle on the other, so I don't know which of them it is. One would always protect the other, and the other would always follow the lead of the other, if you get my drift. Bah. I'm not saying it well. But you'll see."

"So you want me to take the position?" Gabriel asked.

"I do. But I tell you, two likely fellows have already failed, and my entire staff, though loyal to a man and woman, couldn't spy out a thing. I tell you, sir, it's almost uncanny. I bought this house just this past summer because it was the best on the street. The former owner just up and disappeared one day, and so it took forever for the estate to be settled, and longer to sell because of the price. It's on the park, which pleased me, because to tell the truth I miss my estate and don't care much for London. But I wanted to get the girls settled with proper gentlemen, and there weren't that many eligible ones for them back home."

The baron looked uneasy. "But it turned out that the woods are thickest in this end of the park, and it's altogether too dark and wild for my tastes. There are ancient trees, and it's all tangles and brambles in places, like something out of a witches' tale of gingerbread houses and trolls and such. Even my horse doesn't care to go cantering on the paths near here. Others must have thought the same, because the house was empty a long time before I took it. I thought that was because of the price, but now I wonder. And I am not a fanciful fellow."

"Nor am I," Gabriel said. "I don't believe in spirits

or magic. I believe in my own eyes and ears. I think what you have are two clever lasses and one villain. I'll discover the whole of it, sir."

"More than one villain," the baron grumbled. "At first, the girls were occasionally seen walking in the park with this fellow, but no more. I could find out nothing about him, not even where he lives!" he added angrily. "He's covered his tracks too well. But those who saw him say his friends, each one of them said to be more suspicious-looking than the other, usually accompanied him. You'll see, or so I hope. Well, no time like the present," he said, rising to his feet. "I'd like you to meet my girls."

Gabriel got to his feet too. "And you'll tell them I've been hired on as what, sir?"

"No sense lying," the baron said. "They're too clever, and you don't look like any footman, butler or manservant I ever clapped eyes on."

"Too true," Gabriel said with a pained smile. "But if you didn't tell them, I might be able to discover more."

"What? Not tell them? Good heavens, man, how could that help? I expect you to stay on here with us for the duration. No sense in your staying outside. Thing is, the girls somehow leave here with no one knowing how they do it. It's part of your job to find out. I had a fellow slept in the garbage bins in the alley by the back door for a week, and he slept like a top while my girls literally danced off into the night. No, sir, I need a man on the spot. Still interested?"

Gabriel hesitated. He didn't want to stay on in another man's house, like a servant. But if he wanted to be able to make Christmas jolly for those he was responsible for, he would have to take this job. "Yes, sir. I am," he said.

"Good," the baron said with sympathy. "I'll raise the wages because I can see it ain't to your liking."

"Thank you, sir. But I don't think it will be that costly in the end. I intend to settle the matter by Christmas, at the latest. It's only a matter of two weeks, but if I can't do it by then, there's either nothing to settle or I'm not the man for the job."

"Fair enough," the baron said. He went to the door,

opened it and called, "Beecham. Tell my daughters to come in here now. I want to talk with them."

Gabriel got out of his chair and stood, leaning on his walking stick, waiting. He expected the girls would hate him, and didn't blame them. But he didn't need to be on good terms with them. He was never on good terms with the French, and though they'd wounded him, he had eventually won. Or at least, he thought ruefully, he still stood, even though it was with difficulty.

His musings were cut short as the baron's daughters entered the room. Gabriel was glad he was holding his walking stick, or else he believed he might have staggered. He couldn't remember ever having seen two such lovely young women, nor two that looked less like sisters, and even less like the spoiled and arrogant young wenches he had expected.

One of the young women was fair as the dawn, slender and lithe, with wide blue eyes and long silky blond hair. She looked more like a vision from the fairy world than London town, and gazed at him with a sweet and tender smile on her lips. But it was the other that his eyes were drawn to and had difficulty straying from. She had masses of jet curls high atop her well-shaped head, an amazingly plush pink mouth, a perfectly etched little nose, finely arched brows and dark, tilted sloe eyes that brimmed with curiosity and sparkled with intelligence.

But Gabriel hadn't survived as a soldier all those years by letting himself be disarmed for long. He gripped his walking stick and took a deep breath. These lovely creatures were now his responsibility and it didn't matter that they looked like angels. They had behaved badly, and he was here to stop that.

"Sylvia, Rosamund, here is Major Blanchard," the baron said. "Blanchard, here are my daughters: Rosamund's the dark one, Sylvia's the blonde. Girls, the major is going to stay on here with us for a while."

The baron's daughters didn't so much as blink. They looked at Gabriel with interest and, he thought, secret amusement. They didn't question their father or ask their visitor his reason for staying on. They only looked at him, summing him up the way he supposed opposing generals took stock of the troops they saw before them.

"Happy to make your acquaintance, ladies," Gabriel said as he sketched a brief bow. "I fear it won't be a long acquaintance, though, since I can only stay on until Christmas Day."

"Oh, fine!" Sylvia said, and then blushed, and added, "Because I'm sure you wish to be with your loved ones on that day, of course."

"Of course," he said, and added with as much innocence as he could muster, "Don't we all?"

Sylvia smilingly agreed. But her sister gave Gabriel a long and measuring look. He returned it, and he could swear he almost could hear the clash of swords raised, and met.

The bedchamber that Gabriel was given was better furnished than his entire set of rooms, and the bed in it looked warm and inviting. But he'd no intention of sleeping tonight. After he'd been introduced to the baron's household staff and they'd been instructed that he had the run of the house, he'd gone back to his own flat rather than sending for his bag because he had his own instructions for Hart. He was putting away his things when there was a tap on his door.

"Major?" the footman said. "The baron wonders why you haven't come down to dinner, sir."

"I brought no formal clothes with me," Gabriel said.

"No matter, sir. Dinners are informal here."

"Very well," Gabriel said with a sigh, because he'd planned a solitary dinner and short nap before a long, wakeful night. "Tell the baron that I'll be there shortly."

But it was a while before he navigated the long stair and entered the baron's dining parlor. Nevertheless, he could see dinner had been held for him. "Forgive me," he said as he entered the room and saw the baron and his daughters. "I hadn't expected to be asked to dine with you."

He was sorry he'd made them wait for their dinners, but pleased that his entrance had stopped all conversation. They obviously saw how awkwardly he made his way to the chair that a footman held out for him. He'd wanted them to.

His leg *was* stiff. It hurt like the very devil to bend

his knee. But he could, and could manage well enough with it. Tonight he didn't manage well at all, because no one would worry about being tracked by a man who could hardly walk. After he sat, he looked at the baron, and saw first worry and then a dawning look of comprehension and admiration on the man's face.

But the baron's daughters seemed shocked by the extent of his infirmity. Gabriel was delighted. He made a show of putting his stiff leg out to the side when he finally sat after hobbling to his chair. He felt a pang of remorse when he saw that the blond sister, Sylvia, looked as though she were about to cry as she watched him. But he felt more guilty seeing how valiantly the dark-haired one, Rosamund, tried to recover her poise.

They both looked lovely tonight, but he doubted they could look any other way. Sylvia wore a filmy green gown, making him think of fairy hills and sweet new grass in the springtime countryside. Her amazing hair was done up so that soft curls fell to either side of her ethereal face.

Her sister wore red, which reminded him of autumn bonfires and the heart of the blazing fire in the hearth. Her ebony hair was pulled back and tied in a knot at the back of her smooth neck. The severity of her hairstyle and the purity of her profile contrasted with her lush figure, and the contrast was dazzling.

"Well, you're here at last, Major," the baron said heartily, "and I, for one, am glad of it. I'm particularly sharp set tonight," he added as a footman served his soup. He picked up his spoon and looked at the bowl eagerly. "Winter gets into a fellow's bones. No wonder I put on at least a stone every Christmas. But then I ride every day after, to get my girlish form back." He looked up with a grin. As he'd hoped, everyone at the table laughed, and the moment was lightened.

"Truth is I look forward to going home," the baron went on. "I like our old manor at this time of the year maybe best of all, though it's a treat in the spring and pleasant in the summer and autumn. But I love to see every window lit to welcome neighbors come to sing carols. The place glows like a lamp—you can see it from miles around," he told Gabriel.

The baron's eyes took on a distant look. "I like to share a cup of wassail with friends, and it's good to see all the old familiar rites of Christmas every year: the kissing bough up over the doorway and the Yule log blazing in the main hall. The mistletoe too, and lashings of holly and ivy wound round the stair newels, though it's unlucky to have pagan trappings in the house before Christmas Eve, nor would I tolerate all that folderol other times of the year. But Christmas at home is a real treat."

The baron paused, and heaved a mighty sigh. "Can't wait to go back. London just don't seem like the right place to spend Christmas to me."

Sylvia's spoon fell with a clatter to her plate. "But we are staying here for Christmas this year, Papa," she cried. "You *promised.*"

Her sister gave her a warning look. "Papa, surely you recall you said we could stay at least until Christmas Day," she said. "Sylvia and I have invitations we've accepted for parties and galas and such here in London for the entire week before it. It would be wrong for us to go back on our word, and we were so looking forward to all the festivity. Surely you can wait until after Christmas Day to leave?"

So Christmas is the day by which they hope to accomplish whatever it is they're after too, Gabriel thought with interest, as he waited for the baron's response.

"Oh, aye," the baron said gruffly, looking hunted. "It was only wishful thinking. But I'm as good as my word. We'll leave for home the day after Christmas, then. So, Major," he said more briskly, turning to his guest, "where are you going for Christmas? Home too?"

"It's been so long since I've been there that home is just a memory to me," Gabriel said smoothly. "And since my brother is in Europe now, and the family home is empty, I don't think I'd find Christmas too merry there. I'm used to foreign places, and so though I don't come from London, it seems more like home to me than anywhere I've been in many a year. I'll remain in London, I think." He paused to put his hand over the top of his plate as a footman came to his side, a full ladle poised to tip soup into his bowl.

"It is very good soup," Rosamund said, seeing his refusal.

"I don't doubt it," Gabriel said. "But you see, as I said, I hadn't thought I'd be asked to dinner, and I've already dined."

"A glass of wine then, surely?" she said, her eyes very dark and very wide.

He shook his head. "I'm afraid it would interfere with the medicines I take for this blasted limb of mine. It's giving me difficulty; it always does when the wind comes from the west. Another night, perhaps."

He smiled at her. There was no way he would eat or drink in this house, where the master and his servants slept like rocks through the night.

Was that admiration he saw in her eyes, Gabriel wondered? He would never know. It was gone in a fleet second, as she lowered her gaze.

"But I don't want to make you feel awkward," he said immediately. "So if I might have a glass of water? And some of that bread, if I might? It looks very good. And if there's any fruit?"

He was famished. But he'd faced hunger before. And he'd packed his own food for this night. He'd have that later, but he couldn't refuse to break bread with them now, especially since bread was the hardest thing to add poisons or potions to. And though water could be tampered with too, he thought he'd taste anything added to it. Fruit, at least tonight, when no one had expected him to dine on it, would be safe enough, if only because he meant to inspect the skin of any apple, orange or hothouse pear offered.

"You are a man of ascetic appetites, Major," Rosamund said.

"No," he corrected her. "It's only that life has made me so."

"But the Blanchards were Puritans, weren't they?" she asked.

Gabriel's smile was wide. "I am flattered," he said, inclining his head in a sketch of a bow. "I didn't know you knew my family."

She smiled, showing even white teeth. "I didn't," she said sweetly. "Papa told us."

His laughter was real and his grin honest. To his surprise, she grinned right back at him.

A worthy opponent, he thought, as he picked up an apple from the tray of fruit a footman brought him, and turned it round and round in his hand. That was exciting. He found himself hoping she was the one who went out every night to watch her sister, and not the one meeting her foreign lover in the dark.

It was bizarre, Gabriel thought as dinner went on and they chatted about Christmas and holidays and other safe topics, how they all ate their dinners and carried on light conversation without a hint of the fact that they knew he'd been hired to spy on them. But the baron's daughters were, after all, ladies, and so, well-schooled in the arts of deception. They might call it tact or diplomacy, or even social grace. Still, when all was said, Gabriel believed perfect manners were merely another form of deception.

The sisters sang after dinner. They sat side by side by the pianoforte in the salon and sang like a pair of Sirens, Gabriel thought. At least, their songs soon had their father nodding off in his chair by the fireside. A quick look at the footmen poised by the doors to the salon showed their eyes growing heavy too. Gabriel kept seeing their heads dip and then snap up, as if the poor fellows were exerting every effort to stay awake and upright.

But Gabriel was wide-awake, his every sense humming with interest and speculation. Although they sang beautifully, Gabriel doubted the baron's daughters had the magic of Sirens. Something else accounted for the torpor he saw in his host and the servants. The food had been plentiful, true. And the room was warm, and the hour growing late. Still and all, he was very glad he hadn't dined in this house tonight. Another reason, Gabriel thought with a touch of amusement, was that he wouldn't have wanted to take his eyes off Rosamund, even for a minute.

He had spent his life among men. But he liked women very much, and regretted the fact that he'd never really loved as he believed a man might love if he were lucky. Once or twice in his hard-fought and essentially lonely life he'd thought to marry, but a lack of funds as well as a lack of conviction that he'd survive to see his children, if he ever begot them, had ended hopes of that. He'd found female companionship without marriage, although not often. He'd had too much discrimination and too faithful a heart to be a rake. But the body had its demands.

And so he'd known rough women and gentle ones, and even wellborn ladies in his time. He'd known both passion and chaste admiration, but was willing to swear he'd never felt the powerful pull of attraction he experienced now whenever he looked at the beautiful Rosamund, the baron's deceitful daughter.

So he began to think that maybe there had been something in the water, after all.

After the songs, they sat and talked. The baron closed his eyes and settled deeper into his chair. Rosamund sat chatting with Gabriel, while Sylvia drifted over to the pianoforte again and began softly playing an old sweet song. The beauty of the melody was somewhat ruined by the baron's increasingly loud snores.

"No need," Rosamund laughed when Gabriel suggested he retire. "It's only ten o'clock. Papa always dozes before bed. He calls it the sweetest sleep, an appetizer for the coming night. If we wake him now to say we're going to bed, he'll be embarrassed that his behavior sent you off to your room so soon. Unless," she added quickly, glancing at his leg, "you'd rather retire now, of course?"

Roses, he thought dreamily. Every time he inhaled he could scent a trace of white roses, and jasmine, yes, definitely jasmine. If the food hadn't sent him into a trance, her perfume certainly did. But he had no wish to leave her now, in any fashion.

"If you and your sister are in the habit of keeping late hours," he said, "I'd be only too happy to remain here with you." He'd wanted to sound courtly, but it had come out pompous. "Forgive me," he added with a warmer smile. "It's been awhile since I spoke to a young lady. I mean to say that I'm not tired in the least. And I'd be delighted to have company. It's always hard to sleep the first night in a strange place."

One perfectly arched jet eyebrow went up. "But you

were a soldier," she said. "Didn't that make it difficult for you? A soldier must often sleep in strange places."

He laughed. "A soldier can sleep on a barbed fence as well as on the floor. Exhaustion makes a man a sound sleeper. Peacetime will be the ruin of me."

"Well, then," she said briskly, "I'll have to see if we can find you a frozen floor, or a bit of wire to rest upon."

He laughed. She seemed pleased.

"Is there anything we can do for you?" she asked. Light color appeared high on her cheeks as she added, "I mean to say, are you in pain now?"

"No, not more than usual," he said, suddenly wishing he could tell her the truth, which was that his knee only pained him when he insisted on bending it too much. But he reminded himself that no matter how entrancing those parted lips looked as she seemed to breathlessly await his answer, those same lips parted to speak lies, or else he wouldn't be here tonight. And so he couldn't tell her he could move without too much pain, not when he knew he'd have to do so without her knowledge in the coming nights.

"It happened at the last great battle," he told her. "I'm lucky to have the limb at all, no matter that it's a nuisance."

"Oh," she said with relief, "so it's your own. I mean, it's not artificial?"

He bit off a curse that sprang to his lips. He'd talked too much. How much better if she'd thought he had a wooden leg!

"Pardon me," she said earnestly when he didn't answer at once. "It was a rude question and not my business."

"But of course it is," he said as earnestly. "Now if you hear woodworms chewing you'll know it's your house and not your guest they're dining on."

He smiled at her.

She returned his smile with twice the brightness and a hint of warmth he hadn't seen before.

"So," he said, tearing his gaze from hers and stretching out his stiff leg in front of him to give him something else to look at, "why don't you want to go home for Christmas?"

Her smile vanished. He knew because he'd looked to see her reaction.

Her head went up, and her voice, though no less sweet, was a deal cooler. "I didn't say that, Major. I love Christmas at home too. In fact, I weary of London as much as my father does." Her expression grew faraway and sad. "But I have obligations and responsibilities." Her gaze and her voice sharpened as she added quickly, "We've given our word to attend so many functions. Speaking of which, surely you will grow weary of following us to all the musicales, routs and balls we're promised to?"

"Gloves off now, is it?" he asked with amusement. "Well then, truth for truth. I won't grow weary so long as I stay interested. And believe me, I am, and will be, until I find what it is I'm looking for."

She nodded. "Yes, I thought so. But, Major, whatever you're looking for you will not find. There's been a great deal of nonsense spoken in this house lately. And nothing to support any rumor. But, you'll see, I promise you."

It was said sweetly, but he knew a challenge when he heard one.

He nodded. "So I will, Miss Latimer. So I will."

They talked for a half hour after that, though it seemed like minutes to Gabriel. Time and place slipped away when he was with Rosamund. And that, he thought in annoyance with himself when he rose at last to go to his bedchamber, had nothing to do with drugs or potions.

Gabriel's room was cozy this chill night, and the fire in the hearth turned his bedcovers a warm rosy bronze, making it look even more inviting. But he turned his back on it and reached into his bag to take out his dinner of cheese and cold bread instead. He ate quickly, without tasting, because a soldier learned to respect his rations, and could only do that without tasting them.

Then, when the house was still and the moon rode high, he drew off his boots. He left his room in his stocking feet and made his way stealthily down the hall.

A small high lamp on the wall lighted the hallway, and so Gabriel easily found the alcove he'd seen and remarked earlier. It was near the head of the stair, where no one could go up or down without passing it. He took off his jacket and laid it on the floor. Then he withdrew some string from his pocket and carefully tied one end to the topmost stair newel, then took another string and tied it to the next one, and another to the next. At last, with some difficulty and many a stifled curse for the pain of it, he went back to the alcove and finally sat down on his folded jacket, one leg straight out, his back resting against the wall. He tied the ends of the strings he held to the fingers of his left hand, drawing his almost invisible web taut between the stair newels and himself. Then he leaned back against the wall.

The house was still. All Gabriel could hear was the muted ticking of a clock somewhere below stairs, and the assorted creaks, groans and snaps of any old house settling down in the night. He could even hear the distant sawing of the baron's sonorous snores.

The night moved on. Gabriel had lied to Rosamund. She'd been right: A seasoned campaigner could sleep anywhere and at any time. He couldn't sleep now, of course, but allowed himself to relax. Though weary, he was confident. He was trained to wake quickly and completely, so even if he dared sleep, if anyone went up or down the stairs, he'd feel the tug of the strings as they passed them and he'd be ready. He was as prepared as he could be. He leaned back and closed his eyes for a moment to refresh them.

Morning came instantly to Gabriel, blindingly bright. And loud.

He shot to his feet, blinking.

"Oh, the master will be wickedly grieved!" lamented the maid scurrying down the hall and toward the stairs.

Gabriel was at her side in a moment. He laid his hand on her arm to stop her, and had to steady her because his sudden, silent appearance almost made her trip and go hurtling down the stairs. But it didn't make her relinquish her grip on what she clutched to her breast.

"What will he be grieved at?" Gabriel asked.

"These, sir," she said, holding out a pair of pink dancing slippers.

He took them from her and turned them over. A

pretty pair of slippers, elegant, made of some shiny material and light as feathers in his hands. The soles were worn almost to parchment, and the silk or satin they were covered with was shredded and dirty, as though they'd been danced in at a hundred balls, and trod upon by some partners as well.

He looked down at the maidservant. He recognized her. "You are Iris, the baron's daughters' maid, are you not?" he asked.

She nodded.

"And these slippers?"

"They're new," she wailed. "Just bought last week and never worn. And now look at them. And her best rose gown, the new one, is all rumpled and crumpled and still warm from her wearing it, though she's in her bed and sleeping sound."

"Whose slippers? Whose gown?" Gabriel demanded.

"Miss Rosamund's, sir, but I don't doubt Miss Sylvia's are the same. They always are. I sleep in the dressing room betwixt them these days, with the doors open too! I tried to stay up all night, but I must've closed my eyes for a minute. But I heard nothing, I promise you, sir," she said a little hysterically. "I heard nothing at all!"

Nor had he. So, he thought, a familiar feeling of dread and anticipation flooding through him, this is war.

"He's following us," Sylvia said with a giggle, as she and her sister paced down the path through the park.

Rosamund didn't turn her head. "I know," she said.

"He moves a deal better than he let on yesterday, doesn't he?" Sylvia whispered. "The wretch, to make us feel sorry for him! It's not pleasant to see, but he can move fast enough. Now I'm not a bit guilty about him."

"I am," Rosamund breathed. "I like none of this."

"You liked the dancing well enough," her sister whispered so the footman a few paces behind them didn't hear. "I vow you didn't sit down all night. And Robin liked it as well, except when you were in Tom's arms."

"In his *hands*," Rosamund corrected her. "I don't let any of them take me into their arms, and neither should you, no matter what Alberon says to you."

"I don't," Sylvia said merrily. "I don't want him to lose interest before the day he can ask me to be his—with all legality. I may be entranced, sister dear, but I am not a fool."

"I wonder," Rosamund said. "No matter, don't bristle. I'm too tired to fight with you. Now, let's make the major earn his fee. He doesn't know we're not meeting anyone, so let's take him for a little walk so he can sleep all the more soundly tonight, shall we?"

Gabriel followed them down the long park paths. He no longer tried to conceal his presence. It was all he could do to conceal his anger and his bafflement. Seven nights now they'd eluded hm. Seven nights they'd left their rooms to meet their lovers. He'd only slept the first night. He napped the next day to be sure of it. Now he vowed he'd never sleep again until he found out how they did it, and what they did when they did it.

And every day at some time before the night, they'd sit with him and chat about inconsequential matters, as though they'd nothing on their minds but the parties they'd be going to and the ones they'd just come from. Rosamund would ask him questions that didn't matter and he'd reply with answers that weren't true. And she'd smile her bewitching smile and he'd smile back, though frustration and thoughts of slow murder were growing in his heart.

He'd followed them to musicales and routs, to grand balls and social teas, to the theater and to morning calls. And never had he seen them with the same gentlemen twice, nor had he ever seen them show special favor to any gentlemen either. They didn't exchange secret glances with any men, nor had they received any secret notes. That he was sure of.

And yet they stole from the house each night when the moon was high, and danced the night away.

At first, he'd wondered if it wasn't some bizarre jest. He'd stood with his ear to their doors, wondering if they were dancing with each other. But there wasn't a sound from either woman's room. He'd prowled the outside of the house by light of day, and would swear there was no way they could climb from their windows. There were no nearby trees, handholds or balconies. He'd even sent to Hart to have him watch the house through the night to be sure no rope ladders were lowered.

There was no way the baron's beautiful daughters could escape the house. But they did. Gabriel was getting worried. Not for their welfare: Whatever they did, it was obvious that though it ruined their slippers and their gowns, it made them glow with happiness. They were safe enough, he supposed, though he had a bad feeling about such safety and suitors who shunned a woman's family and the sunlight. He had a bad feeling about his prospects for success as well.

Christmas was coming closer. Vendors were crying it in the streets, and the feeling of Holiday was everywhere in the air. And yet he was no closer to finding out what was happening. It wasn't only that he'd miss receiving his fee for services if he failed in his mission: Now Gabriel was determined to solve the mystery for his own sake. He couldn't ask to stay in the baron's daughters' bedchambers in order to spy on them, but he was beginning to wonder if he'd have to hide in their chimneys.

Gabriel scowled. He didn't like this park any better than the baron did. Even without the leafy recesses it would have in summer, there were too many places for things to hide. Wherever bare briar thickets hadn't woven their brown cages along the sides of the paths, the crisscrossed trunks of saplings made impenetrable barriers. Overhead, the many-fingered branches of giant trees laced, preventing the infrequent winter sunlight from showing much on the browned leaf-littered ground. It was a place made for secrets, and though the baron's daughters wore red and white capes today, even their bold colors were muted by the false twilight as they hurried farther into the park.

Gabriel didn't think he'd discover much if he followed them. Their transgressions were always by night. And they always took a maid or footman with them when they went walking in the park, as every lady should. It would be hard for them to be up to anything smoky. If they did see an occasional lady or gentleman they knew, they'd nod, exchange a word and move on, as they did now, when they saw a gentleman riding by on his horse.

But then, they never treated any man they met with more than cool civility. Gabriel wondered if that might just be what they wanted him to see. The girls walked faster and so did he, though his knee was aching savagely, and he found himself leaning on his walking stick whenever it touched the ground. It made him lurch, and he felt he must look a hobgoblin as he tracked them. Still, his heart pained him more than his vanity or his leg whenever he thought about how every smile Rosamund gave him hid another deception.

He didn't trust her. And yet, sometimes he thought he caught a glimpse of regret or sorrow in her fine dark eyes when she looked at him, and that, strangely enough, pained him even more.

He'd grown to like her, even though he kept her deceptions in mind. He'd grown to admire her too. Why not? She was more than lovely; she was intelligent, charming and clever, and he sensed a commonality. . . .

Of course, nodcock, he told himself angrily, and walked faster. What beautiful and rich female of the nobility wouldn't want to attach a broken-down penniless soldier?

He was in a vile, dark mood as he tried to catch up to his quarry, when he saw the old woman standing on the path ahead. She was very old and seemed very cold, even though she was dressed in what might have been finery, once upon a time. And she was wringing her hands. There was a large, lumpy string-tied parcel at her feet. Either the weight of it had proved too much or the growing cold of the oncoming evening had numbed her fingers.

He stopped. He could not have done otherwise. "May I help you?" he asked.

"Oh, thank you, sir," she said with gratitude. "I've just bought this bag of cat's meat for my tabby. The butcher sells it half price when it starts growing dark and he knows he must soon close up shop. He doesn't want it spending another night in his establishment, for cats *are* picky eaters, though you'd never guess it. And what must I do but drop it when that fine gentleman rode by and his horse brushed against me! It might have been my fault for not stepping aside fast enough, but did he stop to so much as ask? Alas, no! My hands are half-frozen now, and I don't know how I'll get it home tonight. It cost two shillings and my poor puss is hungry. I hate to leave it here, for there's no doubt wild animals will have it if I do."

Gabriel had a second's remorse for losing the track of his quarry. But only a second's. He could no more desert the old woman in the lowering dusk than he could skip down the path to catch up to the baron's daughters. "Allow me," he said, on a sigh, as he bent to pick up the parcel.

"But you were on your way somewhere," the old woman protested, "and I can scarce reward you enough for your time. It's only cat meat, after all."

But it was worth more than diamonds to her, he thought, and probably cost her as dear. Nor could he leave her in the growing twilight. She mightn't have much, but no defenseless female should be out alone in the park after dark. "No reward is necessary," he said.

"But your leg, sir," she protested.

"It carries me, and I can carry a parcel," he said, offering her his arm. "Where shall we go?"

"Back to the entrance to the park, my dear boy," she said. "I am so grateful to you." She prattled to him about cats and their tastes all the way to the park gate. There she stopped. She took her parcel from him, and though he offered to carry it home for her, refused.

He didn't blame her. He was, after all, a stranger to her. The cat meat might be for her own dinner, or for a dozen tabbies. Her ancient clothes could just as easily be those of an eccentric wealthy miser as a beggar's. He wouldn't judge by appearances. If a beautiful young woman's seemingly innocent smile could hide a multitude of lies, an old woman could also have her secrets.

"You shall be rewarded, though," the old woman told him, a smile wreathing her wrinkled face. "If not in the ways you can readily see. Advice can be as good as gold. So remember, lad, in this life, don't look only to the doors you can see, but also to those you cannot. Good night."

It was nonsense, but well meant, he knew. He bowed

his thanks to her. When he straightened, she was gone into the growing dark.

"We missed you on our walk this evening," Sylvia told Gabriel with a catlike grin that evening when they met again at dinner.

Her sister gave her a minatory look. "Were you well, sir?" she asked Gabriel, with every evidence of real concern.

"Well enough," he said. "I met up with an old friend, or should I rather say a new one, and so couldn't follow you further."

"Was she pretty?" Sylvia said with a giggle. The girl seemed merrier with each passing day.

"Sylvia!" her father admonished her. "Mind your manners, girl. The major has his own life, you know. He can't follow you every moment."

There was a silence. Gabriel tried not to wince. That was entirely too true.

"Come," Sylvia whispered, looking back to see if her sister was there.

"I follow," Rosamund said as she gathered her skirts in one hand so they wouldn't impede her as she followed her sister down the long, dark passage. She could not do otherwise, she thought sadly.

They came to the end of the passage, and, once again, she found herself bathed in soft, silvery light. The great ballroom ahead was always lit subtly, so it seemed that they always danced by the light of the moon.

"Ladies," the Duc d'Alberon said, bowing low over Sylvia's hand. "At last, you are here."

"We left a little late tonight, so as to be sure we weren't followed," Sylvia said anxiously, looking up into his astonishingly handsome face.

"Any second I wait seems like a year," he said, his hand on his heart.

Ugh. Far, far too much, Rosamund thought, and looked up to see he'd caught her unspoken thought, because his lips curled in a mocking smile. As ever, it was impossible for her to know if he was mocking her or himself.

"But so it is," he told Rosamund as he took her hand and bowed over it.

She drew her hand away. His clasp was cool and smooth and strong as the coils of a huge exotic snake. The thought dismayed her. She felt he knew it and was again amused.

"Come," he said, bowing low again. "The company awaits."

They did, they always did, Rosamund thought with sudden despair. His friends and relatives were always there. Well, he said he was an expatriate, and it made sense that he'd have his court with him in his exile. It should have reassured her about his motives toward Sylvia, and it had at first. But as time went by it unsettled her. His friends and relatives or courtiers—she couldn't be sure because they seldom spoke about themselves—were always present. As were her dancing partners: flaxen-haired Robin, always filled with mirth; Tom, with his sparkling eyes and ready quips; light-footed Will, who claimed he couldn't sit still; mischievous Jack, who always grinned; and even poor, sad Tam, full of sighs, the only one who never smiled—perhaps, she thought, because that made him seem tragically handsome. They, and more like them, always partnered her.

They were all handsome as the devil, she thought, but far merrier than he could ever be. They were charming, though they were clearly peacocks. They were fond of clothes and jewels, and, of course, dancing. Some nights they wore fantastic costumes, some nights they dressed like exquisites from courts of other times, and this night they dressed like the finest gentlemen in London, although, as always, they looked finer.

They were difficult for her to talk to because they only wanted to laugh, and impossible to feel kinship with because she sensed they were cold at heart. They weren't cold in body. Still, every time any sought more than a dance, she denied them, and they accepted her refusals with smiles. They seemed to have less heart than beauty, but then, it was hard to think of anyone who had more beauty.

Alberon loved to surround himself with beauty, and

so he often told Sylvia. Indeed, the ladies who always danced there were also beautiful, if less friendly, because they never deigned to speak to the baron's daughters. They were so exquisite that Rosamund often wondered why, lovely as Sylvia was, Alberon bothered with her. But he'd known those ladies forever, he'd said with a laugh when Rosamund had first hinted at it, before he swept Sylvia away in the dance again.

Whenever Rosamund accompanied her sister, she was filled with apprehension and doubt. And then, every time the music struck up, it was wonderful. Every time the night bled into day, Rosamund could scarcely believe she'd danced until dawn. Never before had she loved dancing so much, and she couldn't understand why she did now. She felt light as a feather as she whirled around the silver ballroom, and her heart felt as light as her feet. The pain in both only came later, when she was home again.

She hated deception, and the anxiety, guilt and doubt she felt about her role in deceiving her father about these meetings was growing so acute that she yearned to end them. Whenever she mentioned it, Sylvia would weep and plead, and vow to go alone, and so then Rosamund had to go with her again. And again, once the music began, all her doubts fled, like the hours of the long nights she passed dancing.

But now she thought about Major Blanchard, and that made her hesitate again. She felt more than sympathy for him—she felt a commonality with him, as well as strong attraction. He had natural dignity and poise. He was intelligent, intuitive and knowledgeable; his smiles were real, and caused by things that made her smile too. He too was doing something he didn't want to do, but in his case, he did it to earn his bread. She admired him for it. And somehow, in his ruined fashion, he was more appealing to her than any of the incredibly handsome gentlemen who would partner her in the dance tonight. Her heart ached for his courage in carrying on against all odds, and she hated to see him fail. But fail he would, and then she'd never see him again.

She sensed he felt the same attraction to her, but

though they talked about so many things, he never spoke of it. He was an honorable man, so she supposed it might be because he'd already given his heart away.

They didn't speak of such things. Now, she vowed to remedy that before they parted, so she could have that at least to remember him by. She knew she'd never see him again when he discovered how she'd duped him. He had pride, and she would wound, if not kill, his self-esteem by the time this was over.

But she couldn't let Sylvia go by herself. And it wouldn't be for much longer. Soon, very soon, it would be Christmas. Alberon would declare himself and Sylvia would marry him and go away forever, or so it would seem to her sister. Then all of Rosamund's doubts about her role in their courtship would also be gone. But tonight, like each successive night, they weighed more heavily on her spirit.

Rosamund sighed, and almost turned back. But then the music began, and she had to step into the dance again.

The sky was changing from black to gray when Rosamund and Sylvia stepped back into their house. Sylvia wore a dreamy smile. She waved languidly at her sister as she drifted off to her room again. But Rosamund paused in the hallway.

The major was sitting upright, sleeping, in the alcove where he usually passed the night, the strings tied round his hand still drawn taut, connected to his hand that was flung across his heart.

Poor fellow, she thought, as she dared step toward him. It had been foggy and damp all the day, and his leg must have ached as badly as the soles of her feet now did. He had very long eyelashes, she thought in surprise as she came closer and saw them fanned against his high cheekbones. She'd never have guessed it. But then, she'd never dared look so closely at his eyes and wouldn't have done so now if they weren't closed. Now she didn't have to worry about being caught in that clear gray gaze.

And that scar on his cheek, now she could see it was deep, and pitiless. It must have been from a saber, and must have pained him cruelly when he'd gotten it. She bent, without thinking, and knelt by his side. His breathing was slow and deep and even, so before she could resist the urge she reached out a hand and traced that reminder of his hard past, keeping her finger a hair's breadth from his skin. She sighed, and then, on an impulse even deeper than the need to dance every night, she bent closer to him. She lowered her head until her lips were a fraction from his. She hesitated.

Then she gasped and shot upright. She turned and ran lightly back to her room, glad she'd had the strength to fight off the imperative impulse to touch his lips—and equally sorry she had not kissed him.

Her door closed without as much as a sigh.

Gabriel's eyes snapped open. He'd have known her scent even in his coffin. He'd heard her light step first, then scented roses, and had closed his eyes. He didn't want her to know he was aware in the hope he could discover what she was up to now. It was too late to see where she'd come from, but at least he might find out where she was going. It took every ounce of his determination to remain still and keep his breathing even and his eyes closed. It took more resolve than he knew he had to keep breathing at all when he sensed her hovering over him. He'd waited, and when he felt the warmth of her so close, as close as his breath itself, he'd dared watch her through slitted eyes.

He'd heard her sudden indrawn breath, and then she left in a rush.

He was glad she hadn't actually touched him, because he couldn't have resisted that. It was bad enough how he'd longed to reach out and capture her. Now he saw it was dawn. She'd visited him on her return home, because he never doubted she'd been out dancing again. And he didn't dare wonder why she'd come so near. But now, he had another reason to discover what was happening beneath his nose and outside his vision and in his heart of hearts.

This innermost part of the park was never filled at any hour, but it was almost empty now, as Gabriel followed the baron's daughters and the footman who accompanied them. Evening was coming on. A chill wind made the dead leaves of autumn skitter across the frigid paths. Snow threatened, and though Gabriel was glad it hadn't begun yet, because walking in it would have been difficult for him, still he thought it might at least have softened the gloom of the place.

It was a bad evening to be out, but Gabriel couldn't bear being inside much longer. He had to walk to clear his mind. And he had to follow the sisters as they strolled down the paths as though it were a May morning.

At length, they turned back. He stopped and waited, then bowed as they came abreast of him. No sense hiding what he did now, not with his term of employment almost up, not with Christmas coming on as sure as the night was. Two days more, and it would all be over. When the bells on Christmas morning tolled, he'd be gone from here forever.

Maybe that was what made one of the sisters stop when she saw him.

"Major," Sylvia said, with a great show of surprise, cocking her head to the side. "What an hour for you to be traipsing through the park, and you burdened by having to use that walking stick. Whatever could you be thinking? Ah, I know! You're trying to build up an appetite for dinner. I vow I've never seen a grown man eat so little as you do. Well, I hope your walk in the park will give you healthier appetites."

"Sylvia!" Rosamund gasped in shock. Her sister's face wore a spiteful smile, and her voice echoed the sly innuendo she'd often heard in Alberon's conversations. Sylvia was sometimes thoughtless, but this was malicious. "The major was looking after us, as well you know! And do you know?" Rosamund added coldly. "I believe you can return home with George this evening," she said, gesturing to their footman. "I shall take the major's escort, if he'd be so kind?"

Gabriel bowed, and offered her his arm. As Sylvia gaped at them, Rosamund put her hand on his arm and walked off with him.

"I'm sorry," Rosamund told him once they were out of Sylvia's hearing.

"No need to be," he said. "You did nothing out of the way. Your sister was the one singing a victory song. Prematurely, I think. I know that had one of my men done that before a battle, I'd have had something to say about it too."

"You think it tempts the Fates?" she asked.

"No. I don't believe in Fate, or superstition. I believe in what I can see. And that is that confidence is always necessary, but overconfidence is never good."

"Good? Would that be good for you, or for us?" Rosamund said before she could stop herself.

He smiled. "No doubting, Miss Rosamund, you have the upper hand now. But it isn't over yet. I'm glad we can speak about it openly at last. I assume that's because you believe it's done, and you've almost won?"

She looked down at her fur half boots. "I can't say. Surely you know that."

"Surely," he said softly, "I do."

They paced along slowly and saw Sylvia, head high, nose in the air, march past them, the footman trailing behind her.

"So," Rosamund said too brightly, to cover her embarrassment, "Christmas is coming. And you will be leaving us, or so you said."

"So I shall," he said.

"You're staying on here in London as well?"

"Maybe," he said. "Maybe not. Now I'm not sure. I had a bit of good news yesterday. I received payment on an old debt." He smiled just remembering his shock when Hart had showed him the letter from his brother and the bank check with it. "And so I sent my valet back to Devon, to the house left to me by my uncle. It's a grand old place on the Tamar. He's going to see if it's habitable, at least for the twelve days of Christmas. I have go there anyway to see what its future can be. One day, I hope to fix it up and stay there forever, as my uncle did. But I won't until my fortunes change and I can do it right. I'm a handy fellow, but Uncle's estate needs more than roof tiles and a coat of whitewash.

"Don't look like that!" he said with a laugh, seeing her discomfort. "I'm not trying to win your sympathy and so your confidences. I play the game by the rules. I was just answering your question. If I'd wanted your sympathy, I'd say I had no funds at all, and hobble more when I walked, and be sure, I'd groan while I was at it."

"You'd never!" she laughed.

"No, I wouldn't," he agreed. "I think I'd hop all the way back to your house, pretending I loved doing it, to keep you from knowing I felt even a twinge, whatever my aims. Only beggars court pity."

"Is there nothing you can do?" she asked impulsively. "I mean, to heal it? If it's a matter of money, I'm sure my father . . ."

"No," he said, patting her hand. "No, it's not that. I've friends who'd pay for a cure in a twinkling, and I wouldn't be too proud to ask them if it was only a matter of funding. But it isn't. I've seen many physicians. There is an operation that might ease my problems. The fault lies inside the knee. Healing caused scars that bound it up after they removed the shot from it. Breaking, or cutting loose, those inner scars might cure it, they say. But it might not. And as I've had surgery on it once before, near the battlefield where I got the wound, great coward that I am, I'm loathe to lie down again, leather between my teeth, for a cure that never comes."

" 'Great coward'!" she gasped. "But you've more honors for valor than any man in your regiment. . . ." She stopped and bit her lip, because she didn't want him to know how thoroughly she'd researched his history.

"Then say, 'great skeptic' instead," he said with a smile, "if that makes you feel better. If my infirmity becomes worse, I may opt for the knife. If not, I won't. Enough about my war wounds. I tell you, Miss Rosamund, never ask an old soldier about his wounds. He'll go on about them as long as he will about his battles, and the only thing worse than being in them is hearing about them, endlessly."

They walked on in silence, because neither could think of a thing to say that wasn't too personal or too filled with longing.

"I think you should rejoin your sister," he finally said. "You've made your point. The shadows are lengthening and your footman, though a stalwart lad, is beginning to look anxious. I don't blame him. This is an ominous-looking patch. But I haven't seen hide nor hair of any malefactors lingering, and I looked hard. I think this park discourages even them. So you can rejoin her. I'll follow behind at a slower pace to make sure all's well. But be sure, I'll see you later tonight."

She nodded, because she didn't dare ask exactly what he meant by that last promise. Then she hurried to catch up to her sister.

The trio was soon far ahead of Gabriel, and soon gone into the deepening dusk. He walked on alone, deep in thought.

"Oh, be damned and be bothered," a rough voice shouted. "Oh, foul mischief and black luck!"

Gabriel spun around, all his senses alert, the sword hidden in his walking stick out and raised and shining in the last of the light.

At first he saw nothing. Then he made out a blockish figure struggling in the brush at the side of the footpath. In spite of the pain to his knee, Gabriel charged into the thicket, and stopped when he saw that the man wasn't fighting with anyone but himself.

The man was very short, stout and bearded. He wore a heavy coat and a fur hat, and he was struggling furiously, trying to free his leg from some sort of a trap. Gabriel was immediately sympathetic.

The man was instantly horror-struck. He cringed, raised an arm to protect his head and cried out, piteously, "Nay! Dinna assault a helpless old man! Put down yer sword! I'll give ye all me gold, I swear it!"

Gabriel looked at his raised sword, and instantly sheathed it in his walking stick again. "I meant you no harm," he said. "I was trying to save you from your attacker." He knelt as best he could, grimacing at the pain that caused him, and inspected the trap the fellow had stepped in. "It's ancient and rusted," he said. "Lucky you're wearing good stout boots."

Privately, Gabriel thought the boots were as thick and ancient as the trap. But that was all to the good. They looked indestructible. "I daresay your leg's not touched at all," he said.

"No, no, it ain't. But I can't spring meself from the trap. Give us a hand, will ye, eh?" the fellow said, his tone now wheedling.

"Aye," Gabriel said, as he rose to his feet again. "I'll need a long strong stick, but I think I can spring it. Hold on. I'll be back."

He found a suitable tree limb nearby and returned to see the fellow still cursing and muttering as he tried frantically to free himself. "I told you I'd be back," Gabriel said. "O ye of little faith," he laughed.

The fellow winced.

"Does it hurt?" Gabriel asked at once.

"Nay, it dinna. Hurry, hurry, spring me."

Gabriel put his legs apart and, bracing himself hard in spite of the pain it caused him, inserted the stick into the teeth of the trap at the side near the hinge. Using all his strength, he pushed down until his muscles knotted and finally he felt the trap parting. "When you see you can, pull free," he told the trapped man from between gritted teeth. He strained until the trap's cruel mouth gaped wider, and as soon as it did, the fellow hopped aside, his leg free. Then with slow patience and infinite care lest the trap somehow catch him in its teeth when it snapped back, Gabriel slowly eased pressure until the trap shuddered and bit back into place again, snapping the stick in two.

He heaved a sigh, and straightened, only to find the man gone. He looked around to see the fellow running off into the dusk without a word of goodbye. Another look at the trap and the ground around it told him why. The earth looked freshly turned. Mischief had been done here; the trap had guarded something that had been dug up. Gabriel didn't want to know what it might have been. He picked up the trap and flung it far into the wood. Then he stepped back on the path. It was getting very dark, and now even he didn't relish being alone here in the park.

He picked up his pace as he hobbled back to the gate, his arms as well as his knee aching.

"Well, I like that!" a familiar voice said.

Gabriel paused. Then he frowned. The little old woman he'd helped with her package of cat's meat not a week past stood looking at him, another untidy parcel in her hands. "My good woman," he said harshly. "Whatever can you be thinking of? Alone in the park at this hour?" And then, hearing an eerie echo of the hurtful thing Sylvia had said to him, he added, more gently, "This is no place for you, ma'am."

"Nor you, lad," she said. "But you can't help helping folk, can you? He owes you a reward, that rude fellow. And not just because it's clear your heart is bigger than your purse."

"My dear lady," Gabriel said, torn between laughter and annoyance, "that's not to the point. He's a rogue, and the world is full of them, and so you shouldn't be out here at this hour."

"But I am," she said, "and so what luck to have met up with you again! Will you take my parcel, lad? This time the butcher had a heap of cat's meat for me, for with Christmas coming, even the poor are buying better cuts."

Suppressing a sigh for her foolishness, and his own aching limbs, he took the parcel from her, offered her his arm, and while she chatted about cats and rogues, escorted her to the gate.

"Now, please don't go out of an evening on your own again," he warned her when they arrived there. "I can't be here every time. Indeed, I'm only visiting and will soon be gone."

"So you all are, lad, or so it seems to me," she said sadly. "But don't worry about me." She gave his arm a gentle pat and gazed at him with serious concern. "My boy," she said, "you give advice and expect me to take it. But you didn't listen to my advice last time either, did you? Now, mark me well. I told you to look for doors where you don't see them. I still do." She scowled. "Young people today don't have the hang of a good hinting riddle anymore. Or is it just that I'm so old you think me daft? Never mind answering that," she said with a grin.

"Now," she said, "hear me out. I have lived here long and long, before the baron came, before the man he bought the house from, and aye, before even that man was born. I knew this land, this place, this park, and that is why I venture out at odd hours without concern. I am well protected, though you mightn't think so. Now, listen well. The baron's house itself is not what it seems. No more can I tell you. That much I do. Good luck to you, because you deserve it. And my wishes for luck are not idle."

He put his hand over her small frail one. She was likely addled, but gentle and without guile, withal. She had nothing to give him but her best wishes, and so he treated them like a great prize. "Thank you," he said sincerely, "and if we don't meet again, I wish you a happy Christmas too."

It seemed she startled; at least she dropped her hand from his and stepped back. And then she said with a small, sad smile, "Ah, well, that you cannot do. Nor can I wish that for you. Good night, my lad, and don't sleep well."

Gabriel watched her go, and then walked slowly back to the baron's house, deep in thought. It was a strange, unpleasant reward she'd wished him this time, but he'd no right to belittle it, whatever it was, even in his thoughts. He had not much more to offer anyone but his best wishes himself. That, and his own battered body and soul. Not much to give to anyone for Christmas, and nothing to offer a woman in exchange for her hand, and too well he knew it. He ached in heart as well as body. He had one more night to earn his wages. And he knew he could take one thousand and one, and even if he did, that wouldn't be enough to offer the woman he wanted.

Then, because a good soldier can't dwell on his defeat lest he defeat himself again, he began to think about what the old woman had said in order not to think about what he could never say to Rosamund, the baron's most beautiful daughter.

He was still thinking as he came to the front of the baron's town house. He saw the baron's daughters go up the stair and safely into their house. But he remained outside a long while, not feeling the cold or seeing the night settle around him. He stood so lost in thought that he didn't move when light snow began to sift down over him.

At last, his head snapped up, suddenly, as though he'd

been struck hard across the face. His eyes widened. And then, forgetting his bothersome knee, he dashed into the house, startling a footman as he rushed past and raced up the long stair. He was in such a hurry he didn't even use his stick. Nor did he feel pain, though pain there was. There was a time for thinking and a time for action. He had to plan his actions now, and he had too many things to do in too short a time. There was no time to think of pain, or sorrow, or regret.

The huge ballroom was suffused with a glorious, gentle silver light. It looked as though the evening star itself was set in the great chandelier that hung above the room, and all the lesser stars in the night sky gathered close around it to twinkle in the other many blazing sockets. The light was pure and subtle, and seemed not of this earth at all.

Gabriel stood at the doorway to the ballroom, breathing hard as he stared at the light. And then, at last, he began to see the faces of all the heartbreakingly beautiful people who were dancing in that light. Then, without warning, he found himself feeling ashamed. Ashamed of being crippled, of being badly dressed, of being less than perfect in face and form, of being as human and damaged in the eyes of the world as he knew he was in this glittering company.

Hidden musicians were playing a waltz with strings and pipes, the strains summoning summer in the midst of winter. It flowed like honey into the ear, and fed the heart of the listener with sweet delight. It clearly inspired the dancers as they wove round and round the white marble floor, tracing patterns as intricate as those of the music. They were all handsome, all elegantly dressed, and as they danced they seemed almost not even to touch the floor beneath their flying feet.

Gabriel was enchanted.

But he was a professional soldier who had fought for his life and his men's lives too many times. It took only another moment for him to remember where he was. A soldier had no time for poetical musings. He had to assess the situation, and act.

He saw her then, in the arms of a magnificent male

in the midst of the dance. The fellow wasn't brawny, no one Gabriel feared besting him in battle. But he feared his effect on Rosamund, because the man was incredibly handsome—though not, Gabriel thought, half a patch on what Rosamund herself was.

Tonight, in this secret eerie ballroom, she reminded him even more forcibly of the roses whose scent she bore. She wore a gown of red trimmed with pink, and when she waltzed, flashes of yellow like those in the heart of a ripe rose peeked out from under her swirling silken skirts.

"Enough," Gabriel said. And though he'd said it low to himself, the music, and all the dancers, stopped.

"And who is this?" a dark and incredibly handsome gentleman asked.

The gentleman still held one hand on his partner's waist, and that partner was Sylvia. She stood arrested, a secret glutted look upon her face as she gazed up at her partner, a look that Gabriel had seen in the eyes of some lovers he had just satisfied. A look he'd seen on the faces of women who had wanted him to satisfy them. It made him shudder, seeing that look on Sylvia's young face.

"I am Major Gabriel Blanchard," Gabriel said, clutching his walking stick hard as he sketched a bow. "And I've discovered your secret, sir. It was effective because it was so simple. Simple enough to be foolish, really. At least, I feel a fool for not having thought of it before. A door in the house next door. A concealed door hidden behind a panel in a wardrobe leads from Miss Sylvia Latimer's bedchamber to a long passage, which in turn leads to this house, next door, and in turn to this ballroom. I've no idea who built the door or the passage, but it's as old as these old houses. I discovered it this night. And as I'm charged with watching over the Misses Latimer, I followed them, and now I'm here."

"So you are. And now, what do you intend to do, my uninvited guest?" the dark gentleman asked.

Gabriel swore he could feel as well as hear the gust of scornful snickering that filled the room. "I'll take the ladies home, and now. Their father knows not of their presence here, nor would any father permit his daughters to go dancing with men who have not met him or asked his permission to call on them."

"And if I refuse you this honor?" the gentleman asked, with a beautiful smile and even more amusement.

"I'll do it anyhow." Now Gabriel smiled. "I know you are many, and I am one. Those odds would never avail on a battlefield. But this is London."

"And you think that makes a difference?" the gentleman asked with a less beautiful smile. "This is not my land. I'm only a visitor here. And so your rules don't apply to me."

"Well, they do if your guests obey them," Rosamund announced. She stepped away from her partner and moved to Gabriel's side. The music had stopped and her head was clear; suddenly seeing Gabriel made everything in the room less wondrous and everything she'd done more wrong.

"Rosamund!" Sylvia cried, as though struck to the heart.

"You don't have to leave, my lovely one," Alberon said, turning his attention to Sylvia. "We can go on as we began. I leave this night to go home again. If I return, I can't say when. Not at least until the year turns to springtime again. So come away with me tonight, my lovely girl, and I'll show you my world."

"She has to come back with us," Rosamund declared. "Oh, Sylvia, you must."

"Indeed, Miss Latimer," Gabriel said, "you must. Your dancing partner can't offer you more than his hand in the dance. He has no intention of marrying you." It was a guess and a stab in the dark, but Gabriel saw it hit its mark.

Alberon's eyes narrowed. He took Sylvia's hand and gazed down at her. "I can't wed you, at least not in the way your people do. That's true. But come with me," he said again with another lustrous smile. "I'll make you happy every day. Come with me and see."

"But that's not what you wanted or expected, Sylvia!" Rosamund cried. "Dancing isn't living. What do you know of him or what he plans? He has lied to you—to us—in everything. Come away now. There can't be happiness in deceit."

Sylvia hesitated, still staring deep into her dark gentleman's eyes.

"You'll never see us again if you stay," Rosamund said. "Not me, not Papa, not England itself. I feel it in my heart. Is what you feel now worth that? Christmas is coming, in a day," she went on urgently, seeing her sister's gaze slowing turning toward her. "We'll be going home. Christmas at home, remember? The carols, the comradeship, the house ablaze with light, the sleighing, and carols sung in the night, the neighbors, and the wassail, the holly and the ivy, and oh, the mistletoe."

At that, Alberon stepped one pace back.

Sylvia hesitated.

"He lied," Rosamund went on urgently. "All of this is a lie. You still don't know where he comes from or where he goes. And he cannot, will not, marry you. Come home—it's time."

Sylvia bowed her head. Then she looked up at her partner and slipped her hand from his clasp. "I have to go home," she told him in a small voice, looking at him as though she wished he had a way to call her back.

He bowed. "You must do as you will. I cannot take you without your permission. It's not my land, but some rules apply. It is true I can offer you no more, but remember, I will give you no less."

Rosamund snatched up her sister's hand. "Let's go," she told Gabriel nervously. "Please."

"We'll go. Don't worry," he said, keeping his eyes on the dark man. "He can do nothing and he won't try. This is England, after all."

"Not mine," Alberon said enigmatically. "Good-bye." He waved his hand, and the musicians struck up again.

But Gabriel didn't wait to see or hear more. He held Rosamund's hand, and she held her sister's hand tightly as they backed toward the hall. They stepped into the secret passage and fled from the sight of the silvery ballroom, the wonderfully beautiful dark man and the dancers who danced through the night.

It was a sad and solemn ending of the night for the baron's daughters. Now it was morning, and they sat in

Rosamund's chamber because their father and a pair of footmen had gone exploring the passage in Sylvia's room at first light. Their father knew all, because he'd been woken by their return in the night.

He had rushed into the room in his nightshirt and nightcap, gaping at his daughters in their gowns, and Gabriel leading them. "So you've caught them at it!" the baron had cried, and then fell still, clearly torn between excitement and disappointment as he looked from Gabriel to his daughters.

"Sir," Gabriel had said. "There's no point in involving your daughters any further tonight. It is done. All was discovered. Let them go to bed. We'll talk now or in the morning, whichever you prefer."

"Do you think I can wait until morning?" the baron roared. "To bed, girls. The major and I must talk."

And so he and Gabriel had done, in the baron's study until dawn. The baron had only been dissuaded from immediately charging into the secret passage by the major's insisting there was no point in doing it right away. He told the baron his daughter's suitor would keep, or would be already gone. It would only upset his daughters further if he went charging into their room again, because they were likely already sleeping. Or so, at least, the baron's daughters' maid reported to them.

So the baron's daughters were weary this morning, having slept not at all.

Sylvia was the first to be called to her father's study.

Rosamund paced until she returned.

"We're going home tomorrow morning," Sylvia said dully when she returned, "even though it means traveling on Christmas Day." She looked more wan and exhausted than she had an hour before. It was as though an inner light had been extinguished. "And I don't believe we're ever coming back. At least, not to this house."

"Well, that's good," Rosamund said. She hesitated. "What is our punishment to be?"

"None," Sylvia said. "He says there's no point. The major convinced him we saw our error and left when we did. They searched for Alberon, but he's gone, he and his whole company. Papa and the major can't find a trace of him or his household. They seemed to have vanished, like a fairy ring in the morning sun."

"Oh, poor Sylvia," Rosamund said.

"No," Sylvia said. "No, not really. I see now that I didn't see anything before. Thank you, sister. And, oh! Papa's waiting for you."

Rosamund raised her head high and went down the stair to see her father. She braced herself as the door to his study closed behind her.

He only shook his head and looked at her sadly. "You did wrong to deceive me," he said. "But right in defending your sister, the major said. This foreign fellow was uncannily persuasive, and you are both young and impressionable, just as the major said."

"He meant 'stupid,' I'm sure. But I'm not that young, nor so stupid as I behaved. I didn't mean to deceive you, Papa. It may sound like a lie, but in truth, I seemed to have little control over what I was doing. I hated to do it, but I did, and I'm so sorry."

"There's no crime in being young," her father said. "But it is time to go home. I'm selling the house, or else I'd brick up the secret door right now, but it ain't fair to endanger anyone else. Let them see it and know it, and be warned. I can't discover who owns the place next door. This Alberon fellow, if that was even his name, isn't on the records as the owner, so he must have let out the place. But he won't anymore. I've told the Watch, and sent a note to my friends at Bow Street. He won't be welcome in England again. So there's an end to it." He saw her sorrow and added, "Buck up. We'll have us a fine old Christmas at home, and do our best to let the holiday heal us. For I don't blame you or your sister. Let's have an end to blame."

She nodded. "You're too good, Papa. . . . And the major?"

"Never fear, he's been paid. He packed up and left not an hour past. A good man—his reward was well deserved."

"Oh," Rosamund said softly, sadly. "Did he leave no message for me? I mean, for Sylvia and me?"

"No," the baron said, in surprise. "Oh," he said, echoing her sad word as understanding came to him. "Rosie," he said gently, "he had a job of work to do and he did it. We can ask no more of him."

Rosamund nodded and left him. She slowly climbed the stair to her room. Sylvia was no longer there. Rosamund went to her sister's room to see how she was faring, and was staggered by the change in her.

Sylvia glowed. She wore a new gown and she twirled round and round before her looking glass. Rosamund couldn't help glancing over to the wardrobe, to make sure the door to the secret passage was closed.

"Guess what?" Sylvia sang. "Arthur came to call," she said before Rosamund could answer. "He's downstairs now. He wants to see me and talk with me. He didn't go home for Christmas. He sent me a note saying he'd waited to see what I was doing. Isn't he a dear? I'd have thought he'd given up on me, but no! I think I'll ask him to share Christmas with us. Wouldn't that be wonderful? Just like the old days."

"Wonderful, indeed," Rosamund said quietly. "I'll just go to my room now. I think I could nap for a while."

But she didn't sleep or even close her eyes as she lay on her bed and watched the day pass outside her windows without seeing it, just as the nights had done, all those nights she'd danced away. Only this time, she couldn't see it for the tears in her eyes.

At length she heard a tap on her door. She raised herself on an elbow and was shocked at how the daylight had fled. It was time for dinner, and so she wondered if she ought to tell them it was her stomach or her head that hurt, though it was her heart. She couldn't send to the major on any pretext. She felt so close to him, such a bond and so much affection. But now she realized she actually knew less about him than her sister had known about Alberon, and the major had no cause to trust her at all.

"Rosie?" her father called.

She sprang to her feet. It had to be important, because he always sent a maid to her room.

"Get dressed. That is to say, put on something special," he said, when she opened the door. He was smiling hugely. "It's our last night here, so let's make a celebration and a peace with it. Come down to dinner. We have visitors too, Sylvia's old friend, Arthur, and a special guest. I've just passed a very interesting hour with him. Come, girl, shake a leg."

He didn't have to tell her that. Rosamund picked her best new gown, crimson velvet for the holiday season. She was glad Iris was there, because her hands were shaking too much to fasten her gown or tend to her hair. It couldn't possibly be him. But since it might be, she could hardly contain her excitement.

"Miss Rosamund," Gabriel said, looking up at her as she came down the stair.

She smiled, or tried to, because she was shocked to discover she was about to cry.

He took her hand. "Your father has given me permission to spend a few moments alone with you. May I?"

He was dressed exquisitely. In fact, she wondered just how rich his reward had been, because his clothes looked new. He wore a bottle-green jacket and biscuit breeches, his linen was finely made and immaculate, his half boots were Spanish leather, shining and unscarred. And his smile was warm, and real, and just for her.

She couldn't leave off looking into his eyes as he led her to the empty salon and sat beside her, never releasing her hand.

"Where to begin?" he said. "Yes, at dawn. What better time to start a story? I went back to my rooms to find my valet waiting for me. I'd sent him to inspect my uncle's house, and so he had. He had a lot to report to me, so he rode like the wind, arrived back in London in the night and sat up waiting for me. He's a thorough fellow, and had gone poking around Uncle's house, tapping on walls, lifting tiles, peeling back carpets, trying to estimate the extent of the repair the place needed.

"He found woodworm, and dry rot, and water damage, but all possible to repair." He paused, and grinned. "That is to say, with the money my odd uncle left me. You see, he also found a sack of ancient gold coins beneath a floorboard he noticed pried up in the master's chambers!

"Rosamund," he said more seriously, looking deep into her eyes, "I couldn't court you, or ask to do so. I couldn't ask for anything but your smile not even a day past. But now I'm well off—very much so. My brother paid back *all* his debt. My uncle left me a rich man. And my investments, which I hope to add to with your father's sound advice, will doubtless make me richer, as will the income from the estate when I get it on its feet again."

He hesitated. "Speaking of feet," he said slowly, "before I go any further, you must tell me how far you wish me to go. I won't presume. I know too well that money won't solve all my difficulties. You're young and lovely. I'm an old soldier. Not ancient, not even a decade older than you, but centuries older in the life I've led. I'm not titled or handsome. I'm scarred inside and out. But whatever I am and have, and whatever life I have left to me, I would share with you. I don't know if I've grown too full of myself with my good fortune to see truth. But I thought I detected some fellow feeling in you."

She smiled, though now she was weeping. "I lied, and cheated, and deceived you," she said.

"And in the end, aided me, remember?" he said. "In fact, were it not for how hard I saw it was for you to lie, I don't think I'd have kept at the puzzle so long. That's in the past. As for the future? How you feel about me now is all that matters."

She bent toward him, hesitated, and then put her lips on his, lightly and tentatively, because she'd never initiated a kiss with a man before. He took her in his arms and kissed her deeply and soundly, because he'd never wanted to kiss any woman so much.

It was just as well that dinner was waiting, because it took a tap on the door to remind them that they weren't wed yet and there were proprieties. Gabriel finally left the salon with Rosamund's hand on his arm, her promise to marry him and the memory of her kisses to make him feel he was gliding two feet above the floor.

Dinner was riotously happy for the baron and his two beautiful daughters that night. One was promised to be married to a gentleman her father roundly approved of, and the other couldn't stop smiling and laughing up into her old friend and new suitor's eyes.

They sang around the pianoforte and traded stories until near midnight, when the baron yawned. "We leave early tomorrow, Christmas Day," he said as he rose from his chair. "So we must get *some* sleep. We'll take two coaches so there'll be room for all of us. I'll see you at seven, gentlemen. I'll walk you to the door now, Viscount. Go to bed, Sylvia. Major, you and Rosie may take an extra half hour together alone because you're affianced. But don't take advantage of my holiday spirit," he said, shaking a finger at the man who'd soon be his son-in-law.

"Never," Gabriel said, bowing as the baron, Sylvia and Arthur left the room.

Then he opened his arms to Rosamund. She stepped into them, and raised her lips to his. But he didn't kiss her; he only took her hand in his again. "One dance," he said softly. "You and I, we have never danced."

She bit her lip. "It's all right," she said. "I'm really not that mad for dancing. I don't know what got into me in that silver ballroom, because I don't always dance."

"But you sometimes do," he said with a small smile. "And you love it too."

"It doesn't matter," she said. "I don't want to cause you pain."

"You won't," he said simply, as he put his hand lightly on her waist, and humming softly, led her in a waltz.

She moved with him, slowly, and then faster, and spun and twirled, entranced as she had never been before. But after a moment, she stared up at him in astonishment. "Your leg! Your knee. How did this come to be? It must be magic! You dance beautifully!"

He laughed aloud. "It came from you. I saw a physician today, and he confirmed it. I am cured." He stopped and looked down at her, exultation in his clear gray eyes. "No, really. I did it myself, all unknowing, and all of it because of you. I followed you through the park every day instead of sitting nursing my pain, as I'd been doing before. That was wonderful exercise. And when I tracked you in the park yesterday, I came across a strange little fellow who needed aid getting his leg out of a trap. I thought I'd wrenched mine beyond repair helping him. But I did it. Then I met an old lady. I'll tell you about her someday: She's odd and old as the hills, but she'd lived here all her life. She gave me a clue about the secret door, and when I understood it I flew up the stairs, without my stick. It hurt like the devil. Then I raced through the passage, so excited that I didn't feel pain.

"All that, the physician said, was likely what did it. All that activity must have broken through the knot and untied the scars that bound my knee, because now there's no pain and I can move as well as any man. But he cautioned me to exercise regularly. So, my dear Rosamund, will you promise to keep waltzing with me for so long as we both shall live?"

"Yes!" She laughed. "Oh, yes. But no matter what you say, it is magic!"

"No," he said seriously. "I don't believe in magic. We make our own. It's what happens when you kiss me. It's what brings a man and a woman together, though their fortunes couldn't be further apart. It is, God willing, what will happen when our love creates another being. That is magic. There is no other, and it is enough for me."

She didn't argue. She was too busy kissing him.

"I like that!" the old woman in the park across the street from the baron's town house exclaimed. "No magic, indeed."

"Aye, well. Humans. Huh," the odd little man at her side grumbled. "And ye wouldn't rest until I paid him a sack of gold, would ye?"

"He earned it," the old woman said primly. "You can find more in your mountain halls. And don't tell me you didn't like helping thwart our old friend's plans."

"Huh," the odd little man said. "Old friend! He might fool them, but not us. 'Duc d'Alberon' he calls hisself now. Like he was a furrener, when there ain't a body more English than he—or we."

"Well, but the new world is become very learned, you know," the old woman said. "He can scarcely lure mortals if he names himself 'Oberon,' can he? But whatever he calls himself, we've put a knot in his net. Not only did the king and his faery troupe have to leave the house and the land, but without his mortal maid. He won't be back until Midsummer's night, but I doubt he'll show that pretty face anywhere near here again for at least another century. Best of all, he'll never know who vexed him so, will he?"

"Aye, I'll give ye that," the little man allowed.

"So what if the major doesn't believe in us?" she asked. "Better for us, I'd say."

The old man gave her a curious look. "Do ye? Well, there's some that say that when they don't know us no more, not one of them, we won't be here no more, neither."

"There's some that say the most ridiculous things," she snapped. "We're bone and blood of this land, you and I: sorceress and dwarf, little folk and large, we of the green earth and deep caverns. Now come, we must go. It's time. Their holiday bells will ring and we must be gone before they do. They sound silver but strike iron to the heart in such as we."

The odd man gave her an even more curious look.

Her cheeks flushed. "We still have our places and powers, though they be hidden. But the bells are bane to old magic, and such as we who once ruled in this land. We'll go now, but not forever. Children of the earth still need all the help they can get."

"There's that!" he said, clearly heartened.

They stood silent a moment, and were gone in the next, before the first bell to signal the coming of Christmas chimed.

Gabriel lifted his head and brushed a lock of Rosamund's hair back from her flushed face. "Listen," he whispered. "It's Christmas Day. Happy Christmas, my own."

"Happy Christmas, my love," she said as the bells of London began tolling Christmas, echoing around the sleeping city, through the streets and over the rooftops, and down the length and breadth of the wild and suddenly empty park across the street.

The Enchanted Earl

Barbara Metzger

Chapter One

Once upon a time (all proper fairy tales begin that way, you know) there was a beautiful young maiden.

Well, Laurel Mumphrey was not precisely beautiful. Her nose was too long, her mouth was too wide, and her hair was neither blond nor brunette. She was the type of female who one said had a pleasing personality, or a well-educated mind, or fine eyes. Her eyes were indeed her best feature, being a clear green, as deep as the laurel leaves she was named for.

To be perfectly honest, she was not quite young, either, not when a woman past her twenty-first year was considered past her prime. Laurel had seen twenty-five birthdays, and was looking forward to her twenty-sixth on Christmas Day.

She was definitely not a maiden.

Married since she was eighteen, Laurel Mumphrey, née Lady Laurel Haddington, daughter of the Marquess of Haddington, had been wed for seven years. She would have been a widow for one year on Christmas Eve, and she was ready to celebrate both events. Coming out of mourning and into her majority, free to spend her deceased spouse's money and her own settlements without censure or supervision, she was more than ready to revel at the grandest party Upper Shepherd's Neck, Somerset, had ever seen. Lower Shepherd's Neck, too, for Laurel intended to invite every family for miles in either direction, be they gentry, aristocrats, farmers, or servants.

She intended to throw open the gates of Mumphrey Hall, its ballroom and its barns and outbuildings, the orangery and the armament room. There would be dancing and caroling, wassail and wine, food fit for a king and ample enough for an army. She had hired an orchestra from London and fiddlers from the village. Besides dancing, she planned to have mimes and tumblers, games and contests, fireworks and fortune-tellers and a magic show, if she could find a magician willing to come entertain the children.

She recalled village fairs when she was a child, sitting enthralled when a caped man in a pointed hat pulled coins from her brother's ear and silk ribbons out of her hair. She had laughed and laughed when his rabbit had scampered out from under his hem instead of appearing when he tapped his wand against a painted box. That was the magic she wanted for her party, that laughter, that fun, the innocent joys of childhood, the carefree holiday spirit.

Her neighbors, tenants, and staff deserved it after living under Felix Mumphrey's thumb. Heaven knew Laurel deserved it.

Her late but not lamented spouse had been wealthy beyond measure and as tight as an oyster with its pearl. He squeezed his shillings so hard they cried for mercy, which he never gave. He neglected his tenants, mistreated his servants, and despised his wife.

Mumphrey had expected his well-born bride—and his fortune—would gain him and his sister entry into the Polite World. In the *ton*, a woman took her standing from her husband, however. It did not work the other way round, and the Mumphreys remained what they were: rich, rude, and rejected by the beau monde. Lady Laurel, which title she kept at her ambitious husband's insistence, was no longer invited to her own aunt's at-homes, much less Almack's.

To compound her failure in her husband's eyes, Laurel had not been able to produce a son to inherit Mumphrey's fortune, losing two infants to miscarriages. His dreams now bitter ashes, Mumphrey turned on his wife.

Her dreams of a loving husband and a family of her own died, too. Sold into matrimony the year of her come-out, Lady Laurel had not known how to refuse the rough-mannered East India Company nabob, or her father, or her conscience. If she did not wed Mr. Mumphrey, they all told her, her frail mother would not get the medical care she needed. Her brother might be sent to the workhouse, her feckless father to debtor's prison.

Now they were all gone. Her mother had died of the consumption, her father of consuming too much brandy. Her brother had tried his luck with the Trading Company and had fallen to malaria. Mumphrey had tried every fallen woman in London, until his heart gave out. Even Laurel's aunt was dead, having choked on a fish bone.

Laurel had no friends left, either, for Mumphrey had not let her mingle with the lower classes, and the uppers wanted nothing to do with the taint of Trade. Laurel was all alone . . . except for Mumphrey's money.

Her father might have been a gambler and a wastrel, but his solicitor was a clever chap. He'd made sure that the marquess's debts were paid, but he'd also insured that the young lady would never be in want. With no entailment and no heirs, everything—Mumphrey Hall, Mumphrey's millions—went to Laurel. Her fortune would be made final on her Christmas birthday, three weeks away. Independence and inheritance, in one fell swoop.

If that was not cause enough for celebrating, nothing was.

She might not be the princess of fairy tales, but Lady Laurel was a genuine heroine to her dependents. She had already lowered the rents and raised new roofs. She'd started schools and erected a hospital, hired honest estate managers, and underwrote repairs to the church.

Everyone was delighted to help plan her party—except, of course, the least desired guest, the ill-wishing witch, the cruel stepsister. The sanctimonious, self-serving, shrewish sister-in-law, in this instance.

Bettina Mumphrey White lived in the estate's dower house, at Laurel's sufferance, and suffering it was. Widow of a merchant sea captain who had lost his ship along with his fortune and his life, she was beholden to her late brother's wife for her very bread. Bitter, she blamed Laurel for her woes. If Lady Laurel had not been such a failure, Bettina could have made a grand marriage into the *ton*. If Laurel's solicitors had not been such fierce bargainers, Bettina might have been left her brother's fortune. Now she hated to see a farthing of it spent, especially on frivolous, flighty fetes for her sister-in-law's birthday.

"It is not seemly, I say. You are in mourning for my brother."

"The year of wearing blacks will be over soon." Laurel had switched from black to gray and lavender and dark blue, with black bands, at the sixth-month mark. She had ordered a green velvet gown for the party, with joy. "No one will count the days, not when they are drinking our wine."

Bettina sniffed, wrinkling her hooked nose and fingering the black bombazine she wore like a shroud around her tall, bony figure. "You should have shown mourning for two years. I intend to, for dear Captain White. If not longer."

This was the first Laurel had heard of the captain being anything other than that demmed witless White, sailing off without insurance. "One year is sufficient to express my respect for Mr. Mumphrey." One day of marriage was sufficient to erase any affection or admiration that might have developed between the innocent young girl and the middle-aged merchant. The man was a boor and a brute, and smelled of the bottle and the brothel—at their wedding. The wedding night was a memory Laurel chose to forget, along with the ensuing years of abuse and anxiety. "I am done with mourning, for my family and for Mr. Mumphrey. It is time to move on."

At thirty years of age, Bettina had nowhere to move to, not without looks or pleasant manners or a groat to her name aside from the allowance Laurel made to her. Laurel also provided servants and supplies for the dower house; never enough, however, in Mrs. White's estimation. She wanted it all. If she could not enjoy Felix's money, she saw no reason for Laurel to enjoy it. "My brother would be outraged that you are wasting his hard-earned blunt on such a vain, useless entertainment."

Laurel smiled. "Yes, he would, wouldn't he?"

Bettina ignored the satisfaction in Laurel's voice. "I heard you have invited the entire populace for miles. Farmers and shepherds, peasants and paupers alike, the very parasites my brother despised. I would not be surprised if you took to dancing with the blacksmith, you ungrateful chit."

"Mr. Botts has promised to teach me the reel."

Bettina sniffed again. "I doubt any of the important people in the neighborhood will come, then. Lord and Lady Thaxter would never rub shoulders with such scum."

The viscount and his wife had never invited the Mumphreys to their home, either, but Laurel did not mention that. "Lady Thaxter penned a lovely acceptance, asking if she might bring her houseguests as well." Laurel consulted her ever-present list. "Squire Hildreth replied, on behalf of his family and visiting company, as did Sir Percival."

"Humph. They are all coming for the free food, just like those idle aristocrats. No matter, it is disrespectful, holding a common revelry on the eve of Christmas. I insist you cancel your plans and hold a quiet dinner instead, or a dignified gathering where a few choice guests might sing carols. I should be willing to play the pianoforte for the company."

Laurel showed great restraint, she felt, in not reminding Bettina that she had no right to insist on anything. "Nonsense," she said. "There is no disrespect in celebrating the birth of the Holy Child with laughter and good cheer. Quite the opposite, I believe. In any case, the fete will be over in time for everyone to attend midnight service at St. Jerome's, so not even the vicar can object."

Bettina meant to call on the vicar herself, as soon as she was done with Laurel. "He will have a word or two, I swear, about having a magician practice his ungodly arts at Christmas Eve. I heard you were asking about the gypsy band that robs and lies its way through here in the spring, asking if they knew of an illusionist. How could you think to bring a pagan charlatan into my brother's house?"

Since Mr. Mumphrey had been both unchristian and unscrupulous, and was now unavailable to protest, Laurel thought the idea was an excellent one, all the better for rankling her overbearing sister-in-law. "You need not worry, for I have been unable to locate a magician," she said now, more than ever determined to have one to entertain her guests. Perhaps she would advertise in the London newspapers.

While Laurel was thinking of the note she would pen, Bettina was thinking of what she could do to ruin the party, or at least her sister-in-law's enjoyment of it, without jeopardizing her allowance. She could harass the servants and spread rumors of tainted foodstuffs through the village. Mostly, she could destroy Lady Laurel's new and unwelcome confidence. While Felix lived, his wife was as timid as a mouse, acquiescent and nervously accommodating. Bettina did not like the mouse showing its teeth.

"They are only coming to gawk, you know," she told Laurel now. "To laugh at the widow trying to buy her way into their favor. The swells will eat your food and dance to your music, snickering behind their hands at your ambitions. The villagers will take what you give, and still despise you for being better off than they are. And if you are thinking to attract a new husband, be warned. You might trick yourself out like a tart—I heard in the emporium about that green velvet you intend to wear—but any man who looks at you will only see the color of your gold. No man wants a barren widow with no looks to speak of and no connections. They'll toss compliments and flowers at your toes, but it's not you they are after. Never you. Only the money."

Ah, the poisoned apple of truth.

Chapter Two

No man was going to want her. Laurel knew that and accepted it, gladly. She did not want a husband any more than Bettina wanted her to find one. Bettina could lose her allowance and her home if Laurel wed, but Laurel could lose a great deal more. What, give her new fortune into the hands of some wastrel who could gamble it away? Be a slave to some other man's whims and wishes? Act as the docile puppet of yet another despot? No. She was free, with no father or husband to order her life, and she was going to stay free. Those girlhood dreams of love and happiness, of sharing her life with the perfect soul mate, were tucked so far away in her heart that she could not find them if she tried. She did not try. She tried to find a magician instead.

A man in tattered clothing arrived the following morning, declaring himself an illusionist. He did not even give the illusion of sobriety, much less sorcery. He was so inebriated, the best trick he could perform was staying on his feet. Laurel sent him to the kitchens for coffee and a decent meal, then sent him on his way.

The next would-be mage arrived in a painted wagon, wearing a pointed hat and a flowing robe. At least this one looked the part, Laurel thought as she accepted the bouquet of flowers he pulled out of thin air—or out of the voluminous sleeves of his robe. He proceeded to pull coins from her butler's wig. The gawking footmen had their mouths open in amazement, while the watching maids were giggling as yet another coin appeared. Unfortunately, Frederick the Phenomenal was equally as deft at making silver candlesticks disappear from the hall table.

Laurel had her servants turn him upside down to see what fell out, then threw him out, with three grooms to escort him to the local magistrate. Heavens, her neighbors could have been robbed of their jewels and their purses while watching her paid performer. Laurel would have been robbed of their respect. A fine divertissement that would have been, watching her guests flee, bereft and blaming her. She vowed to be even more careful with future interviews. She thought of asking for references, as one did when hiring a maid, but a shady sleight-of-hand artist could easily forge a note of commendation. Time was growing too short to check the references, anyway. She would have to trust her intuition and her intelligence.

Or she could hire a troupe of circus performers. Acrobats, fire-eaters, and rope-walkers appeared at her doorstep later that week, having heard of her search for entertainers. Their caravan was followed by all the village children and half of their parents, hoping for a free show while Lady Laurel considered hiring the band. Their magician had doubled as the dancing bear's trainer and was no longer available, the troupe's manager confided while the tumblers tumbled and the jugglers juggled. Marvello should have stuck with his pet pigeons and counting pig. He should have put a muzzle on the bear.

The children were entranced, so Laurel took on the troupe, minus the magician who was now minus a limb or two. They could stay at the inn in the next village until the party, earning their fare by entertaining travelers passing through on their way home for the holidays.

Lady Laurel was glad to have the little circus. Besides, they needed the work, with winter shutting down the country fairs and bad weather halting outdoor performances. She still wanted a magician, though.

What she did not want was another lecture.

"I have been informed of your coming gala," Vicar Chalfont said after sipping delicately at his sweetened tea.

Laurel was sure he had been, knowing her sister-in-law. Bettina had been busy leaving the greenhouse doors open, trying to change Cook's menus, accidentally knocking over a bucket of ashes on the Axminster rug.

"I was certain your invitation would have been delivered by now," Laurel said. "I was hoping you called to accept in person."

The vicar's thin lips pursed, as if the tea were still too bitter. His lips were the only thin thing about the man, except for his dark hair, combed in strands across his forehead. The vicar did like his desserts. He'd downed two raspberry tarts already. Now he scowled, at both Laurel and the remaining refreshments. "You must know I find the event unseemly. *I* am hoping to persuade you to cancel the fete."

Laurel set her own cup down. "What, after all of the invitations have gone out, the refreshments are half prepared, the performers hired? I could not cancel the party if I wished. And I do not wish."

"But you must listen to older, wiser heads, my dear young lady. You will be made a pariah in the neighborhood if you go through with this ill-conceived gathering."

"Fustian. Nearly everyone I invited was delighted. If they disapproved, they would not have accepted."

The vicar's mouth twitched up in what might have been a smile, or indigestion. "But they have not heard my sermon about keeping the solemnity of the Christmas season. I shall remind the congregation that this is a time of prayer, not partying."

"I thought yuletide was a time for rejoicing. 'Comfort and joy,' 'Joyful and triumphant,' 'God rest ye merry.' To say nothing of the Hallelujah Chorus."

"A time for gladness, certainly, joy for one's soul, not for base entertainments. Circus performers, bah! You show no respect for the sanctity of the season."

"Of course I do. We shall be singing those very carols, and the Sunday school children will be reenacting the Nativity in the barn. Their instructor, Mrs. Jessel, was delighted." Mrs. Jessel was also delighted to have a wider audience for her young charges than ever attended the Reverend Mr. Chalfont's tedious church services. Laurel did not say that. She did consult the watch pinned to her gray gown, hinting that the vicar had overstayed his welcome.

The vicar reached for a macaroon, not his favorite, but it would do. Holding it in the air, he sneered. "The barn? The children's pageant is in the barn while the decadent, debauched, and most likely drunken partygoers dance in your ballroom? Sinful, that is what it is." He swallowed the pastry in one gulp.

Laurel moved the dish out of his reach as she tidied the tea things. "The Christ child was born in a barn, or have you forgotten, sir? And I cannot agree that our neighbors, most of whom are your own congregants, are such transgressors. Nor would they entertain the devil's spawn in their own homes. The solemnity of the occasion will be preserved, as will the spirit of celebration."

"With magic? You might as well invite a warlock into your home, a druid, a heathen witch doctor. How could you think to debase this holy day with such ungodly entertainment? Magic is anathema to true religion."

"Rubbish. I am not planning any pagan rites or bacchanals, merely a merry night's entertainment. You make it sound as if I were sacrificing maidens to appease volcanoes, trying to awaken the dead, or predict the future. You are far wide of the truth. I assure you, my only wish is to see the children laugh and clap in wonder."

Mr. Chalfont eyed the distant dish of macaroons, then his hostess. "I fear it is you who is mistaken and misguided. Mrs. White and I agree. You are too young to know what is proper. You need a man to direct you from this immodest levity onto the path of righteousness. Mrs. White hinted that you might be amenable, now that your mourning period is over."

Outraged, and determined to confront her sister-in-law over this latest interference, Laurel stood up, indicating the conversation was at an end. The vicar did not stand. Instead, he sank to his knees and grabbed for her hand. "I am prepared to be that guiding man."

Good grief! Laurel was not in the least prepared for a priestly proposal, although she should have been. Chalfont was nearing fifty, with no use for sons. He had innumerable uses for the widow's wealth. Laurel tugged on his hand to raise him to his feet. "Please cease, sir. I do not intend to remarry."

"You see how far you have gone astray from the Lord's will? All women are meant to marry, to be protected and sheltered from the chaos of their own wayward emotions by a man. It is a woman's duty to marry. I am offering to be your earthly guide as well as your spiritual leader."

Laurel tugged harder. "I am honored"—she gasped as she pulled his leaden weight—"but fear we would not suit. What you find unseemly levity I see as seeking the joy in life. Now please get up before we are both embarrassed."

Instead, Chalfont began kissing her fingers.

"Sir, you forget yourself!"

"No, I am remembering the appetites of my youth, seeking that joy of which you spoke. I do not want you thinking that I am too old to enjoy conjugal relations."

Laurel thought he was a slobbering old goat, with a vise-grip on her now dampened hand. She tried to pry his fingers loose with her other hand, while she prayed none of the servants came into the room to witness this mortifying spectacle. "You forget your calling, then."

"No, I am devoted to my church and my vocation. That was what made me decide to take a wife after all these years of celibacy. Your good deeds, my dear, have made me see what a fine helpmeet a woman can be. Think of all that we can accomplish, working together. We can transform St. Jerome's chapel into a magnificent edifice, one the bishop would commend. Who knows how high I might rise in the church hierarchy with you at my side?"

Her money, his ambition. Laurel had heard enough. She made one last attempt to free her hand from his hot, fleshy fingers and his wet kisses, then reached for the plate of macaroons.

"No, thank you, my dear. Later, perhaps, after I have had your answer and we can celebrate."

"My answer is no, you . . . you . . ." Laurel could not think of a word suitable for a jackass in collars, one a lady might use. So she hit him over the head with the dish instead.

Mr. Chalfont left, rubbing his head and blowing over-heated gusts of steam into the cold winter air like an irate dragon. His last words, however, were cold and mean: "May you live to rue this day, when you are leading apes through the fires of hell."

A maiden, a mischief-maker, a malevolent curse—where the devil was the hero? What kind of fairy tale had no dashing knight on a white charger riding to the rescue? A poor one indeed.

The damsel's desires aside, a flurry of gentlemen sought the role of hero as soon as the invitations to the party were delivered. Lady Laurel Mumphrey was out of mourning. She and her bank account were available for wooing.

As Bettina had predicted, the suitors brought floral tributes and false compliments. They also brought their mothers, their motherless children, their financial statements, and their pedigrees, anything to convince her of their need and their worth.

Viscountess Thaxter accompanied her second son. The lad was two years Laurel's junior, and two inches shorter. He had no fortune, no career, and no chin. No matter. His mother thought he would make Laurel the ideal husband. "No backbone," the doting parent whispered in Laurel's ear. "You'll be able to lead him around by the nose."

Laurel could have found herself a dog if that was what she wanted. A dog might have had more intelligence than Mr. Thaxter.

Squire Hildreth brought his brood of unmanageable, motherless brats to tea, to prove that Laurel's inability to bear children was unimportant to him. If all children were as unpleasant and unruly as these, Laurel was glad of her lack. Now she was missing two matching teacups, the antique urn in the hall, and one footman, who gave notice after the little beasts poured glue into his gloves.

A dog? Laurel could have taken in a litter of puppies if she wanted her house and her peace of mind destroyed.

Lord Brownwell arrived with an invitation to a private luncheon, and a leer. A London buck down on his luck and down in the country, he put the other callers to shame with his elegant apparel, sophisticated gallantries, and town gossip. He flashed his practiced smile while his eyes darted from framed masterpiece to priceless jade figurine.

Laurel decided she'd rather adopt a wolf.

Sir Harold Canaday was a connection of Lady Montrose's, supposedly come to court her granddaughter. Laurel was the bigger prize, of course, so he brought her a bigger bucket of Spanish coin. He also pinched one of the maids.

A tomcat would be a more loyal companion.

Laurel told herself she was content as she was. She did not need a husband, or a pet, or even a magician. That evening, though, while a sudden storm came up to obscure the full moon, Laurel put down her book and went to close her opened bedroom window before the pounding rain could come in. She could not help looking out at the wild night and the wind-tossed trees, wishing she had someone to share it with. All she had was a boring treatise on agriculture. Perhaps she ought to get a dog after all.

With her luck, she thought, she'd find a mongrel that hid under the bed at the first clap of thunder.

Laurel was awed by the violent storm, not frightened. Her house was made of stone and had stood on its hill for centuries. The trees had weathered worse. Her friends and neighbors and servants should all be safe in their beds, although she was not certain of Sir Harold or Lord Brownwell, or that maid Lizzie.

Then, as she stayed watching, all that power of the thunder and lightning, all that fury of untamed nature, made her feel small, dull, alone. She wished— Oh, she was not going to wish for anything as foolish as eternal love or happily ever after. That was the stuff of picture books and broken dreams. All she wished for was . . . a bit of real magic in her life.

Chapter Three

An old gamekeeper's cottage had been struck by lightning and an ancient oak had been felled by the wind. That appeared to be the storm's only damage, thank goodness. Laurel went out with her bailiff to check on the progress in removing the tree from the lane so deliveries could be made, and to inspect the cottage to see if it was worth repairing. While she was there in the woods, she made note of the stands of holly, the evergreens, and the high vines of the mistletoe she would have her grooms and gardeners cut for decorations soon. The woods seemed quiet to her, with no birdsong or scampering squirrels, and the air was still, as if the raging tempest had left the very earth exhausted. She was exhausted, too, after a sleepless night.

She had to rub her eyes when she returned to the Hall. No, she was awake. She had not dreamed up the figure that waited in the carriageway. She was no magician to conjure up the tall, handsome stranger or his stomping, snorting black steed. He obviously was. A magician, that is.

He had ink-black hair and a straight nose, a cleft chin, and eyes of midnight blue. He was coatless, with white shirtsleeves billowing against well-muscled arms. Laurel would have been enthralled by the stranger's devastatingly masculine beauty even if he had not been juggling balls of fire between his hands. Suns, stars, streaking comets flew over his head, seemingly without effort. Her stable men were fascinated, too, keeping their distance from the dangerous-looking stallion while edging closer to the performer. Mobcapped heads were at every window that overlooked the drive, and footmen crowded the front doorway. Now here was a magician worthy of Mumphrey Hall's Christmas Eve birthday ball.

Laurel clapped her hands in delight. The man gathered his flaming balls into a scarlet silk pouch, then made her an elegant bow. "My lady. I am Cauthin and I have answered your call."

His accent sounded foreign to Laurel, but she could not identify its origin. Then his words registered in her mind. "My call? Oh, you must have heard that I was looking for a magician to entertain my guests on Christmas Eve."

The man raised one dark winged eyebrow. "A . . . magician?"

"Yes, I adored magic shows when I was a child and was hoping to give the tenants' children that pleasure. You know, pulling rabbits from hats, naming hidden cards, that type of thing. You can do that, can you not, Mr. Cauthin?"

Cauthin snapped his fingers and a book appeared in his hand: *Elementary Prestidigitation.* He thumbed through the pages and nodded at Laurel. "I can amuse the children, yes. You did not want any of them to disappear, did you?"

Laurel laughed, but with a tinge of uncertainty. She was not sure that the children's parents would enjoy Mr. Cauthin's humor. There was something about the man's handsome dark visage that was unsettling, like looking at a fallen angel. "Ah, have you performed anywhere nearby, or for someone who might vouch for you? Not that I mean any disrespect, of course, but one of your brethren turned out to be a thief. I have to be careful what manner of man I invite into my home."

Cauthin bowed again. So did his horse. "A wise woman, besides beautiful. I assure you, my lady, that creature was no brother of mine. Your valuables and your guests will be safe." He produced a cascade of gold coins that fell into a neat pile at Laurel's feet. "I do not need your money."

A chill went up Laurel's spine. "Then what do you wish in payment for your time and efforts?"

"Your firstborn son, of course."

Laurel gasped. "That is not amusing. Everyone knows that I was not able to give my husband an heir."

While Cauthin adjusted his shirtsleeves, he stared at Laurel, leaving her colder than ever. "Yet you shall bear a child. Three healthy infants. Two will be boys. I would claim one."

Laurel was shaking. "Please leave. I find that I do not require your services. Perhaps a magic show was not a good idea."

Cauthin sneered. "It is never a good idea to dabble in what you do not understand, madam."

For a moment Laurel worried that the lunatic would not leave, that he would threaten her or her staff. His brute of a horse could trample any number of them. She looked down at the gold coins at her feet, but where they had fallen were only pebbles. "Go, sir. Go now. Or I shall be forced to call—"

"Whom? Your cowering servants? Your pompous vicar? The magistrate?" He laughed now, an ugly sound, made worse coming from such a stunningly handsome face. "I obey no laws except one: My minions must be willing."

With those cryptic words Cauthin vaulted onto his horse's back, causing the stallion to rear up, sending stones and sparks in all directions as he thundered off.

Laurel wiped at a tiny cut on her cheek from a flying pebble. She shook her head, wondering what she would have done, in fact, if the madman had not ridden off. She left the grooms staring down the carriageway and went inside, hoping no one could tell that her knees were shaking and her palms were wet.

Her butler met her inside the front door with a glass of sherry.

"Thank you," she said. "I need that."

The butler looked longingly at the drink he'd been about to swallow, then mopped at his sweating brow. "There are more of them," was all he said.

"More of . . . ?"

"Magicians, if that is what you would call them. Unnatural, that is what I say, ma'am. One started a fire in the Gold Room, where no logs had been laid. The two in the library keep fading into the wallpaper. As for the one who insisted on bringing that, that dog into the house . . ." He shuddered.

"Why did you let them in?" Laurel wanted to know.

"They said you sent for them. Besides, who am I to argue with a wolf?"

If Laurel had felt alone before, she was positively quaking now, wishing she had a strong, forceful gentleman at her side. Or in front of her. With a pistol. She could not ask the servants to step into danger; she had to do this herself.

The occupant of the Gold Room was a short, round gnome of a man. He grinned at her, showing a gap between his teeth, the ones that were not capped with gold. Laurel could see nothing to burn in the hearth, yet a merry fire was warming the room. She nodded politely and said, "I fear there has been a mistake, Mr. . . . ?"

"Sparky, my lady. Sparky will do. And there is no mistake. You called for real magic. Here I am." He patted the Staffordshire pottery dogs on the mantel and tongues of fire flew from their mouths. Then he touched the bouquet of silk chrysanthemums and the orange and yellow and amber flowers burst into flames. He turned toward the draperies.

"No! That is, you appear a very fine magician, Mr., ah, Sparky. But I find that I do not wish to engage one after all. I have, ah, decided to play charades instead."

His slightly slanted eyes lit up and he skipped in place. "I love parlor games! Here, what am I?" He got down on his hands and knees, wagging his rear end like a dog, but breathed out bursts of steam and fire.

Laurel leaped back before the flames reached her skirts. "I am sure I have no idea. Please stop, though, before the rugs are scorched."

"A dragon, of course! Now look at—"

"No!" she shouted before he could burn the entire house down.

"No?"

"That's right, no. Now please leave." She remembered Cauthin's odd words. "I am not willing to pay your price, whatever it is."

Sparky seemed ready to weep, but he did drag himself from the room.

Laurel understood what her butler meant about the two men in the library disappearing into the wallpaper. They were so thin, so pale, that she almost thought she could read the book titles on the shelves right through them. They introduced themselves as Agron and Agred, but she had no idea who was who, or where one ended and one began, for that matter. She was beginning to get a headache— No, she already had a headache, Laurel realized. She was beginning to grow weak from the pain of trying to delineate these tall visitors, like imagining elephants in puffs of smoke. Her guests were too real, though, picking up books and taking on the hue of the leather bindings. No, she was simply ill, Laurel told herself, rubbing at her temples. She must have contracted an ague while standing at the window last night. Now she was suffering brain fevers. How else to explain such troubled, peculiar, waking dreams?

"Thank you for coming, gentlemen, but I have changed my mind about the entertainment at the party. In fact, I am feeling so weary, I might have to cancel all the preparations. I do not require your services."

She could not swear the Aggregates left via the window, but they did not pass her on the way out.

Trembling from the tip of her head to the toes on her feet, Laurel made her way to the breakfast room and her last caller, the man with the dog. She liked dogs, and was thinking of getting one for company and protection. Perhaps this one did tricks, she tried to convince herself, like sitting up and begging or dancing on its hind legs wearing a tutu.

It was too late to find Mr. Mumphrey's old blunderbuss. This dog was not going to perform pirouettes in anyone's parlor.

Only crumbs remained of what was to have been her morning repast. A huge silver wolf was licking its lips while the man sat nearby, smiling vacantly at the empty dishes. The wolf growled until the man made a bow.

"Good day, madam. Thank you for the fine repast. Traveling is hungry work," the wolf said.

The wolf said? Laurel blinked. Twice. "Ah, you are a

ventriloquist. I have seen performers throwing their voices, but never one so proficient."

The wolf licked his foot. The man bowed again, with that same empty smile.

"I have nearly decided not to have a magic show," Laurel said, "but out of curiosity, do you have any other tricks?"

The wolf licked his privates. The man smiled.

"Yes, well, I, ah, do not feel that is suitable entertainment for the children I have invited." Nor was a ravenous wild beast. "I am sorry you had to come all this way, but at least your stomachs are full." And her shepherds' flocks ought to be safe.

The wolf whined. "You don't want us?"

She shook her aching head. "No. Thank you."

They left and Laurel sank onto a chair, her head leaning back against the chair rail. If she slept, she might wake up soon to find this had all been a nightmare.

The servants came in to remove the empty plates, and the empty sugar bowl, the empty butter dish, the empty flower vases. "Coffee," Laurel ordered her butler. "Hot coffee. With a dash of brandy. Or brandy with a dash of coffee. I do not care. And I am not at home, not to anyone."

Her sister-in-law was furious to be turned away, but Bettina did meet a handsome gentleman on a black horse on her walk back to the dower house. He smiled at her in a way no man had ever smiled, not even her husband. She invited him for tea.

Laurel did manage to rest despite the servants' excited chatter—the ones who had not given notice to quit. By the afternoon she was composed enough to walk to her sister-in-law's house to make amends. She hated to be at odds with anyone, even Bettina.

On her way to the dower house, however, she passed a bent old man pushing a cart. On top of the cart was a battered trunk decorated with stars and moons in peeling paint, lettered with the faded name: SPINROD THE SORCERER. Oh, no.

Before the old man could say a word, Laurel pointed back toward the village. "We are not interested. I have changed my mind about magic. I am sorry you came all this distance for nothing."

Since he seemed old and rather ragged, in worn leather breeches, fraying wool cape, and scuffed boots, she tossed him a coin to see him on his way.

He caught the coin with an agility surprising for an ancient with a long white beard and white hair tied back with a leather thong. His voice was stronger than she expected, too, as he said, "Nay, my lady. I came for something."

"Then you have had your recompense. There will be no performance."

He shrugged, then stretched, showing he was not as crippled as she had thought, merely bent from pushing the heavy cart. He must be a poor magician indeed, that he could not afford a horse and wagon. "I fear there will be a performance, my lady, will you or won't you. I doubt you will enjoy it, nor your neighbors."

Laurel was confused. "I hired no one."

He waved a gnarled hand. "But they are here. They won't miss the opportunity to win you over, now that you have called them."

"I called no one," she scoffed. "I did put an advertisement in the newspaper for a magician."

"No, my lady, you called for real magic."

"No, I did not! I wanted a bit of happiness for the children, that was all."

Spinrod shook his white head. "No, you wished for far more. Here on this sacred hill, amid a circle of holy oaks, and coming from a family of sympathetics—"

"My grandmother was fey, they said. That did not make her—"

He ignored her interruption. "A lady named Laurel, which has magic of its own, on a night of possibilities, wished for true magic. That is what you got. Wizards, shape-shifters, apparitionists, pyromages. Such as they are not easily swayed from their course. They mean you no good."

The old man's words rang true, as odd as they were. He spoke kindly, so Laurel was not afraid of him, yet fear entered her heart like a burrowing insect. "And what of you?" She gestured toward the name on his trunk. "You claim to be one of their ilk. What do you mean to do?"

He smiled, showing even white teeth, and laugh lines formed around his clear blue eyes. "Why, I mean to protect you, my lady."

Her hero was a crazy old man in a dusty cape, with a scarred trunk? Faugh.

Chapter Four

"Why should I trust you? You might not be who you seem."

"Oh, I am definitely not who I seem. You must learn not to trust appearances."

Her head was aching again. "If you admit to being a charlatan, why should I believe a word you say?"

"Because I am your best hope." He tapped his chest. "I still have a human heart. The others have become . . . something else."

"I do not understand."

"Of course you do not, poor puss. It took me ages to figure it out. You see, true magic gives a man more power than he is meant to have, and makes him want still more. More gold, more knowledge, more years to his life, no matter who dies in his stead. He always wants more. Magic, money, and power, they all go together to steal a man's soul."

"And you?" she asked, nearly whispering, although no one was nearby to hear. Grooms and gardeners would come if she shouted, she knew, but such an old man could not mean her harm, could he? "What of you?"

He looked at her with longing and sadness. "I am not yet entirely a true wizard, and I pray never to become one." Then he brightened and smiled once more, and the chill in Laurel's heart eased. "But that is a tale for another day. Will you accept my aid?"

He really had a lovely, gentle smile, Laurel thought, but he himself had warned her to beware of appearances. "Can you do any magic tricks at all?"

He frowned, as though insulted by her request. "I do as little as possible, just to earn my keep, so that I do not become one of them." Seeing her still doubtful look, he tossed the coin she had given him up into the air. The coin became a white feather that floated to his shoulder, turning into a tiny white owl.

"Merlin," he said, stroking the bird.

No, a merlin was a small hunting falcon. This, unbelievably, was a tiny owl, round yellow eyes and all.

"That is his name," Spinrod said, as though he could read her mind, his lips curving up at her astonishment.

Laurel gathered her wits. "You pulled him from your sleeve. You shall have to do better than that if you wish me to believe even half of your words."

"I told you, true magic has too high a price." Spinrod stroked his beard, then reached into his cape. He pulled out a small, pale gold egg. "But here, this ought to convince you of my bona fides."

Laurel took the little egg into her hand. It did not fill a quarter of her palm, but felt warm. She could feel it stirring. "Oh, it is going to hatch!" She heard a tiny pecking, and the shell started to crack, then bits of it fell away. Laurel held it higher, to see the emerging infant—and found herself inches away from a baby snake. "Yiee!" she cried, throwing the egg and the snake away from her.

"Uh-oh, wrong egg." Spinrod caught the newborn serpent before it reached the ground and tucked it into a pocket of his cape. He took out another egg, but Laurel would not hold the thing. He held it out where she could see, although she did step back a pace. This time a butterfly hatched out of the egg, a brilliant, glittering gold and scarlet butterfly that flapped its wings to dry them off, then flew up to land on Laurel's shoulder.

"It is magnificent," she whispered, so as not to disturb the resting beauty. "But butterflies do not hatch from eggs."

Spinrod smiled, taking decades off his appearance. "Magic," was all he said, and his smile was as bright as the butterfly.

Oh, how the children would love this gentle man, Laurel thought, setting aside all the far-fetched, sinister warnings. If he could not perform a lot of tricks, he could amuse them with his fairy stories, like some bard of old telling tales of derring-do and dragons. The adults would enjoy him, too, she thought, once he was washed and made presentable for company. She could have her entertainment, yes, and give the old fellow decent meals and a warm bed to sleep in before she sent him off with a heavy purse.

She was well pleased with her decision, but had to ask, "What payment do you want, then?"

"Oh, I seek no recompense. Except a kiss."

Laurel was disgusted, both at the licentious old goat and at herself for nearly being taken in by another trickster. "At least one of the others wanted my firstborn son."

"Oh, I'd like that too, as long as he were my son also, but I think a kiss has to come first, don't you?"

Both the owl and the butterfly flew away when she slapped his cheek. "I shall have no sons, and you shall have no kiss, you cad." Laurel spun on her heel. She was going home, and to the devil with her sister-in-law's wounded sensibilities.

"Wait, my lady," Spinrod called after her. "I beg you, please stay so that I might apologize for being forward. I did mean what I said about the danger, so you must not send me away. You need me."

"What, to frighten away warlocks and wizards with butterflies and baby snakes? Go tell your fairy tales elsewhere, sir. I am not interested." The butterfly returned to her, though, landing on a stray lock of her fair hair so its wings brushed against her cheek. She did not want to frighten it away again, so did not rush back to her house as she had intended to do.

Spinrod took advantage of her hesitation. "I cannot leave you unprotected. Please, my lady, accept my help. I swear I will not ask for anything more than you are willing to give. In fact, I will accept nothing."

Now the owl alighted on her shoulder, looking up at her with head cocked, making small chirping sounds. Laurel looked at the owl, not at the man. "I always pay for services rendered." She spoke softly, so as not to disturb either of her companions. "I shall pay you what you are worth, after the performance. Is that acceptable?"

"That is fair, my lady. Perhaps I might even prove worthy of that kiss. Who knows?"

"I know," she declared, turning on her heel. "There will be no more talk of . . . of taking liberties or our bargain is off." She moved so fast the owl toppled off her shoulder and the butterfly tangled in her hair. "Oh, dear, it will be hurt."

He came closer and said, "Let me."

As the man's hands touched her hair, Laurel could not help noticing the clean, lemony scent of him, despite the layer of travel dust on his cape. His hands were those of an old man, or one who had pushed a cart for years, but they were gentle, like the touch of a breeze, as he freed the fragile creature.

"Trust me," he said. "I would never hurt you."

She did not know if he was speaking to her or the butterfly.

"You can sleep in the stables," she said by way of acknowledging that he was going to stay. "The grooms have rooms above."

"No, I do not think that wise. Animals do not like me. The horses will be disturbed."

"Fustian nonsense," she said as the butterfly flew toward his trunk and the owl landed on his shoulder again.

Spinrod shook his head as he took up the handles of his cart. "These are magical beasts. Natural animals are afraid of what they sense but do not understand. People would be better off if they had not lost those instincts. But do not fret over it. I can sleep under the stars. I am used to that. When it rains I crawl under the cart."

"This is December, however. The nights are too cold. I would not have anyone in my employ"—especially not an elderly man—"sleeping out of doors. Too bad that old gamekeeper's cottage burned down. But there are empty rooms in the attics where the staff sleeps. We have them prepared for the guests' servants."

He bent lower over the cart handles. "I doubt these old bones will thank you for the stairs, my lady."

She could not take a strange man into her home—and

Spinrod was one of the strangest she had encountered—as a guest, especially not a traveling performer. No matter that she was a widow and he was old, people were bound to talk.

On the other hand, he spoke like a gentleman and treated her with respect. And he was old. For once Laurel decided to follow those instincts he had mentioned. Intuition told her Spinrod was to be trusted. Besides, she did wish to hear more of his stories. "Very well, then. There must be an unused chamber somewhere in Mumphrey Hall. Heaven knows it is big enough."

He smiled in satisfaction as he followed her along the path.

After a few minutes of walking toward the Hall, Spinrod raised his head and looked back, in the opposite direction. "Who lives there?"

"My sister-in-law. Why?"

He was suddenly running in that direction, leaving his cart behind. So much for his old bones, Laurel thought as she trailed after him, constrained by her narrow skirts. When she reached the dower house, she saw that other madman Cauthin's wild stallion waiting outside, with no tie or tether. The door was ajar and Spinrod was already inside, shouting. Laurel headed toward the raised voices, giving the snorting horse a wide berth.

"No, lady. Do not drink that!" Spinrod was yelling as he leaped between Bettina and the handsome gentleman who was handing her a cup of tea.

Bettina's mouth was hanging open, but Cauthin was shouting back at Spinrod. "Get out, you maggot, you miserable half-mage, you ensorcelled slug. Do not interfere with my business unless you want me to put another spell on you!"

Spinrod did not even look at the other man. He stooped to Bettina's level and told her, "He means you ill, madam. Do not drink anything he hands you."

Bettina had found her tongue. "What is the meaning of this? Who are you, old man, to barge into my house and insult my guest?" Then she noticed Laurel coming into the parlor. Her eyes narrowed. "I know what this is about, missy. You are jealous, that's what, jealous that such an attractive gentleman is visiting me."

Cauthin smiled and preened, straightening his cuffs, patting a curl into place.

"No, Bettina, I do not envy you your caller. If Spinrod, ah, Mr. Spinrod thinks you ought not drink that beverage, you should listen."

"Why should I heed either of you? Your old uncle does not resemble a physician or apothecary. He does not even resemble a gentleman, while Mr. Cauthin is everything pleasing."

"He is not my—"

Spinrod did not wait for the women to establish his social standing. He picked up the cup of tea. Cauthin reached into his jacket, but before he could retrieve a weapon or a wand, Spinrod poured the tea into a potted fern. Cauthin cursed, Bettina called them all Bedlamites, Laurel held her breath while Spinrod panted after his exertion, and the fern shriveled up and died.

While the others were watching the fern turn to dust, Cauthin headed for the door, leaving a curse behind him.

"Tell him not to come back, Bettina. Tell him you will not pay his price."

But Bettina was shrieking and kicking her feet against the floor.

Spinrod shouted out a parrying curse that Laurel could not understand, thank goodness. She was too busy trying to stop her sister-in-law's fit.

When he was certain the black wizard had gone, Spinrod returned to Laurel's side. He pulled a white feather from his sleeve and stroked it down Bettina's cheek. She was so startled by the soft touch, the gentleness, and the sweet smile of the old man kneeling in front of her that she stopped screaming.

"Are you truly a physician?" she asked him.

"Oh, no, I am a sorcerer, ma'am. When I am not an earl."

This time Bettina did not bother with apoplexy. She swooned instead.

Laurel rang for Bettina's maid, but Spinrod picked up the thin woman with surprising ease for an old man, although Laurel had ceased being surprised by anything this day. He carried Bettina's inert form to the stairs, up to her bedroom and the maid's care.

He returned to the parlor to make sure all signs of Cauthin and danger were gone. Then he turned to Laurel, smiled, and said, "You see, my lady? You need me."

Chapter Five

"What do you mean, about being an earl?" Laurel clutched at the one thing she might understand, something that was not about sorcery and spells and insanity.

"Later, my lady. You would not believe me now."

She did not believe her own eyes, much less whatever had just happened. She wanted to believe something, anything, that was real and solid and ordinary. The kindly old man who was pushing his barrow again seemed as commonplace as dirt, despite the small white owl on his shoulder. "How do you know I will not believe you?"

"Do you believe in ghosts?"

"Of course not."

"What about divination? Communion with the afterlife? Curses? Vampires? Were-creatures?"

She walked faster, putting distance between them. "That is the stuff of ancient myths and old pagan religions."

"When people believed that magic surrounded them." Somehow he was able to keep up with her, walking at her side along the carriageway.

"Bah, those are tales told to frighten children."

"Which is why you would not believe me. Yet. But tell me, lady, do you believe that Cauthin is a wizard?"

"I believe that he is evil."

"Good." He smiled his approval. "You are not entirely without the old instincts and understandings." The look she gave him made him add, "Not that you are without intelligence and education. Mankind's senses have become dulled. I am glad you listen to what lies in your heart, not merely what fills your brain."

Laurel was as confused as ever, but found his smile so reassuring that she decided to let the matter rest for now. With her party and Christmas both approaching, she had too much to do to fret herself to flinders over the impossible, the improbable, and the incomprehensible.

Thinking of the party, she said, "I think I should like to see you practice your performance tomorrow." She'd had enough surprises. If Spinrod turned out to be a complete fraud or a Captain Sharp, she wanted to know it before all her guests found out how she'd been taken in by somebody's grandfather. Of course he did not act like an ancient, pushing that cart effortlessly, without breathing heavily or perspiring. All the more reason for her to make sure he was what he said he was—an earl?

Oh, dear. Could she truly let a lunatic with grandiose delusions practice illusions in her parlor? "Perhaps you should use the barn for your performance. We will look it over tomorrow."

"No, we will be too busy tomorrow. You have to come with me."

Laurel thought she had hired the man to do her bidding, not vice versa. She stopped before they reached the front doors of Mumphrey Hall and drew herself up into her best daughter-of-the-nobility demeanor. "I beg your pardon. If I say you shall rehearse tomorrow, that is what you shall do. Otherwise you might turn your wagon about and find a room at the inn with the circus folk. Perhaps they will let you join their band. No, I believe they were looking for a magician who could also be the animal trainer. That leaves you still looking for employment, does it not?"

Instead of being humbled, Spinrod grinned. He let go of the cart's poles and applauded. "Excellent, my lady. Perhaps you ought to go on stage yourself. That was a fine imitation of one of the Almack's hostesses, telling some poor blighter that he could not enter their sacred portals without knee breeches."

"How do you know about Almack's and— No, you

would only tell me another taradiddle. If you are to continue here, you need to understand that I will not suffer disrespect or disobedience. I have made allowances for your age, but I must demand the proper attitude, especially in front of my staff."

He bowed. "Your servant, madam," but the twinkle in his eye told her he did not really mean it. Before she could protest, or dismiss him, he said, "Forgive my presumption, my lady. But we have to establish defenses around your property as early as daylight permits. No one will be safe otherwise."

"Rubbish. We have never had any crime in this area, no more than some boys stealing apples."

"You have never had bogeymen at your borders, either."

"But I did not hire you to protect me."

"Nevertheless, my dear, *that* is my job."

She could not toss him out with night quickly falling. She would have her butler do it in the morning, inform old Spinrod that his services would not be required, give him a coin, and send him on his way. Meanwhile she had merely to find him a cot somewhere and see that Cook fed him, and she'd be done with the attics-to-let actor.

Somehow, though, her butler, who had never before mistaken a peddler for a peer, accepted the presence of a sorcerer in their midst as if he were visiting royalty. He escorted Spinrod to one of the best guest chambers, ordered a hot bath for him, unearthed a cigar and a bottle of aged cognac, and even raided the attics for some of the late Mr. Mumphrey's attire.

Without a by-your-leave, Laurel found herself sitting down to dinner . . . across from a cork-brained conjurer. He was washed and trimmed and garbed in almost fashionable, albeit ill-fitting, attire. He was quite attractive, Laurel thought, for an older man, of course.

"What?" she asked, laughing to cover her surprise at finding her newest employee at her table. "Did you cast a spell on the servants?"

"Only a small one. I told you, I try not to use magic when I do not have to."

Laurel ate the rest of her meal in silence. She was not

about to encourage the poor man in his madness. That handsome Cauthin was a scoundrel, that was all, and the others were oddities and eccentrics, nothing more. She should never have placed her address on that advertisement, Laurel admitted to herself, but word would quickly go out that she was no longer interested in hiring a magician for her Christmas Eve party.

She credited the day's tumult to lack of sleep, the headache, excitement over the coming celebration, and a vivid imagination. Looking at the older man now, one could never suspect him of anything worse than falling on hard luck. His bearing was refined, his table manners excellent.

Not so her sister-in-law's. Bettina arrived during the fish course, having heard from the servants that Laurel was entertaining that strange old man. Very strange indeed, Bettina declared Spinrod, as if he were not sitting right there. Bettina had arrived in the nick of time to protest, to protect her brother's wife's reputation . . . and to enjoy a free meal.

She went on and on, as course followed course, about people knowing their place, about the proper conduct of a lady toward her inferiors, about wasting money on charlatans and churls. She refused to acknowledge Spinrod, no matter how nicely dressed he was nor how politely he put up with her insults. Her husband and her brother might have been working men, in Trade, but they held respectable, profitable—until Captain White's ship sank—positions. They were not itinerant tinkers!

Embarrassed, Laurel tried to stem the tide of Bettina's tirade, to no avail. Spinrod kept eating, as if he had not had a decent meal in ages or as if he were deaf.

Then he winked at her and rubbed his chin. He jerked his head in Bettina's direction and winked again.

Laurel looked, and saw a mole on her sister-in-law's chin that she had never noticed before. As she watched, it grew bigger. Bettina put down her fork long enough to scratch her chin, then went back to her meal and her maligning of Laurel's intelligence, upbringing, and intentions.

Laurel took a hasty swallow of her wine. Then she

started choking when the mole on Bettina's chin sprouted three long black hairs. The butler hurried to pound her back, and Spinrod asked if she were all right.

All right? Heaven help her, she might never be all right again. There really was magic in the world. More astounding, it was in her house!

She dreamed that night of ogres and elves and enchanted earls, which is to say she barely slept at all. Her maid awakened her at dawn "on Mr. Spinrod's orders, ma'am."

Who the devil did the man think he was, giving orders in her household? Laurel dressed and marched into the breakfast parlor ready for a fight. Spinrod and her bailiff were poring over maps—of her estate!

"Eat well, my lady," he told her, "and quickly. We have a lot of ground to cover."

"But I—"

Her bailiff spoke up: "Odd things are happening, ma'am. I don't rightly know how those sheep got on top of Mrs. Gilding's cottage, or who wove all that mistletoe you wanted into a huge nest on top of the tallest oak, or why three of Sam Hooper's eggs hatched two-headed chicks, but it's worried I am. Mr. Spinrod here says he can tend to matters, and I have to believe in something. He already filled in the moat."

"What moat? We do not have any moat."

"Not anymore, we don't, thanks to Mr. Spinrod here. If he thinks you ought to go along instead of me, I'll add my tuppence. Please go with him, ma'am."

"Oh, very well. Have my carriage brought around as soon as I finish my coffee." She had decided tea or chocolate were simply not fortifying enough for this morning's work. "And have hot bricks placed by the feet, for there is frost out."

"No, my lady, we will be walking." Spinrod looked up from his—her—maps. "I have asked your maid to bring your heaviest wrap and your stoutest boots."

He was already dressed in his own old cape, now darned and brushed clean of the road dust.

"You might be used to traipsing the countryside, Mr.

Spinrod, but I assure you, we shall cover a great deal more territory, faster and far more comfortably, in the carriage."

"That may well be, but horses do not like me. Besides, our feet need to be on the ground we would protect in order for the charms to work."

"You go on, then, and sprinkle your garlic and silver crosses. I shall follow in the coach."

He shook his white-maned head. "Those are for vampires. But you are the keeper of this land that is rife with potential. You have to be the one to say the words."

"Gammon. My husband would not have bought an estate that was encumbered with enchantments and such."

"Mumphrey? He would not have recognized magic if a flying pig bit him on the nose. You do. You are starting to, at any rate. Furthermore, you are the one who most needs protection. It is you they seek."

"Me?" Laurel was dismayed at the squeak she heard in her own voice. "But I am nothing out of the ordinary. There are far wealthier widows, with better connections."

"You are this marked land's keeper," he repeated. "And your blood shows promise of breeding back to that grandmother with the old arts. You are the prize, but your tenants and servants will be pawns in the game they play."

"Game?" she whispered.

"It is all a game to them, the competition for more power, more slaves, more territory under their sway."

Before she had time to think—or panic—Laurel found herself wrapped in her cloak and sent out the door. She had a wool scarf around her throat, wool stockings and extra petticoats under her skirts, and a fur muff for her gloved hands.

Spinrod wore neither hat nor gloves. He did not slow his speed for her shorter legs, either. If an old man could set such a pace, she decided, then she could jolly well keep up, even if it killed her.

Every so often he would stop and bend a twig, or leave a feather, or sprinkle on the ground a bit of something he took out of his pockets. He spoke words she could not understand, and then had her speak.

"What am I to say?"

"You must merely declare that you will not accept anyone's bargain, that you refuse their gifts."

"What gifts?"

He pointed to a cherry tree she had not noticed. The tree was in blossom . . . in December.

"The fruit will be tainted, subverting the eater's will. And see here, this pool?"

Laurel could not recall a pond here, but the vista was lovely enough for an artist's brush. The clear water was reflecting the December sunlight and the last of the autumn foliage. "How pretty!"

"How deadly. One drink of the water would make you slave to the pool's creator for the rest of your life. That stand of wild roses? A prick of a thorn unites your blood with its maker. That new well beside the gatehouse? A water-dowser lurks in its depths, ready to snatch the soul of anyone leaning over. Those are the gifts hunting wizards bring to bait their traps."

Laurel licked her suddenly dry lips. "What am I supposed to say again?"

" 'I decline' ought to do the job."

It had not worked with the vicar, but Laurel decided to humor her odd companion and the prickle down her spine. She declined from one end of her estate to the other, through fields and woods, across streams and over rock walls. Surely the old man would tire soon, she thought, desperate for a hot drink, a warm fire, a stool for her aching feet, and an end to this accursed magic.

Besides, her nose was running. What kind of heroine had a dripping nose?

Chapter Six

Spinrod was striding as fast at midday as he had in the morning.

To slow him down and give herself a rest, Laurel tried to engage him in conversation. Perhaps interrupting a wizard mid-spell was not the best course, but how was she to know? Laurel was as confused as the spotted frog that kept croaking "Miss me, miss me" before Spinrod sent it back to whatever realm the addlepated amphibian ruled.

Spinrod spoke intelligently—if one ignored the occasional intonation and incomprehensible chant. He obviously had a gentleman's education, and, unlike any gentleman she had ever met, seemed interested in her opinions too. He was widely read and widely traveled, far more than she on both scores, yet he did not speak of himself or his origins. Nor did he stop their mad dash from pigsty to fence post to pianoforte.

What the deuce was a pianoforte doing in the cow pasture?

While he dealt with the aberration, Laurel leaned against a tree trunk, wishing she had a pot of hot tea, a smaller estate, and an extra handkerchief. As soon as he was done with the ill-gotten instrument, he handed her his, a once fine linen square, somewhat frayed at the turned hems, embroidered in one corner with an *S* and an *R*. He did not offer an explanation, and she did not think she could pry.

Spinrod consulted the map, plotting their next course. Laurel blew her nose, and then had a dreadful thought.

"You are not ensorcelling me, are you? I mean, what other reason could there be for me to be alone with a stranger, out in the empty fields, in freezing weather? I must not be in my right mind to have accompanied you at all."

He looked up from the map and smiled at her. Suddenly Laurel was not half as cold. In fact, she felt quite warm now, under his seemingly fond regard. She even forgot for a moment that he was old enough to be her grandfather. "There, you see? You must be casting spells on me, too."

"No, that would not be allowed. I have to win your kiss fairly, without paying for it or coercing it by force or by manipulation."

Laurel ignored that bit about the kiss. "Could you, if you wished?"

"What, seduce a woman with glamour? I would not." He appeared affronted, muttering that he had never needed to resort to subterfuge or spells, not when he was a carefree youth, and not now, when he was a wizard. He marched off, leaving her to follow or not.

"Yet you are using magic here," she called out to his back, hurrying to catch up. The pianoforte had disappeared, leaving nothing but a tinkling chord behind in the chill air. "I thought you said you would not use sorcery," she said as he followed the owl's flight to the next suspicious spot on her property's perimeter, "because it drained one's humanity."

He slowed down a little so she could walk beside him. "These are minor spells, for defense, not attack. Besides, I would have to use a great deal more sorcery if any of the others truly gained a foothold here, fending them off. More magic than I possess, possibly. One has to weigh the risks. I chose to ward off the danger rather than confront it later." His head was cocked, listening for the owl's call. "If I lose, I lose my humanity. You and your people could lose your lives and your wills."

"But why are you doing this?" she asked. "Why are you taking such a chance? You say you do not want money."

"Money puts food in your belly; it does not feed your soul. But what good is being a man—or a magician—if I cannot save the woman who can save me?"

She was supposed to save him? That was the first she had heard of it. All she had been doing was declining December-blooming daffodils and sugar-coated caterpillars. "What am I supposed to rescue you from, and how do you expect me to go about it? I know nothing of your spells and potions."

"Later. You will know the way later. I am wagering my future on it."

"On me?" Laurel had never been responsible for another person her entire life until Mr. Mumphrey died. Then she had solicitors and bailiffs to help her manage the staff and tenants of the Hall. Now this odd person was counting on her, if she believed a word he spoke.

"Of course you. That is why I came. I trust your wisdom and your goodness of heart to know what to do."

She knew nothing but cold, sore feet. "Bah! Conundrums on top of confusion. I wish I had never thought to have a party, much less a magic show. Perhaps the vicar was right after all and such a thing is indeed doomed to failure because it offends the heavens."

"How could a Christmas party be offensive?"

"Because it is frivolous, Mr. Chalfont says. And because he believes magic to be sacrilegious, not in keeping with the spirit of the Holy Child's birth."

"What is more magical than that? Magic or miracle, who is to say? One's vision of the supernatural dictates one's choice of words."

"Now that is heretical. Do not let Mr. Chalfont hear you say that or you shall be the subject of Sunday's sermon."

He shrugged. "I shall not be in church to hear it."

"You do not believe, then?"

"It is hard to believe when one's prayers are not answered."

"But that is what faith is, of course."

"For now, I have faith in you. Come, we must complete our circle before darkness falls."

By hurrying her along, Spinrod made sure they did. In fact, they returned to their starting point at Mumphrey Hall's front door late in the afternoon, hungry, tired, and cold. At least Laurel was worn out. Spinrod seemed as spry as ever.

The man must thrive on thin air, Laurel thought bitterly, for the loaf of bread and wedge of cheese they had eaten at one of her tenants' kitchens had not sustained her for an hour. Her nose was still dripping, her stomach was rumbling, and her feet had blisters. At least she thought they did. Her toes were so cold she could barely feel them.

As Spinrod helped her up the last few steps, he said, "I know you are weary and irritable, but it was worth it. I do not think we missed any evil incursions."

They had. Three suitors were waiting in Laurel's parlor. They refused to leave, her butler reported, until they had seen her for themselves. They had heard of dire happenings at Mumphrey Hall and demanded to wait until Lady Laurel was home, safe and sound. Otherwise they were prepared to ride hell for leather across the country to rescue her. That is, the hunting-mad Sir Percival Cotter was ready to ride. So was Major Gilmartin, despite his missing limb. Mr. Boone of Boone's Bank was ready to call out the militia.

Laurel knew all of the gentlemen, by sight, at least. They were no wizards, thank goodness. They were not much as prospective husbands, either. Sir Percival was a penniless rake, toadying up to a wealthy aunt in the neighborhood, Major Gilmartin was a penniless recluse, usually inebriated, and Mr. Boone was a bore, with a penchant for boys, although no one spoke of it in the town.

They brought her gifts: flowers, a book, a picture. Unfortunately, the flowers were her own, from her forcing houses; she had been saving them for the party. More unfortunately, Major Gilmartin's book was his own, recounting his war years and injuries. Mr. Boone's print was of his bank.

Laurel declined all the gifts. Her tongue could have spoken the words without her brain behind it by now. She rejected the flowers on grounds of a sudden sensitivity to pollen, proved by her reddened nose. She gave the book back to Major Gilmartin, saying her sensibilities were too tender. She refused the bank's portrait because she already had one, Mr. Boone's gesture of condolence after her husband's passing. It was lining her glove drawer.

Still the three men sat on, sipping tea and exchanging sneers and barbs. No one wanted to be the first to go, leaving the field to the others. They all wished to reserve dances with her at the party, except for Major Gilmartin, naturally, who asked to sit out a set of dances with her. She declined all three again, saying that, as hostess, she would not be dancing much.

Darkness was falling, yet the men stayed on, hoping for an invitation to dine, she supposed. She ordered another dish of tea sandwiches, so they would realize supper was not going to be served soon. It was not going to be served at all, if she had her way. She wanted a bath, a nap, and a tray in her room, with her feet up. Spinrod could do as he pleased. He usually did, she realized.

The men ignored him for the most part, especially after he declined to give a preview of his coming performance. He merely told them he was planning a surprise, but that he was too tired now to exercise his skills. He pointed to the owl, asleep atop a portrait's frame, lucky bird. "It has been a wearying day," he hinted.

Laurel smiled at him as she passed around the plate of sandwiches, silently thanking Spinrod for his efforts. She tried not to limp, lest her callers think she needed carrying or, worse, their sympathy. When she reached Spinrod's chair in the far corner, she whispered, "Do something, for heaven's sake."

"What, my lady wishes me to perform magic?" he said with a grin, showing a dimple she had never noticed before. "Horrors. Are you sure it would not be a sacrilege?"

Laurel stepped on his foot, intentionally by accident. "Get rid of them and I might consider that kiss."

"Ah, a devil's bargain indeed. I might forfeit my soul, or I might win it back." He stroked his bearded chin in mock deliberation.

Laurel felt like giving that beard a good tug, and his long hair, too. She'd been wanting to since she'd met him, in fact, to see if the snowy white locks were truly his own. Spinrod acted so much younger than his hair indicated, she suspected they were part of some intricate disguise, some convoluted plot. He was not going to confide in her until he was ready, she knew. She was ready to dump the remaining sandwiches in his lap if he did not get rid of the plaguesome trio. "Please," she begged.

He stood and waved his hand. Nothing happened. He mouthed some unintelligible words. Nothing happened. He sprinkled something into his tea: sugar. Then he said, "I wonder that you gentlemen are not in the village. I understand the circus performers are holding an impromptu rehearsal. The girls are trying on their new costumes."

Sir Percival stood.

"And two of the men are to hold a marksmanship contest in the courtyard."

Major Gilmartin got up, with his cane.

"A great deal of money is to be wagered, I suspect."

Mr. Boone bade Laurel good evening.

"That was not magic," Laurel said after they had all left. "That was a parcel of lies."

"But one believes what one wants to hear or see," Spinrod answered. "And therefore it might be the truth. If they go to the village inn demanding a performance, they might get one."

That was too devious for Laurel, but she was grateful anyway. Not grateful enough to kiss an old man, though, so she hurried up the stairs to her bath and her bed. "You can dine in your room if you wish, or in the parlor. I will not be down, so you can have the company of my sister-in-law to yourself."

Bettina was not coming to Mumphrey Hall for the evening repast, though. She was too busy at home in the dower house, lamenting the mole on her chin.

Her maid had put hot compresses on it, then lemon juice and vinegar, then strawberry jam, since there were no fresh strawberries at this time of year. She had sent over to the Hall's kitchens for cucumbers, all to no avail. Bettina had a huge mole on her chin, with three black hairs in it, no matter how often they were cut away.

"I am ugly!" Bettina moaned into her mirror. "I look

like a hag. Oh, why did this have to happen now, just when that wretched woman is holding her cursed ball? What am I going to do? How could this happen to me?"

The mirror did not answer. Wrong story.

Chapter Seven

Sometimes a bit of magic would not come amiss. Laurel would have been happy to sprinkle fairy dust and have her house left sparkling clean. She'd speak any number of arcane words, to have her home decorated with garlands and wreaths. She would have loved to wave a wand and have the kissing boughs woven.

Her resident magician, though, had disappeared. Oh, he was not performing some marvelous trick with smoke and mirrors; Spinrod was in the library reading and resting, as if paltry matters like her party were beneath him. He was not going to expend his energy making ready for any harum-scarum gathering, his attitude seemed to say, although he never missed dinner. Aside from the danger to his own psyche, he explained to Laurel, magic begat magic. If he started using his powers over trivial matters, others would know. They would come, and they would fight to steal what power he had.

So he stayed in the library except for taking the evening meal in the dining room with Laurel. He ate Cook's meals with enthusiasm, and conversed with pleasure and intelligence and interest. He listened to Laurel recount her days, her plans, her hopes. He wanted to hear about her friends and neighbors and her dealings with the servants and tradesmen. No facet of her life was too unimportant, his smiles of encouragement seemed to say, because she was important. To him.

Laurel found that talking with Spinrod about small things was far more enjoyable and entertaining than listening to any of her suitors—nay, than any other man of her experience—expound on weighty matters. Not that Spinrod could not converse about serious topics. They discussed the war and the Corn Laws, affairs of state, and the state of the poor king's mind. He knew the current novels and poets, too, and laughed with her at the foibles of society as noted in the newspapers sent from London.

Then he would disappear into the library again.

Laurel missed him. She found herself waiting for the next day's dinner. How peculiar, she thought, but how nice, to look forward to someone else's company. She had dreaded her husband's presence, and was too often bored among her neighbors. Spinrod was never boring, not even when they did not speak. Silence could be companionable, too, she was learning.

Laurel thought she might try to convince Spinrod to stay on after the party. He could be a . . . what? Schoolmaster? Secretary? She could not hire him as a lady's companion, to her regret. Such a fine man, however, should not live the rest of his life as a traveling peddler, giving demeaning performances at country fairs, living hand-to-mouth out in the elements.

She would invite him to stay on as a guest, Laurel decided. She could do it without censure, for he was old enough not to cause gossip, and one could have any number of old relatives and connections in residence. If people did talk, so what? Laurel did not care for her sister-in-law's opinion, nor the vicar's. Her neighbors had ignored her while she was Mr. Mumphrey's wife; she did not care if they ignored her now. She did care about Spinrod and his opinion.

The more she thought of the notion, the better she liked it. She could have a congenial companion without hiring some Friday-faced woman to add countenance to her widowhood, and she would not have to give up her independence. She would not be so alone, trying to make important decisions on her own, decisions that affected so many other people's lives. She could have a friend to share her little pleasures and big worries. Spinrod might even be able to shed light on that odd reference Cauthin had made about her future children. If such a thing were possible, then she ought to be looking around her for a husband. Spinrod could advise her, for if he could detect the presence of magic, surely he could tell when a man was honest.

Yes, she would ask Spinrod to stay, as soon as Christmas was over. She was too busy now. She was active from morning until night, working alongside the staff to clean and decorate the house when she was not ordering the menus, selecting the music, arranging the flowers, or being fitted for her gown. She also had to see about the baskets of gifts for Boxing Day, after Christmas. Every family on her estate would have preserves and produce, coins and small toys for the children, dress lengths of fabric for the women, warm scarves for the men. All of her servants would have new uniforms and livery, handkerchiefs and perfume or cologne, plus bonuses. Her bailiff was getting a series of books, and Bettina had already selected her gift, a new black gown to wear to the party of which she disapproved—and which she was threatening not to attend unless the mysterious mole disappeared. Laurel offered to speak to a physician she knew. A metaphysician, perhaps, if he ever stirred himself from the book room.

All of this took time, too much time to worry about a lazy lumpkin in the library who did not offer to help, with or without magic. She would have to think again about offering Spinrod a permanent place in her household if he could not bestir himself to tie a single red bow. Why, he ought to be happy if she gifted him with his paltry kiss, much less a Christmas present, after his lack of assistance.

She did look into the library at first to make certain he had not suffered an apoplexy or a heart seizure, of which older men were often victims.

He snored.

He looked older in repose, with worry lines and weathered skin. She was no longer tempted to tug on his silvered beard or white hair. He was old, more the pity. She let him sleep and went back to her chores.

At least the unwanted suitors left her alone once word went out that they would be put to work. The first time she set one of them to weaving evergreen boughs and wreaths—not even kissing balls—was the last time she saw any of the fortune-hunting fribbles.

She had no more magicians apply for work either, thank goodness. Or thank Spinrod for putting up his safeguards before going to sleep.

Somehow everything was getting done. Her house was looking more festive than it ever had while Mr. Mumphrey was alive, festooned with red ribbons, smelling of clove-studded oranges and pine. The indoor servants were happier than they had ever been under her husband's employ, singing carols as they went about their duties. The stable boys whistled, looking forward to the tips they would earn from the guests. The farmers and shepherds tended their fields and flocks without incident, eager for the party and a day of rest. Even the weather cooperated, staying cold but not miring the roads with rain or hindering deliveries with snow and ice.

By the day before the party, Laurel declared them ready, except for the last cooking preparations, of course, and the arrival of the musicians. Her gown was hanging in the wardrobe, the maids were giggling under the mistletoe, and Bettina's mole had disappeared as mysteriously as it had arrived, leaving a tiny black spot. Bettina called it a beauty mark; Laurel thought it might be a reminder.

Then Hubie Eckles disappeared. The orphaned grandson of Laurel's housekeeper, Hubie had come to stay at Mumphrey Hall the past summer. He made himself useful helping the butler polish the silver, the cook knead her bread, and the gardeners rake the leaves when he was not at lessons in the village. The entire household liked the boy and tried to make him feel welcome, important, and not so abandoned.

Hubie was six years old, and he was missing.

Everyone went out on the search. How far could the lad have wandered, between school and the Hall? They walked the fields, rode the lanes, searched the attics. The bailiff went from cottage to cottage. Laurel herself asked every shopkeeper in the village if they had seen him. No one had.

Mrs. Eckles was wringing her apron, the maids were weeping, and the footmen were muttering about Dark Doings.

Laurel saw nothing for it but to enlist her slacking sorcerer. She went into the library without knocking. After all, it was her house, her library, her resident wizard. She shook his shoulder, feeling muscle beneath her hand. He was old, but he was strong enough to push his barrow. Strong enough to find Hubie Eckles for her.

"He is not on your property," Spinrod said after he rubbed his eyes and stretched.

"How do you know?" Spinrod had not left the house once since their inspection as far as Laurel was aware.

"What do you think I have been doing these past days? I have been keeping watch, maintaining the wards against magic. No wizard came to steal the boy, no evil befell anyone on your land."

Laurel believed him. She did not know why or how, but she had ceased questioning him. Spinrod simply followed other rules, outside her understanding. She would have to apologize for thinking him an idler, but the boy's disappearance was more urgent. "If he is not here, where is he, then? We asked at every house and shop in the village."

Spinrod shrugged. "I do not know."

"But you can find out, can't you? You have ways of knowing these things. I know you do. You could tell if someone had cast a spell on him or spirited him away. You could get him back for us. I know you can!"

He did not answer, but turned his back on her to stare out the window.

"What, is it money you want? I will pay you whatever it takes," she begged. "Or that stupid kiss."

"A kiss in payment will not do," he replied, turning to face her. "It must be heartfelt and free."

"Then what? What do you want, to help us?" Laurel was nearly in tears, and Spinrod was not much better off, ashen-faced and trembling, looking like an old, old man.

His voice was a hoarse whisper, torn from his despair. "It is more magic than I can safely do. I will be lost."

"No, no, you won't! We'll save you, and save Hubie, too. I swear."

He gave her a fleeting smile. "But you have no understanding of the mystical realms such matters inhabit."

"I do understand that a little boy's life might be at stake, a frightened, orphaned child."

"I am frightened, too," he whispered, so softly that Laurel could barely hear the words, but then he opened the window and sent the white owl outside.

"Can Merlin find the boy, then? He is small to fly any distance, isn't he?"

"He cannot fly far from me. And he cannot travel off the protected land or he would be preyed upon by larger raptors or rapacious wizards. But he can bring me what I need."

They waited silently then the bird returned with something clutched in his talons.

"An acorn?" Laurel asked, dubious of Spinrod's skills, now that he had seemingly agreed to help. She had supposed he would consult a crystal ball or wave a magic wand. That was what sorcerers did in the old stories. "An acorn?" she repeated.

"Oaks are sacred to those who know all the secrets of the earth. What can be more miraculous than the tiny seeds of such majestic giants' births?"

He called for a kettle, wine, more wood for the fire, and a jar of water from the well, not from the pump in the kitchen.

"Don't you want a lock of Hubie's hair or something?"

"Hmm. An apple."

Laurel was relieved. This was more like it.

When the first footman arrived with a tray, Spinrod poured the clear water into the kettle and set it on the fire to heat. Meanwhile he ground the acorn with his knife.

"What is the wine for, then?" Laurel asked as she watched.

"For you. You seem discomposed."

Of course she was discomposed. Her housekeeper's grandson was missing on the day before her party, and her last hope was making acorn soup. She swallowed a glass of wine.

"What about the apple?"

He picked up the apple and polished it against his sleeve. "Oh, that is for me. I'm hungry."

At least he waited until the bits of acorn were simmering in the kettle before taking the first bite. Laurel watched and waited for something to happen. He took another bite, chewing loudly.

"Nothing is happening," she complained.

"Of course it is. Even though you cannot see them, events occur. Mountains move, volcanoes erupt, puddles dry up in the sun. Things constantly happen that you cannot see."

Laurel kept still, rather than appear more foolish than she already felt. Who was she to be telling a wizard his business?

When his apple was done, Spinrod tossed the core into the fire. Then he sat cross-legged in front of the hearth, staring. Laurel tried not to breath out loud.

She saw steam rising from the kettle, nothing more.

Spinrod saw a graveyard.

"But we checked. Hubie goes to visit his parents' graves in the churchyard every once in awhile, so we looked there first, after the house."

"There is an empty crypt."

"Yes, Lady Foggerty had one built for her eternal resting place when she turned seventy. She is eighty-four now. All the village children play around it, trying to frighten one another into nightmares. The door has always been propped open."

"It is closed now. I cannot tell if by accident or on purpose. Hurry. The boy is afraid."

Laurel was already halfway down the hall, shouting for horses. She turned back. "Aren't you coming?"

"You can make better time without me, but here, carry this in case neither the wind nor some other mischievous boys shut the door." He took a white feather out of his pocket and held it out.

Laurel recalled how the stables erupted in whinnies and hoof stompings when Spinrod walked by. On their circle of the estate, the sheepherders' dogs had slunk away, and Mrs. Barnett's cat had tried to hide under her skirts. No, he could not ride to the church.

He seemed weak, besides, as if the effort to find the

boy had drained all of his physical strength as well as his spirit. Laurel came back to his side and took the feather out of his cold hand. "You wait, then. I will hurry back. You'll be fine." She quickly placed a kiss on his cheek. "Thank you."

She left, but Spinrod sat on the floor, stroking the limp body of his owl.

Chapter Eight

No, no, no. Only the evildoers die in fairy tales, not the heroes or their pets. Definitely not their pets.

They found the boy, right where Spinrod had said he would be. Hubie was curled up and asleep, having exhausted himself with crying and shouting before anyone was looking for him.

They carried him home, and everyone wanted to thank the man who had sent them in the right direction. Laurel thought it better not to admit to having a divinator in her drawing room, so she merely said Spinrod recalled seeing the door to the crypt loose when he passed through the village.

Mrs. Eckles rushed in and threw herself into Spinrod's arms. The boy bowed, but needed a hug so he clutched at Spinrod's legs, nearly toppling the old man. The rest of the staff and half the villagers wanted to touch his hand for luck and to show gratitude. He seemed embarrassed by the attention, standing stiff and unsmiling.

Laurel was worried that he looked tired, too, so she declared an early celebration in the kitchens, with ale and cake for everyone.

When the others had gone, he remained in place, not speaking, hardly looking at her at all. She embraced him anyway. "You are a good man, Mr. Spinrod. And a good friend."

The owl opened its eyes.

"I would like you to stay here forever."

Merlin fluttered his wings.

Spinrod's voice was raspy and low. "Do you know,

lady, how easy it would be for me to accept? To stay, to bind you to me? To ensnare you, yes, and all of your people who are so eager to shake my hand. Do you understand that now, because of who I am and what I did, I could cast a spell over all of you, stealing your wills? You would be mine, forever, to do my bidding, be it for good or ill. Your lives would not matter to me, only my own. I could be master, with a snap of my fingers." He held up his hand, as if he were going to do it, click his fingers together.

Laurel took his hand in hers. "But you won't."

"How do you know? I am hungry for the knowledge that lies here in this place, starving for the power dominion over it and your friends will bring. You especially. I want to own you, Lady Laurel, body and soul, so no other man can ever look at you, so I can make you adore me and serve me and restore my youth, against your will or not."

"I have only to say 'I decline.' You taught me that."

"But I could teach you glories, show you hints of a paradise you cannot imagine so you will not want to decline."

"But you won't," she said, still holding his hand. "You will not do any of those things."

Merlin stretched out a taloned leg.

"You cannot know. You cannot comprehend the yearning for power, like a landed fish strains toward the water. Run, my girl, run while you can."

"I will not, sir. I could never run from you. Your wiles could catch me if you wished, anyway. But you would never hurt me, or anyone. You are not that kind of man."

"I am hardly a man any longer."

"You are a man! A fine, caring, wise man. The best man ever put on this earth, for whatever reasons and with whatever skills. You are a man!"

The owl flew to his shoulder.

"And you will trust me to entertain your guests without ensorcelling them?"

"I would trust you with my life. I think I have, bringing you into my home. You say words I cannot decipher, and I believe them. I believe you, and I believe in your goodness. Stay, Spinrod, stay and help us rejoice at the gift of Hubie's return and at the Holy Child's birth."

"And your birthday, my lady."

"Help make it a happy one, please. Say you will stay."

The owl bit his ear.

"Ow. If we are staying, you better feed us, so we might practice our performance. I think you mentioned cake and ale?"

Laurel's party was the finest, most lavish, most enjoyable assembly in anyone's memory. Lanterns lighted the entire carriageway, welcoming those who drove in wagons and carts and fine carriages, as well as those who walked from the village at dusk. All the children were presented with whistles and gingerbread men. The men were given sprigs of holly and berries to pin to their lapels, and each woman received a silk rose, tied in silver ribbon.

Food and drink were everywhere, with music for dancing and music for listening and Christmas music to sing along with. Laughter filled the ballroom and the barn, with groups of friends and neighbors going between the two locations, men of the land greeting lords and ladies, shepherdesses dancing with sirs, a viscount's children playing snap-dragon with the vintner's.

Some of the titled guests found it a novel experience, delightfully different and in keeping with the season, where the Three Kings visited the humble manger. Such blending of the classes need not be repeated, of course, but for one night they could all celebrate together.

The circus folk mingled with the partygoers, juggling, tumbling, walking on ropes tied between rafters in the barn. Two men walked on stilts, and an old woman told fortunes in the orangery. There were waltzes and jigs, country dances and minuets, children's games in the morning room, card tables in the library, charades in the drawing room. Wassail bowls were kept filled, as were the tables of shaved ham, lobster patties, stuffed geese, and Christmas puddings.

What the wine and the music did not make merry, the mistletoe did. Kissing boughs hung from every doorway, it seemed, far more than Laurel had planned. Giggles and good cheer rang from almost every inch of Mumphrey Hall and its surrounding buildings. Truly, this was the best party the neighborhood had ever known, and Laurel was overwhelmed with praise and felicitations and so many offers of friendship that tears of joy filled her eyes. This night was everything she had wanted . . . almost.

At nine o'clock, she had the servants announce that the children would perform the Nativity in Mumphrey Hall's chapel, renovated for the occasion. More people than could fit walked to the stone building, but no one minded standing outside, watching the Sunday school students reenact the Christmas story. The Star of Bethlehem fell off the ladder, and two shepherds fought over who held the lamb. Melchior forgot his lines, and Mary was too frightened to say hers above a whisper.

In other words, it was beautiful. Laurel was not the only one who needed a handkerchief. Even the vicar nodded his approval.

Then Laurel invited all who wished to return to the barn for a magic show.

Some eyebrows were raised, and some of the villagers carried their sleeping children home. A few of the gentlemen chose another round of cards instead, and a handful of dowagers chose a nice round of gossip in the drawing room. They had had enough of egalitarian entertainment, amateur acting, and plebeian performances.

The remaining children were awed. The adults were amazed—and Spinrod had simply stepped onto the makeshift stage. He wore a red velvet robe with trailing sleeves and white fur trim, with a white feather in his scarlet cap. His snowy hair and beard flowed loose, and a small white owl sat on his shoulder. He was a figure from a fairy tale, a mystical being, a living legend.

Laurel could not have been prouder than if she had produced him out of thin air herself. Then he began with simple tricks, ones any fairground magician could perform. He pulled coins out of the air and flowers out of his silver wand. He made a white rabbit appear in an empty sack, then he made six eggs disappear into the same empty sack.

That was what Laurel had wanted for her guests, especially the children: the enchantment of the unknowable.

One guest was not enchanted whatsoever. The Reverend Mr. Chalfont stood at the foot of the stage, making certain, he swore, that nothing blasphemous was done. Now he said, "Bah! This is sleight of hand and trickery. Keep an eye on your watches, gentlemen, and your jewelry, ladies." He looked at Laurel, standing at one side of the stage. "Your magician is nothing but a Captain Sharp. I warned you how it would be."

Laurel was ready to order him from her property, but Spinrod laughed and said he was simply getting started. He made a halo of smoke appear over the vicar's head, then turn into horns. The watchers laughed uproariously, more so at Chalfont's confusion when he could not see what was above his eyes.

Spinrod turned away from the vicar, as if he were too minor an annoyance to be given heed. He motioned for Laurel to come forth and began to pull silk scarves from her hair, her sleeves, her neckline, and her hem. He handed all the silk squares to little Hubie Eckles, who was at least an inch taller than he had been yesterday, all puffed up with pride. When he was done gathering the silks, Spinrod waved his wand over them—and they changed into white doves that flew over Laurel's head in another, swirling halo.

The applause was thunderous. It was so loud, no one noticed the vicar creep out of the barn, or Bettina, Mrs. White, follow him, a determinedly matrimonial gleam in her eye. Ah, there was magic in the air. And mistletoe.

Spinrod went on to make a dragon out of smoke, a phoenix out of fire, a maiden out of water. He plucked the silk rose from Laurel's hair and made it multiply until he held a whole bouquet—of real flowers, the scent filling the barn instead of the smell of hay and manure and all the human bodies pressed close to the stage to see better. He presented the bouquet to Laurel with a flourish and wished her a happy birthday, which was loudly seconded by every person there. Then he wished the audience a joyous holiday, bowed, and started to step down from the makeshift stage.

Marveling at her bouquet, Laurel could only smile.

The crowd cheered wildly, stamping their feet, calling for an encore.

"More, more! Give us one more trick!"

Spinrod raised one eyebrow at Laurel, who shrugged. "If you are not too tired. Or think it might be dangerous."

He thought a minute, then held up his hand. There was instant silence. "I cannot perform more tricks for you, forgive these old bones, but I can offer a different kind of entertainment. What say you to a tale of magic and marvel, spells and sorcery?"

"Aye! We say aye! Let's hear it, Master Spinrod."

Someone carried two chairs up to the stage, one for Spinrod, one for their hostess. Spinrod sat, but he held onto Laurel's hand. He paused for effect, and then began: "Once upon a time . . ."

Chapter Nine

"All good fairy tales begin that way, you know," he said. Everyone nodded. The haberdasher's daughter sighed.

"Yes, well, once upon a time there was a foolish youth."

"What one isn't?" a woman called from the side.

Spinrod smiled. "But this one was more foolish than most. The son of an earl, he had every boon and blessing known to man. He had an honorable name and a respectable fortune, a loving family and a fine education. The young men considered him a good sport, and the young ladies considered him handsome."

"Where is this paragon?" one of the Londoners shouted. "I have three daughters."

"Ah," Spinrod went on over the laughter. "But I said he was foolish. And he was the earl's third son. The eldest son was a fine young man, taking his responsibilities to heart. The second went for a soldier, making his mother weep but his father proud. The third son, Spencer, was meant for the clergy."

The lord with three daughters clucked his tongue. "More's the pity to waste such a promising *parti*."

"Young Spencer thought so too. He argued with his father and went off to London, to learn more of the world."

"I'd wager he learned more'n our good vicar knows from all his books!"

Spinrod nodded. "He learned to gamble and wench and drink and outspend his allowance. His family was furious. His father decided to cut off his allowance until young Spencer came to his senses, came home, and took up the profession chosen for him."

"Hear, hear. That's what you have to do with headstrong boys," shouted someone who had never tried to raise one.

Spinrod held up his hand again before a disagreement arose in the audience. "Spencer did not go home. He wanted to prove to his father that he could manage on his own, in his own manner. He sold his horse, his watch, and his fine clothes, and tried making his living with the pasteboards, but he had no head for numbers. He left London and worked as secretary, tutor, and newspaper reporter. He even took a position as barkeep at an inn. While he was at the inn, an itinerant magician came by to hang broadsides for his show. Spencer went to the performance and was fascinated. The magician sawed his own wife in two!"

"Go on with you. He never did!"

"I swear to you, he did. And yet she was whole after the performance. Now here was something Spencer thought he would enjoy doing, traveling the countryside, entertaining the folks."

"But he were a swell, not a common actor!" someone protested.

"Oh, he did not intend to be a common conjurer—he intended to be the best ever. To that end, he apprenticed himself to the traveling magician. He rode along with the man, Abamista, he called himself, and his wife, Clorisande, who read fortunes in the tea leaves. In return for caring for the horses, hanging the playbills, and collecting the fees, Spencer learned the secrets of Abamista's act. To his sorrow, he also learned that Abamista was not what he appeared."

"Stole the lad's money, did he?"

"No, far worse. Abamista was no mere magician. He could perform tricks that were impossible, that could never work in this world." Spinrod looked at Laurel. "He performed real magic. Wizardry."

No one said a word to that, but they looked at their neighbors with fearful glances. There had been rumors . . .

Spinrod went on. "Abamista's wife was a true sorceress too. Spencer learned that all of their former apprentices had suffered fatal 'accidents.' Still, he was young and fearless. He thought he could learn from them without risking anything, and he did, for a while. Spencer became a competent magician, but not a great one. Then one day Clorisande took a fancy to the lad."

"Uh-oh."

"Precisely. How do you refuse a sorceress?"

Laurel jumped to her feet, dropping his hand. "You say 'I decline!' "

Spinrod stood too, looking at her, his blue eyes asking for understanding. "Yes, but Spencer did not know that yet. Perhaps he was ensorcelled, or perhaps he was merely young. And foolish, as I said. He dallied with the wizard's wife. Abamista discovered them, of course, and called a curse down upon the young man's head. 'You want to learn magic?' he shouted. 'Then here is your magic!' He struck Spencer with his wand, and the boy became an old man, a silver-haired, careworn ancient with powers he never dreamed of. Spencer was suddenly a wizard, set apart forever from his fellow men."

"What's so bad about that?" someone called out. "A wizard can have anything he wants, can't he?"

The old man stared at his empty hands. "He could not go home." Spinrod paused to clear his throat. "He found out years later that his parents had both perished in a carriage accident. His older brother, the heir, had succumbed to a putrid throat. And his middle brother had died a hero, in battle. Spencer Roddell never got to make his peace with them or say good-bye. He was now the Earl of Roddermore, but no one would believe him."

"Why, I knew the Earl of Roddermore," Viscount Thaxter declared. "I sponsored a bill in Parliament with him. He was heartbroken about letting his youngest go off, and sent Runners across the country looking for him. They sent the Runners out again when the old earl died and both of his other sons shortly after. Never found the lad, by George. Are you saying that he . . . ? That you . . . ?"

Laurel was staring at Spinrod, who had always said he was an earl's son, who carried a handkerchief embroidered with "SR." He did not answer the viscount.

One of the dairy maids started weeping. Someone handed her a cloth and told her to stubble it so they could hear what happened next.

Spinrod shrugged. "Next? Why, Clorisande took pity on the old man, knowing she had caused his downfall. She could not lift her husband's spell, but she could temper it with a counter-curse. She said that Spencer could be restored with a kiss, an honest, heartfelt kiss, freely given from a loving woman."

"So what happened? Did he find a willing wench? Did she kiss him?"

"I think— That is, not yet, I fear."

"Lord love you, I'll kiss you!" Mrs. Eckles, Hubie's grandmother, rushed up and smacked Spinrod on the lips. Everyone laughed, but the old magician was still an old magician.

They all looked at Laurel.

"No, no, it cannot be true," she cried. "It is a story only, to pass the time."

"Why not try, mistress?" called one of her tenants. "You'd be a countess."

Another tossed her a sprig of mistletoe. "So no one can say you're being forward."

Two youths who had imbibed too much wassail started chanting, "Kiss him. Kiss him." The crowd took up the call, laughing and slapping one another on the back, not really believing, but enjoying the good-natured joke. This was a party, after all, and Christmas kisses were part of the merriment.

Laurel's cheeks were as red as Spinrod's scarlet cap. To stop the tomfoolery, she told herself, and to put an end to this madness once and for all, she held the sprig of mistletoe aloft and pressed her lips to Spinrod's. They were soft and warm and made her lips tingle and . . . and his beard tickled.

"You see?" she called to the cheering crowd. "He is still our Spinrod the Sorcerer. Now it is time to leave for church, unless we wish the good vicar to be cursing us, as well. I bid you all a good night and a happy Christmas, and thank you for sharing my birthday celebration."

Everyone cheered and filed out of the barn to join

those from the house in a long line of lantern-lit coaches, wagons, and walkers on their way back to town for the midnight service of Christmas.

Laurel and Spinrod stayed behind on the steps of Mumphrey Hall.

"I am sorry," she said.

"For what?"

"Because the kiss did not work. I have no magic to offer you."

"You are magic, my dear. You have brought joy to so many tonight."

"But not to you. You are still sad."

"I am still an old man. Too old to offer for a beautiful young woman like you."

"Would you, if it were otherwise?"

"In a flash." Fireworks flew from his fingers.

"Don't!" She reached for his hand, ignoring the sparks. "You have done enough magic tonight." Still holding his hand, she whispered, "I would accept, in a flash. You are already dear to me, and everything a husband should be. I wish . . ."

"Don't! Your wishes brought you trouble."

"My wishes brought me you, my love."

He dropped to his knees, groaning just a little when his bones creaked. Another bouquet of flowers appeared in his hand.

"You must not use your skills," she said. "You told me that you might lose yourself that way."

He offered her the flowers. "I think I am lost either way. I love you, Lady Laurel. I love you, and not because you are my best hope of salvation, but because you are the best woman I have ever met. I will love you forever, as an old man, although I would love you longer and better, with the vigor and appetites of a man nearing his thirtieth birthday. Will you kiss me, my dear heart?"

"But I did, and nothing happened."

"What, no tingle, no warmth spreading from your lips to your toes? I could have sworn I heard you purr with pleasure. I know something happened to me."

She blushed, glad he could not see in the dark. "You know what I mean. You did not become a handsome young man, earl or not."

"But that kiss was to please your company. A mistletoe kiss. There is no kissing bough now. No one urging you, except me."

Laurel closed her eyes and wished—not for true magic this time, but for true love—and placed her lips against his. And they were soft and warm and made her lips tingle and . . . and his beard did not tickle, not in the least.

He did not have a beard. He had a tanned, square jaw in a handsome face with dark wavy hair and laughing blue eyes. And dimples. Laurel sighed. "Happy Christmas, my Lord Roddermore."

"Happy Birthday, my Lady Laurel, Countess Roddermore to be."

"But will you miss it?" she worried. "The power, the ability to shape people and things to your will?"

"No power is greater than love, nor gives its owners more joy. If I have the power to make you happy, then I am content."

"Being your wife will make me the happiest woman on earth."

Which statement called for more kisses, endearments, promises. His joy and her delight lasted through all the years of their lives, raising their three children and clutches of owls, devoting themselves to their estates, their responsibilities, and each other.

Which is to say they lived happily ever after.

Of course.

The Green Gauze Gown

Sandra Heath

Chapter One

It was Christmas Eve, 1818, and Puckscroft Park, Rosalind's stately new English home on the coastal downs above Brighton, was filled with seasonal excitement. She had thought the drafty Palladian mansion gloomy and inhospitable after her elegant but cozy American home left behind on upper State Street, Albany, New York, but nothing could have been more joyous than the atmosphere here tonight.

Rosalind's breath caught with wonder at the reflection gazing back at her from the oval floor-standing mirror. The plowman's gauze evening gown shimmered bewitchingly in the candlelight, and was surely the most lovely, enchanting, absolutely exquisite garment in all creation. It was perfect to the very last stitch, and so exactly what she would have chosen that she could not believe what she was seeing. A foolish smile played on her lips, and her green eyes shone, for she was happier than she'd dreamed possible. Never had she felt so beautiful, so special. And, incredibly, she had her eight-year-old son Jake to thank; as well as Master Dobbs, of course, and heaven alone knew how old *he* was!

"*Now* do you believe me, Mother?" Jake said from the doorway behind her. He had lived all his life in America, spoke with an American accent, and regarded himself as American, even though his mother and late father were British, and his older brother, Peter, had just become the sixth Marquess of Southdown.

Not realizing the little boy was there, Rosalind turned with a start. Crossing the room, she knelt to hug him warmly. "Of course I do, Jake. Can you forgive me for doubting?"

Jake nodded, and flung his arms tightly around her neck. "I said I'd prove it about Master Dobbs, and I have."

"Yes, you certainly have." She was still a little bewildered about the gown, which had come as a great shock when her maid opened her wardrobe earlier tonight. There was no logical explanation, nor even an improbable one; which left only the downright impossible . . . the downright magical. She smiled at her serious little son. "You must forgive me for being such a Doubting Thomasina, but as a mere grown-up I fear I am not privileged to see and hear things as you do. I now realize that back in Albany you really did see the spirit of a Mahican sachem dancing on the burial ground, and the old Dutch ghost ship sailing up the Hudson, *and* Captain Kidd's pirates reburying his treasure on the riverbank every full moon."

She sat back on her heels, smiling fondly as she pushed his hair away from his face. He was in his nightshirt, with his tartan scarf around his throat. His dark hair was tousled, and his big brown eyes—so very like his late father's—had at last lost their reproachfulness. Jake was a dreamer, thus taking after her in temperament. Her other son, Peter, was nine and had her auburn coloring, but had much more his father's down-to-earth character. So it was as well that Peter had inherited the Harwood family title, because Jake would have been eminently unsuited to such responsibility.

Right now, however, Jake was determined that none of his past claims were omitted from the new reckoning. "And don't forget I saw old man Lydius looking from the upstairs window of his house on Elm Tree Corner," he reminded her.

"It's *Mr.* Lydius to you, sir, but yes, I accept that you really saw his specter as well."

Jake beamed. "So now I can have roast goose with you and Peter tomorrow after all?"

Rosalind laughed. "You were never in true danger of bread and water on Christmas Day."

"I really thought I was."

"That was the intention, for I was convinced you were telling enormous fibs all the time."

He looked at her. "So you won't mind if I talk to Master Dobbs from now on?"

She hesitated, but then admitted to herself that she could not really stop him, and after all, if he'd obeyed her recent strictures, she wouldn't be wearing this gown tonight. "Of course not, but you are not to do anything of which you know I would disapprove. Promise?"

"Promise," he said, well satisfied that his first Christmas in England was going to be excellent after all. He hugged her again. "You look very beautiful tonight, Mother."

"Fit for a ball at the Marine Pavilion?"

"Much too good for *that,*" he answered valiantly.

She laughed. "You, sir, will do well with the fair sex."

"Girls are silly," he replied. "Anyway, you'd better go now, for *he* has arrived with his sister and her beau." With that he hurried off to the rooms he shared with Peter.

Rosalind rose to her feet again, and surveyed herself one last time in the mirror. Tonight she was being escorted to the Prince Regent's ball by the man who had always been her secret love. Yet a mere two days ago she had been so harassed and unhappy that it did not seem possible she could have reached this point. Leaving her apartment to go along the curving external corridor that linked the private west wing to Puckscroft Park's majestic central block, she considered the astonishing sequence of events that had taken place since only this past Tuesday. Her thoughts returned to that midmorning, and the moment she'd been hastily summoned to the echoing marble entrance hall to deal with another quarrel between Peter and Jake.

The new Marquess of Southdown and his little brother had been discovered tussling ignominiously in the middle of the Christmas greenery they'd just gathered in the park, and the servants had been obliged to separate them. The boys glared fiercely at each other across the freshly gathered, exceedingly wet holly they'd thrown on the marble floor between them. So much for Yuletide goodwill, she remembered thinking as she confronted her troublesome offspring. Both boys wore rain-soaked merino overcoats, peaked hats, and disgracefully muddy boots, and neither looked in the least like members of the British aristocracy. They did, however, look what the local people of Sussex would, with masterly understatement, call "middling wet."

Rosalind's rich auburn hair hadn't been dulled by the wintry morning light from the dome overhead, and her indigo silk evening gown, three years old and marked with tailor's chalk and dressmaker's pins, was a welcome splash of femininity amid the masculine slate grays and murky creams of the surrounding Corinthian columns. But she was cold, and in no mood to be amenable.

"Well, here we are yet again, gentlemen," she observed in the crisply British tone she had never lost during her ten years in the Hudson Valley. "I confess I'm agog to hear what you have to say for yourselves *this* time." She fixed the elder boy with a gimlet gaze. "Peter?"

"I'm sorry, Mother," he mumbled, shuffling his boots and keeping his gaze on the floor.

"Jake?" Her younger son's response was a mutinous glower, so her tone became a touch angrier, as did her green eyes. "I await your answer, sir!"

He flinched. "I'm sorry too, Mother," he said, although that was the very last thing he looked.

They were both fast running Rosalind ragged with their endless bickering, and this latest spat had interrupted her important consultation with Mrs. Addiswell, Brighton's most fashionable dressmaker, who had graciously agreed to undertake some very hasty alterations to the indigo silk. The royal invitation had been overlooked in the general uproar of arriving at Puckscroft, and there just wasn't time for a new gown to be made. The indigo silk was all Rosalind possessed for an occasion as brilliant and important as the Christmas Eve ball at the Marine Pavilion. The Prince Regent's exotically oriental palace-by-the-sea was surely the most amazing and desirable place to be seen, yet she was to go there in a gown that had originally been chosen for its just-out-of-mourning seemliness after the death of her father rather than whether or not it suited her. She would much have preferred yellow, her favorite color, for her unforeseen return to British society. Dislike of the gown was bad enough, but her children's time-wasting squabbles were the last straw.

"Why must you argue day in and day out?" she demanded. "This is genteel 1818, not barbaric 818. It's also Christmas, and we have come to England to commence a new life, so can't you at least *try* to be civilized?" The boys shuffled again. "Well, sirs? Is it your intention to have the servants think you have been badly brought up?"

"No, of course not!" Peter answered hotly. "It's all Jake's fault, if he—!"

"It takes two to quarrel, Peter," Rosalind interrupted.

He drew back slightly. "Yes, Mother."

She turned her attention to Jake. "I suppose that yet again we have Master Dobbs to thank for this?"

Jake's jaw jutted. "He *does* live here, Mother. He sleeps in the pantry, and all the servants know about him. He puts silver coins in their shoes on Christmas morning."

Peter was provoked. "The cook only told you he was in the pantry to stop you eating all the Christmas cakes and preserves!"

"She didn't do it because of that! It's true about Master Dobbs!" Jake was almost in tears.

Peter was without pity. "Oh, yes, of course it is! Just like when you said you saw Mr. Lydius's ghost in his window! You're always telling lies, Jake Harwood!"

"I'm not!" Jake said through gritted teeth, his hands clenching into little fists.

"Of course you are!" Peter insisted furiously. "You don't really expect us to think your pesky Pharisee can make cold figgy pudding hot *and* magic a jug of steaming custard from nowhere as well, do you?"

"He did, I tell you!"

Rosalind struggled to maintain some measure of outward calm. She and the boys had only arrived here three weeks before, but in that short time the seemingly invisible Master Dobbs had managed to invade their lives. To be honest, she rather sympathized with Peter's increasing wrath, and she could cheerfully have choked the cook.

Questioning the servants hadn't brought forth any sensible explanation for Master Dobbs; they simply insisted that there was indeed a Pharisee at Puckscroft. At that she had firmly decided it was all stuff and nonsense. Not only was it extremely unlikely there would be a Pharisee in Sussex, but it was even more unlikely that his name would be something as Anglo-Saxon as Dobbs!

Right now, with Christmas Eve, and therefore the Prince Regent's ball, the day after tomorrow, she had more important things to think about than fights, figgy puddings, and Pharisees. "Very well, sirs," she decided, "if you cannot behave yourselves together, you can amuse yourselves apart. Go to your rooms."

"Oh, Mother!" they protested in unison.

She held up a hand. "No! My mind is made up. Off with you both, and stay there until I say you may leave."

They glowered at each other, then trudged wetly away across the hall toward the corridor to the west wing. Only then did she notice that Jake's scarf was not the one he had been wearing when he went out earlier. "Jake?" she called after him.

He turned, still scowling. "Yes, Mother?"

"Whose scarf is that?"

His eyes were swiftly lowered. "It's mine, Mother."

"But you don't have a tartan scarf," she pointed out, knowing for certain that this was the case.

"I've always wanted one," he said.

"I know that, sir, but you still haven't explained how it is that when you set out after breakfast you were wearing a red-and-gray striped scarf, and yet are now resplendent in blue tartan."

Peter turned to look back. "I didn't notice that!" he gasped, and he and Rosalind looked intently at Jake, whose cheeks were a dull red, and whose eyes were not raised from what was evidently a highly interesting spot on the floor.

"Jake?" Rosalind prompted, her spirits sinking as she anticipated yet another magical act on the part of the confounded Master Dobbs.

Peter guessed the same, and was furious all over again. "I don't know where you got the scarf, Jake Harwood, but I don't believe your stupid Pharisee had anything to do with it. You think you're *so* clever, don't you! Well, I'll show you who's clever, because I'm not going to speak to you at all from now on, so there!" With that he stomped away to the west wing.

"Oh, Jake," Rosalind murmured. "When will you ever learn?"

The little boy remained defiant. "It's all the truth, Mother. Master Dobbs came out with us, and when I grumbled that I wanted a tartan scarf, he changed mine into this. He said it was a Christmas present."

"Go to your room," she ordered.

"But—"

"Your room! *Now!*"

Rosalind watched him scuttle away as if his heels were in imminent danger of bursting into flames. She was close to tears, for it was becoming nigh impossible to continue making allowances. Both boys were still deeply affected by the loss of their father two years ago, but was that an excuse for Jake's present behavior? Yet how could he not have been shaken to the very core by Oliver's sudden demise? Oliver Harwood had been a vigorous man who hadn't suffered a day's illness in his life until struck down out of the blue by what the doctor termed "a malevolent miasma from the summer-heated Hudson."

She looked away distractedly, for it was still hard to believe Oliver had gone forever. Her thoughts winged back eleven years, to the time when she and her parents—now both deceased—had come to Sussex from Monmouth because her clergyman father had been appointed to St. Luke's parish church in Roecombe, a village two miles east of Puckscroft Park. The new residents of the rectory had received an invitation to the great annual picnic here at Puckscroft. It was at the picnic that she first encountered a trio of young gentlemen friends, Oliver Harwood, nephew of the then Marquess of Southdown, Francis Tempest-Connell, a Scottish gentleman engineer, and Sir Henry Trafford, who was newly returned to his ancestral home just outside Roecombe. Of the three, the one who'd impressed her most that day, and to whom she had been inexorably drawn, was the fair-haired, aesthetic Sir Henry, who was so embarrassed by his lame leg and thick-lensed spectacles. It had never bothered her that he needed a walking stick, and if his thick lenses exaggerated his wonderful gray eyes, it was only to make them seem more arresting and lively.

"Oh, Harry," she whispered, remembering so very much. Then, to the astonishment of a passing footman, she struck a heroic attitude and declared loudly, *"Cry 'God for Harry! England and Saint George!'"*

She laughed as her voice rang around the dome and columns, but at the same time tears pricked her eyes. Harry Trafford had been everything to her. She'd loved him at first sight, and heaven help her, she loved him still. How could she not adore the gentle poetic man whose eloquent gray eyes spoke with the briefest glance, whose smiles illuminated her very soul, and whose disability made him more dear and beloved to her simply because it was *his* disability. Harry could summon Shakespeare's words from the very air, recite them as tenderly as might the Bard himself, and he seemed to understand her more than any other before or since.

Rosalind closed her eyes for a moment. He had so clearly been her other half, yet they had never become one. Instead he had distanced himself from a mere clergyman's daughter, whereas Oliver paid her constant court. How could she ever have been such a gull as to believe that *Oliver* had composed those wonderful love letters? There had never been a poetic bone in his body, yet it was through heartfelt prose and the beautiful words of a Shakespeare sonnet that he'd won her hand; and, she naively imagined, her love as well.

It was later, in far-off America, where Oliver insisted they reside, that common sense told her he had merely copied letters written for him by Harry. When she questioned Oliver, he had confirmed her suspicions, saying that Harry had offered to help him win her. Such knowledge ought to have taught her a lesson about the folly of loving Harry Trafford, but it didn't. She still thought of him every day, but since returning to Brighton had been afraid to inquire after him. What if he had married? What if he worshipped his wife and children? What if he had found the happiness that the former Rosalind Beaufort had lost forever? Worse still, oh, how much worse . . . what if he were dead? It was better by far to dwell in the past, no matter how sad and fleeting.

Pushing the memories aside, she made her way toward the west wing to continue the fitting of the gown, but as she entered the connecting corridor she heard someone behind her, and turned. There was no one there. She walked on, and again heard the steps, small and childish. "Is that you, Jake?" she inquired, gazing back toward the hall. No one answered, and there wasn't another sound of any sort. Thinking she'd imagined it, she proceeded to her apartment, and by the time she entered she had forgotten the odd little footsteps.

Chapter Two

Later that Tuesday, a fine maroon chaise splashed through puddles on its way to Brighton from Trafford Hall, a handsome medieval manor house on the outskirts of the village of Roecombe. Its two passengers, Sir Henry Trafford and his unmarried sister, Ellen, were en route for Mrs. Addiswell's fashion emporium at the top of Ship Street, where Ellen was hoping to find that her gown for the Prince Regent's ball had been satisfactorily completed. Under normal circumstances, their mother, Lady Trafford, would have accompanied them on account of her own gown for the ball, but she was in poor health at the moment, and often confined to bed.

Heavy rain continued to fall, and a boisterous wind blew in from the sea as the chaise toiled up out of the valley, crossed the lower downs, where a thin layer of springy turf covered the chalk, then approached the town of Brighton. The weather was so dire and disagreeable that lamps and lanterns had already been lit, twinkling like stars through the December murk. The brightly illuminated shop windows were filled with seasonal delights and garlands of holly and ivy, but the weather was doing its very best to spoil Christmas trade. Few people had ventured out, and those who had were suitably attired, the gentlemen in greatcoats, huddled beneath large black umbrellas, the ladies in hooded cloaks, with pattens on their feet to raise their hems well clear of the dirty streets and wet pavements.

Harry Trafford looked out of the chaise's rain-dashed window, and ran a gloved hand uneasily through his mop of dark blond hair. His clothes were in the very tippy of London fashion, but there was nothing in the least foppish about him. Beneath his charcoal-gray Polish greatcoat he wore an olive coat, dark mustard waistcoat, and cream cord pantaloons. Black gloves and a top hat lay on the seat next to him. His gray eyes grew troubled at a brief announcement he'd seen at breakfast in an old copy of the *Brighton Herald.* A Shakespeare quotation came to his mind, twisting anew the dagger that had pierced his heart for so very long. He said the words beneath his breath. *"How like a winter hath my absence been From thee, the pleasure of the fleeting year! What freezings have I felt, what dark days seen! What old December's bareness everywhere! . . ."*

Twenty-year-old Ellen heard, and gave him a cross look. "Not Shakespeare again, please, and so dismal too! I vow you will wake up one morning and find you have turned into old Will." She sat opposite him, neat and trim in cherry and cream merino, her glossy brown hair tucked beneath a jockey bonnet.

"The Bard has much to say," Harry replied rather pompously.

She rolled her eyes skyward. "Too much by far when you're around," she grumbled, then made a very obvious point of changing the subject. "I think we are going to get very wet, even simply stepping from the carriage to old Rest Assured's hallowed door." She always referred to Mrs. Addiswell as Rest Assured because of the lady's propensity for scattering the expression throughout conversation.

"Well, on this occasion getting wet is in a good cause," he replied, trying to concentrate on Ellen's priorities instead of his own lost cause.

His sister studied him. He had a sensitive face, finely wrought, with lips that were quick to smile, and his hair always flopped over his forehead no matter how often he tried to comb it into obedience. His gray eyes were large and expressive, but shielded behind ugly spectacles to correct his myopia. He was charming and witty, and his taste in clothes was faultless, but the silver-handled walking stick propped beside him was no mere fashion accessory.

At the age of fifteen, after a very brief illness from which he had seemed to recover, he went out for a walk one day and his left leg collapsed beneath him. He'd been carried home and the physician sent for. The leg did not improve, and it was soon decided that Harry suffered from "a debility of the limb," a very serious condition that would never heal. At first he had needed crutches to move around, but now he managed with just the stick. He was very conscious of his infirmity, and had become shy and retiring with all but his closest family and friends.

"Don't you know it's rude to stare?" Harry murmured, glancing at his sister.

"What did you read this morning in the *Herald*?" she asked rather impishly, hoping to catch him off guard. All had been well last night when he'd arrived from London for Christmas, but at breakfast he'd been deep in a weeks-old edition of the Brighton newspaper when a noticeable change had come over him. Ellen had gained the strong impression that he wished he'd never left his rooms in Piccadilly, so the moment he'd gone out for his morning ride she had scoured the columns—but to no avail. She had even taken the paper up to Mama, to see if she could shed a little light on the matter.

"The *Herald?*" Harry pretended not to understand.

"Don't try to gull me, for it will not work. I know you saw something that upset you at breakfast, but try as we would, Mama and I couldn't find what it was."

"Then you cannot have been very thorough."

She pounced. "Ha! So there *was* something!"

He smiled and declined to answer, but she noticed how his right hand moved absently over the left breast of his greatcoat. It was an unconscious action, a habit of his to which she was so accustomed she barely noticed anymore. But now, it caught her attention.

She searched his face again. "Well? Are you going to tell me about it?"

"No."

"Harry—"

"Look, Ellen, it really does not concern you, nor is

there anything at all that you or Mama can do to change matters, so can we please leave the subject alone?"

She fell silent, but had already decided to examine the newspaper again. Whatever Harry's secret was, she would find it.

He changed the subject. "What is your wondrous new evening gown like? Lurid lilac? Shocking scarlet? Odious orange?"

She flushed. "Well, it *is* orange, but a sort of reddish mandarin taffeta that is definitely not odious. I've gone to considerable trouble to look just right for Francis." She had formed a deep but thus far unrequited attachment to Harry's old friend, Francis Tempest-Connell, who was always too engrossed in inventing steam engines to notice that she had grown up.

"Francis is far too old for you," Harry observed.

"He's thirty-three, not fifty-three, and I'm twenty, not fifteen."

"You're a mere chit of a thing," he declared crushingly, then cleared his throat. "Brighton is filled to overflowing with young blades. Surely you can find *someone* a little closer to your own age?"

"You're so stuffy, Harry Trafford, that rooms in racy Piccadilly seem ill-chosen for you. A cell in a secluded monastery would suit you better. A closed order, of course."

He ignored the acid comments. "Well, you may as well forget Francis, because when he arrives for dinner tonight I intend to strangle him."

Ellen's eyes widened. "But he's your very best friend!"

"So I thought, but as he and I are all that remains of the old triumvirate, there's something I would have preferred to know *before* coming to Brighton for Christmas, not by chance after my arrival."

A small beam of light began to dawn upon her darkness. "Would this, by any chance, have something to do with Oliver Harwood?"

"Why do you say that?" he asked quickly.

"I'm old enough now to do basic sums," she replied pertly. "There were three of you, now there are two.

The missing one is Oliver Harwood. I may have been a child when he left the country, but I did know the three of you had been inseparable. You and he fell out around the time of his marriage, and he and his new wife, who I believe was the daughter of Mr. Beaufort, the last-but-one vicar of Roecombe, went to America. You then moved to London, and Francis stayed here to squander his fortune on his vile steam contraptions."

"Francis is too levelheaded a Scot to squander anything."

His droll attitude hurt her. "You are the only person I confide in, yet you laugh at the things that matter to me most. No wonder I keep a diary; at least the written page doesn't make fun of me."

Harry suddenly became very serious. "Never believe that a diary, or indeed any written page, cannot make a fool of you, Ellen. Burn the wretched thing, and make a resolution never to keep such a journal again."

"Burn it? Whatever for?"

"Because other people can read your words and use them for their own purposes. Take my advice, destroy the thing now." He leaned forward to kiss her hand, then sat back again to continue gazing shortsightedly out of the rain-distorted window.

Ellen was deeply puzzled. "Are you speaking from experience, Harry?"

"Mm?" He didn't want to enlarge upon anything.

"About keeping a diary. Did you keep one?"

"Not a diary exactly. I wrote letters to someone I cared for very deeply, but did not have the courage to send them." He gave her a sideways glance. "And the only reason you never found them was that they were well hidden from your prying eyes."

Specks of color warmed her cheeks. "I wasn't all *that* nosy."

"You were an omnipresent little pest, and sometimes I fear you still are."

She was offended. "If I'm a pest now it's because I'm worried about you."

"There is no need." With that he hoped to close the conversation, but it didn't do to underestimate her tenacity.

"So where *did* you hide the letters?" she pressed.

"Can't we leave the subject alone, Ellen?" he answered, a little irritated.

"What harm is there in telling me now?"

He sighed resignedly. "Oh, none, I suppose. Very well, I kept them in the bottom drawer of my private desk, in the box of Spanish cigars procured through Oliver Harwood's friend at the Madrid embassy."

Ellen stared at him. "There were . . . *letters* in that box?"

Harry nodded. "Yes, and I had poured out my every foolish emotion into them, so you can well imagine my dismay when the box disappeared."

"Yes, I . . . I can." Ellen looked away to hide the sudden consternation that flooded her brown eyes. "Why didn't you say something about the letters at the time? You must have missed them almost immediately, yet all you said was that the cigar box had been mislaid."

"I preferred not to mention the letters. Besides, it happened when Mama decided the Hall had to be properly cleared out and all rubbish disposed of on a bonfire. I thought the box had simply been thrown out and burned by mistake. At least, that was what I hoped. I was wrong, and I later realized that Oliver Harwood had taken it."

Yes, he did take it, Ellen thought wretchedly, for looking back she realized she'd happened upon Oliver in the very act. If only she'd been fully aware at the time, if only she'd said something about what she'd seen. Oliver had called at Trafford Hall one day when Harry was not at home, and she encountered him as he was coming out of the library. He'd halted rather awkwardly, then grinned and indicated something flat and rectangular that he'd tucked into his coat. "I trust you do not mind, but I came to borrow a book. My mother desires to read *Gil Blas.*"

She remembered returning the smile, and had even accompanied him out to his horse to watch him ride away. It had been later, in the circulating library on the Steyne, that she'd seen a volume of *Gil Blas* and realized what a very thick book it was; too thick by far to have been hidden in Oliver Harwood's beautifully tailored coat. Looking back now, she realized that it could very well have been a slender box containing Harry's precious letters.

Harry gave a wry smile. "But there again, maybe Master Dobbs had been at work, not Oliver."

"There ent no gurt ol' Pharisee at Trafford Hall, as you rightly knows," she replied, putting on an exaggerated Sussex accent.

"No Master Dobbs? Well, so we modern souls are supposed to think, but I'm not so sure."

"You don't really believe in such things, do you?" Ellen was taken aback.

"Let's just say that I don't entirely disbelieve." Harry sighed. "Anyway, Pharisees aside, perhaps now you will understand why I urge you never to keep a diary. I went through torture because of putting unwise pen to paper, and then I went through heartbreak when unfolding events made it clear Oliver had taken all but one of the letters. Apart from Francis, he was the only other person who knew about them. I was idiot enough to bare my soul to Francis, whom in this respect I would trust with my very life."

Francis knew all about it? Ellen resolved to browbeat that gentleman into telling her what had happened.

"But neither of us realized Oliver had overheard me," Harry went on. "He told Francis later, and Francis promptly told me, but by then it was too late. If I'd known earlier I could have forced Oliver to return the letters, and maybe . . ." He broke off, for he would never know if he'd had a chance of winning Rosalind's hand.

"You say Oliver took all but one of the letters?"

"Yes. It had somehow become wedged behind the drawer, and was discovered later. It was the one I wrote the actual day I met—" He looked away. "Well, it doesn't matter now."

"Met whom? Oh, do tell me, Harry, for I want to help if I can."

"No one can help after all this time, Ellen, dear as it is of you to want to." He gave her a fond smile.

Her mind was racing. The letters could only have been of the loving variety, but to whom had they been written? Rosalind Beaufort seemed the obvious candidate. Ellen remembered that once, when in his cups—an unusual circumstance—Harry had whispered a quotation she had never heard him use before or since. *"From the east to western Ind, No jewel is like Rosalind."* There being no other Rosalind of his acquaintance, at least, not of whom his sister knew, the obvious conclusion was that Harry *and* Oliver Harwood had been in love with the vicar of Roecombe's daughter. If Francis was in possession of the facts, she would have them out of him like water from a pump. "Where is the letter now?" she asked.

He patted the breast of his coat. "I keep it with me at all times. Whatever clothes I wear, the letter stays upon my person."

"So *that's* why you're always patting your coats."

"I'm not always patting my coats."

"Yes, you are, although I don't think you even know you're doing it." She gave him a look. "So, with you it's a case of 'don't do as I do, do as I say.' "

"Mm? What do you mean?"

"Only minutes ago you advised—nay, instructed—me to destroy my diary because keeping such a private thing was a risk. Yet here you are, after all this time, still carrying an old love letter against your heart."

He colored slightly. "That does not make my advice to you any less wise."

"Have we ever had a copy of *Gil Blas*?" she asked suddenly.

The abrupt change of subject left Harry rather bemused. "I beg your pardon? A copy of what?"

"*Gil Blas.* The book by Le Sage."

"Not to my knowledge. Why?"

"Oh, nothing . . ." Even now she had secretly hoped to be wrong about what she'd witnessed, but there was no denying it. She *had* seen Oliver taking the box of letters. Guilt settled over her like a wet cloak, making her feel as if she had aided and abetted the thief. To her relief the chaise drew up at last at Mrs. Addiswell's, but almost immediately relief turned to further dismay as she saw another carriage was already there.

Harry heard her stifled exclamation. "What is it?"

"That is the Caldicot chariot. Dear spiteful Laurinda is the very last person I ever delight in seeing."

"Spiteful? I take it you do not care for her?"

"She is a *chienne* of the first water, a troublemaker extraordinaire, and a scandalmonger par excellence. I assure you I describe her most accurately. In fact, I even have a Shakespearean quotation to suit her. *Hamlet,* I think. *O most pernicious woman! O villain, villain, smiling damned villain!*"

"Good heavens, that's strong! You really aren't very fond of her, are you?"

"I loathe her."

Harry had never met Laurinda Caldicot, but knew she was reckoned one of England's great heiresses. Her fond father was Yorkshire's wealthiest man, and well-known for lavishing thousands on his only child. Harry recalled something about Laurinda having been betrothed to Oliver Harwood's cousin, the fifth Marquess of Southdown, who a year ago had unfortunately met his demise while attempting too big a ditch during a hunt in Gloucestershire. But for that tragic incident, it would have been Laurinda, not Rosalind, who was now mistress of Puckscroft Park.

Chapter Three

Ship Street was one of the most prosperous and handsome in Brighton, with fine houses, shops, and hostelries. These included the Old Ship Inn, which stood at the bottom, close to the sea, and from which the street took its name. The dressmaker conducted her flourishing business in a double-fronted, bow-windowed property at the other end of the street. The fluted Doric doorway seemed rather far from the carriage as the coachman, umbrella at the ready, opened the door for his passengers to alight. The smell of roasting chestnuts drifted across the cobbles from a nearby pavement stall, and the sound of carol singing could be heard on a corner further down the street, but there were very few people about to appreciate either. Rain fell relentlessly, beating on the pavement stones and gurgling in gutters and drainpipes.

Harry and Ellen sheltered beneath the umbrella as they crossed to the doorway, then the bell tinkled pleasingly and they were inside. The reception room, which stretched across the entire front of the house, was bright and cheerful, with lighted chandeliers and two roaring fires. Christmas garlands festooned the mantels and picture rails, flowered Chinese silk adorned the walls, and blue-and-white striped furniture had been placed around. Resembling a drawing room, it was intended for use by those who accompanied Mrs. Addiswell's lady clients. As these often included gentlemen, the necessary propriety was ensured by a large black lacquer screen that prevented any male gaze from penetrating the fitting rooms beyond when the connecting door was opened and closed. At present there was only one other person present, an elderly, rather hawkish gentleman seated on a sofa in one of the bow windows. He was, Ellen whispered, none other than Theophilus Caldicot, Laurinda's doting Papa.

Ellen made her way toward the screen, and Harry limped to the sofa in the other window and made himself comfortable, propping his walking stick beside his knee. But as he was about to wipe stray raindrops from his spectacles, from behind the screen he heard a brief but rather feline exchange between two young women, one of whom was Ellen. Almost immediately the second woman swept into sight, wearing a lovely evening gown for which Harry guessed she was taking a final fitting.

The woman was very beautiful and golden-haired but with anger-reddened cheeks and a positively vitriolic flash in her lovely blue eyes. She paused to take a deep breath, evidently striving to calm her temper after the brief contretemps with Ellen. Then she commenced to twirl affectedly around the room to show off her delightful green plowman's gauze gown, from time to time addressing Theophilus Caldicot as Papa. So this was the dreaded Laurinda, Harry mused as she halted to admire herself in the glass. There was something so disagreeably prideful about her that he could not help thinking she seemed everything Ellen said, and more.

Mrs. Addiswell had accompanied Laurinda from the fitting rooms, and every now and then hastened forward to put a new pin in here or tuck the material there. The dressmaker was a small, rather plump lady dressed in wine red fustian, and had a bland face and manner. Her brownish hair was scraped back from her face and hidden beneath one of the frilliest lace bonnets Harry had ever seen. Laurinda was sorely taxing the dressmaker's patience, seeming unable to stand still for more than a second, and yet constantly demanding adjustments to the gown.

A tall, rather gawky assistant hastened from the fitting rooms in a flurry of fawn wool and starched mobcap. "Oh, madam," she said to Mrs. Addiswell in a very nasal tone, "I simply cannot get the old indigo silk gown to drape properly. No matter what I do, the previous stitches show, and it looks all of its three years! The bright lighting at the Marine Pavilion ball will be most cruel! I cannot understand, for when Mrs. Harwood tried the gown on earlier it seemed . . ."

Mrs. Harwood? Harry's ears pricked, but Mrs. Addiswell was appalled. She gesticulated urgently to silence further indiscretions, knowing it would do her business no good at all if clients' private affairs were spoken of so publicly. Fortunately the dressmaker saw that Laurinda Caldicot and her father were talking and had not heard, but the same could not be said of Sir Henry Trafford on the other sofa. "That is quite enough, Edwards!" Mrs. Addiswell always addressed employees by surname only. "Have you no wisdom at all? Get back to your work, and see that you do it well or it will be the worse for you! Rest assured that if I find a single clumsy stitch you will be dismissed."

"Yes, Mrs. Addiswell." Edwards gave her employer a look of ill-concealed dislike, then returned to the fitting rooms.

The assistant's days were clearly numbered, Harry thought as he rose awkwardly to his feet, leaned on the walking stick, and caught the attention of the now very flustered dressmaker. "A word, if you please, Mrs. Addiswell."

The woman came over. "How may I be of assistance, Sir Henry? I fear Miss Trafford will be some time yet, and—"

"This does not concern my sister," he said to the dressmaker. "Tell me, the lady whose indigo silk gown was mentioned a moment ago—would she by any chance be Mrs. Harwood of Puckscroft Park?" He noticed Laurinda's eyes were suddenly fixed coldly upon him now that she knew he was Ellen's brother.

Mrs. Addiswell was faint with dismay. "Er, no, Sir Henry, rest assured my foolish assistant was referring to someone a long way from here."

He dropped his voice to a whisper. "Someone called Harwood who just happens to be attending the Prince Regent's Christmas Eve ball? Come now, Mrs. Addiswell, I am not a fool."

"Sir Henry, I must beg you to overlook my assistant's grave error of judgment. I assure you that—"

"Mrs. Addiswell, I am not concerned with anything other than whether or not Mrs. Harwood of Puckscroft is the lady of the indigo silk gown. I am not about to delve into her secrets. It is simply that it's been many years since I last saw her or her late husband, and I wonder how she is? She does well, I trust?"

"She does, Sir Henry." The dressmaker eyed him curiously, obviously thinking his query strange. If he was acquainted with the Harwoods, he only had to call at Puckscroft Park to find out for himself.

"And she is attending the ball?"

"Yes, Sir Henry."

Harry's heart sank, for he wasn't ready to see Rosalind again. Not now; maybe not ever. His emotions had been such a maelstrom since breakfast that he really did not know what to think. Ten years was a long time, and he'd believed himself healed from the trauma of what Oliver had done. *What's gone and what's past help Should be past grief.* But now, it was as fresh and painful as ever.

The dressmaker was still anxious. "Sir Henry, I assure you that nothing should be read into the fact that she is to wear an altered gown. It is simply that, due to an oversight, her invitation was not handed to her in time for a new gown to be made. That is all, and I beg you to be discreet. It is more than my trade is worth for a rumor to be spread that the lady is financially . . . er, embarrassed. She is not, I assure you." Mrs. Addiswell's glance slid uneasily toward the Caldicots, who were now clearly trying to eavesdrop.

Harry raised his voice for Laurinda's benefit. "I am not given to spreading gossip, Mrs. Addiswell. That is all I wished to ask, so please feel at liberty to return to Miss Caldicot, whose interest in us would seem to indicate an urgent need of your attention."

Laurinda's eyes met his, and she flushed angrily. In that second he knew he had made an enemy. Ellen's savage indictment of the famous heiress seemed fully confirmed by the hardening of Laurinda's cornflower blue eyes, the slight pursing of her rosebud lips, and the barely perceptible toss of her golden-curled head. She had already marked Harry as Ellen's brother; now her whole aspect warned that he would be sorry, not only for having such a sibling, but also for his sarcasm.

As Mrs. Addiswell scurried over to reexamine a portion of the green gown's hem, Harry resumed his seat, propped the walking stick again, and watched the dressmaker try in vain to placate the increasingly difficult client. Laurinda carped and complained even more, twitching the gown as if it were a rag. The disagreeable creature really did not deserve such an enchanting garment, he thought, which anyway would look far better on someone with Rosalind's wonderful auburn curls. It would have fitted the Rosalind he remembered, and he wondered if it would now.

Harry was deeper in thought than he realized, because Ellen suddenly whispered in his ear. "Are you so intent because you have a fancy for the Caldicot fortune?"

He started and glanced around into eyes that were a little too bright with their owner's effort not to think about cigar boxes and stolen letters. "Certainly not," he answered in an undertone, "for I believe you are right about her."

"Most gentlemen manage to overlook her faults and concentrate only on her expectations. Anyway, enough of that. What do you think of my gown?" Ellen stepped around to the front of the sofa and did a little twirling of her own. She was deliberately flamboyant, knowing full well that the mandarin taffeta was far more dazzling than the subtler shade of Laurinda's green gauze, and that it rustled more deliciously as well. Harry's mischievous sister had only come out of the fitting rooms to irritate the conceited heiress, who did not like sharing the stage with anyone.

But it was Theophilus Caldicot, not Ellen, who really upset Laurinda's applecart. "My dear," he said to his parading daughter, "I wonder if it would have been better if . . . ?" He thought better of it, and fell silent.

"Better if what, Papa?" Laurinda whirled about to look at him, thus snatching the gown from Mrs. Addiswell's busy fingers.

"Nothing, my dear," Theophilus replied.

"It is clearly something, Papa, so I *demand* that you tell me!" Laurinda stamped her foot, and Ellen gave Harry an eloquent look that was encyclopedic in range.

Theophilus took the nascent tantrum in his stride. "Very well, my dear. It just occurred to me to wonder why you chose green instead of blue."

Mrs. Addiswell, still on her knees, closed her eyes as if in prayer.

Laurinda had been wondering the same thing herself, but did not like being obliged to face the matter. "Is there something wrong with green?" she inquired edgily.

"No, of course not, but—"

"—but you think blue would be better," she interrupted.

He cleared his throat and declined to respond.

Laurinda looked down at the green gauze, then at Ellen's citrus-orange, then at her own reflection in the glass. The green came a very poor second. Mrs. Addiswell's lips moved in silent supplication, but the damage was done. Laurinda gave a dramatic sigh. "You are right, Papa. This green is very dull. I will have blue instead."

The dressmaker scrambled hurriedly to her feet, intent upon diverting the imminent calamity to her overflowing timetable. "Miss Caldicot, there is no time to stitch an entire new gown."

"Then you must make time, Miss Addiswell," Laurinda declared airily.

"It has taken weeks to prepare the green gown, and the ball is the day after tomorrow. Even if I had a suitable material in my stock, I do not—"

"Have I or have I not been a good client?" Laurinda interrupted rudely.

"Yes, of course, Miss Caldicot."

"Then show proper respect and appreciation by attending to my wishes. The green will no longer do. I will have blue, or nothing at all. Ever again," Laurinda added.

"Miss Caldicot, what you request is impossible to carry out, no matter how much you insist. Please rest assured that the gown is perfect as it is. Do you not agree, Sir Henry?" Mrs. Addiswell suddenly beseeched

Harry's assistance, catching that gentleman quite off guard.

"Eh? Er . . . yes, Mrs. Addiswell, it is indeed," he managed to say.

Laurinda looked at him, then at his walking stick, and tossed her head with disdain. "I'm grateful for your opinion, sir, but do not think you can possibly know about such things."

It was very rudely said, and Ellen leapt to her brother's defense. "I am sure my brother knows a great deal more about good taste than you do, Laurinda."

Laurinda's eyes flashed, and her lips parted to say something scathing about mandarin taffeta, but Theophilus knew when to intervene. "Enough, my dear. Clearly the gown is no longer of even vague interest, so I think you had better change out of it, don't you?"

Laurinda's face was a picture of mixed emotions. Too late she realized she would have nothing new to wear to the ball, but all she could do was stalk back into the fitting room. Mrs. Addiswell followed, and as they vanished behind the screen, Ellen smothered a giggle. Conscious of Theophilus Caldicot's continuing presence, she made much of fussing about her own gown. In a few minutes Laurinda reappeared, elegant to the fingertips in lavender and pale pink. Her father rose to offer his arm, and they left the premises, the bell jingling almost mockingly behind them.

Ellen immediately turned to Harry. "Well, did you ever see such behavior in your life?"

"Not since school days," he replied dryly.

"Can you imagine how absolutely *awful* it would have been if she'd become Marchioness of Southdown? She'd have thought herself more important than the Prince Regent!"

"Yes," Harry murmured, his thoughts returning to the green gauze gown, now so unhappily without an owner.

"What are you thinking, Harry?" Ellen inquired quickly, noticing the reflective gleam in his eyes.

"Mm? Oh, nothing. Hadn't you better continue your fitting? I do wish to be home in time for dinner."

Ellen looked at him a moment longer, images of stolen cigar boxes hovering wretchedly before her eyes, then the orange taffeta rustled pleasantly as she retraced her steps behind the lacquer screen. He spoke after her. "Would you request Mrs. Addiswell to give me a moment of her time?"

The dressmaker came soon enough, still looking very harassed and upset by the contretemps with Laurinda Caldicot. "You wished to see me, Sir Henry?"

"Yes, Mrs. Addiswell. It concerns the green gauze gown."

The woman was taken aback. "Sir?"

"Is Miss Caldicot likely to change her mind and accept the gown after all?"

"I would not surrender it to her even if she did!" the dressmaker answered firmly, all thought of discretion having flown. "She was most disparaging about its style and quality, and to be truthful, I do not care if she never patronizes me again."

"I see. Well, I only ask because it would not do for what I am about to say to cause any embarrassment or awkwardness. You see, circumstances permitting, I am interested in purchasing the gown for another."

Various expressions crossed Mrs. Addiswell's face—relief, puzzlement, a whiff of scandal, and, finally, suspicion. "Circumstances permitting?" she repeated. "What do you mean?"

"The lady for whom I wish to purchase the gown may not be as she once was. Oh, there is no other way of saying it . . . she may be somewhat larger than I recall of old."

"May I presume we are speaking of Mrs. Harwood?" the dressmaker inquired.

"We are."

Mrs. Addiswell smiled. "Then the gown will do perfectly, Sir Henry."

Harry wasn't quite satisfied. "Of course, it wouldn't be wise if Miss Caldicot were to immediately recognize the gown, so perhaps a few adroit alterations would be advised?"

The dressmaker froze, perceiving something impossibly time-consuming after all. "I fear that a green plowman's gauze gown is a green plowman's gauze gown, Sir Henry, and nothing can change that."

"Quite. So perhaps some frills added and furbelows removed? Some bows here and there? Oh, you know what I mean, Mrs. Addiswell. Just make it superficially different." Harry was also conscious that acquiring the gown for Rosalind was risky for her reputation if word got out. "I am anxious not to jeopardize Mrs. Harwood's character, so please take the gown to Puckscroft Park and tell Mrs. Harwood exactly what happened here today, but do not mention me. Simply tell her that the gown is on your hands and you thought immediately of her. I don't really care what story you invent, provided my name doesn't enter into it. All I want is for Mrs. Harwood to have the chance to wear the gown to the ball."

The dressmaker was pleased again. "Of course, Sir Henry. Rest assured that I will be the soul of discretion. It pleases me immeasurably to think the gown will be worn after all, for if I say so myself, it is certainly one of my finest creations."

"It is almost to be described as delectable, Mrs. Addiswell, and if I delve deep for a criticism of any kind, it is simply that I wish it were in a shade of yellow, because I happen to recall that yellow is Mrs. Harwood's favorite color," said Harry. "But such a trifling matter in no way detracts from the gown's exquisiteness. Simply send the account to me at Trafford Hall. Add it to my sister's bill, since I am already paying for the orange taffeta. And remember, this transaction is to be strictly between you and me. I don't want a single word of it to get out, not even to your seamstresses." *Perhaps especially not to them.*

Chapter Four

Trafford Hall dated back to the sixteenth century, and with its gray stone gables and tall mullioned windows it might have been created by nature in the wooded glen formed by the River Traff. It was no less picturesque inside, possessing a wealth of Tudor oak furniture, great stone fireplaces, paneled walls, and intricate plasterwork ceilings. Portraits, tapestries, and needlework abounded, and at Christmas, when Ellen continued the family tradition of decking the house with all the ancient Yuletide leaves, the old house's history seemed almost tangible.

Dinner over, Francis Tempest-Connell departed Trafford Hall for his house on the Steyne. Lady Trafford, always in poor health, especially in the winter, complained of a headache and took herself to bed early, and Harry retreated to the library to be on his own, so Ellen decided to retire for the night as well. She had much on her mind, and wished to think. Poor Francis had not enjoyed the most comfortable of evenings, for she had interrogated him before the meal, and Harry had torn him off a strip in the library afterward. Ellen had eavesdropped rather shamelessly at the library door, having already dredged the old newspaper anew, discovering a tiny but very pertinent announcement of arrival. It was barely half an inch of narrow column, informing Brighton society that Mrs. Harwood, widow of the Honorable Oliver Harwood and mother of the new Marquess of Southdown, had returned from Albany in America, and was now in residence with her sons at Puckscroft Park. By the time she went to bed, Ellen was in possession of all the necessary facts, and had begun to hatch a devious little plan that could be put into effect the very next morning.

While his sister lay in bed plotting, Harry was alone in the firelit library, a Spanish cigar in one hand and a glass of cognac in the other as he sat in his green leather armchair, staring into the flames. He had set his spectacles aside, and his shortsightedness denied the flames their clarity and delineation. The room was quiet, except for the ticking of the longcase clock and the crackling and spitting of pinecones on the fire. Sparks winked and flashed as the winter wind drew down the chimney from the rain-drenched clouds that still scudded over Sussex from the storm-whipped sea.

Harry knew it was time to think long and hard about the Marine Pavilion ball. He knew his absence would disappoint Ellen, but it wouldn't prevent her from going, for Lord and Lady Braithwaite would gladly take her under their wing. The Braithwaites were sticklers for all rules and regulations, but they were old friends of the family and very kind.

Exhaling slowly, Harry leaned his head back to gaze myopically at the scarlet ribbons and gold-painted apples on the old stone mantel. Oliver could never be forgiven for what he did, but at least Rosalind could be absolved of complicity if she had truly believed Oliver wrote the letters. But what if she *did* know the letters' true authorship? It was Harry's deepest fear that his beloved idol would be found to have feet of clay. All was fair in love and war, or so it was said, but only the victorious really believed it. The vanquished were left bitter and betrayed, nursing hearts that remained broken forever. "Like yours, Harry boy, like yours," he murmured.

Harry thought back to the great July picnic a decade ago at Puckscroft Park, which was then the seat of Oliver's uncle, the fourth Marquess of Southdown. It seemed society from all around the Brighton area had been invited to the picnic, and among the crowds were Oliver Harwood, Francis Tempest-Connell, and foolish Sir Harry Trafford, a lame savant who really ought to have known better that day than to let his heart run wild among roses.

Oliver and Francis were prepared to lounge on the grass indefinitely, but sitting for long periods had never been easy for one whose withered leg still retained sensation. Oliver did nothing but comment on the charms of every young woman he noticed, and Francis scribbled scientific matters in a notebook. Such company was hardly inspiring, and Harry's physical discomfort soon obliged him to get up and walk a little. He made his way toward the rose garden, which in early July was in its fullest glory. Indeed, he recalled that the playful sea breeze carried the fragrance long before he reached the wrought-iron gate in the high garden wall.

Once inside, Harry discovered that the wall kept the breeze at bay, and the almost still air was so intoxicating that he paused just to inhale it. At first he thought himself alone, but then he saw the women's quiet, pensive figure seated on the edge of a raised fountain. Her gloriously wayward auburn hair was gathered loosely on top of her head, and she wore a primrose muslin gown, with a pink-and-blue cashmere shawl draped idly over her arms. She made a beautiful picture as her fingers trailed in the fountain's dancing water, and the vignette had haunted him ever since.

There was something so captivating about her that one of the Bard's sonnets slipped unbidden from his lips. *"Shall I compare thee to a summer's day? Thou art more lovely and more temperate . . ."*

She turned quickly, then smiled. "You flatter me I think, sir."

"That would be impossible, as I am sure Shakespeare himself would agree." He ventured closer, miserably conscious of his lameness and of how like a startled owl his spectacles made him appear. "Sir Henry Trafford, your servant," he said, inclining his head.

"I know who you are, sir."

"Indeed? Should I be flattered?" He doubted it, for she had clearly inquired about the poor crippled fellow.

"Well, I do not know if you should or not, Sir Henry, for I asked the name of the gentleman who had brought a volume of poetry with him today."

His preconception melted away. "You noticed that?"

"How could I not? I wondered if we had a Nordic Byron among us."

The preconception rushed back, for Byron too had been lame. Realizing what he thought, she hastened to add, "I meant that I thought you were a handsome poet, Sir Henry," she said.

He was surprised to know he was being gently chided for leaping to incorrect conclusions. "Forgive me, but I am rather too accustomed to, well . . ." He didn't finish, for further words seemed superfluous.

"You are oversensitive, Sir Henry, and although I cannot speak for other occasions, you have my word that this time there is no need."

He was mesmerized, enchanted, bewitched; call it what he would, the effect was the same. *Why, this is very midsummer madness* . . . He had come upon Titania herself in this haven of roses, and he knew his life would never be the same again. The temptation to kiss her was almost too great, so he sought a distraction. "I am at a disadvantage, for although you know who I am, I confess to having no idea who you are."

"Miss Beaufort. Rosalind Beaufort."

He gazed at her. "Newly of Roecombe, perchance?" He knew of no other Beauforts apart from the new incumbent of St. Luke's.

"Yes. My father has been appointed from Monmouth."

"Monmouth's loss is Roecombe's gain," he said rather clumsily, then colored. "Forgive me, I don't usually resort to such obvious compliments."

"My vanity will become insufferable if you continue in this vein, Sir Henry," she answered.

"Do you mind if I join you, Miss Beaufort?"

"The fountain is not my private domain, sir."

"And if it were?"

She smiled. "Then I would gladly let you join me."

"I need no further permission," he observed, trying not to be too ungainly as he sat a few feet from her on the edge of the fountain. But when he tried to prop the walking stick, it clattered noisily onto the mossy flagstones. He stretched down to retrieve it, but she was quicker, her slender fingers closing over the ebony and placing it firmly against the fountain. Their eyes met, and for the first time he truly saw the lovely green depths of hers, so very like a cool, clear stream where dappled sunshine glimmered amid waving fronds. He had never seen such eyes before, never felt so instant and abiding an attraction that it was almost as if she had rescued his heart, not just the walking stick.

Perhaps he stared, for she looked away self-consciously. "We appear to have chosen the same hiding place, Sir Henry."

"I do not know why you are here, Miss Beaufort, but I have escaped from my companions, one of whom is concerned only with categorizing the ladies, the other with the intricacies of steam engines."

His answer amused her, and as their eyes met again, Harry fell further and further in love. She was utter perfection, the most flawless, adorable, witty, smiling, winsome creature the Almighty had ever created, and here in this wonderful rose garden she was his alone.

She searched his face. "Do you write poetry, Sir Henry?"

"A little, but not with any success. I cannot compare with Shakespeare . . . or Byron," he added.

"I am sure you write beautiful verse, Sir Henry."

"Now *you* flatter *me*," he replied with a grin.

"That cannot be done either, sir. Why, even Will Shakespeare lauded you." She struck a mock heroic pose. *"Cry 'God for Harry! England and Saint George!' "*

He laughed. "If that is to be the way of it, Miss Beaufort, then let me remind you *From the east to western Ind, No jewel is like Rosalind* . . ."

She clapped. "Oh, how well you know the Bard! It is such a pleasure to talk with someone who can pluck quotations from the air!"

They both laughed then, and for the next hour talked of their shared love of Shakespeare. They recited their favorite lines, discussed the plays, deliberated on the sonnets, and argued amiably about the modern genius of Byron. Color flushed their cheeks and kindled emotions in their eyes, and they were so completely in harmony that it was as if they'd known each other forever. Harry had never felt so at ease with anyone; nor had he been so hopelessly stricken with love. She cast such magic over him that he was enslaved, heart and soul, and incredible as it may have seemed, he was already certain that he wished to marry her; indeed, nothing could have been more certain. But the joy ended as suddenly as it had commenced, and it was his fault.

She became aware of the passing time, and stood. "I think we will arouse whispers if we are discovered like this."

"I could sit here with you forever," he said, needing to let her know how deeply she had affected him.

For a moment she met his eyes. "You do me a great honor, Sir Henry. . . ."

". . . but?" He voiced the word his insecurity felt certain hung on her lips.

"There are no buts, sir." She smiled. "I was about to say you do me a great honor on so brief an acquaintance."

He still felt she was endeavoring to cool the ardor she must see in his gaze. How could she not shrink from such a poor fellow as he? *But I, that am not shaped for sportive tricks, Nor made to court an amorous looking-glass; I, that am rudely stamped, and want love's majesty* . . . An instinct for self-protection overtook him, and he reached for the first face-saving remark he could find. "And . . . and I merely meant that I am very comfortable sitting like this after having to sprawl very uncomfortably on the grass with my friends. I fear I am prey to aches and pains." As he spoke he realized how fretful and churlish he sounded.

"Oh." She blushed.

"I . . . I mean . . ." he began, but she stopped him.

"There is no need to explain, Sir Henry."

He was appalled with himself. What a moaning curmudgeon she must think him. After starting out so well, his damned insecurity had within seconds managed to ruin everything!

She was now intent upon leaving, and he could not blame her. "Well, it was most agreeable to meet you, Sir Henry, but I think I had best return to my party."

Catching up her muslin skirts, she fled from the rose garden, leaving him so angry with himself that he could almost have dashed his walking stick to pieces. Fool, fool, *fool!* Why had he been so birdbrained? When he stepped into this garden, something incredible had happened to him, and he'd bungled it so monumentally that he wondered if he could ever look her in the eyes again. How long he had remained by the fountain he didn't know, but when he returned to the picnic it was to see that Oliver had not only perceived Rosalind but inveigled a mutual friend into an introduction.

Francis, slender, sandy-haired, and somehow unmistakably Scottish in appearance, was now alone on the grass, Oliver having joined the large group of which Rosalind was part. As Harry eased himself down beside him, Francis glanced up from his drawings and notes. "Ah, there you are. Had your surfeit of the rose garden?"

"How did you know I've been there? Please don't tell me I smell like a boudoir."

Francis chuckled. "I wouldn't suffer you near me if you did. No, as it happens I know because a certain delectable Miss Beaufort apparently said she'd encountered you there, and that you'd spouted Shakespeare as gushingly as a fountain."

"She said that?" Harry was hurt, even though he knew he didn't deserve more. *Roses have thorns, and silver fountains mud . . .*

"Mm? Oh, I don't know exactly what she said, but it must have been something along those lines. Oliver came back for your book. He said it would serve him well."

"Oh?" Harry looked across at the other party. "In what way?"

"God alone knows. He had a rather sly look about him, though. He's up to something, you mark my words."

And so he had been, although weeks passed before the eventual extent of his deceit had been fully realized. By then it was far too late, and Rosalind Beaufort had been lost to Sir Henry Trafford forever. *Farewell! Thou art too dear for my possessing . . .*

Harry's thoughts returned to the present, and the flickering firelight in the library. Even in the depths of winter he was sure the scent of the rose garden warmed the air, and in the distance he could hear Rosalind's gentle laughter. He knew it would be foolish to go to the ball because the old wound could only bleed anew, but he did so want to see her again, to feast his eyes upon the woman who'd filled his consciousness since that fateful day so long ago. Yes, he would go to the ball, but before then he would do something he should have done this morning, the moment he'd read the newspaper. Getting up, he grasped his walking stick and left the library, calling for his horse to be saddled. Behind him the longcase clock struck eleven.

Chapter Five

It was gone midnight as Rosalind walked slowly along the wide external passage into the east wing of Puckscroft, where the kitchens and other offices took up the ground floor and cellars. She shielded a candle with her hand as she ascended an unlit staircase to the shuttered rooms on the deserted second floor. Shadows leapt, the wind moaned outside, and she felt a chill draft as she reached the landing.

The lonely atmosphere was intimidating, as if Puckscroft were trying to tell her she didn't belong. It might be Peter's birthright, but it wasn't his mother's, nor would it ever really be her home. Just somewhere she was obliged to live for the time being, until . . . Until what? The answer to that question eluded her, as had so many other answers over the past ten years. She felt as if she were waiting for something, anticipating, yearning, craving . . . *hungering.* A dream lay just beyond reach, like the moon itself, precious, mysterious, and infinitely alluring.

Tonight she was so restless that she felt she would scream with frustration and bewilderment. It was as if her whole life had been a sham, a painted canvas that placed a false view between the window of her eyes and the truth beyond. Oh, what was the matter with her? Why must she be forever hounded by phantoms? Her steps quickened and the candle flickered, sending grotesque shapes lurching along the passage. The shuddering light fell upon marble consoles, Grecian urns, gilt statuettes, and alabaster busts that seemed to watch her as she passed by.

Why had she been so drawn to the east wing tonight? She hadn't set foot here since arriving in the house, because these rooms overlooked the rose garden. The taboo was of her own making, raised by memories she wished to forget. But those memories had already resurfaced once today, and—if she were utterly honest—had been with her every day of the past ten years. She had simply pretended to herself that Harry Trafford no longer mattered. Yet tonight he mattered so much that the painted canvas had to be removed and the past gazed upon properly once more.

Rosalind paused by the immense double doors of the music room, her breath silvery in the candlelight. From here, even on a dark, wintry night such as this, the view would be perfect. But as she reached for the doorknob, she again heard the patter of childish footsteps along the dark passage behind her. "Who's there?" she called, and her voice echoed eerily. The footsteps halted, but no one responded. "Jake? Is that you playing silly games?" she asked, even though she had just left both boys fast asleep in their beds. There was still no answer. She listened intently for the slightest sound, but heard nothing.

After a few moments Rosalind decided her imagination was playing tricks again, and she opened the door to go into the music room. Ghostly outlines in white cloths loomed from the shadows, a harp, a pianoforte, a double bass, all standing like silent sentinels to observe her every move. But she hardly glanced at them as she crossed the room to the shuttered windows. Placing her candle on the floor, she folded the shutters back and at first saw only her own reflection in the glass. Her hair was loose about the shoulders of the rose merino wrap she wore over her nightgown, and the glow of the candle was set too low to reveal her eyes. It made her seem blind, and maybe that was entirely appropriate, for she had certainly refused to see what was real and what was not.

She went closer to the rain-dashed glass, which misted slightly from her breath, but she wiped it clear again and at last made herself look down into the walled rose garden below. It was hard to see anything, just the square walls and the pale lines of the winding paths between the naked beds. Ah, but there was the fountain. It was motionless now, unlike that July day when Harry had found her. His voice carried across the years, reaching out tenderly, caressing her senses, stealing her everlasting love. *"Shall I compare thee to a summer's day? Thou art more lovely and more temperate . . ."*

As she gazed down, seeing the past shining brightly against the cold, wet darkness of the present, something moved along a path toward the fountain, a man, cloaked and top-hatted, visible only as a silhouette in the stormy night. He didn't simply walk along the path, but limped, maybe even hobbled. There was something so beloved and familiar about his gait that she did not pause to think that it might belong to someone other than Harry. It *was* Harry, come to see her at last!

A sob caught in her throat and she snatched up the candle to flee from the room. The candle had fluttered and gone out long before she reached the staircase, but she hardly noticed as she hurried down to the linking corridor, where she knew there was a door to the gardens. She fumbled with the key, but at last she was out in the night air that carried the smell of the distant tide. Cold rain stung her face, but she thought nothing of it, or of being in her night attire, as she ran toward the rose garden. The postern was already open, and a foam-flecked horse was tethered to a nearby walnut tree. She knew it was Harry's horse because of the special saddle he needed to accommodate his damaged leg.

She went inside, and the racket of the wind was immediately excluded, leaving only the sound of the rain and the rustling of the shrubs as she gazed toward the fountain, where the cloaked man stood.

"Harry?" she called, his first name slipping unguardedly from her lips.

He turned so swiftly that he knocked over his walking stick, which had rested against the edge of the fountain. Even had that dear sound not been sufficient to identify him, what little light there was revealed the face of which she'd dreamed for so long. "Oh, Harry, how good it is to see you again," she said, moving toward him. The rain and cold did not seem to touch her, oblivious as she was to the bizarreness of such a meeting.

Harry stared as if at a phantasm. He'd been unable to help coming here tonight, but had not anticipated an encounter with Rosalind. In the dead of such a terrible winter night it was the last thing he'd expected. Now he felt vulnerable, caught off guard, and painfully defensive. Even the dislodging of the damned walking stick would remind her of how clumsy and unfinished a creature he was. Damn all idle whims!

Rosalind blinked back foolish tears, taking comfort that in the rain he could not possibly see them. Somehow she restrained herself from running the last few steps and flinging her arms around him. Instead she retrieved the walking stick, rested it in its former position, then stood uneasily, her hair beginning to drip in rats' tails, her nightclothes clinging to her form in such a way that in daylight would have been most improper. She was improper anyway, going to him in her wrap and nightgown like a common trollop. Maybe that was just what she was, for how many times had she made love to him in her dreams? How many times had she surrendered to his kisses? Lain with him until dawn? Been his and only his . . . ?

She managed an embarrassed laugh. "I do not think you will compare me to a summer's day tonight."

He knew he had to say something. "How are you, Rosalind? You're looking well." *You haven't changed at all, but are as lovely as ever.* So ran his thoughts, but his tone was level and polite, his unease making him seem disinterested.

The spontaneity of Rosalind's smile froze into disappointment, and her joy began to twist with renewed hurt. Nothing had changed between them, and she had been deluded to read anything in his presence here tonight. "I . . . I am in good health. And you?"

"I'm well enough."

She floundered a little. "And . . . and your family?"

"My mother is unwell at the moment, but Ellen is in fine fettle."

He did not mention a wife! Or children! She tried not to show her relief. "What brings you here like this? And to the garden, not the house?"

He shifted uncomfortably, and told a blatant lie. "I'm

on my way home from a magistrates' dinner at the White Hart in Henfield. My horse is tired, and I'm resting him a while before I continue."

"And you would have done so without coming to the house?"

"It's late, and I did not wish to impose."

Perhaps he simply did not wish to see me, she thought. "Do you still adore Shakespeare?" she asked then.

"Of course." He wanted to smile warmly, but mortification kept him awkward. "I understand you have two children now?"

"Yes, Oliver and I were blessed with fine boys."

"I . . . er, was sorry to hear about Oliver's passing." He was ashamed of himself. *Liar! You felt nothing when you learned of his death, nothing at all!*

Rosalind looked away. "It was very sudden."

"So I understand."

He didn't care a jot, she thought, stricken. She could be a widow thrice over and his reaction would remain the same. Those bewitched minutes here in this very garden on the day of the picnic had clearly meant nothing at all to him. She had perceived far too much in his smiles and gentle voice, read nonexistent volumes in quotations that to him were but idle words thrown away. How she wished she could have accepted that fact the moment he returned to the picnic and chose to sit with Francis Tempest-Connell instead of joining her party. She had persuaded herself it was but shyness on his part, but now she saw the truth. He simply wasn't interested, and a line should have been drawn beneath her love there and then. No wonder he'd found it so easy to compose those letters for Oliver! She felt so shabby for never having loved her husband as much as she loved his friend, that she couldn't stop herself from speaking tenderly of Oliver. "We were very happy together, and he was a perfect husband," she said.

"Perfect? That doesn't sound like the Oliver Harwood I knew."

"I cannot help that," she answered defensively. "To me he was kind, considerate, strong, and always there to talk to. And he was a fine father to the boys, of course."

Harry looked at her in the darkness. "Of course." *Oli-*

ver was also muscular, athletic, and vigorous. Everything I am not.

"I am sorry that you and he fell out," she said then. "You did fall out, didn't you? Oliver never said very much about it, but I knew something had happened."

The letters happened, he thought. "We went our separate ways. Outgrew each other, I suppose."

"Oh." She shivered as the wind and rain struck through her clothes. "I . . . I thought perhaps it was simply that you did not like me."

"I didn't not like you," he corrected quickly.

No, you were simply indifferent, she thought, casting around for something else to say. "Are . . . are you going to the ball at the Marine Pavilion?"

"It is my intention, yes, for I am escorting Ellen."

"Then no doubt I will see you there."

"No doubt." He was conscious of the distance between them growing by the second, and it was the very last thing he wished to happen. He wanted to blurt out his love, to lay bare his heart, to fling himself upon her mercy, yet all he could do was make stilted conversation and sound increasingly formal. Suddenly there were harsh words on his lips, words he couldn't hold back no matter how he tried. "So Oliver was perfect, was he? No doubt he proved to be the romantic you always yearned for."

She recoiled a little. "I'm surprised you, of all people, should say that."

"Oh?"

"Please don't play the innocent, sir, for I *know* you wrote the letters."

His breath escaped with pain that he found hard to conceal. "I had hoped you were unaware." *Heigh ho! Sing, heigh ho! Unto the green holly: Most friendship is feigning, most loving mere folly . . .*

"We're getting very wet, sir. Perhaps you would care to come inside after all . . . ?" *Please say no.*

His eagerness to be gone was a match for her own. "Er, no, thank you. I ought to be getting home." They were strangers, and except for enchanted minutes on a single July afternoon long ago, they always would be. "I don't think I'll be attending the ball after all, Mrs. Harwood, so I will take this opportunity to wish you a very happy Christmas." Grasping the walking stick, he bowed his head to her and limped out of the garden to his waiting horse.

But as Rosalind listened to the sound of hooves dwindling into the turbulent night, she knew she could never be truly free of him. No matter how cold and distant he was, no matter how uncaring and uninterested, she would love him forever.

Chapter Six

Wednesday, December 23, dawned clear, calm, and bright. Brighton seemed fresh-washed and dazzling against the sparkling sea, where sails billowed white and a torn wisp of smoke marked the latest outing of Francis Tempest-Connell's steamboat. Such a change in the weather augured well for Christmas trade, and Ship Street was already thronging with people. The carol singers once again sang lustily on the corner near Mrs. Addiswell's address, and the delicious smell of roasted chestnuts hung appetizingly between the buildings. A small flock of geese was being driven past as Mrs. Addiswell's premises opened for business, and a man led several donkeys that were heavily laden with holly and mistletoe.

There wasn't a cloud in the dressmaker's sky either. The first thing she had done that morning had been to dismiss Edwards, whose surliness and complete lack of all discretion had become a veritable liability. The creature was even now packing her belongings, and would hopefully be gone before the first lady client arrived. Then, a little later, there would be a visit to Puckscroft with the green gauze gown, for which, if cards were played with care, payment would be made twice over, by Sir Henry *and* Mrs. Harwood.

However, the dressmaker's sense of seasonal satisfaction was short-lived. Within moments of opening time, a carriage halted outside and Laurinda Caldicot swept through the door. Mrs. Addiswell's spirits plummeted. *Please don't let it concern the green gauze gown. . . .*

Laurinda halted in front of her and declared imperiously, "I am persuaded that the gown will do after all, so I wish to take one last fitting, to be absolutely sure."

The dressmaker felt ill. "I . . . I fear . . ."

"Yes?" Laurinda's voice took on an ominous note.

"Well, I . . ." Mrs. Addiswell smoothed trembling hands on the front of her chalky-gray skirts, then took a huge breath. "I fear the gown is no longer available, Miss Caldicot."

Laurinda froze. "I beg your pardon?"

"The gown has been purchased by someone else, and—"

"But it's *my* gown!" Laurinda cried, outraged.

"With all due respect, Miss Caldicot, you said very publicly that you no longer wished to have it."

Publicly? Laurinda's mind raced back to those moments in this very room. Who else had been there who might constitute the public? Why, Ellen Trafford and her ungainly brother! The heiress's blue eyes became diamond-bright. "Am I to understand that Miss *Trafford* now has my gown?" she demanded.

"Oh, no, Miss Caldicot, most certainly not."

"I expect a name, Mrs. Addiswell."

The dressmaker drew herself up. "Rest assured that is not my policy to divulge information about one customer to another, Miss Caldicot."

"Then make it your policy this instant!" Laurinda stamped her foot. "It is *my* gown, and I wish it to be returned to me without further ado."

"I cannot, Miss Caldicot, but please rest assured that—"

"Rest assured?" Laurinda squeaked. "*Rest assured?* And how, pray, do you think I will accomplish that? I am without a new gown for the ball because you have given mine away. Well, I expect it to be returned to me this instant! I will ruin you for this, I swear."

Mrs. Addiswell found unexpected backbone. "With all due respect, Miss Caldicot, you are without the gown because *you* rejected it on a whim over color, not through any fault of mine. Now, I consider this conversation to be at an end, and would be grateful if you would leave." She went to the door, and held it open.

Laurinda was stunned, and was about to launch a

scene to end all scenes when another carriage drew up, bearing two distinguished ladies, so her lips clamped closed, and she swept from the shop like a galleon in full sail.

Laurinda was just getting into her waiting carriage when Edwards hastened up to her from the alley that led to the rear of the dressmaker's establishment. The summarily dismissed employee, bent upon revenge against her former employer, saw her opportunity. "Begging your pardon, Miss Caldicot, but may I have a word?"

Laurinda gave the woman a disparaging look, and continued to get into the carriage.

Edwards spoke quickly. "I can tell you who has your gown."

Laurinda paused, then stepped back down to the pavement. "Indeed?"

The woman's tongue passed nervously over her lips. "It will cost you," she said then.

"And how do I know you will tell me the truth?"

"I'm not fool enough to lie about such a thing."

Laurinda hesitated, then opened her reticule and took out some coins, which she dropped into the woman's outstretched palm. The palm remained open, and the woman's eyebrow raised a little, so with ill grace Laurinda surrendered several more coins. The grasping palm closed at last. "Mrs. Harwood of Puckscroft Park is to have your gown, Miss Caldicot, and intends to wear it at the ball."

Laurinda knew all about Rosalind, whom she actively disliked for becoming mistress of Puckscroft, a position to which Laurinda herself had, until recently, aspired. The Caldicot heiress was the sort of creature to always blame someone else for her woes. Her late fiancé, the fifth marquess, was no longer there for her to accuse of deliberately dying in order to prevent her from becoming his marchioness, but Laurinda's spitefully illogical nature permitted the easy casting of Rosalind Harwood as a usurping adventuress. "Mrs. *Harwood?* But how on earth did she—?"

"Sir Henry Trafford purchased it for her," Edwards interrupted.

"Did he indeed?" Laurinda almost purred the words. How very interesting . . . and shocking too, if one spread whispers with malice aforethought. "Just how well acquainted is the lady with Sir Henry?"

Edwards was Laurinda's match when it came to malice. "Judge for yourself, Miss Caldicot. He's buying her a gown, so I'm putting two and two together."

"So am I," Laurinda murmured vengefully. "So am I . . ."

A light breeze picked up across the downs, and rustled the ivy around the window of Rosalind's private drawing room. She wore a butter-yellow velour gown with lavish lace at the throat and cuffs, and a warm red-and-bronze shawl she drew tightly around her folded arms as she pondered what to say to Jake. There had been yet another Master Dobbs episode, and she knew she really had to deal with it before the whole silly business got quite out of hand.

There was a timid tap at the door behind her, and she turned as the little boy came in. Judging by the jut of his lower lip, he was prepared to stand his ground over Master Dobbs.

Rosalind drew a deep breath. "I think you know why I've sent for you."

"Yes, Mother."

"Have you anything to say?"

"Just that there *is* a Master Dobbs, and he told me it's because of him that Puckscroft got its name."

"Enough!" Rosalind held up a stern hand, but was distracted by the sound of a carriage outside. Turning, she saw to her surprise Mrs. Addiswell's brown chariot drawing up by the double steps that led up to the portico at the entrance of the main block. Forgetting Jake for a moment, she moved closer to the window. A footman hastened out, and the dressmaker and an assistant climbed down, bringing with them the cloth bag containing her gown. At least . . . Rosalind was a little startled when a gust of wind fluttered the open end of the cloth bag and revealed not indigo silk, but what appeared to be green gauze!

"May I go now, Mother?" Jake spoke at her elbow.

He'd come to see what she was looking at, and was highly delighted to realize that it was Mrs. Addiswell. Things like new gowns were guaranteed to relegate him to the background for a while.

"No, sir, you can stay right where you are, for I haven't finished with you yet."

His face fell. "Oh, Mother . . . !"

"Sit over there, and not a word from you. Is that clear?"

"Yes, Mother." With a theatrical sigh he went to the chair and wriggled his bottom onto it. Then he sat with his legs swinging, his face a study of suffering.

Mrs. Addiswell was announced, and soon produced a very different gown from the hated indigo silk. The dressmaker explained about the green gauze having been ordered and then refused. "So I wondered if . . . Well, Mrs. Harwood, if you would consider the gown for yourself? I realize that it is impertinence on my part, but I do know how disappointed you were not to have time to order a new gown for the ball. I also know that I am left with a gown on my hands that would suit you most admirably. The measurements are perfect, quite perfect."

Rosalind's eyes shone delightedly. "Are you absolutely sure the young lady will not change her mind?"

"You may rest assured on that score, madam. Besides, the gown is no longer exactly as it was. I've removed some frills from here, added some there, and changed the decoration around the bodice. It is essentially the same garment as before, but with sufficient difference to make it exclusively yours."

Rosalind adored the gown on sight. If only . . .

"Is something wrong, madam?" Mrs. Addiswell detected the reservation in her client's eyes and became anxious.

"Mm? No, not wrong exactly, just a foolish little quibble."

"Perhaps it is something that may be changed?" Mrs. Addiswell's fingers were crossed behind her back.

Rosalind laughed. "No, it is merely something concerning the color."

The dressmaker's face took on a fixed look. Not another tiresome whim about not liking the green?

Rosalind was at pains to reassure her. "I was merely wishing it was yellow, that's all, because yellow is the color that suits me best of all."

Jake, still observing sullenly from his chair, sat forward with sudden interest. Yellow? Yes, the gown *would* look better that color. Master Dobbs would be able to change it in a trice, but Mother didn't believe in Master Dobbs. . . .

Unaware of her son's interest, Rosalind smiled at the dressmaker. "But the green is lovely, of course, and I am well satisfied with it."

"How very odd you should mention yellow, for that is just what Sir—" Mrs. Addiswell's lips clamped shut.

Rosalind looked curiously at her.

"Oh, nothing, madam. It was something and nothing."

"My mind is made up: I will definitely take the gown. Why, it might have been made for me. I do not know how to thank you, Mrs. Addiswell. I will expect your invoice in due course."

The dressmaker beamed with relief. "And *I* do not know how to thank *you,* madam. We are each other's salvation, I think." *Oh, the joy of being paid twice!*

"We are indeed."

There were smiles all around at such a satisfactory outcome, except from Jake, of course, who still awaited his mother's wrath. When Mrs. Addiswell and her assistant had departed, he was summoned from the chair to stand before Rosalind by the fireplace. "Right, young man, enough is enough. I absolutely forbid any further mention of Master Dobbs."

Jake gave a long-suffering sigh. "That's not fair," he muttered under his breath.

"Yes, it is, sir," Rosalind replied, her ears sharp enough to miss very little.

"Nor are you to go anywhere near the pantry. If I hear so much as a single word about your disobedience on either of these scores, I will resort to other means. There may be no Christmas presents, and you may be confined to your room with bread and water while Peter and I tuck into roast goose. Am I understood?"

"Yes, Mother."

"Right, you may go."

Jake went grumpily toward the door, then turned. "I'll *prove* to you that there's a Master D— That there's a Pharisee in the pantry! Then you'll *have* to believe me!" Without giving her a chance to reply, he opened the door and fled.

Chapter Seven

Harry was just about to set off on his morning ride. Clad in a pine-green coat and beige breeches, he made his way across the great baronial hall, his walking stick tapping on the uneven stone flags. Two maids were putting the last touches to the Christmas decorations, and he smiled as one laughed in surprise and said to the other, "My, Dolly Jenkins, you finished that garland double-quick. Did Master Dobbs sneak up to help you?" He entered the screened passage at the far end of the hall, then emerged to the shallow flight of steps beneath the Tudor porch. Two horses were saddled and waiting in the courtyard—Ellen had rather taken him by surprise at the end of breakfast by leaning affectionately over his shoulder and informing him that she would accompany him today.

Now her blithe tones rang along the passage. "Well, here I am, Harry, all ready to show the world what an indifferent rider I am compared to you."

Leaning on his walking stick, he turned to see Ellen hurrying toward him, still drawing on her buff gloves. She wore a crimson woolen riding habit, and her hair was pinned up neatly beneath a black beaver hat. There was a cheerful smile on her lips, too cheerful by far, had he been alert enough to notice. She had tossed and turned most of the night, thinking and plotting, and had now hatched a plan she hoped would salve her conscience about his stolen letters.

But Harry was not alert. "I still can't understand why you want to come with me. You hate riding." She saw his hand move automatically over his left breast, and for a moment was afraid that he would realize the precious letter was no longer there. Ellen had sneaked it from its hiding place when she'd leaned over him at the breakfast table. To her relief he didn't seem to notice anything amiss.

She flexed her fingers in her gloves, then admired the perfect fit. "Harry, you are supposed to say something about it being a wonderful notion for me to come too, and how delighted you are to have my company."

"Oh, what a wonderful notion. I'm delighted to have your company," he said dutifully.

She gave him one of her arch looks. "You can be such a beast at times, Harry Trafford, that I wonder I bother with you. I trust you mean to be agreeable while we ride?"

He grinned. "Of course . . . Well, from time to time, anyway."

The waiting groom helped them both to mount, and Harry attached his walking stick to his unique saddle by a special strap, for he never ventured anywhere without it. A moment later they rode out of the courtyard, over the permanently lowered drawbridge, and across the ancient deer park with its equally ancient oaks, toward the village of Roecombe.

Laurinda was at that moment seated in the dining room of the Ship Hotel in Brighton. It was considered a fashionable place to be seen, and she and a number of her lady friends had congregated to take a dish of hot chocolate before venturing forth to the shops with their attendant maids and footmen. For the time being, however, all thoughts of shopping had been set aside as they listened open-mouthed to the shocking tale of Sir Henry Trafford, Mrs. Harwood, and the green gauze gown.

The ladies went their separate ways, spreading the scandal to all and sundry, which was exactly what Laurinda intended. It wasn't long before Harry and Rosalind were being discussed in the circulating library on the Steyne, in the Castle Inn, and in every shop of consequence. Soon their names were passing from lip to lip among the crowds riding and parading in front of the

Marine Pavilion itself, where even the Prince Regent was informed of the infamous green gauze gown.

Brighton had swiftly become a hothouse of rumor and innuendo, but the unfortunates whose names were being bandied with such salacious delight did not know a thing, of course.

Harry and Ellen rode through Roecombe, with its delightful tile-hung houses, and past the church lych-gate that was overhung with holly. The slender, shingled spire and lichen-covered roof of St. Luke's church, where Rosalind's late father had once delivered his sermons, loomed above the yews in the churchyard, and on the valley side beyond rose the beech hanger wood that in summer offered coolness and shade from the sun. Coppiced hazel was scattered in the meadows close to the River Traff, but as the two riders made their way up through the hanger toward the open downs, the sound of their hooves was softened by a carpet of beech leaves.

On such a fine December day it was very agreeable to hack along, just enjoying the winter sunshine. Ellen chattered a great deal. Oh, how she chattered, for she wished to lure Harry toward Puckscroft Park, the roofs of which were just visible ahead. She distracted his attention, pointing at this and that, questioning him about London, and generally making certain that he had little time to consider their increasing proximity to Rosalind's home. The nearer to the gates she could lead him, the better for her plan. It did not occur to her that Harry might not be pleased with her interference, or that anything might go very wrong. To her it was a simple matter of black and white, without any gray in between, and in that she was very much still only twenty.

Harry suddenly realized where they were going, and reined in sharply. "We've ridden far enough," he said, and began to turn his horse.

Ellen reacted like lightning, and with a frightened squeal made her mount appear to bolt. With much show of being frightened, she gave the animal its head toward the fine wrought-iron gates bearing the coat of arms of the Marquesses of Southdown. The gatekeeper's lodge had been unoccupied for several months now, and the gates were always left open. Next to the gravel drive about fifty yards into the park she knew there was a convenient carpet of the Saint-John's-wort shrub, which would be the very place for her to fall safely, and this she proceeded to do. Galloping through the gateway she gave another squeal and jerked the animal's head one way, at the same time flinging herself to the ground the other, and she landed quite perfectly in the midst of the shrubs. Unharmed, she lay as if in a faint, perhaps even dead.

Harry galloped up and reined in so swiftly that his horse almost went down on its haunches. "Ellen? Are you all right?" he cried, slipping lightly to the ground, all the while holding the saddle for support. He didn't bother to unfasten the walking stick, but lurched awkwardly to where she lay. "Ellen? Can you hear me?" She was a little ashamed when she heard the anxiety in his voice, and even more so when he struggled to kneel beside her, but she stuck doggedly to her plan, only permitting herself a feeble moan, as if barely conscious.

He removed his glasses and leaned over her, his hand warm against her cheek. "Ellen?"

She made another convincing noise. "Mmmm . . ."

"Please open your eyes."

She managed only a brief flutter of her lids before giving a splendid impression of sinking into complete unconsciousness.

"Oh, dear God," Harry breathed in dismay, sitting up straight to hurriedly replace his spectacles then peer toward Puckscroft Park. It was the very last place he wished to call, but there really wasn't any choice. To his relief Ellen's riderless horse had already attracted the attention of two keepers taking a supply of Christmas game to the house kitchens in a pony and trap.

Soon Ellen had been laid gently on Harry's coat amid the trap's load of pheasant and partridge, and was on her way to the house. She regretted causing her beloved brother so much anxiety, but did not doubt she was doing the right thing. As the trap shuddered to a halt by the portico of the house, she became more certain than ever of the justice of her cause when she glimpsed the statue of Venus atop the pediment.

A footman was immediately sent to inform Rosalind that an injured lady had been brought to the house. In the meantime Jeffries, the butler, took it upon himself to instruct the keepers to carry Ellen into the state bedroom, which adjoined the entrance hall in the main block, and had last been occupied by King George III himself. It was a sumptuously gilded chamber hung with exquisite blue brocade, and the great crimson velvet bed, as majestic as any monarch could desire, had an elaborately swagged canopy that rose almost to the ceiling. The staterooms were always warmed with fires in the winter months, and there was a rather festive smell of spices from the opened potpourri jars in the hearth.

Ellen lay very still on the bed, seeming oblivious to the consternation all around her, and Harry stood by the white marble fireplace, his walking stick now safely in his hand. He was agitated, not only because of Ellen, but because at any moment he was bound to come face-to-face with Rosalind again. After the meeting the night before, when he'd realized she knew he had written the letters, he felt more ill-prepared than ever to speak to her. The coward in him would have avoided the matter entirely by staying well away from her; now the coward was being forced to confront the issue.

As the seconds ticked by, Harry's disquiet increased, and his walking stick tapped impatiently on the polished oak floor as his temper deteriorated. At last, seeing his sister apparently lying at death's door, with the keepers, the butler, and several maids clustered uselessly around the bedside, his anger bubbled over. "Has someone been sent to bring a physician?" he demanded of the butler.

Jeffries turned, his expression one of dismay. He was a thin, pale-faced, rather foxy man, always clad in brown, and he took himself very seriously. Nothing could have been more abhorrent than being found lacking in his duty, but before he could answer there came the sound of light hurrying footsteps, then Rosalind arrived in a flurry of lemon velour, her shawl dragging behind her. "What has happened, Jeffries?" she asked as she leaned over Ellen. She didn't notice Harry.

"The lady's horse bolted, madam, and she was thrown near the lodge."

"Do we know who she is?"

Harry spoke. "She is my sister."

Rosalind turned, her face draining of color. "Harry?" she whispered, her hand creeping to her throat. The scent of the rose garden seemed to drift fleetingly in the room, with the melancholy wistfulness and never-forgotten pain of lost first love.

Chapter Eight

Harry gazed back at Rosalind, keeping his face as free of emotion as he could. "Perhaps something could be done for my sister? Such as sending for a physician?" How cold and unfriendly the words sounded. He could almost feel her recoil from them.

"You're right, of course, Sir Henry," she responded civilly, and turned to Jeffries. "Send a rider immediately. The doctor is to be told it is urgent because Sir Henry Trafford's sister has met with a riding accident. Be quick now."

"Madam." The butler bowed and hurried away into the adjacent great hall, so far forgetting his dignity as to shout for a footman.

Next Rosalind turned to one of the maids. "Bring the medication chest."

"Madam." Dipping a curtsy, the girl caught up her skirts and ran from the room.

Then Rosalind waved the keepers out, before turning to Harry again. "Please wait in the state drawing room, Sir Henry."

"I would prefer to stay," he replied. The state drawing room was on the other side of the marble hall, and seemed a great distance from Ellen.

She held his gaze. "I am not asking you, Sir Henry, I am telling you. Miss Trafford would not wish you to be present when the maid and I undress her and put her properly into the bed."

He flushed. "And how long am I expected to kick my heels in grand seclusion?"

"I will come to you directly." Gazing into his eyes, as chilly and gray as the sea, she wished she had never left Albany.

Harry hesitated, then hobbled awkwardly from the room, his walking stick tap-tapping. Rosalind watched him leave, seeing how the light from a window fell upon his fair hair, remembering a time when his eyes and lips had smiled, and he had quoted Shakespeare's sonnets. She listened to the diminishing sound of the stick as he crossed the marble hall toward the state drawing room, then she looked briskly at the remaining maid, who was observing her rather curiously. "Go to my private apartment and bring a nightdress. I will begin to extricate Miss Trafford from her riding habit."

"Madam." The maid followed everyone else out of the room.

Rosalind bent to unfasten the tight-fitting riding habit, then straightened with a gasp on finding herself looking into Ellen's wide brown eyes. "Miss Trafford?"

"Mrs. Harwood." Ellen made to sit up, but Rosalind prevented her.

"Don't do that, for heaven's sake, you've had a bad fall!"

"But I'm not Humpty Dumpty, and do not need putting together again," Ellen replied coolly. "There *is* something that I think needs putting together, however. At least, I hope it does. Mrs. Harwood, this may seem a dreadfully impertinent question, but did you love your late husband?"

Rosalind took offense. "You are right, Miss Trafford, it *does* seem an impertinent question."

"Please don't be angry with me, because I'm trying very hard to right a wrong that I think was done a long time ago. But first you *must* tell me if Harry means anything to you."

"You presume too much, Miss Trafford!"

Having come this far, Ellen had no intention of giving up. "It is a very simple question, Mrs. Harwood."

"One that I do not intend to grace with an answer," Rosalind replied. But she avoided the brown eyes of her interrogator in such a way that the truth was laid only too bare.

Ellen smiled. "Harry thinks I am still a child, and no doubt you do too, Mrs. Harwood, but I know about love." She took Harry's letter from her cuff, pressing it urgently into Rosalind's hand. "You must read this, Mrs. Harwood. It's the only one that wasn't—" She broke off and collapsed back on the bed as the unmistakable sound of her brother's walking stick and irregular steps approached the doorway.

Bemused—and unable to think of anything other than concealing the letter among the folds of her skirts—Rosalind turned as he limped back into the room. "Sir Henry, I . . . I thought I asked you to—" she began, but he interrupted.

"I cannot idly dally around elsewhere when my sister is badly injured."

"Badly injured?" Rosalind glanced down at Ellen, but that young lady once again seemed nigh to being a corpse.

Harry misunderstood Rosalind's response, and was somewhat outraged. "Surely you are not about to tell me Ellen *isn't* injured? For heaven's sake, Rosalind, she's unconscious! Lord knows what injuries she may have incurred."

Rosalind was in a cleft stick. "Harry, if you wish to be disagreeable toward me, that is entirely your prerogative. I'm sure I do not know why you should feel thus ill-disposed, but there is no reason at all why I should remain in this room with you. So if you intend to stay here, I will leave."

The letter forgotten, she began to leave the room, but his bitter reproach followed her. "Of course you know why I behave this way! You aren't a fool, Rosalind, so please don't treat me as if I am."

She whirled about. "I have no idea what you're talking about, Harry."

"Really?" The word was uttered dryly.

Now her anger sparked too. "Yes, really. So tell me, if you please, for that is the only way I am going to understand."

He came toward her, his gray eyes filled with something that only at the last second did she recognize as hurt. "You knew about the letters, Rosalind. You knew

I'd written them, yet it suited you to pretend you thought they were Oliver's."

She stared at him, remembering the letter in her hand. Her fingers closely tightly around it, but she did not look at it. "Yes, I knew you'd written the letters, Harry. I didn't at first, I confess, but I guessed later."

"Would that I could believe you."

"Believe me about what? Harry, what is there to not believe? I was fooled at first into imagining Oliver had composed them himself, but common sense prevailed in the end, when I realized he wasn't in the least interested in or appreciative of poetry. Therefore it had to be that you wrote the letters for Oliver to copy and give to me."

He was astonished. "That I wrote them *for* him?" he repeated incredulously.

"Well, yes, of course. What else?" She blushed a little, and tried to hide the emotions on her face. "I have never understood you, Harry. That day in the rose garden I thought . . . Well, it doesn't matter what I thought, because it was wrong anyway, and when I left the garden you could not have made it more abundantly clear that I had read more into your compliments than you intended."

Now he was the one to go a little red. "I rather thought you wished it that way."

"I *wished* it that way? Oh, yes, every lady desires to be snubbed, but I more than most."

"That isn't how I meant it!" he replied, running his hand agitatedly through his hair.

Her eyes were bright with tears that she desperately wanted to hold back. "Then what *did* you mean? That it was a case of *I must be cruel, only to be kind*?"

"I meant only to release you from the embarrassment you were undoubtedly caused by my earlier remark."

She looked blankly at him. "I still don't understand."

Suddenly Ellen sat up in exasperation. "Oh, for *heaven's* sake, why can't you simply sit down together and be reasonable?"

Harry turned to her in amazement. "Ellen?"

She had the grace to look a little ashamed. "As you can see, there is nothing wrong with me. My accident was a fabrication because I need to salve my conscience.

My intention was to bring you two together, so that you could settle your differences, but instead of doing that, you seem so intent upon perpetuating this misunderstanding that I vow I could strangle you both!"

Harry was incensed. "Ellen, I am going to find this very hard to forgive," he said in a tight voice.

"Well, I fancy I can endure until you stop being in a silly huff," she replied a little saucily. "Look, I will be absolutely honest. Ten, maybe eleven years ago, I saw Oliver Harwood leaving the library at Trafford Hall with something tucked inside his coat. He came when you were out, Harry, and said he was borrowing our volume of *Gil Blas* for his mother. But we have never had *Gil Blas,* nor could that thick volume have been what he had in his coat. I now feel certain he had taken your cigar box, and if I'd known at the time, if you'd only said something, things might have turned out very differently."

Rosalind gazed from one to the other. "Cigar box? What cigar box?"

Ellen answered. "The one in which my brother kept all the unsent love letters he'd written to you, and which your late husband copied and pretended he'd written himself," she said bluntly, and swung her legs from the regal bed. "There, it is said, and if neither of you speaks to me ever again it will be too bad, but at least I can live with myself once more. I have felt dreadful since I realized what I'd witnessed back then. Now I am going to leave you together, and if you do not settle your differences, it will not be my fault."

Gathering the cumbersome skirts of her riding habit, she hurried from the state bedroom before anyone could say anything to stop her, but in the doorway she looked back at Rosalind. "The letter I gave you is the only one your husband didn't take, and you may care to know that Harry has carried it next to his heart ever since." With a final imploring look at them both, she hastened away.

A heavy silence settled over the bedroom as the sound of her swift footsteps faded. Harry was so mortified to have his great secret blurted in such a fashion that he didn't know what to say or do. He could not bring himself to look at Rosalind, for fear of seeing disdain written large on her face, so he turned away, snatching off his spectacles as if in some way his shortsightedness would protect him.

Rosalind was shaken to realize just how greatly her husband had deceived her. "Oliver told me you'd written the letters for him," she whispered, looking down at the crumpled paper in her hand. It was such a creased, dog-eared article that she knew Ellen had told the truth. "I asked him if you had written them, and he admitted it, but said you'd done it at his request."

"He lied," Harry replied.

She gazed at him. "You wrote them to me? It had nothing to do with him?"

"Nothing." Harry exhaled slowly, and limped across to lean against one of the magnificently carved bedposts.

Her pulse had quickened, but she was still cautious. He had rebuffed her so many times in the past that she dared not believe things would be any different this time. "If that is so, why were you always so cold toward me? Why didn't you come to sit with me at the picnic? Why did you give me such a cruel congé? Why did you go out of your way to avoid me for the rest of that summer? We lived in the same village, but you did all you could to stay out of my company."

He had done all those things, but not for the reason she thought. "Have you any idea how incredible I believed it would be if you truly liked me in the way I liked you? Can you imagine how utterly beyond possibility I thought it would be for you to actually *love* me? I knew how poor a thing I was beside a great strong fellow like Oliver, and how even Francis was a god compared to me. There I was, a shuffling invalid whose only talent was to be able to *spout* Shakespeare like a fountain." He emphasized the last.

"A shuffling invalid? I didn't see you like that! As for spouting Shakespeare, why, I thought it was truly wonderful to meet someone whose knowledge allowed him to do such a thing with so little effort. I admired you, liked you . . . adored you. Yes, I did. Those hours in the rose garden were the most wonderful of my life, and, God help me, I've dreamed of them ever since."

His lips parted and he gazed at her as if at something so ethereal it was bound to disappear again at any moment.

"Harry, are you telling me that you behaved as you did because you thought I was embarrassed by your lame leg?" she demanded.

Somehow he managed to meet her eyes. "Yes," he admitted. "Yes, of course that's how I felt. I'm a half-blind cripple who needs a stick to walk, and such thick lenses to see that I have trouble keeping my spectacles in place! How could I not see it in your glance, and hear it in your voice? Damn it all, I was so accustomed to that sort of reaction that I thought it was bound to be repeated with you."

"Even though I told you it didn't matter to me?"

"Kind words, perhaps," he answered.

"True words," she corrected. "Oh, Harry, how could you do me such an injustice?"

"As easily as you did me the injustice of believing I would write such letters for Oliver," he replied.

She nodded. "Yes, we are both at fault." She held out the letter. "This is yours."

"No, it's yours, Rosalind." Harry took off his spectacles and placed them carefully on the coverlet on the bed. "I wrote those letters for your eyes alone, but did not have the courage to send even one. It's time you read my words with truly opened eyes."

Chapter Nine

Harry straightened from the bedpost as Rosalind slowly unfolded the letter. At last she gazed upon the words as she had been meant to when they were written.

My dearest Rosalind. I pray I may be so forward as to address you by your first name, for that is how I think of you. Rosalind: my lady of the roses, my jewel, my shining Grail. Rosalind: my dream on awakening, my last thought on going to sleep. Rosalind: my past, my present, and my future. You are more to me than a summer's day, more gentle than a night breeze, more delightful than the sun through morning dew. To be with you is to become happiness itself.

If romantic foolishness fills my soul, it is because in you I see the perfect bloom. But when you look at me you will never see perfection, for I am a withered stem that will never flourish as you flourish. Yet I am not without passion, without hope, or without dreams. I dream of you, Rosalind, and of a future shared . . . a future blessed with countless joys.

Read these words, and know that I adored you at first sight, and that my love will endure until my eyes close forever. Read these words and think kindly of me; think fondly of me . . . perhaps even think lovingly of me. Know that I am here for you forever, as is my ring. Wear that ring, sweet Rosalind. Be my bride. Let me cherish you as I have yearned. Let me worship you, be your husband, your guardian, your knight, your lover, and your dearest friend. We are two, but we should be one, Rosalind, my fairest jewel.

And should you find it hard to even recall my name, it is Harry.

Tears ran unashamedly down her cheeks. Not recall his name? Why, it had been part of her soul for as long as she had been part of his, and if this letter had been placed in her hand when it had been written, she too would have carried it next to her heart.

Could she forgive Oliver for what he had done? It would not be easy, but then perhaps his punishment had been always to believe she hadn't truly loved him. Besides, she had him to thank for her two beloved boys. She folded the paper again, and slid it into her bodice. "Now it will rest next to *my* heart," she said softly, and smiled at Harry through her tears.

"Oh, Rosalind," he whispered, taking an unsteady step toward her, but she went to him, slipped her arms around his waist, and put her lips to his. They cleaved together, exulting at last in the kiss that had yearned through them both for such a very long time; the kiss that should have been given life in the warmth and fragrance of the rose garden . . . All the suppressed passion and hunger for true love flared into being, running fiercely through their veins and blazing through their hearts.

She had dreamed of him, wanted him, keened for him for so very long that it was almost possible to know complete ecstasy just by being so tightly held within his arms. Her lips moved luxuriously against his as one by one the lost years were dashed aside. That single exquisite kiss eased the pain of heartache, assuaged the sorrow of unrequited love, and freed their hearts at last.

At length it was Harry who drew back to cup her flushed face in his hands and gaze adoringly into her eyes. "I love you, Rosalind. I have always loved you, and I always will. You are the only woman I have ever wanted, and that is how it will be forever."

"And you have my heart forever," she whispered.

He smiled, feeling almost ridiculously happy. "Attend the ball with me tomorrow night! Well, with Ellen too, of course, but . . ." He was too overcome to finish.

"I would love to attend the ball with you. Why, I even have a new green gown because one of Mrs. Addiswell's other ladies decided at the last minute not to accept it after all."

"I'm . . . pleased to hear it.

"The years may have passed, Rosalind, but I mean to ask the question I contemplated at our very first meeting, and which I put to you in that letter. Will you marry me?"

"Yes, oh, yes," she whispered, fresh tears springing to her eyes.

Their lips came together again, and there were tears in his eyes as well, for such incredible joy was almost too much to bear. The future was no longer lonely and unfulfilled. If it hadn't been for Ellen, whom he had wronged so much by treating her as a child . . .

Suddenly there was a scuffling sound and a crash as one of the potpourri jars in the hearth somehow managed to fall over. The sound was so loud and unexpected that Harry and Rosalind leapt apart. As they both looked askance at the broken jar, its spicy contents spilled on the warm marble, there was a squeak, followed by the unmistakable patter of footsteps.

This time Rosalind knew it couldn't be Jake. "You *did* hear that, didn't you, Harry? Someone knocked over that jar and then ran from the room!"

"The heat of the fire probably proved too much for the jar, and the footsteps were a trick of the wind outside."

"But there's hardly any wind today," she pointed out.

"In that case I fear you and I are rather long in the tooth to actually see the likely culprit," he teased.

"Culprit? Who?"

"Why, Master Dobbs, of course."

Rosalind's lips parted. "Just who is this wretched Master Dobbs that everyone talks about? The servants insist he's a Pharisee, which I find totally ridiculous!"

Harry began to laugh. "You haven't lived in Sussex long enough to realize that 'Pharisee' is local dialect for fairy. Master Dobbs is peculiar to this county, and whenever anything untoward happens, it's said that he's been at work again. You know, in the same way that people say anything that's lost will be found in Grandmother's bedroom behind the wallpaper, or that Jack Frost is responsible for ice patterns on windows. It's just a silly country saying, that's all."

"I have enough of Master Dobbs from Jake," she said with feeling. "He has driven me to distraction with his insistence that a Pharisee resides in the kitchen pantry, that it changed cold figgy pudding into the hot variety, that it transformed a red-and-gray scarf into a blue tartan one, and oh, I don't know what else. I am so tired of Master Dobbs that I could scream."

He pulled her close again and rested his cheek against her hair. "Then let us simply leave it that the fire broke the jar, and the steps belonged to a . . . a rat!"

She pulled sharply away and shuddered. "That's even worse than Master Dobbs!" she cried in horror, then saw the laughter in his eyes and began to laugh too.

It was laughter that culminated in another kiss, and another, and many more after that.

Come the evening of the ball, Laurinda had fomented such an air of scandalized anticipation throughout the Brighton hive that a loud hum was almost audible above the most fashionable rooftops. Everyone who would be attending the ball was filled with secret glee at the prospect of the scene that was bound to ensue when Rosalind appeared in Laurinda's green gauze gown. Even the Prince Regent was guilty of looking forward to someone else's embarrassment rather than his own. He had so often been the butt of gossip and innuendo that it would be a refreshing change to be an onlooker for once. It was for this reason, and this alone, that he did not peremptorily cancel the invitations that had been sent to Trafford Hall and Puckscroft Park.

Harry, Rosalind, Ellen, and Francis had agreed to attend the ball as a foursome. Harry and Ellen awaited Francis's arrival before setting off for Puckscroft Park, with no notion at all of the awful drama awaiting at the Marine Pavilion. Happiness glowed from both brother and sister as they dressed for the occasion. Harry had not stopped smiling since his reconciliation with Rosalind, and Ellen was in seventh heaven as well, not only because she had succeeded in bringing her brother and his love together, but because that afternoon she had received flowers from Francis. They were not just any flowers, but very rare and expensive red roses from a hothouse in the neighboring town of Lewes.

The flowers had been accompanied by an unexpectedly tender note that at last made plain that Francis Tempest-Connell was not indifferent to her after all. Mind you, there was an oily fingerprint in the corner of the note, which told the recipient that the writer had been working on his wretched steam engine just before writing, but somehow that made the note all the more affecting. Ellen could live with a thousand steam engines provided Francis loved her. So she pinned one of the red roses to the daringly low bodice of her mandarin gown and another in her beautifully dressed hair, and she could do nothing about the foolish smile that lit her face.

Never had Christmas seemed more special than it did when Francis arrived and Harry and Ellen went down to greet him in the great baronial hall. As luck would have it the Roecombe wassailers arrived at the same time, and came in to fill the house with carols. The smell of mince pies and hot cinnamon punch hung in the warm air, and Ellen's Christmas decorations cast holly and ivy shadows in the swirling light of the log fire and the wassailers' lanterns.

Harry's only regret was that Rosalind was not at his side, but when the singers departed he learned something from Francis that stirred far greater regrets than that. Francis had driven from Brighton, having been made late because as he was about to depart he had heard the rumors and speculation Laurinda had set in motion.

Harry ran his white-gloved fingers through his hair. "Oh, dear God," he breathed, "I wish I had never even seen that cursed gown."

Ellen was shocked. "What have you to do with the gown, Harry?" she demanded.

He confessed his part in things, and his sister looked at him in dismay. "You did *what*? Oh, Harry, have you no sense? It would have been bad enough were the gown connected with another lady, but when it was *Laurinda's* . . ." She left the sentence unfinished.

Francis was in full agreement. "It was a wee bit daft of you, old man."

"You think I do not know that? I acted on the spur of the moment, encouraged by the thought of Rosalind having a new gown after all."

Francis was unimpressed. "It was still monumentally clumsy, if you don't mind my saying."

"As it happens, I *do* mind you saying," Harry replied. "What on earth would you know about the rights and wrongs of the situation? You, the man who has only just awakened to the fact that he is in love with my sister! Let me see, how many years has it been . . . ?"

Ellen intervened before the disagreement became more serious. "Sirs, neither of you is exactly in a position to throw stones. The damage has been done, and we must think hard about how to thwart Laurinda's troublemaking."

Both men fell silent, for there seemed no way out, apart from somehow preventing Rosalind from attending the ball at all.

"That will only postpone the problem, leaving Rosalind to face the music later on," Ellen pointed out with a wisdom beyond her years. "If Rosalind could be persuaded to find another gown in her wardrobe, something that definitely is not green gauze, then perhaps . . . ?" Again she didn't finish, remembering that Harry had just explained Rosalind didn't have such a gown.

Francis looked at her. "What of your wardrobe, Ellen? Do you have anything that would do?"

Ellen was cross. "Francis, I am a good six inches shorter than Rosalind. I vow that wearing any gown of mine would make her the object of even more shocking chatter!"

Harry's walking stick tapped the floor impatiently. "There must be *something* we can do. Wait a moment—maybe there is still time to remove the sting from things by asking the Braithwaites to enter the ballroom with us. They *always* arrive late, so are unlikely to have left home yet. If we send a rider . . ."

But Ellen gave a sleek smile. "They already expect to join us," she said, "well, Francis and me, at least."

Harry was startled. "They do? But—"

"You *did* tell me you weren't coming tonight," she reminded him, "which meant that I could hardly go on my own with Francis. So I sent an urgent note to Braithwaite Manor. I would have notified Francis to meet us at the Pavilion if you hadn't changed your mind yet again, Harry Trafford. As it was I had to send to her ladyship again, telling her you would be able to escort me after all, and suggesting they join us at the ball. So that is what they will be doing."

Harry smiled with relief, but Francis pulled a face. "If only Laurinda Caldicot's rumors were entirely unfounded, but they aren't, I fear. Mrs. Harwood may not be a kept woman, but she *is* going to wear that confounded gown tonight. I don't like to think what Lord and Lady B. will make of *that* small detail."

Ellen wasn't quite so pessimistic. "Harry, you asked Mrs. Addiswell to alter the gown a little, didn't you?"

"Yes."

"Then maybe there is hope. The most that can be justifiably whispered is that Rosalind is wearing a green gauze gown, but not necessarily *the* green gauze gown. Francis and I can busy ourselves telling all and sundry that it isn't the gown Laurinda ordered. We may not be entirely believed, but we can create doubt in people's minds, enough maybe to make the whole thing redound upon Laurinda herself." A glint entered her brown eyes. "I will certainly enjoy doing my utmost to see that it does."

The two men looked at each other, then Francis grinned. "I'm game."

Harry was reluctant. "But it's all risky for Rosalind. Maybe if I could simply persuade her to cry off tonight . . . ?"

"No, Harry!" the others cried together, then Ellen added, "You will have to confess to Rosalind, of course, for we cannot allow her to arrive at the ball unaware of the furore. Grasp the bull by the horns, or whatever it is that matadors are advised to do." She gave a sudden grin as years of Harry's quotations brought a suitable line from Shakespeare into her head. "What was it Old Will said on the subject? *Out of this nettle, danger, we pluck this flower, safety.* So put a stop to Laurinda's mischief right now, because I promise you that postponing the business will merely make things worse."

Harry gave in, but grave doubts remained, and as their carriage drove away from Trafford Hall, the note to Lord and Lady Braithwaite having been duly dispatched, he wished he had never clapped eyes on Miss Laurinda Caldicot or the green gauze gown.

Chapter Ten

And that was how matters stood at the beginning of this story as Rosalind, having conceded to Jake that Master Dobbs existed after all, made her way to the marble hall. She was about to go to the ball with Harry, whom she adored as much as life itself, and she was clad in a very special, very beautiful, very magical gown. No heart could have beaten more joyfully than hers.

Hearing her light steps approaching, Harry, Francis, and Ellen turned uneasily to greet her, their thoughts fixed on the trouble Laurinda had so willfully created in Brighton. But when Rosalind entered the hall, their eyes widened and their lips parted in utter amazement, for her appearance was not at all what they'd expected. Far from wearing the ill-fated green gauze gown, she was clad in golden yellow, her favorite color. Francis blinked, not knowing what to think after all the things he'd been told. Harry and Ellen stared at the gown, which was still made of plowman's gauze and was in the same style as Laurinda's, yet was the wrong color entirely. There really hadn't been time for Mrs. Addiswell to make a new gown, and it simply wasn't possible to dye green into such a glorious yellow. It must be a different gown altogether, already made for someone else, and acquired in some way as roundabout as she had received the green gauze. What other explanation was there?

Rosalind smiled at them all, and then particularly at Francis, for this was the first time she had seen him in a very long time. "I'm delighted to meet you again after all this time, Francis."

He was still riveted by her gown, and stumbled over his reply. "Er . . . yes, and—and I you, Rosalind."

His manner puzzled her, and then she saw the looks on the others' faces as well. "What is it? Is something wrong with my gown? Is it marked, or torn?" She fluffed out the skirts, glancing down anxiously.

Harry stepped swiftly forward, and took her hand to draw the palm to his lips. "You look breathtaking, my darling," he said softly, "but . . . I thought you said your new gown was green?"

She laughed. "Ah, yes, well, I much prefer yellow, so someone had a word with Master Dobbs."

Being well acquainted with Sussex folklore, and little realizing she wasn't joking, they laughed with her. It didn't cross their minds for a moment that the Pharisee really had anything to do with it; they simply thought Rosalind was making light of it because she preferred not to say where or how she had acquired such a remarkable new gown in such a very short time.

Francis was glad the fuss was going to come to nothing, and Harry was overjoyed about the gown because his clumsy interference had ceased to matter. The star-crossed green gauze would not make an appearance at the ball after all, Lord and Lady Braithwaite would add respectability to their party, and Laurinda Caldicot would get her just deserts. Only Ellen wondered a little more about the miraculous new gown, which, yellow or not, still bore a suspicious resemblance to Laurinda's. Well, maybe tonight wasn't the time to ask Rosalind for the truth, but questions would certainly be put some time over this Christmas.

Rosalind could tell from Harry's face that all was not yet resolved. "What's wrong, Harry? There's still something else, isn't there?"

He looked wretchedly at her, his eyes magnified by his owl lenses. "Yes, I fear there is." He glanced at the others, then took her hand and led her out of earshot, across the hall. There, among the shadows of the marble columns, where a shaft of moonlight found its way down from the skylights in the dome, he confessed how she had really acquired the green gauze gown.

Rosalind was dismayed. "So . . . it wasn't Mrs. Addiswell's idea at all? It was yours?"

"Yes. I know it was a silly thing to do—"

"It certainly was! I know you acted with the very best intentions, Harry, but a lady's reputation is beyond price to her, especially when she is a widow with two sons to consider!"

"I know, I know!" He ran his hand unhappily through his hair. "All I thought was that you'd have a new gown after all, and that if it were altered so it didn't quite look like Laurinda Caldicot's . . . Anyway, it's done now, but you aren't wearing Laurinda's gown, so everything will be all right. Well, almost everything."

She was dismayed anew. "There's still more?"

He nodded, and told her about Laurinda's poisonous scandalmongering.

Rosalind went pale. "Are you telling me that Brighton society in its entirety is waiting for us to arrive tonight, convinced that you are my protector and that you have purchased Laurinda Caldicot's gown for me?"

Harry felt sick. "It would appear so," he admitted, "but you're wearing yellow, and Lord and Lady Braithwaite will be with us. It will be all right, truly it will."

"I imagine that right now you have your fingers crossed behind your back, Harry Trafford."

He managed a weak smile, because that was exactly what he was doing. "You must still come to the ball, Rosalind. Not to do so would be to hand Laurinda victory. Or so I'm advised, anyway." He looked back at Ellen and Francis.

Rosalind drew a long breath. "I think they are right. I will look the vixen in the eye, and everyone else, too. You are *not* my protector, and I have paid for this . . . er, the . . . gown myself. Which means, of course, that Mrs. Addiswell is sitting rather prettily, having been paid twice for the same item. She will get away with it, too, because if either you or I make a fuss, we'll merely be stirring the talk again. Were I wearing a hat, I would take it off to her."

Harry shuffled as guiltily as had Peter and Jake in this very hall, and Rosalind had to laugh. "Am I such a scold that I reduce you to the same behavior as my sons?"

His gray eyes swung to meet hers in the moonlight. "I deserve your scolding, for I behaved with complete thoughtlessness, but if you are up to attending the ball and snapping your fingers at them all, then let us to it." He offered her his arm.

She did not immediately take it, but instead moved closer, removed his spectacles, then slipped her arms around his neck. "I love you, Harry Trafford. I love you so much I might burst."

"Not in that gown, please."

"I will restrain myself. After all, Master Dobbs worked very hard with his needle and thread." She stood on tiptoe to kiss him. Oh, the feelings that ran through her, the excitement, wonder, and swift desire. No matter what happened at the ball, she was living a dream come true—a Christmas carol of a dream.

A few minutes later, when Harry had placed Rosalind's evening cloak around her shoulders, they all went out into the starlit night for the drive down to Brighton. As the carriage drove away, Jake watched from the window of the bedroom he shared with Peter. He was apparently alone, except that he addressed someone at his side whom only he could hear and see. "I told you Mother would be pleased."

"Does she believe in me now?" asked Master Dobbs in his high-pitched, apparently disembodied voice. He was a little brown manikin no more than twelve inches high, with slanting eyes and long pointed ears, and looked a little like a satyr from Greek mythology, except that in an English winter he was obliged to keep warm in thick clothes made of green laurel leaves lined with the best swansdown. He even had a rather battered laurel hat.

"Shhh." Jake put a finger to his lips and glanced around uneasily as Peter turned in his sleep, disturbed by his brother's voice but unable to hear or see the Pharisee. Jake lowered his tone. "Yes, Master Dobbs, Mother does believe in you."

"Well, that's something, I suppose. And please don't stand on ceremony by calling me Master Dobbs all the time. I am Puck of Puckscroft, and you may call me Puck."

"Can I really? Thank you!" Jake's eyes shone at being granted such an honor.

Peter's eyes opened. "Mm? What's that you said, Jake?" he murmured sleepily. "Is something wrong?"

"Go back to sleep. Everything's all right," Jake answered.

Peter muttered something unintelligible, and snuggled down beneath the bedclothes. In a moment he was lost in dreams again.

Jake nudged Puck. "Let's go to the pantry and have some figgy pudding," he suggested.

"Hot or cold?"

"Hot, of course. Oh, and Puck, can we have clotted cream with it this time?"

"I suppose so, if you must, but I prefer custard. And anyway, you're asking a lot of me tonight," Puck grumbled. "After all, I *did* change the color of the gown."

Jake was prepared to concede the point. "All right, custard it is," he said, making for the door.

Puck sighed and pattered after him. "I can't dither around for long because I must put silver coins in all the servants' shoes before they wake up in the morning, and first I have to get the coins from the hiding place in the beech hanger above Roecombe. I can only get them on Christmas Eve."

"Can I come with you?"

"Certainly not, it's Pharisee business."

"Then can I help you put the coins in the shoes?" Jake wheedled.

"No. That's Pharisee business too."

"Oh, but—"

"You can't come with me tonight, and that is the end of it," Puck declared firmly.

"I could share the job of carrying the coins," Jake offered hopefully.

"I can manage well enough on my own."

"*Please,* Puck."

The Pharisee couldn't stand any more. "No! A thousand times! If you ask me one more time I'll change you into a figgy pudding and eat *you*, hot *or* cold!"

At that, Jake fell prudently silent.

* * *

The Marine Pavilion was brightly illuminated both inside and out. Torches flickered in the gentle night breeze, every window and doorway was lit, and there was a veritable jam of fashionable vehicles on the Steyne. Everyone who was anyone in Brighton had been invited to the grand Christmas ball, and the lesser beings who had not, congregated outside to watch every arrival. A military band was playing "Good King Wenceslas" on the green as the Trafford carriage drew up at last at the main doors.

Footmen in the prince's livery hastened to assist the four guests, who entered the brilliant, overheated royal residence as two couples. As luck would have it Lord and Lady Braithwaite had arrived at almost the same time, so in fact there were six people to be announced in the newly finished music room, which was so vast and luxurious a chamber that it could easily accommodate a ball.

Luck did not remain with the Trafford party, however, for a waltz had just finished and there was a lull as the master of ceremonies struck the floor with his staff and gave the six names. His voice rang out clearly. The lull became a deathly silence as all eyes, royal included, fixed upon the new guests, and in particular upon Rosalind . . . and her *yellow* gown! Yellow? A wave of chatter circled the room, and all eyes swung toward Laurinda, who was wearing a pearl satin gown trimmed with blue lace, a garment that had seen the light of other chandeliers before tonight's. Laurinda stared at Rosalind as if cloven hooves would be perceived beneath the glittering yellow hem.

Some wag was daring enough to speak anonymously from the depths of the gathering. "Merry Christmas, Laurinda. Where's the green gauze gown?"

There was laughter, even from the Prince Regent, and Laurinda's face went the color of Ellen's mandarin taffeta.

Lady Braithwaite, as tall and angular as her husband was short and round, and looking a little like a salmon-pink flamingo in figured silk, did not shrink from expressing her disapproval. "The Caldicot chit is a disgrace for spreading such infamous untruths," she declared only too audibly. "She no longer deserves to be on any genteel guest list."

"Hear, hear," murmured various people.

With a choked sob, Laurinda fled from the ball, closely followed by her anxious father. Even more chatter, liberally laced with laughter, broke out behind them. The sting had most definitely been removed from all the scandalous gossip, and as Ellen thought entirely appropriate, it was Laurinda's bones that were now being picked. As Harry conducted Rosalind to where the prince waited to receive them, Ellen smiled wickedly at Francis. "Oh, the poor dear, she can't have been enjoying herself if she left so very early."

"It would seem not," he replied, and took her hand to lead her after the others.

After the ball, Harry took Rosalind home as the first hint of Christmas Day dawn lightened the eastern sky. Francis had walked to his house from the Marine Pavilion, and Ellen had been dropped at Trafford Hall before Harry and Roslind drove on to Puckscroft.

The moon was still hanging in the star-scattered azure sky, and the Christmas bells of Brighton echoed up the downs as the carriage halted before the great portico. Harry alighted, and then handed Rosalind down. His walking stick tapped the steps as he escorted her up to the open doors, where lantern light shone with seasonal cheer on a red-ribboned spray of holly.

Harry halted and turned her to face him. He looked anxiously into her eyes. "You are certain I am forgiven for the foolishness of buying that green gown for you?"

"Oh, Harry, of course you are forgiven. I couldn't be angry with you tonight if I tried, for I'm the happiest, proudest, vainest woman on earth. Just to be with you is all I ask."

"Even though I am so poor an escort that I could not dance with you at the ball?"

She smiled. "What's this, sir? Are you still determined to cast yourself in the glum role of Lord Byron? If so, I presume I am to be Lady Caroline Lamb, so perhaps we should return to the ball so I can make a terrible scene and cause an even greater scandal than Laurinda tried to bring about." She pretended to catch his hand to descend once more to the carriage.

His fingers tightened around hers and he pulled her back to him again. "Not so fast, my lady, for I'm being serious."

"I can see that." She stood before him again. "My dearest darling, I do not need to dance. Besides, I was never all that graceful at such antics, and would probably insult this gown if I attempted a reel!"

"But—"

She silenced his protest with a gloved finger. "Don't say another word, Harry."

He slipped an arm around her waist and drew her to him. "I love you, *From the east to western Ind, No jewel is like Rosalind,*" he whispered.

She smiled and leaned coquettishly back to survey him in the light from the lantern by the holly-adorned doors. "One thing I do ask of you, my love, and that is an early wedding. For I am impatient to quote . . ." She let the words die away tantalizingly.

"Yes?"

Her smile deepened. "Well, because I am impatient to use a line from *Henry V.* Act Four, I think it is. Anyway, it has been most improperly in my mind these past few days."

"And what line might that be?"

"Why, *A little touch of Harry in the night,* of course."

"Madam, you will have far more than a *little* touch of me!" he breathed, and brushed his lips against hers, tenderly at first, but soon with much more urgency. The walking stick slipped from his hand as he put both arms tightly around her.

The clatter of the stick disguised the jingle of Master Dobbs and his sack of silver coins as he slipped by them into the house.

"This is one romance that will not fail to enchant."
—Booklist (starred review)
SIGNET
"Romantic and funny—
I loved this book!"
—Mary Balogh
Wedded Bliss
BARBARA METZGER
A Signet Paperback
0-451-20859-5